Justice Bitch

Written and Illustrated by

Coyote Paria

DISCLAIMER

If you have experienced physical abuse as a child or as an adult, you may find some of the events that take place in this series offensive or personally triggering. I would like to state for the record that I do not condone violence or corporeal punishment outside the realm of mutually consensual sexual role play. I realize that that's a controversial statement, since those who *do* condone violence and corporeal punishment do so as a sort of secular religion. However, I'm not here to pass judgment on anyone's world view, anymore than I am to offend or trigger anyone who has suffered physical abuse in real life. Read deeper meaning into what's written here at your own discretion. My function is merely to entertain.

Table of Contents

Coyote Paria

Chapter 1:
After the Accident

After the accident, Harriet had been plagued by a bizarre compulsion. Her fingers twitched when she watched the news, and she watched the news everyday through blood shot eyes, and with zombie-like absorption. This was a maddening, irresistible need; a neurotic, relentless obsession.

At one point the compulsion became so overwhelming that she found herself unable to tear her gaze away from the flashing, murmuring screen for even a moment. She lost her job curating at the art museum. It didn't matter though, because she didn't need to work. She was an heiress. Her father (now dead from the accident) had been a wealthy CEO.

In the aftermath of her accidental exposure to the radiation, the dark and twisted parts of Harriet's personality became destructively magnified, resulting in a disturbing and debilitating mental breakdown. At one point, the madness became so great that Harriet stopped showering. She stopped eating. She stopped sleeping. She stopped brushing her teeth, shaving her legs, combing her hair, and putting on makeup. None of it mattered. The only thing that mattered was that television screen; those stories on the news.

Through tired, twitching eyes, Harriet watched towns reduced to flaming ruins, banks and museums emptied by radiation altered thugs abusing their godlike powers, and greedy politicians using the fear of the people to turn these tragedies into votes. The faces of murder victims and missing people were paraded for the amusement of the viewing public by each news station with perky optimism and callous indifference. It filled Harriet with a violent and frightening rage that was very new to her in its extremeness and totality.

In response to these new and overwhelming feelings, Harriet donated a small fraction of her considerable fortune to charities. However, this in no way managed to alleviate her compulsion to watch the atrocities on the news with bloodshot, unblinking eyes and gritted teeth for countless hours on end. She stood in front of the television for days with out sleeping, eating, or drinking water. It did not occur to her to do any of these things. There was something else that she needed to do first.

But what was it?

The people who knew Harriet began to suspect that she was on drugs or mentally ill. The latter was closer to the truth. The accident had fundamentally altered her brain chemistry, fixating her on a *new* need; one far more pressing than the consumption of food and water.

But what *was* it?

Harriet needed to know. If she went on much longer without whatever it was that her crazy brain was telling her to do, it was going to kill her. Her ribs were beginning to show through; her fake blond hair to grow out, revealing the dark roots underneath. She did not bother to re-bleach them. She had more pressing issues to attend to.

The accident had changed other things as well. Harriet had acquired a superhuman strength, which allowed her to move entire automobiles without the slightest bit of difficulty. Her skin had become impervious to cuts, bruises, and abrasions. And when she walked down the street, (on the rare occasions when she was able to pry herself away from the news long enough to do this) she sensed the auras of passers by.

It was this ability more so than any of the others that interested her. For herein lied the possible answer to what mysterious new need she was feeling; herein lied the key to her release from this tumultuous and fanatical new mind.

Harriet noticed a blinking, red light on the answering machine, which still sat on her father's desk in his extravagant office. She inched toward it, in the darkness, extended her hand slowly, and pressed the button next to the blinking light. A message began to play.

"Hey, girl, what's going on?" said a female voice from

the answering machine. It was Viola Davis, an old friend of Harriet's from high school. "You're not answering your cell phone, so I figured I'd give this number a try. Anyway, I heard your brain was sick since the accident...so I'm calling to tell you that you should come party with me and my pals tonight. Get your mind off of it. Have some fun. Call me, kay?"

Strange, Harriet hadn't talked to Viola for years apart from the occasional message on social media. Viola must have heard about the accident and about Harriet's unusual new abilities.

Perhaps it was a good idea to call. After all, Viola was known for having some supernatural abilities of her own. In high school, she had been known as Hawkette because she had the power to glide from roof top to rooftop like a bird. She had long, sharp talons at the tips of her fingers instead of fingernails and talons at the tips of her toes that she could use to snatch things off of the ground as she flew.

Perhaps Viola would understand what was wrong with Harriet's newly altered brain.

Harriet retrieved her cell phone and dialed Viola's number.

"Hey girl," Viola answered the phone, "I heard about the accident. *So*...how're you doing?"

"Good," Harriet lied.

"Oh that's good," said Viola, "The effects of the radiation take some getting used to...and I think they're different depending on the personality of the person who is exposed to them. There are some people who say that the radiation magnifies your personality quirks to the point of manifesting them as themed supernatural powers. I mean, some people say that's a myth. But, I don't know. There's probably some truth to it."

"Yea," said Harriet, "About that...when you were exposed to the effects of the radiation, did you ever have this weird obsession with stopping criminals and injustice...like a…rip your eyeballs out of their sockets with your bare hands unless you can stop criminals and injustice feeling?"

"Sure a little bit. I think that a lot of the people exposed to the radiation feel that way, to varying degrees. Kind of a violent metaphor, though."

"It's not a metaphor. My hands literally want to snatch the eyeballs out of my own head. I catch them creeping up to my face every time I think about not lashing out violently against criminals," Harriet said.

"Wow, dude. You're a fucking psycho."

"Yeah…I know, right? I don't know what it is. Since the accident, I've just felt different…"

"I see that with superhumans all the time. They always get a kind of crazy, fanatically obsessed, post-radiation hangover that, like, makes them want to save the world, or overthrow the government, or destroy all ham sandwiches on planet earth or something crazy like that. Its like a proven science thing or something, they call it a post-radiation brain chemistry fluctuation."

"I guess that makes sense. But I feel like I'm going to die if I don't do something about it."

"Well there's only one cure for that," said Viola, "Come hang out with me and my pals tonight. We fight criminals in masks like for real heroes. You interested?"

"Yes. Oh *god* yes. Anything to stop my hands from ripping my eyeballs out of their sockets."

"Keep those eyeballs in their sockets, girl," said Viola, "At least until tomorrow night."

…

Harriet met Viola and her friends at a little café on the corner of 5th and Rose Street. It was on the lower floor of a Victorian-style building, painted white with green awnings.

"Hello," said Harriet to Viola as she walked through the door of the café. Viola smiled and waved back. She was a pretty black woman with yellow, hawk-like eyes. Since high school, she had cut her hair short and let it regain its natural fuzziness. However, she seemed to have retained her habit of dying it unnatural colors. Today, it was a vibrant shade of cotton candy pink that matched her hot pink tank top.

To Viola's left sat an attractive, muscular man with short blond hair and very blue eyes.

"This is Stuart," Viola said, pointing to the man. Stuart waved. He had unusually large hands.

"Hello," he said.

Viola pointed to a skinny young-looking fellow with slightly curly, auburn hair, sitting to her right.

"And this is Benjamin," she said.

"Hi," Benjamin greeted Harriet.

"And Lilly," Viola said, pointing to the woman who sat across from her. Lilly had thin lips, lank, white-blond hair with bangs cut into it, and eyebrows that were so fair as to appear non-existent.

Lilly nodded in Harriet's direction as a way of greeting her.

Harriet glanced around the table at Viola's rag-tag team of young heroes. They stared back at her with frozen smiles on their faces, noticeably uncomfortable and awaiting her response. Despite being taken aback by Harriet's startlingly disheveled appearance and twitchy withdrawn demeanor, the group seemed to be making an effort to be polite and friendly. Perhaps they were accustomed to the eccentricities of newly altered superhumans. Or perhaps they were only tolerating Harriet at Viola's insistence.

"Hi everybody, Harriet said and she sat down at their table with them.

Her fingers began to twitch involuntarily. There was something about Benjamin that felt….*unclean*.

"Tell us about your powers," Lilly asked. Her voice was breathy to the point of almost resembling a whisper.

"Oh…I guess I'm really strong now," said Harriet, "I moved my car the other day by pushing it and then by picking it up. Also I might have some other things. I'm not really sure yet."

"Oh," said Lilly. Her breathy monotone was creepy. Like her white-blond eyebrows, it was understated to the point of being almost nonexistent. "My power is that I can be invisible and teleport."

"Cool," said Harriet.

"We call her Ghost Gal," said Benjamin.

"Oh," said Harriet. "That's....*clever*."

She paused and then added.

"So I heard you guys 'fight criminals in masks like for real heroes.' Is that true?"

Benjamin laughed. He had a nice laugh and it made his green eyes crinkle in a manner most genuinely benevolent. For a moment it almost made Harriet forget the aura of corruption that she felt about him. *Almost.*

"Yea, that's true," Benjamin said, sipping his coffee cautiously. "After Hawkette heard about your accident, she was hoping you would join us."

"So...does that mean you guys all have powers?" Harriet asked.

"Uh huh," said Stuart, "I have the super strength too...also I can fly. I guess that makes me like blond Superbro or something."

"We call him, *The Copy Right Infringer*," said Viola dramatically, waving her hand to emphasize the phrase "Copy Right Infringer."

"Actually, It's The Patriot Eagle," said Stuart.

"Except we already have one bird-themed hero on our team and that's me," said Viola pointing at herself. "I'm Hawkette because I can fly and I thought of naming myself after a bird because I can fly before you, so that makes *you* 'Copyright Infringer.' Deal with it."

"Yea, but I'm The Patriot Eagle because I'm patriotic," said Stuart.

"You're such a nerd," said Viola.

Harriet turned toward Benjamin who was sipping his coffee slowly. He seemed so mellow and pleasant. So why did she have such a bad feeling about him?

"So…" said Harriet suspiciously, her stern brown eyes locking onto Benjamin's pleasant green ones. "What can you do?"

"Oh…" said Benjamin, "It's kind of hard to explain. Let me show you."

Benjamin picked up the metal napkin holder from the table and placed it in front of himself, then, he put his hands out in front of him. His eyes began to glow green and a Safire electrical current flowed from the tips of his fingers. The napkin holder absorbed the green bolt of energy and sprouted legs. A disturbing, twisted-up face emerged from the tissue paper in the front of it and the thing screamed as though in unbearable agony.

"Stop it," Harriet snapped angrily.

Benjamin put his hand on the paper towel holder and it went back to normal.

"Sorry about that. It can be a little disturbing. Comes in handy though," said Benjamin.

There was definitely something wrong with Benjamin; Harriet could sense it. Something in her brain was telling her that he deserved to be obliterated completely and was urging her to take action.

The conversation continued. Harriet was only half listening to it. Her fingers twitched to close around something, perhaps Benjamin's throat. Perhaps a weapon.

"Green Lightening has the ability to electrocute things and also to give inanimate objects life," said Viola, "If you think about it though, bringing things to life is really the best power of them all. It's like he's a god or something."

"Aw man, Hawkette," said Benjamin modestly, shaking his curly head with some degree of disdain. "You act like its some kind of an incredible gift or something. It's really more of a curse, actually."

"Aw...*Benji*," Viola crooned lovingly. "Don't be like the man who shat gold bricks and called it a curse, even though he got to be rich and then everything became awesome after that."

"Yea, until he died from shitting gold bricks," said Benjamin.

"Ok, so maybe that's a bad example," said Viola waving a hand dismissively. "But my point is that nobody likes a guy who bitches about having superpowers."

"Still a valid point," agreed Stuart.

Lilly nodded silently in agreement.

Harriet remained unresponsive. Her eyes remained trained on Benjamin. As pleasant as he seemed to be, his aura still reeked of that incessant corruption. She could not bring herself to ignore it for very long.

"What do you think, Harriet?" Benjamin asked her. Perhaps he had noticed the strange way that she was staring at him. Harriet fumbled for a reply. A great deal of her energy was currently being used to stop herself from grabbing the fork in front of her, lunging across the table, and stabbing Benjamin in the throat with it:

"Oh...ha ha...um....I guess...everything has its drawbacks," she said.

"Truer words were never spoken," Benjamin sighed in agreement and then he picked up his coffee mug, tilted his head back, and gulped down the remainder of its contents in one swift motion.

"Alright, team," said Hawkette, standing up. "Dinner has concluded! Its time to suit up and begin tonight's patrol.

"Uh...Hawkette, I haven't finished my coffee yet," Stuart pointed out in annoyance.

"Also...Harriet hasn't eaten yet. Even if we have," murmured Lilly timidly.

"Oh...no...that's ok," said Harriet, shaking her head and putting her hands up in protest. She stood up as well. "I'm not even hungry. Let's get right to it."

—

Chapter 2:
Of Costumes and Heroes

The team walked out into the parking lot, and toward a large van, with a pink and yellow hawk airbrushed onto the side of it. The hawk had its feathered wings expanded, and was dive bombing magnificently, its yellow eyes narrowed in deep concentration as its sharp talons pierced a diseased-looking viper. A rainbow of blood splatter shot from the viper's dead body. The whole thing was very ostentatious. Harriet wasn't sure how she had managed to walk right past it on the way from her car to the restaurant without noticing it.

"That's my van," said Viola, pointing in the direction of the van. "Alright, let's get changed."

"Changed?" Harriet repeated cautiously.

"Yea, like I said, we fight villains in *costumes*," said Viola.

"She carries a bunch of costumes with her. Just incase someone wants to join," murmured Stuart. He pulled his shirt off, and rolled it up into a ball in one of his hands. Underneath, he was wearing white spandex that was tight over his broad shoulders and large muscles. There was an angular S on the center of his chest, which was painted like an American flag.

Viola dug her keys out of her purse and pushed a button on a key fob, popping the door on the back of the van. There were several laundry bins filled with costumes in the back, a floor-length mirror, a Japanese paper room divider, a pink lava lamp, and a broken disco ball. Harriet recalled that Viola's parents owned a party store. In high school, Viola's room had always been littered with Halloween costumes and party favors that were left over from the discount bin.

"I see not much has changed with you," said Harriet.

Stuart threw his shirt into the back of the van. Viola removed her pink tank top and did the same. Underneath the pink tank top, was a pink midriff shirt with a yellow letter H embroidered on the front of it.

"Pick the costume you like and you can keep it," Viola invited.

Harriet climbed into the back of the van and started sifting through bins of costumes. While she did this, the rest of the team shed their civilian clothes and tossed them in the back of the van.

After a few short seconds of searching, Harriet found a costume that she liked: a pair of thigh-length leather pants; black fishnet stockings; long, black, leather boots with two inch, blood red, platform soles; a long, black, leather jacket with a red lining; and a black leather midriff shirt. She got behind the Japanese paper room divider and put the costume on, then, posed for herself in front of the floor-length mirror. Her disheveled, two-tone hair was wild and greasy, but she supposed that it went rather well with the costume. She pushed a mop of hair out of her eyes and secured a black leather mask over her head, pinning the unkempt mess behind her ears. Then, she smiled at herself in the mirror, before punching the air dramatically. She supposed she looked a bit like a dominatrix prostitute but was also far too eager to begin fighting criminals to nitpick this detail.

Harriet emerged from behind the Japanese paper room divider. The team clapped to congratulate her on her costume choice. They were all in costumes as well now. Viola wore a yellow, beak-shaped mask; a pink, leather midriff shirt; short pink pants; a yellow belt; and long, yellow, leather boots. Stuart wore a white spandex jump suit with an American-flag-patterned, angular S on the chest; and a cape with an American flag on it. Lilly wore a short-sleeved, white dress with knee-length, translucent, white skirts that fanned out like the bloom of a flower; opaque, white stockings; long, white, healed boots; a sheer, white cape; and a white, leather mask. Benjamin wore a pair of green slacks; a black belt; a purple, button-down shirt; a long, green and purple striped jacket; a green, plastic mask; and a green and a purple striped top hat.

To Harriet, this looked more like a villain costume than a hero costume. She wondered darkly, how he had managed to hide all of that under his civilian clothes. Had he actually stripped down and changed in the parking lot?

"Man," Harriet said, while entertaining the mental image of Benjamin stripping down to put on his ridiculous costume in the parking lot, while people stared at him from parked cars at the gas station across the street. "This hero team couldn't be more conspicuous if you all had police sirens strapped to your heads."

Viola laughed.

"Girl, you an't seen nothin' yet," she said grinning.

"Yea, she's probably got those police siren hats ready for us in the back of that van somewhere," said Stuart.

"Alright," Viola said, ignoring Stuart's comment about the police siren hats and sticking her hand out in front of her. Stuart, Lilly, and Benjamin gathered around in a circle and stuck their hands on top of hers. Harriet inched toward the circle and followed their example, placing her hand on top of the others.

"Sexy Rad Super Pals!" Viola shouted.

"Let's rock and roll!" Stuart and Benjamin shouted in reply. Lilly whispered the words timidly. Harriet didn't know what to say so she babbled some nonsense under her breath. The Sexy Rad Super Pals took their hands out of the circle.

Chapter 3:
Sexy Rad Super Pals vs. The Jaywalker

For a few hours, the Sexy Rad Super Pals wandered the streets, looking for criminals. It was dark out and there were not that many people outside, aside from a homeless guy on a park bench, and a pack of loud, drunk college boys on their way to the club.

Lilly pointed in front of her.

"Look," she whispered.

The Sexy Rad Super Pals looked in the direction that she had been indicating. A man wearing a construction worker's yellow jacket, a plastic Ronald Reagan mask, and an orange parking cone on his head was walking up and down the sidewalk, putting parking tickets on cars that were parallel parked along the side of the road.

"5 hundred dollars....6 hundred dollars... ooh a Mercedes Benz, somebody's loaded...aw what the heck....2 thousand dollars," the man sang to himself as he placed parking tickets on the windshields of cars, methodically and in quick succession.

"It's the Jaywalker!" Viola announced.

The Jaywalker turned his head in their direction.

"He has the ability to hypnotize people into sending checks to his personal account for fake parking tickets," whispered Lilly for Harriet's benefit. "Don't look at anything that he writes down on paper. He can only hypnotize with hand written words."

"Enough, evil doer!" Viola shouted.

"Why, if it isn't Hawkette and the Un-sexy Dumb Lame-o Pals," said the Jaywalker, strolling toward them, a pen and pad of blank parking tickets in hand.

"Don't listen to him, Hawkette, he's just jealous of how sexy we are," said Stuart very seriously.

"Yea, we're ten times as sexy as he'll ever be," announced Benjamin proudly.

"What are you retards babbling about?" the Jaywalker inquired with annoyance.

"Sexiness is very important to us," whispered Lilly bluntly.

Harriet shrugged. "Don't look at me," she said, "I haven't been briefed on the importance of sexiness yet."

"Yuh huh," said the Jaywalker, rolling his eyes. "Well I'm just going to keep putting parking tickets on cars and there's nothing you can do to stop me."

Stuart balled his large hand into a fist and drew it back as though to throw a punch. The Jaywalker wrote the words "you are a cow" onto one of the parking tickets quickly, and slapped the parking ticket onto Stuart's forehead. It stuck there by its adhesive edge. Stuart fell down on his stomach and starting crawling around on the pavement, on his hands and knees, mooing like a cow.

"Your friend's a cow now," said the Jaywalker, "Now, leave me alone."

Hawkette charged at the Jaywalker and jumped into the air, taking flight as her healed boot positioned itself for a kick to the face. The Jaywalker stepped sideways to avoid the blow. Lilly flickered into nonexistence, and then reappeared behind the Jaywalker. The Jaywalker turned around quickly and lunged at Lilly with one of his parking tickets, but she disappeared again, before he was able to stick her with one. Harriet charged at the Jaywalker, her fists raised. Her brain reeled with an ecstatic, ravenous, animal passion, and she threw herself at him with all of the obscene pleasure of a starving predator as it sinks its teeth into its kill. She tackled him, and, despite the fact that he was larger than her, easily knocked him to the ground. He gasped in surprise, having lost his grip on the parking tickets and the pen, he now lay helpless; pinned beneath the supernatural weight of her scantily clad body.

"Holy crap, dude, she caught him!" Hawkette exclaimed excitedly, punching Benjamin playfully on his skinny, green and purple striped arm.

"Ow," mumbled Benjamin rubbing his arm.

The Sexy Rad Super Pals gathered in a circle around Harriet and the Jaywalker, eager to learn their long time adversary's secret identity. Except for Stuart, who was still walking around on the pavement, mooing like a cow. He bent his head forward and licked the sidewalk as his pupils dilated, and drool slid down from the corners of his open mouth.

Harriet removed the Richard Nixon mask from the Jaywalker's face, and threw it into the distance. Without meaning to, she sent it flying several city blocks and it landed on some wires strung between telephone poles. Beneath the mask, Harriet found the face of a young man with a buzz cut and profuse pimples.

"...What's your name?" Harriet growled.

The Jaywalker sucked in air, gathered the spit in his mouth, and then hawked it in Harriet's face.

"Go to hell, bitch!" he shouted.

Harriet brought her hand back and slapped the Jaywalker hard across the face. A deep, purple bruise blossomed across his pimply cheek and he cringed, choking back tears.

"Woah, woah, *woah*—Harriet! He's just a petty thief! Go easy on him!" interjected Hawkette rather lamely. Harriet ignored her.

"...What's your name?" Harriet said to the Jaywalker again.

"...The...the J-J-ayw-walker," the Jaywalker stuttered.

Harriet brought her hand back and slapped him across the other side of his face, inflicting another deep bruise.

"Agh!"

"...What's your *name*," Harriet repeated darkly.

"....J-Jason Walker." the Jaywalker stuttered.

"Jason Walker?" Harriet repeated incredulously. "Your name is *Jay* Walker?"

"Yea,yea,yea,yea,yea it is," the Jaywalker said, nodding

vigorously. "Check my driver's license if you don't believe me!"

"I believe you," said Harriet, "Put my friend over there back the way he was."

"Ok. Ok," said the Jaywalker

He took a deep breath and then uttered the words: "woc a era uoy."

"That's 'you are a cow' backwards," whispered Lilly for Harriet's benefit.

Stuart choked, his eyes grew wide, and he stuck his tongue back in his mouth.

"...What happened," he moaned, standing up and rubbing the back of his head.

"It was the Jaywalker, he hypnotized you and–" Lilly whispered.

"–Holy shit, Harriet, what are you doing!" Viola shouted.

Harriet had her hands on the Jaywalker's throat and was strangling him with her tiny hands. The Jaywalker's face was turning purple and his eyes were bugging out of his head.

Viola knelt down and tried to pry Harriet's fingers off of the Jaywalker's throat but had no such luck.

"Not cool — he's like 16!" Viola shouted. Harriet ignored her and kept strangling.

"Harriet, *Harriet*! This is an intervention, not an execution!" Viola shouted.

Stuart grabbed Harriet's arms and with some difficulty, moved them away from the Jaywalker's throat. The Jaywalker gasped for air. Color returned to his bloodless face and he grabbed his pen and stack of parking tickets, quickly writing something down and sticking it to Harriet's forehead.

Harriet's eyes snapped shut and her consciousness faded to black.

Chapter 4:
Harriet and the Drifter

Harriet opened her eyes slowly. Her vision was blurry at first.

"Hey girl, you alright?" Viola asked.

"...Are you....*hurt*?" Benjamin asked.

"No. I'm fine," said Harriet, blinking the cloudiness out of her eyes. The Sexy Rad Super Pals were all standing in a circle around her, staring at her as she lay face up on the pavement.

Harriet removed the parking ticket from her forehead and read what was written there:

You will roll onto your back and sleep for thirty minutes.

"This is a dangerous ability," said Harriet, sitting up. "He could have written 'you will die' and it would have happened."

"Yea, but he didn't," said Viola confrontationally.

"Yea, but he could have," said Harriet, standing up. "No one should have that kind of power."

"So he should die?" Viola interjected confrontationally.

"Yes," said Harriet.

"What about prison?" said Benjamin unsurely.

"What prison could hold him?" said Harriet.

"She has a point," whispered Lilly.

"No. No. No. No. *NO*. I am the leader of the Sexy Rad Super Pals, ok? And *that* is neither sexy nor rad. One more incident like that and you are off the team, Harriet. Do you understand?" said Viola.

"Yea, ok," said Harriet, "I get it. No killing. I understand."

"Alright," said Viola, grinning. "As long as we understand each other."

"Sorry about leaving you in the street like that," said Stuart to Harriet. "But you're actually super hard to move."

"It fine, Stuart. I'm over it," said Harriet.

The Sexy Rad Super Pals all waved goodbye to each other and went their separate ways for the night. Lilly vanished. Benjamin touched a park bench. It sprouted legs and a nightmarish, twisted-up face. Then, he jumped onto its snakelike back and rode it off into the distance. Viola and Stuart walked back to the van, which was still parked a few blocks away, infront of the restaurant.

"Harriet," Viola said, turning back toward Harriet and pointing toward the van. "You want a ride back to your place?"

"No thanks!" said Harriet, grinning wide. In her current state of post-fight elation, she was not at all eager to return home.

The two waved goodbye. Viola got into her van with Stuart and drove away. Harriet continued to walk the streets, thinking. A mad grin twisted her young face and she cackled. The unbearable itch in her altered brain had finally been scratched, along with that gnawing, relentless hunger. For the first time in weeks, Harriet was hungry for real food. Harriet skipped and twirled for joy as she walked. Hunger for real food was a good thing.

As Harriet was walking, she spotted a young man with shaggy, disheveled, black hair and a goatee. He was tall and skinny, with thin lips, a sharp chin, and an impish smirk on his face. Very suspicious. Harriet also noticed the way he was dressed: all in black with a spiky, leather dog collar around his neck and a black acoustic guitar strapped to his back. Harriet had learned not to trust people in costumes, and, though the clothes that this man was wearing were not *a costume* in the technical sense of the word, the punk emo thing that he had going on was just as suspicious as that grin on his face.

The man sprinted up to her, grinning and waving as though attempting to scare off a fly.

"Wassup, beautiful?" the man said. Harriet stared at him with distain as he paused to catch his breath. The man's flirtatious grin alerted her of his true intent, immediately and without words.

"Wassup, yourself," Harriet grumbled. The man was standing close enough to her now that she could sense his aura. There was no detectible corruption in it.

The man took a couple of hundred dollar bills out of the pocket of his black jeans and attempted to hand them to Harriet. Harriet crossed her arms and scowled.

"What is two hundred not enough? I can give you two fifty but that's my dinner," said the man, and he dug a fifty dollar bill out of his pocket.

"I'm confused," said Harriet. "What do you want from me?"

The man chuckled.

"Oh heh heh...*you know*..."

"I don't know."

A faint blush tinted the man's pale cheeks.

"Heheheheh....uh....I've been a real bad boy, if you know what I mean...Like maybe...I need some...discipline," he said. Then he winked a couple of times, rather obnoxiously.

"You miss understand," said Harriet, shaking her head. "I'm not a prostitute."

"Then why are you dressed like that?"

"Why are *you* dressed like *that*?"

"I'm in a band," said the man.

"I'm on a super team," Harriet clarified reciprocally.

"A super team, huh?" repeated the man and then he added with a greasy smirk: "So if I was a villain, would you spank me for free?"

"But you're not a villain, are you?" said Harriet because she could tell that he definitely wasn't.

"But I could be," said the man. He stuck his hand in the pocket of his black jeans and withdrew a business card, which he handed to Harriet.

Harriet observed the card incredulously. It was blood red with dripping, black letters, and had what she assumed was this man's band on it: EAR MUTILATOR.

"You had cards made," Harriet mumbled incredulously. She put the card in the pocket of her leather pants.

"I'm Spencer," said the man, sticking his hand out for her to shake. She didn't shake it.

"Ok," said Harriet. Clean aura or no, she wasn't about to tell this creepo her name. She started walking away. Spencer jogged to keep up with her.

"Let us play for you, sometime," Spencer said and then he blurted out: "I've never seen a woman like you before, pretty lady, won't you be the Wonda to my Severin, tonight?"

Harriet ignored him and started walking even faster. She did not understand whatever reference he was making and also did not really care to understand it. *Why is he even talking like that? Who talks like that? Is he insane? What the fuck's wrong with him?* Harriet thought with derisive incredulity.

"Heheheh...*you* know it's uh...it's a book about kinky French Aristocrats? I thought that maybe you *uh*....I guess not..." Spencer mumbled unsurely. A blush crept over his pale cheeks and he fell back, watching her stroll off into the darkness. "Wanda, *Wanda*!...Call me if you ever need a band!"

Chapter 5:
A Stranger's House

Harriet lived in a large, Victorian-style mansion, known as The Ross Manor. The Ross Manor was built into the side of a natural cliff, near the shoreline. Most of the mansion's large, arched windows held a spectacular view of either the Propopolous city skyline or the adjacent private beach, which, like the mansion, had been the property of the Ross family for multiple generations. The manor also had an extensive staff, consisting of many maids and servants, who could often be seen, flitting around, dusting, preparing meals, and conversing with each other in a businesslike way. Harriet's father had designed and decorated the manor's interior before he died, so the furniture and all of the decorations had already been selected without Harriet's consent and had nothing to do with her. Everything was white and minimalist. Abstract paintings in plain white frames scattered the walls and bouquets of white orchids garnished the tables and flat surfaces. There were so many large, tall windows throughout the building, that, in places, it seemed that the walls must have been made almost entirely of glass. The vast living room was filled with light, and gave Harriet a panoramic view of the distant city.

After a night of crime fighting, Harriet felt good again, so she ordered a pizza and ate it by herself in the massive living room. Then, she took a long shower, shaved her legs, and cut the blond tips off of her two-toned hair with a pair of scissors, whistling happily as she did so. Everything was good again and all she had to do was keep punching in criminal faces. Probably for the rest of her life.

She stared at herself in the bathroom mirror for a moment. A gaunt, dark-haired woman with circles under her eyes stared back. She glanced down at the business card that the vagabond musician had handed her last night. It had a number on it, written underneath the words: For Information call Spencer Tuckerson at:

Harriet cackled raucously.

"...What an idiot!" she said, smirking. "As if anyone would ever be interested in his stupid band!"

She picked up the card and walked over to the waste paper basket in the corner of the bathroom with it.

"No. I'll hold onto it," said Harriet to herself. "Viola will get a kick out of this."

Harriet walked back out into the living room, where she saw the butler, Reynolds, conversing with a maid by an arrangement of white orchids at the center of a low, square, white, coffee table with a glass top.

"These are the wrong orchids. The master of the house instructed us to use dendrobium aberrans not dendrobium chrysanthemums, before he died," said Reynolds. He was an old man with a bald head, who wore a black tuxedo and spoke with a pompous British accent.

"Its ok," said Harriet, "I don't care about the Orchids"

Renalds ignored her comment.

"Get the right one's next time, please," he said to the maid.

Harriet groaned. A lot of times it seemed like Reynolds took orders from her dead father rather than her. It didn't feel like she lived here, but rather like she was staying as an unwelcome guest in the house of a stranger. She was not sure who that stranger was exactly. The ghost of her dead father? Reynolds? The French chef that prepared her meals on Saturdays? In any case, she was in no mood to argue the insignificant point of the irrelevant flowers. *Let Reynolds have them the way he likes them,* she thought.

Chapter 6:
Sexy Rad Super Pals vs. Super Annoyo

The next evening, Harriet met the Sexy Rad Super Pals at the restaurant. Lilly greeted her with a weak smile and a wave that was really not so much a wave at it was a barely perceptible jerk of her raised hand.

"Harriet, hi!" said Benjamin and Harriet became immediately suspicious of his (forced?) friendliness. There was still something very wrong with his aura.

"Yes, good. We're all here now, Harriet sit down. We have some very important news to discuss," said Viola.

"Where's Stuart?" Harriet asked, sitting down in the booth next to Lilly and across from Viola and Benjamin.

"He's being an ass," groaned Viola, rolling her eyes. "But that's ok. We don't need him. We already have a team member that can fly: that's me. And we already have a team member with super strength: that's you. Stuart is just redundant. He's replaceable."

"Whoa, did something happen between you and Stuart last night?" asked Harriet, a bit concerned.

"Naw, it's nothing. Forget it," said Viola. "Alright team, down to business."

Viola held up her cell phone for the team to look at. The screen held a news article with a picture of a man in a full-body purple and orange spandex suit, robbing a bank. The suit covered his face entirely and contained a large, protuberant, and very phallic cod piece that made him appear as though he was spouting a perpetual erection.

"It's my nemesis, Super Annoyo," Viola explained, "He annoyed the bank tellers into submission."

"You have a nemesis?" Harriet inquired amusedly.

"Of course I do. We all do," said Viola, "You're not a proper hero unless you have some super personal, backstory-related beef with one of your adversaries."

"Madam Gorge wouldn't date me in high school," said

Benjamin.

"Crunchy Toast Muncher murdered my parents," whispered Lilly.

"Who's your nemeses, Harriet?" asked Viola conversationally.

"....I uh....I don't have one," said Harriet.

"You should get one," said Benjamin.

"Why force a grudge?" said Harriet, waving her hand dismissively. "A genuine spite based relationship is worth the wait."

"That's the spirit," said Viola.

"So why is Super Annoyo your Arch Nemeses?" Harriet asked Viola.

Viola took a deep breath, and stretched her arms out as though settling in for a long backstory.

"A few years back," she said. "I attended the annual Propopolous City Superhuman Bake-off. I was in costume and so was he, so we don't know each other's secret identities or anything. But basically....we both entered lasagna...*so*...he dropped his pants and took a dump on my lasagna to sabotage me. We've been mortal enemies ever since."

Briefly, Harriet contemplated the logistics of Super Annoyo dropping his pants to take a crap in lasagna. Had he practiced the sabotage covertly or had he simply dropped his pants in front of the crowd? Had he jumped onto the table and squatted over the lasagna? *Or* had he dripped the lasagna on the floor first? Harriet didn't have time to ask any of these questions out loud, however, because Benjamin changed the subject before she had the chance.

"You still need a hero name, Harriet" Benjamin said, grinning. All thoughts of a wacky man, with a dildo strapped to his crotch, shitting in lasagna, were wiped mercifully clean from Harriet's mind. The vulgar image had been overridden by her annoyance that the team was now pressuring her to assume a hero alias.

"Jesus, couldn't you just call me Harriet? Anybody who

knows me can figure out that it's me anyway," complained Harriet.

"Justice Bitch," offered Viola.

"Leather Lady," said Benjamin.

"...Midnight Woman?" whispered Lilly unsurely.

"Uh....what about..." Harriet began.

"Ballbuster!" Viola interrupted.

"Short pants girl," said Benjamin.

"....The uh...no never mind...I'm not very good at thinking up names..." whispered Lilly.

A tubby waitress with short blond hair and a piece of gum in her mouth strolled over to the booth where they were sitting.

"Are you freaks gonna' order something, 'cause my boss says you can't sit here unless you order somethin'," she said, chewing the gum slowly.

"How about a round of drinks for all of my new friends," said Harriet humorlessly. She really wanted to skip the *nemesis*, the *backstory*, and the *hero name*, and get straight back to the punching in of faces. A nervous twitch had infected her left eye with relentless, infuriating veracity, and she needed to punch in faces. Now.

The waitress walked away.

"...Wait....I wanted....oh never mind...." Lilly whispered.

"Viola, you like to control things," said Harriet to Viola. "Why don't you choose my name?"

"Justice Bitch it is then," said Viola happily. Harriet could tell that Viola liked having her name chosen.

The waitress returned with four glass bottles and Harriet handed her the money for it.

"Ok, guys," Harriet said, standing up. "Let's walk and drink. Let's drink and walk! Let's go!"

Harriet started walking toward the door with her drink in her hand. The other's followed unsurely.

"Are you sure that Stuart wasn't right about her?" whispered Lilly to Viola, once Harriet was out of ear shot.

"Stuart's an idiot," said Viola. "I've known Harriet for a long time and I can assure you...she's *not* evil."

...

The Sexy Rad Super Pals got into costume and began wandering the streets of the city, searching for evildoers. As they were walking, Harriet decided to bring up her unusual encounter with the wandering musician, the night before.

"Last night, on my way home, this guy saw me in my hero costume and thought I was a prostitute," said Harriet.

Viola laughed.

"It's not very easy to be a female hero, is it?" whispered Lilly almost inaudibly.

"He said he was in this band..." said Harriet and she dug the business card out of the front pocket of her leather shorts. "Have you heard of it?"

Viola stared at the card for the moment and squinted. Then she shook her head.

"I don't know about music," she told Harriet, "Ask Benji. He knows about music."

Harriet pushed the card in Benjamin's direction.

"Have you heard about...*Ear Mutilator*, Benjamin," Harriet asked.

"...Yea," said Benjamin, "They're a local band. They do kind of like a punk alternative rock thing, with a little bit of a goth metal thing sometimes.

"Any good?" Harriet asked.

"They're ok," said Benjamin, "Not really memorable. Sunday Murder Spree does what they do way better...and Bloody Bloody Death Spikes has smarter lyrics."

"Uh huh..." said Harriet, who hadn't heard of any of these local bands, and didn't think that she would care about them if she had.

"It's him!" Viola shouted, pointing straight out in front of her. "My nemesis! Super Annoyo!"

Harriet stuffed the card back into her pocket and looked in the direction that Viola was pointing. A man in a purple and orange, spandex suit, with a dildo-like codpiece sown into the crotch, was running through the parking lot of a bank, holding a massive, heavy-looking sack, presumably, filled with money.

"Woop! Woop! Woop! Woop!" the man squealed at an unbearably high pitch.

"Stop right there, Super Annoyo!" Viola shouted. She sprinted toward him and took off into the hair, the sharp talons on her feet, poised to strike.

"You are no match for my powers of Annoyingness, Hawkette!" Super Annoyo shrieked. His voice was so unbearably high-pitched that it gave everyone who heard it a pounding migraine.

Harriet rubbed her throbbing forehead.

"Ok, this fucker is gonna' die," Harriet said and sprinted toward him with her fists raised.

Super Annoyo dodged Hawkette's impending talon, and then began singing every catchy, jingle designed to sell products on TV, that he could think of.

"Cereal! Ugh! UGH! UGH! UH! YOU need CEREAL! YEA, whoo WHOO woo!" Super Annoyo sang. Super Annoyo's singing was so off-key that Harriet could barely recognize the jingle that he was attempting to sing. Also, Super Annoyo did not seem to know most of the words of what he was singing, and replaced the missing words with random noises. "The BEST PART of boop boop BOOOOOP. IS POO DOOO do MY BAAAAAALLLLLLLSSSSSSS!"

Harriet aimed a punch at Super Annoyo's face, but Super Annoyo sidestepped the blow easily and continued singing.

"Oh myyyy SOMETHING HAS A BLAH blah. It's LOLOLOLOLOL! My SOMETHING ELSE VOVOVOVOVO!"

Benjamin touched a fire hydrant and it grew a twisted face with a pair of mangled, nightmarish ears. The fire hydrant opened its gash of a mouth and squirted a jet of high-pressure water at Super Annoyo's face, but Super Annoyo jumped quickly to the side, avoiding the water, and continued singing.

"RaAAAWEESONDSSSSSSSSOOOOOOOOOOO!" Super Annoyo shrieked stupidly, and the terrible volume of the noise made the living fire hydrant shriek in agony and then explode. Blood dripped from Benjamin's ears and he collapsed onto the brown patch of grass in front of the bank parking lot. Lilly vanished and reappeared beside him. A torrent of blood spilled from her ears as Super Annoyo began singing again.

Harriet charged at Super Annoyo again. She didn't know why it was taking so long to muster up enough enthusiasm to attack him or why he was so difficult to hit. Perhaps his powers of annoyingness were interfering with her ability to think and move. Again, Super Annoyo easily dodged her blow. Viola jumped into the air and tried to slice his face with her talons again, but badly missed and landed in a decorative row of bushes outside the front of the bank.

"HAHAHOHOHO! I'M BORED OF PLAYING with you, NOOOOW! Later, Super Losers! DOOOOOOOOOOOOOOOOOOOOOOOOOOOO!" Super Annoyo shouted as he ran off into the distance, still holding the large sack full of money.

Harriet ran after him but he was too fast to catch. He kept spouting random nonsense, which made her slow down and lose focus. Viola trudged behind her, badly damaged. Dark crimson blood trickled out from her ears and stained her costume. She stumbled and collapsed into the fetal position on the ground.

"God damn it," Viola gasped in exhaustion. "He got away."

Chapter 7:
EAR MUTILATOR Live at the Hornet's Nest

"Shit. Viola, are you ok?" Harriet asked, when she saw the blood streaks trailing down Viola's ears and neck.

"Yea, I'm fine," Viola said, standing up. She stumbled slightly and leaned against the stone wall that was the front of the bank to steady herself.

With some help from Lilly, Benjamin rose to his feet and limped over to them. Lilly vanished and then reappeared by his side.

"Why aren't you bleeding, Harriet?" Lilly murmured.

"I don't know," Harriet replied, "I guess I'm hard to damage now."

"Ugh...I don't feel so good...." moaned Benjamin. Then, he staggered and gagged as though he were about to throw up. Lilly steadied him with one pale, slender arm.

"Shhh....It's ok..." she whispered.

A thought occurred to Harriet. Her aura sensing abilities were probably unreliable. That would explain why Benjamin's aura felt so dark and sinister, despite the fact that he seemed to be such a soft-spoken and nonthreatening guy. *Maybe,* Harriet thought. *I'm sensing the qualities of people's supernatural abilities and not the qualities of the people themselves. Maybe...Spencer doesn't read as corrupt to me because his powers of annoyingness aren't inherently sinister the way that Benjamin's power of turning objects into shrieking, tortured monsters are. He might be Super Annoyo. Even if his aura doesn't feel dark.*

"Listen guys," said Harriet, "I know these super villains like to have themes that relate to their real life identities...you know, like the Jaywalker being Jason Walker....so maybe...this band EAR MUTILATOR...has something to do with this guy that just mutilated our ears."

"That would make sense," said Viola, "We should totally go see if he's a member of the band."

"...I think they're supposed to be playing at the Hornet's

nest tonight. They play there a lot," groaned Benjamin. Then he knelt down and sat in the grass, closing his eyes and grimacing.

"Benjamin doesn't have any super resilience abilities, so Super Annoyo's powers of annoyingness affected him the same way that they would affect a regular person," Lilly murmured quietly. "I think he's really hurt."

Benjamin lurched forward and vomited onto the grass.

"Gotta' go. Bye," Lilly whispered quickly. Then, she knelt down and put her arms around Benjamin. The two of them vanished together.

"Well, I guess it's just us then," said Viola to Harriet. "You up for a concert?"

...

"We are the dead! We are the dead! We are the dead! We are the dead! YEEEAAAAAAAHHHHH!" A man with a bright red mullet screamed into a microphone on the stage. A pair of guys with black and purple Mohawks stood behind him and strummed electric guitars. A fat, bald guy with a black bandana around his head hit the drums like he was trying to beat them to death.

"He kind of sucks, doesn't he?" said Harriet to Viola as they stood in the audience, surrounded by flailing young people in punk and goth attire.

"*Kind of* sucks?" Viola muttered, shaking her head.

"EAAAATTTTT BRAAAAINNNNNSSSS!" the man with the bright red mullet shrieked. He stomped his thick black leather boots on the stage, which was very plain and painted black. The walls surrounding him were painted black as well. Everything in The Hornet's Nest was black. That was kind of its theme.

"I don't get death metal," said Viola.

"No, me neither. But you have to admit, if Super Annoyo was going to hang out anywhere. It would probably be here," said Harriet.

"True that."

"THAT'S WHY MY FACE MELTS WHEN WE. ARE. APART," the man with the bright red mullet shrieked. The two guys playing the electric guitars stopped playing abruptly at the end of that line and so did the drummer. The audience cheered.

"We are Fecal Rot Crotch!" the man announced, clutching the microphone close to his black-lipsticked and ring-pierced mouth. The audience cheered again.

Fecal Rot Crotch walked off of the stage, disappearing behind a black curtain, which hung directly behind the stage. A young man with spiky black hair emerged from behind the curtain and took the microphone.

"Alright, that was Fecal Rot Crotch, singing 'That's Why My Face Melts (When We Are Apart)'. Next up is EAR MUTILATOR!"

The crowd cheered. The man with the spiky black hair walked off the stage, disappearing behind the black curtain. For a moment, the crowd was silent.

"This is them," Harriet whispered excitedly.

"Super Annoyo's band?" Viola said.

"Yea."

A skinny man with scruffy blond hair and a black leather jacket, walked out onto the stage, and took the microphone. He had a red electric guitar around his neck, and was followed by a man with short, spiky, dark blue hair, and a long black coat, holding a black electric guitar. Then, by a man with slicked-back, white-blond hair, who sat down behind the drum set on the stage. Last out was Spencer, wearing a lot of guyliner and holding a black base guitar. He was wearing a sleeveless, black, leather jacket over his muscular, bare chest, and his shaggy, black hair was mussed up with a lot of gel.

"That's him. That's the guy," whispered Harriet to Viola, and pointing at Spencer.

"He's cute," commented Viola.

"I think he might be Super Annoyo," said Harriet.

"Really?" replied Viola, surprised by this startling possibility.

"How are we all doing tonight?" the skinny blond man behind the microphone shouted. The crowd cheered in response. "My name is Devin Forress, lead singer and lead guitarist."

Devin pointed to the blond man on the drums. "That over there is Kalvin Pierce, on the drums."

He pointed to the man with the spiky blue hair: "Danny Plaxman on backup vocals and guitar.

"And Spencer Tuckerson on base," he said, pointing to Spencer.

Devin strummed his guitar and announced the title of their first song: "Funeral March." Then, he began to sing and play a medium tempo melody on his guitar. Kalvin hit the drums in a slow, melodic pattern. Then, Danny began to play his guitar, and finally Spencer began to play his.

"They're not quite as bad as the last guy," said Viola to Harriet.

"Yea, they're almost good," agreed Harriet.

"It makes me sad to know how bad you have it, honey," Devin sang slowly into the microphone.

"When their set is done, we should go see if we can catch Super Annoyo back stage," said Viola, "You are sure he's Super Annoyo, right?"

"Because you're too beautiful to live this way, baby," Devin sang.

"I'm not sure, but to be fair, he is pretty annoying," said Harriet.

"Run away with me. Run away with me. Run away with me. For sure girl, not maybe," sang Devin.

"How will we know if it's him?" said Viola.

"Let's flee this funeral march," sang Devin.

"I don't know," said Harriet, "I guess we'll look through their stuff and see if his costume or the money he stole from the bank is in there."

"That's right, babe," Devin whispered sensuously into the microphone.

"We still won't know for sure," said Viola.

"It's the best we can do right now," said Harriet.

...

After singing a few songs, Devin walked off of the stage and the crowd cheered. Devin's band followed. Harriet and Viola watched as they disappeared behind the black curtain.

"Let's go," said Harriet very seriously, and she and Viola moved quickly toward the stage.

"Hey, hey, hey, whoa, you can't go back there," said the man with the spiky black hair when he saw that Harriet and Viola were headed for the black curtain. Harriet ignored him and kept walking. The man stretched an arm out in front of her to impede her progress and Harriet pushed him violently out of her way.

"I'm so sorry about my friend," Viola chuckled nervously, "She uh...she just really likes EAR MUTILATOR."

Viola disappeared behind the black curtain. The man with the spiky black hair shrugged and got back to announcing the next band.

Behind the curtain, the next band, a pair of women with long black hair and goth makeup, were preparing their instruments. There was lot of junk on the ground here, and piles of crates and clear containers were pushed up against the walls in tall stacks. The containers were filled with spotlights, audio equipment, wires, old TVs, and various other miscellaneous items.

The guys from EAR MUTILATOR were sitting on a bunch of the lower stacks of crates, discussing something with one and other. Harriet and Vila darted behind a couple of tall stacks of boxes, and hid from them, while listening in on their conversation.

"I heard that there's a talent agent in the audience tonight," said Kalvin. His slicked-back white-blond hair looked purple under the blacklight on the wall, near where he was sitting.

"Yea, this could be our big break," said Danny. His voice was much deeper than those of the other band members, as Harriet had noticed while he had been singing the backup vocals. "It's a shame we had to suck so hard tonight."

"Don't look at me," said Devin, "It's *Spencer* who kept fucking up the baseline."

"Hey! I *did not*," Spencer interjected resentfully.

"The talent agent was that guy in the suit. He didn't look too impressed," said Danny.

"But shit. Who knows? Maybe he did like us," said Kalvin.

"We should have played some of the songs that I wrote," said Spencer.

"Oh my god, Spencer, shut the fuck up. You're so annoying," groaned Devin, "Nobody wants to hear the song you wrote about the dominatrix porn star, ok?"

"You didn't even listen to more than the first few chords of it!" complained Spencer. "Why do you never want to play any of my songs?"

"How about because — *shut up* we're talking about something important here," said Devin.

Spencer sulked quietly, while the other band members continued their conversation.

"I heard that a guy from Headless Records is going to be at the Hornet's Nest next Saturday," said Danny, "Not sure though."

"I would practice just in case," said Kalvin.

"Harriet, this is stupid. What are we supposed to be doing here?" Viola whispered to Harriet.

"I don't know. I just thought maybe there would be a clue or something," whispered Harriet back. She poked her head out from behind the stack of boxes that she was hiding behind, and glanced around quickly, in search of clues. Spencer had a black backpack with him and a black guitar case. Perhaps super Annoyo's costume was hiding inside one of those bags somewhere.

"Hey, look'it that. Girls," said Danny pointing to Harriet and Viola.

Harriet walked out from the place where she was hiding and Viola followed nervously.

"Ho yeah. You caught us," said Harriet, "We're *girls*."

"You want my autograph, baby? It might be worth something someday," said Danny, his eyes trained on Viola's cleavage.

Viola blushed.

"Hehehe...ok," she giggled.

Everything was going perfectly. Why should these guys suspect that Harriet and Viola were anything more than horny groupies? Why should they suspect that they were, in fact, heros incognito?

"Sweet," said Spencer, grinning. "We never get girls come back here."

"Spencer, *shut the fuck up*!" said Devin, turning his head to yell at Spencer. He glanced back over at Harriet. "Don't listen to him. We get girls all the time. Like everyday."

Harriet glanced down at Spencer's guitar case. If she could get him to open it, she could also be sure that Super Annoyo's purple and orange spandex suit wasn't squashed up inside of it.

"Play us a song and we'll totally make out with you afterwards," said Harriet. *If the band plays a song*, she thought, *I can kick open Spencer's guitar case and then run off with his backpack while he's distracted.*

"Hey! I never agreed to that." interjected Viola indignantly.

"It's cool. We'll still play you a song," said Spencer, slouching over his guitar nonchalantly.

"Hey. Now *I* never agreed to *that*," growled Devin. "*Spencer*, for the love of fuck, could you please *never talk again*."

"We should probably hang around here a little bit

longer, anyway. Just incase hell freezes over and that talent agent comes backstage to talk to us," said Kalvin.

"So you won't play us a private concert, then?" Harriet moaned disappointedly. That would have been the perfect diversion.

"Oh no. I'm so genuinely disappointed," added Viola rather unconvincingly.

Danny stood up and put his hand in hers.

"Rain check, baby," he said, his deep voice quiet and sensual, not in the slightest bit suspicious of her authenticity.

Kalvin took his phone out and started watching internet videos on it. Devin, now not all together convinced that Harriet and Viola were about to jump in bed with him, lost all interest in the women, and instead watched the tiny screen on Kalvin's phone. Harriet glanced back down at Spencer's guitar case. Then, back up at Spencer. Spencer was looking at her through guyliner-ringed eyes with a distant, entranced expression, which suggested, perhaps, that he had never looked at a woman before.

A thought occurred to Harriet. Why did she need a distraction? Why not just grab Spencer's bag and root through it. What was he going to do about it? If his aura was any indication, not a damn thing.

Harriet kicked Spencer's guitar case open and glanced inside quickly. It was empty except for a broken guitar pick and a few pennies. Then, she swooped down, grabbed the black backpack, unzipped it, and started riffling through its contents.

"...H-hey what're you doing?" Spencer murmured weakly, his eyes getting big as she flipped the bag up-side-down and dumped its contents onto the floor.

A bunch of black clothing fell out, along with a travel tooth brush and a can of cheep cologne. There didn't seem to be any purple spandex mixed in there. Harriet sifted through the pile just to be sure.

"Watch it. Ever thing I own is in that bag," Spencer said

nervously, holding his hand out in front of him. His pale face contorted with a paralyzed confusion and he remained seated.

"Oh my god. Everyone ever has to watch this," said Kalvin. Harriet glanced over at him and saw that he was still staring at his phone. Devin, Danny, and Viola were standing behind him, watching the phone as well. "Spencer, you have to watch this."

"Uh. Ok. In a minute," said Spencer, his eyes still trained on Harriet as she rooted through his bag.

Harriet unzipped the compartment in the front and the compartments on the sides of the bag. There were a few guitar picks and pens in the side compartments and the front compartment had a small notebook filled with illegible, scribbled notes, perhaps they were song lyrics. If Spencer was really Super Annoyo, there was no evidence to support it here.

"What are you doing?" Spencer asked weakly, his eyes still very big.

"Oh...*uh*...." Harriet mused. She pulled a pair of Spencer's black and white striped boxers free from the pile of clothes, which lay next to Spencer's open backpack, and then stuffed the boxers into her front pocket.

"I collect men's underpants," she lied, her light brown eyes locking on his dark brown confused ones. "Because I'm a pervert."

Spencer blinked, looking confused for a moment and then relaxed.

"Heheheheh..." Spencer chuckled, slouching over his guitar. A mop of shaggy black hair slid over his face, obscuring one of his eyes. "Well...enjoy them, pretty lady."

"Spencer, watch the video already," Kevin said, still staring at the screen of his phone.

"Harriet, your life is not complete unless you've watched the video," said Viola robotically.

Spencer and Harriet walked over and stood with the rest of them, behind Kalvin, training their eyes on the screen of his phone. Kalvin clicked the play button on the video, and a quirky pop/electronica dance mix began playing. The screen flashed bright red and purple with seizure educing rapidness. Then, Super Annoyo appeared on the screen, turned his purple spandex clad ass toward the screen, and then started twerking.

"Your life is not complete unless you've watched this video!" Super Annoyo sang at an earsplitting volume and off-key. "Watching this video is your life now!"

Harriet groaned and rolled her eyes.

"You can't be serious," she moaned, noting without surprise that Super Annoyo had chosen the most annoying dance in existence for this video. She quickly glanced at the bottom of the screen to see how many hits this idiotic video had. A little over two million. Perfect.

Super Annoyo pushed his ass closer to the camera and the screen flipped around 360 degrees.

"Lookit mah ass, lookit mah ass!" Super Annoyo sang. Then, a stock photo of some kittens playing with string, with a watermark declaring the property of *Live Vid Stock Photo*, flashed on the screen several times. "Cats-CATS-CATS-cats!"

The screen behind Super Annoyo's twerking ass flashed orange and purple. The camera zoomed in an out on his crack several times and then the screen flipped 360 degrees again.

"Lookit mah ass, lookit mah ass!" Super Annoyo sang again. A picture of a fat grey cat, sitting in a cardboard box, with a squeaky mouse toy in its mouth, flashed several times on the screen. "Cats-CAT-CATS-cats!"

Camera cut to the lower half of Super Annoyo's face.

"Oh my god cats exist," Super Annoyo's mouth informed them. A picture of a fat lady, holding an orange tabby cat flashed briefly on the screen. Then, the camera cut back to Super Annoyo's ass twerking for about four seconds, and then back to the lower half of Super Annoyo's face: "This video is your life now."

Harriet shook her head.

"So you idiots...actually *like* this?" Harriet muttered, confused.

"Oh my god cats exist," murmured Viola robotically.

"This video is my life now," confirmed Spencer in a similar robotic tone.

Hours passed, Viola and EAR MUTILATOR watched the video over and over again, their eyes unfocused, their mouths open and dripping. Harriet tried to get Viola to leave with her, but she refused to move her eyes away from the screen of Kalvin's cell phone for even a second.

"I just need to see the ass one more time," Viola droned robotically when asked to leave. "And the cats....I need to see the cats...and the ass....those are two great things that go great together...."

"This video is my life now," agreed Danny Robotically, without taking his eyes off of the screen."

"I didn't know who I was before I saw this video," said Devin.

"Everything is different now," agreed Spencer. "Nothing will ever be the same."

Harriet grumbled to herself a bit and sat down on one of the stacks of boxes. She waited another twenty minutes for Viola to get tired of the video and leave with her, and then got frustrated, and left by herself.

"Goodbye," Viola said, as Harriet stomped over to the back door, and exited the building. She sounded distant and unconcerned.

Chapter 8:
Super Annoyo Leaves Chaos in his Wake

Harriet exited the Hornet's Nest, through the backdoor behind the stage, and into the narrow alleyway behind the building. The city was strangely quiet. Harriet couldn't hear the engines of cars speeding by, the honking of horns, or the chattering of pedestrians. Absent also was the cloud of human auras that typically swarmed her consciousness when she walked through crowded places.

As Harriet exited the alleyway behind the club and emerged onto the main street, she saw that the roads and sidewalks were empty. As she walked, she noticed the occasional stationary car, or flaming wreck of what used to be a car. A crowd of fifteen or so people stood around a man who was holding a cell phone, their eyes unfocused and mouths open and dripping as they watched Super Annoyo's viral video.

"Excuse me?" Harriet asked, tapping one of these people on the shoulder, a plump middle-aged man with a comb over, a suit, and a briefcase.

The man jerked his shoulder away from her and yelled: "Stop it! Can't you see that this video is my life now!" without turning his head away from the screen of the cell phone for even a second.

Harriet kept walking. Her car was parked five or six blocks away.

In the distance, Harriet saw a large screen built into the side of a skyscraper. The screen, which usually displayed a rotating assortment of paid video advertisements, now displayed Super Annoyo twerking and pictures of cats.

"Lookit mah ass, lookit mah ass!" a massive Super Annoyo sang from the monstrous billboard.

A crowd of spectators was gathered in a circle around the screen, staring at it.

"Cats-CATS-CATS-cats!" some of the spectators sang

back at him. Harriet could sense that their auras had all faded into near nonexistence.

"This is some seriously fucked-up shit right here," said Harriet to herself. "I'll bet anything Super Annoyo's behind it...that dastardly annoying fiend."

Harriet found her car (a black Lamborghini that was worth more than most people's houses) where she had left it, parallel parked next to a meter on the side of the road. A red truck seemed to have crashed straight into it, crushing most of the front of it like an accordion.

"Oh *shit*," Harriet swore, as she walked back and forth, surveying the irreparable damage to her vehicle with disbelief. She slipped her t-shirt and jeans off, and dumped them onto the ground, revealing her hero costume underneath. Then, she dug her mask out of the pocket of her leather pants and her jacket out of the handbag she had been carrying, before putting them on. "Now it's personal."

Harriet peered into the truck that had slammed into her car. The corpse of the truck's driver was hunched over the dashboard; its face mangled and gruesome; its mouth agape with what must have been this man's final emotion: mortal terror. The corpse's torso and abdomen were crushed and pinned grotesquely between the dashboard and the driver's seat. The hand at the end of its limp arm gripped a cell phone.

"Lookit mah ass, Lookit mah ass!" the cell phone droned. Then it made a faint buzzing noise and then went dead.

Chapter 9:
The Hunt

Maniacal, annoyingly high-pitched laughter rang in Harriet's ears. Harriet turned her head in the direction of the large screen mounted onto the side of the tall building where the noise was coming from. The viral video of Super Annoyo twerking had been replaced by what she assumed must have been live feed of him, speaking to the crowd directly. Harriet stopped walking abruptly. She stood still and quiet like the rest of the crowd so that Super Annoyo would not realize that she had not been affected.

"YEAAAAHhh WOOOHOOOO! I hope you all enjoyed my ass and cats! Now you're all UUUNNNNNDDDDEEERRRRR MMMMMYYYYYY COOOOooOOOOoooNNNNTRROooooOOOLLLLLLLLL!" Super Annoyo shouted triumphantly, jumping up and down and punching the air.

Harriet noticed that Super Annoyo seemed to be sitting behind a desk. The wall behind him was grey and there was a calendar with a kitten hanging off of a tree branch behind him. A drawing of a cheeseburger was scribbled on the July 24th box under the picture of the cat.

"You see that huge pile of sacks next to the building?" Super Annoyo asked the crowd. Harriet couldn't see the pile of sacks that he was talking about because the crowd was so thick but assumed that they must have been there. "I want you to take all of the money you have with you and put it in those sacks. Then, do you see that truck over there?" Super Annoyo pointed to a big purple truck parked near the building where his video billboard was mounted. The truck had the word "Annoyo Mobile" scribbled on the side of it in bright red letters. "The purple one, yeessss, the one that says "Annoyo Mobile" on it. You can't miss it. I want you to put all of the sacks into the back of that truck, after they are filled with your money. Then you, *you*, the guy with the glasses and the purple suit–"

"Who me?" asked a black man who wore a bright purple suit, a leopard print shirt, and a bright purple fedora with a pink feather in it. He also wore a pair of bright purple glasses, and carried a gold pimp cane. Perhaps he was a pimp.

"Yea, you. I like your style. After my truck's full of money, why don't you use that GPS in there to drive it down to my secret hideout?"

"...Ok," the pimp replied robotically. His face bore a dazed, zombie-like expression.

Harriet watched with amazement as people everywhere dug money out of their pockets and lined up to throw it all into the sacks provided for them by Super Annoyo. The sacks filled up quickly and Harriet found herself compelled to dump some of her own money in there, just so that Super Annoyo would not become suspicious of her.

"Yes...yessssss...." Super Annoyo celebrated annoyingly, once all of the sacks were full. "Now put the money in the back of the truck."

Several dozen or so people lifted the large, heavy bags on Super Annoyo's command and carried them to the back of the truck. Once the trunk was full, the pimp climbed up into the truck and got behind the driver's seat. He pulled the driver's side door shut, turned the key in the ignition, and started to drive away. This was Harriet's chance. Assuming the pimp was also hypnotized, that truck would take her directly back to Super Annoyo's hideout.

Harriet took a deep breath, and then sprinted after the truck, abandoning her act. She caught the truck easily, and hopped on the back of it with the money.

"Whaahaattt? Why are you not hypnotized?" Super Annoy blurted out furiously. "The woman in the leather fetish costume, DESTROY HER! Rip her EYEESS OUT OF HER HEAD AND CHOKE HER WITH THEM! But I guess we have to keep with the theme here *so*...I guess....DO IT ANNOOOOYINGLY!"

The crowd of people started chasing the car, but by this point it was going at full speed and they could not hope to catch up with it. Harriet breathed a sigh of relief, gripping the side of the truck for stability as it sped away, turned a sharp corner, and headed straight for the first exit, which led out of town. The crowd ran as fast as it could, despite not being able to catch the truck, and, for a time, Harriet became confident that they posed her no danger. Then, the pimp stopped at a red traffic light.

"Fuck," Harriet swore. Harriet stood up as two men climbed onto the truck with their fists raised.

"Oh my God. Did you know that cat's exist?" one of the men informed her robotically. "Ok. I'm gonna' rip your eyes out now."

She grabbled one of the men by his hair, lifted him off of the ground, and threw him at the other one, knocking them both off of the truck. The traffic light turned green, and the pimp sped up again. An old lady hooked her walker over the back of the truck just as the car was picking up speed and got dragged several feet before she finally let go of the walker's silver handles. A crimson smear of blood was left against the rough pavement where her body had been scraped like a peeled potato.

"Caaaatsss...." the old lady moaned as she lay bleeding on the pavement. She attempted to lift herself up, but was then trampled by the zombified crowd as they began chasing the truck again.

The pimp drove for awhile, down the freeway, before taking another exit, and hitting another red traffic light. By this point, the crowd from the city had been left far in the distance. Harriet watched a pack of pedestrians who were strolling along the sidewalk jerkily. Most of them probably had cell phones and could have easily stumbled across Super Annoyo's viral video. The truck started again, and Harriet breathed a sigh of relief.

"This video," a woman's voice huffed. Harriet turned around fast and saw a pregnant woman, holding a baby in a powder blue onesie over her head like a club. *"Is my life now."*

The woman brought the baby down hard like a mallet, attempting to smash Harriet over the head with it.

Harriet sidestepped the woman's blow, while at the same time, kicking the woman's legs out from under her, and sending her flying over the side of the moving vehicle. The woman loosened her grip on the baby as she was slipping and Harriet grabbed the baby out of the air before its soft head hit the floor of the truck. She wrapped her arms around the infant as it began to wail, and its mother shrieked and gargled the lyrics to Super Annoyo's viral video through a mouthful of her own blood. She held onto one of the mud flaps of the truck and was dragged for a total of four seconds before finally letting go.

Harriet shuttered and looked down at the screaming baby she was holding. It was a pretty baby with rosy cheeks and a tuft of blond hair on its head.

"It's too bad you've probably been dropped on your head a few times," said Harriet to the baby. She rocked it back and forth nervously as the truck continued to speed down the road, past houses, strip malls, fast food restaurants, gas stations, and convenience stores. She didn't know what else to do.

After some time, the truck rolled to a stop in front of a yield sign and allowed a blue minivan to cross the street from the right. Harriet took this brief moment of stillness as an opportunity to stick the baby inside one of the sacks full of money, where she hoped that it would not be discovered by Super Annoyo or the pimp, and discarded on the ground like a rag doll. She made a little nest for it in a pile of paper bills, and left the bag slightly open at the top so that it could breath.

"Shh, baby," said Harriet to the baby. "Don't cry now."

The truck started moving again, and then pulled into

an office building parking lot, and parked in a space near the building. A little white sign in front of the parking space had the words: "Reserved for Employee of the Month" written on it in thick, black letters.

Employee of the month, huh? Harriet mused. Had super Annoyo been an employee here? Had he used his powers of annoyingness to annoy his employers into awarding him employee of the month? Or did he simply park where ever he wanted to, while at the same time, making the ears of anyone who complained about it bleed with the intense veracity of his annoyingness?

The pimp jumped out of the truck and slammed the door behind him. Then, he walked to the back of the truck, lifted a bag of money from the back of it, and started to walk toward the building. It was a tall, grey building with a lot of windows and the words: "Bendingo Advertising" chiseled in big, bold, stone letters over the revolving front door. Twenty or so men and women in business attire burst from their parked cars, and then sprinted over to the pimp in order to assist him with carrying the heavy bags. In hindsight, sticking the baby inside of one of the bags of money seemed like a pretty stupid idea.

Harriet jumped into the air and did a backflip over the front of the truck, disappearing from sight before she could be noticed and reported to Super Annoyo. She did this not for self-defense, because these people probably didn't have superpowers and were likely not a threat to her, but to avoid maiming and/or killing anymore normals.

Super Annoyo's minions grabbed sacks full of money, then, darted back through the revolving front door, and into the office building with it. Harriet watched them for a few seconds, contemplating the best ways to get into the building without being noticed.

Super Annoyo's minions moved quickly, and the sacks of money disappeared into the office building with surprising speed. Then, the pimp grabbed the sack with the baby in it and disappeared as well. *Well, shit,* Harriet thought as she watched the pimp run off with the final sack, one white-gloved hand clamped tightly around its opening. *Now you've killed the baby too. Good going, Harriet, some hero you are.*

The parking lot was empty and quiet now. Harriet stepped out from behind the truck and darted toward the office building. To avoid being noticed, she stayed as far away as she could from the front door. Instead, she ran around the side of the building, dug her nails into the narrow crevices between slabs of granite siding, and began scaling the building.

She moved quickly and effortlessly, scaling fours stories of office building without so much as breaking a sweat. Then, punched in a glass window. It shattered easily and pieces of broken glass littered the grey carpet inside. Harriet grabbed the window ledge and pulled herself inside.

She landed on her feet on the glass-littered grey carpet, and scanned the room with her eyes for signs of activity. There were a few desks in this room, covered with computers, mouse pads, desk lamps, and an assortment of personal effects, such as calendars with puppies on them, pictures of people's families, and bobble heads of famous cartoon characters and athletes. There didn't seem to be anyone here.

Harriet tiptoed quietly toward the door at the end of the room and glanced around, incase she had missed someone hiding under a desk, or in a corner behind a large, decorative plant. Still, she saw no one. Absent also was the buzz of human aura.

Harriet exited the room and entered an empty hallway. The presence of human aura grew stronger as she walked toward the elevator at the end of the hallway. Perhaps, Super Annoyo and his minions were in that direction.

Harriet pushed the button on the elevator, waited a few seconds for it to arrive, and then stepped on. She wasn't sure what floor Super Annoyo was on if he was here at all. So she hit the button of the highest floor, 17.

As the elevator rose, Harriet found that the presence of human aura grew steadily stronger and stronger. The intensity of the presence reached its peak at floor 13 and then began to wear off again.

Once at the top of the building, Harriet hit the floor 13 button, her brows drawing together in a look of determination as she did so. If Super Annoyo was anywhere in this building, he was on floor 13.

The elevator sank and so did Harriet's stomach. She assumed a fighting pose, legs apart, knees bend, fists raised, prepared for battle. Super Annoyo would almost certainly be armed and protected in anticipation of her arrival.

The elevator doors slid open. Light poured into the elevator. Harriet blinked. She had been expecting to see an elaborate lair lousy with the eccentricities of her intensely annoying adversary. Instead, she saw what looked like a perfectly ordinary office, filled with cubicles. People in business attire walked back and forth, making copies with the copy machine, talking to each other, holding steaming mugs of coffee. Despite Harriet's bizarre attire and demeanor, they ignored her entirely.

Harriet stepped out of the elevator. The carpets here were gray. The walls were grayish white. The white drop ceiling was lined by fluorescent lights, and the wall at the far end of the room was covered in large windows, which let in a great deal of natural light.

Harriet walked up and down rows of cubicles, searching for Super Annoyo. Instead, what she saw were bored people in suits, ties, skirts, and button-down shirts, working behind desks. She saw computers, keyboards, pencil sharpeners, family photos, and coffee mugs filled with pencils, but nothing to indicate that this was perhaps the lair of an evil super criminal.

Harriet tapped a man in a three-piece suit, carrying a stack of papers in his hands.

"Have you seen Super Annoyo around here?" she

asked.

"Mmm...nope," replied the man, "...Hey did you know, *cat's exist?*"

After circling the room a few times, Harriet concluded that Super Annoyo was not present. Perhaps he had fled. Harriet walked back to the elevator, grumbling to herself, as she felt intensely frustrated by this infuriating anticlimax. She had been expecting a showdown. And blood. Lots of blood. This was just disappointing.

Harriet stopped just a few feet from the edge of the room, and then turned around, grinning evilly. Super Annoyo may not have been present *in costume*. But that didn't necessarily mean that he wasn't *here*. The image of Super Annoyo on the large screen, looking over the city, flashed in Harriet's mind. She recalled that he had been sitting in front of a grey wall, a cubicle wall perhaps. She recalled also that there had been a calendar with a kitten on it pinned to the wall, and that there had been a drawing of a hamburger inside of the box, denoting the 24th. There was a chance, albeit a slim one, that Super Annoyo was still sitting in front of the same calendar. Harriet began her search again with new optimism.

Chapter 10:
My Name is Justice Bitch

Once Harriet knew what she was looking for, it did not take her very long to find it. She spotted the cat calendar that she remembered from the video, hanging on the inside of a cubicle, not to far from the exit. She approached the calendar quietly, while at the same time, pretending to not be too interested in it. There was the picture of the hamburger under the 24th, scribbled there in blue pen, plain as day. Harriet glanced down at the man who was sitting underneath the calendar. His back was turned to her and he was typing away on the computer in front of him, apparently indifferent to her presence.

She stepped closer and felt his heart rate increase. He was afraid of her. Unlike the other people in the room, he was only pretending not to notice her. She could sense it. It was unmistakable. Probably.

Harriet tapped the man on the back of his grey suit jacket. The man turned his computer chair around to face her. He was probably about 40 years old, with a large, sharp, pointed nose that looked like it had been snapped left, and a receding hair line.

"Can I help you?" the man asked innocently.

"Are you Super Annoyo?" Harriet asked bluntly, her eyes locking on his.

The man's eyes got big and he started to sweat.

"Ah ha ha...no....don't be ridiculous," said the man. He pointed to the name plate on his desk, which read: Peter Burgry. "I'm Mr. Burgry."

"Bullshit," said Harriet, slamming her hands down on the arms of Burgry's computer chair. Burgry, startled by the sudden movement, flinched and backed away from her. "You're Super Annoyo, aren't you?"

Burgry rolled his computer chair backward. Then, opened one of the deeper drawers of his desk, and reached his hand inside of it.

"Ok, so you caught me. I'm Super Annoyo," Burgry admitted evenly. "What you gonna' do? Beat me up? Send me to prison? Hmmm? *Hmmmmmmm?*"

"Give up Super Annoyo. Your powers of annoyingness have no effect on me," said Harriet, though, in truth, she really did hope that he would put up a fight so that she could get a little blood on her hands guilt free.

"Oh yea, and who the hell are you?"

"I'm Justice Bitch."

"You are?"

"Yes," Harriet said.

"But are you sure you are?" Super Annoyo asked again.

"Yes."

"But are you sure you're sure?"

"*Yes.*"

"But are you sure you're sure you're sure?"

"YES."

"But are you sure you're sure you're sure you're sure?"

"*Enough!*" Harriet growled, very frustrated by this irritating and likely endless chain of questioning. "Why are you doing this? And why would you set up your evil lair in an advertising firm?"

"I work here," Super Annoyo explained simply.

"Really?"

"Yes, I write commercials," Super Annoyo elaborated further. "I've been doing it for years."

"Really? How could someone as annoying as you write anything even remotely enjoyable?" Harriet mused incredulously.

"Commercials aren't supposed to be *enjoyable*, young lady. They're supposed to make you *want to die*," Super Annoyo said as though this were the most obvious fact in the world.

"Of course," Harriet groaned, thinking of the majority

50

of TV commercials in existence. "How could I forget?"

Growing bored of this conversation, Burgry reached his hand into the deepest drawer of his desk. Then, pulled out the baby in the blue onesie, now sleeping peacefully. He wrapped his arms around the baby, and rocked it gently, staring at Harriet defiantly as he did so.

"Oh, come on, now. You wouldn't hit a guy holding a baby, would you?" teased Burgry, "How about instead we talk about this like adults?"

"You're going to free these people's minds, Super Annoyo, and then I'm taking you to prison," grumbled Harriet impatiently.

"What's the rush?"

"I find your motivations perplexing, Super Annoyo," Harriet said, "Why sit here and talk to me? Why not just sick your room full of brain-dead, zombie henchmen on me instead?"

"You find my motivations perplexing, ay? Well I'll let you in on a little secret there, friend. I'm not really all that complicated," said Burgry. "If I sick my henchmen on you, you'll just kill them, and I don't want these good people to get hurt anymore than you do. I just want to be as rich as it is possible for anyone to be. That's all. Of course, you wouldn't understand that would you, little miss Harriet Ross... since you're already rich.

"You know my name?"

"Of course I know your name, you're a rich bitch, aren't you? I've seen you on TV, going to fancy benefit dinners, and telling the news how much your family doesn't need to be taxed because you give to charity. And you've got nothing but a small, cheap, plastic mask covering your face, how could I not recognize you?" said Burgry.

"You've got me there," said Harriet.

"Sure as shootin'."

"So your plan is to..."

"Steal a billion dollars or so and then disappear, never

to be seen or heard from again," said Burgry, "After that, I'll put everything back the way it was and you'll never know I was here."

"Put it back *now*."

"Nope."

"*Now*, or I'm ripping that baby out of your hands and beating you bloody."

"Not necessary," said Super Annoyo, shaking his head. Then, he started talking to the baby in a high pitched voice. "And you wouldn't like that very much, would you, little guy? No you wouldn't."

"Not necessary....*because*?" Harriet goaded incredulously.

"I just want a billion dollars. I don't really care where it comes from. So...if you give me a billion dollars of your *own* money, I'll give the money I stole back and put everyone back the way they were."

"You're lying."

"I'm not but whatever helps you sleep at night," shrugged Burgry.

"I'm not giving you a billion dollars, Super Annoyo. My family doesn't even have that much money," growled Harriet defensively. Though, in fact, this was a lie. Her father had been one of the richest men in the country.

"Alright, so let me put it this way," said Burgry, "Give me a billion dollars, now and I'll let these people go back to normal. Refuse and I annoy their brains into jelly, making their retardation *permanent*. Do you understand? The whole city will be filled with retards. *Permanently*. They'll have to rename the place *Retardville, Retardopolis, The Land of Drooling, Shitting, Cat-loving Retards!*"

"Ok *fine*," growled Harriet. "I promise to write you a check. I'll write you a check for one billion dollars...Courtesy of the Ross Foundation."

"And if the check bounces you're going to be covered in retards," warned Super Annoyo.

"Of course," Harriet replied, "Let me just go get my checkbook and I'll be right back."

Harriet turned as though to leave. Confident that Harriet was about to bring him the money, Burgry put the baby down on his desk. The instant that the baby was safely away from him, Harriet flipped back around, drew her fist back, and punched him in the jaw. "This is for Hawkette's lasagna!" she shouted (so that she would have something self-righteous to shout) and she felt the bone shatter as her fist connected with his face. Burgry let out the high-pitched scream of a goat getting its testicles removed by pliers, and stumbled to the ground.

"..Augghhh..." he slurred, clutching his bloody, broken jaw with both hands. He tried moving his mouth but found that it was no longer possible. His mangled face refused to cooperate, and instead the attempt to put up an Annoying defense brought on a fresh spasm of white hot agony that made him scream again.

"How do you put these people back to normal?" Harriet demanded.

Burgry lay huddled in the corner of the cubicle for a moment and didn't answer.

"*How* do you put the people back to normal?" Harriet repeated, louder this time.

Unable to speak and therefore, annoy, Burgry rose to his feet, slumped down into his computer chair, and wrote the words: "Play the video backwards," on the back of a scrap of paper.

"That better be the truth or I'm going to break all of your fingers off one at a time and shove them up your ass," Harriet threatened psychotically. A quiet, sinister part of her that she didn't want to acknowledge hoped that he was lying so that she would be able to do it.

Burgry nodded vigorously. He pointed to the computer.

Harriet dug a pair of handcuffs and ankle shackles out

of the inner pockets of her long, black coat. Then, she flipped him around and cuffed his hands behind his back.

"If you try to escape, you're going to be fucking sorry," she growled as she knelt down and fastened his ankles together with the ankle shackles.

Harriet turned her attention to the computer. Something was wrong. She walked over to the computer and shook the mouse a bit to remove the solid blue screen saver. Then, she saw it, the thing that had been open on Super Annoyo's desktop. It was a live video feed.

Harriet glanced up at the tiny webcam built into the top of Burgry's computer. The entire thing had been recorded.

Chapter 11:
An Interview with Justice Bitch

Spencer was in a pretty good mood that day. He woke up, grinning. Visions of Justice Bitch with her big hair and black leather flooded his consciousness. She had a deep and melodious voice that reminded him of smooth, rich hot chocolate.

"Hmmm...metaphor....is that a good metaphor?" Spencer murmured to himself as he sat up and threw the ratty blanket off of himself. He rubbed clumps of guyliner out of the corners of his tired eyes, and then grabbed his black backpack from behind the front seat of his car, removing his notebook from the front pocket.

Spencer flipped the notebook open and then scribbled the words: "Voice smooth and rich like hot chocolate," into the top left corner of the paper, where there was just a little bit of room.

Then, he imagined her say his name.

Spencer.... Spencer, the Justice Bitch in his brain whispered sensuously. He imagined her full, painted lips an inch away from his ear; her breath on his skin. She smelled like heaven. *I know what you did, Spencer. You can't hide it from me.*

Justice Bitch had only just recently saved the city from Super Annoyo by playing his viral video backwards on the big screen in the center of the city, and then distributing thousands of copies of the backwards video to citizens everywhere. The mess had taken a week or so to clean up, with police and emergency medical staff working around the clock to show the backwards video to as many zombified victims as quickly as possible. By the time that Spencer had been released from his own trance, most of the rest of the city had already gone back to normal, Spencer had awoken to discover his pants soaked through with two days worth of his own piss, and Justice Bitch had already started doing TV interviews. Spencer didn't own a TV, but he did own a gym membership. And there was a TV at the gym.

The gym also had a shower. Spencer didn't own a shower. He lived in his car. It was a broken, old, piece of shit, red Honda, with a lot of scratches and dents in it.

Spencer pushed a button under the driver's side backseat window to unlocked the car doors. Then, stepped out onto the sidewalk, where he was parallel parked. There were multiple tickets on the dashboard, stuck under the windshield wipers.

"Noooo...whhhy?" Spencer moaned when he saw the tickets. It was damn lucky that the car hadn't been towed last night as it had been parked next to an expired meter, but he still didn't *feel* lucky.

Spencer ripped the parking tickets out from underneath his windshield wipers and looked at them for a moment.

"Oh man....*oh man*....." Spencer panicked as he began reading the parking tickets. "....I can't afford this..."

Spencer glanced around to see if anyone was watching him, and when he saw that no one was, he ripped the parking tickets into halves, and then into quarters, then, threw the pieces up into the air.

"Ok, problem solved," he said, smiling. If he didn't think about it, then it wasn't a problem.

There was another parking ticket under his windshield wiper that he had somehow overlooked. It was on a different type of paper than the rest of them.

Spencer pulled the ticket out from under the windshield wiper and looked at it. The following words were scribbled on the paper: You *will leave 200 dollars under the rock with the* red x on it, four feet to the left of the tree, planted near the back of your car.

"Well," said Spencer stupidly, as a bizarre urge to do whatever the piece of paper told him overpowered his conscious will. "Can't argue with that logic."

Still smiling, Spencer dug his hand into the front pocket

of his black jeans, and withdrew two hundred dollar bills. Then, he found the rock with the red x on it, in the overgrown front garden of the nearest row house, lifted it, and stuck the hundred dollar bills under it. It was the money he'd received from playing his latest gig at The Hornet's Nest, as the base player for EAR MUTILATOR. It was also, coincidentally, the only money he had.

Spencer grabbed his black back pack and headed for the gym. He walked for six blocks or so, stuck his hands in the pockets of his jeans, and whistled. He was still trying to figure out the baseline of the song that he was working on, and whistling helped with that. Pangs of hunger twisted his stomach. *I'm hungry,* a little nagging voice in his head intruded. Spencer shook his head and ignored it. If he didn't think about it, then it wasn't a problem.

Keep it together, buddy, you won't have to live this way for much longer, he told himself, *EAR MUTILATOR's going to cut a deal with Headless Records. Then you'll be rolling in cash.*

This thought made his grin broaden and his whistling grew louder and more elaborate. The talent agent from Headless Records had shown some interest in the band and there was a good chance that it would see some success in the near future.

Spencer walked into the gym, showed his membership to the woman at the front counter, and then headed to the men's locker room, where he showered and changed his clothes.

Then, he went back out to the gym's front lobby, and sat down backwards in a metal folding chair, pointed away from the large, flat screen television on the wall. Justice Bitch was supposed to be doing an interview today. Spencer wasn't going to miss the opportunity to watch his newest and most awesome imaginary girlfriend talk about crime fighting some more. Nor did he plan to miss her cleavage in that tight, leather, midriff shirt.

"It's great to have you here, Justice Bitch."

"It's great to be here, Tim."

Spencer watched as Justice Bitch shook hands with a news man, who was wearing a black suit with a dark blue tie. She sat down in a round, tan-colored chair on one side of a glass ottoman, and the news man sat down in the round, tan-colored chair opposite her. He cleared his throat and readied his note cards.

"Justice Bitch, since you saved Propopolus City from Super Annoyo's brain washing viral video, everyone has been wondering, will you continue your work keeping the city safe for normal, non-superpowered citizens?"

"The short answer is yes, Tim," said Justice Bitch, "Though, of course, people who misuse their supernatural abilities can be as much a threat to people with superpowers as they are to people without."

"True, true," replied the news man. "The city's growing population of superpowered individuals was affected by Super Annoyo's hypnosis as well. Why do you think you were unaffected?"

"I don't really know," replied Harriet more than a little defensively. "But it sounds like you're trying to imply some kind of a conspiracy and I don't like that."

"Yea, dude. She doesn't like that," interjected Spencer, rocking forward and then backward on the backwards metal folding chair in the gym lobby.

"Ohhoho...sorry, touched a nerve there, didn't I?" laughed the news man. "But still, why do you think that you were not affected by the viral video's hypnotic quality?"

"Resilience to supernatural abilities is one of my power attributes," said Harriet, "I'm not sure why. A friend of mine once said that the radiation affects people differently based on their personality traits. Perhaps I'm a resilient person."

"Well you've certainly shown your resilience recently," said the news man.

"Thank you, Tim," Harriet replied amicably. She smiled big, revealing a mouth full of white, perfect teeth.

Spencer had never seen anyone with teeth that perfect before, except for maybe in toothpaste commercials.

The newsman cleared his throat again.

"As you know, Super Annoyo's trial is fast approaching, and has made big, crazy, media circus, international news," he said.

Justice Bitch nodded.

"It has been argued that some superhumans exposed to the radiation, exhibit a sort of madness resulting from altered brain chemistry. What are your thoughts on Super Annoyo's choice to plead temporary insanity? And how do you feel about the justice system's handling of him?"

"I would have to say..." mused Justice Bitch, "That Super Annoyo's plea of temporary insanity, if we're being perfectly honest here, is utter and complete nonsense. I've spoken to Super Annoyo on several occasions. He's eccentric but he's not crazy. He knew what he was doing when he hypnotized all of those people, and he had a very rational, carefully thought out plan. As for the way the government is containing him, I think it's perfectly appropriate and necessary to keep our citizens safe."

"As you probably are aware, superhuman rights groups are calling the measures put in place to ensure that Super Annoyo cannot use his powers of annoyingness, a 'serious human rights infringement.' Would you agree that the measures put in place to contain Super Annoyo's power are in anyway overly extreme or inhumane?"

"I've seen where they are keeping Super Annoyo, and I have to say, considering how dangerous he is, the accommodations really aren't all that bad," replied Justice Bitch coolly. "Despite what the superhuman rights groups would have you believe, his jaw is wired shut because it was broken in the struggle, and not to contain his powers of annoyingness. It's true that he is being kept in a cell separate from the other prisoners, but he is not, as some people would have you believe 'restrained at all hours of the day.' He is allowed bathroom breaks and showers under strict supervision."

The news man turned toward the camera and then it zoomed in on him.

"Well, that's all the time we have now," he informed both Justice Bitch and his audience.

"Thank you, Justice Bitch, for taking the time out of your busy schedule to come on the show."

Justice Bitch stood up, shook the news man's hand, and gave the audience another amicable smile.

"My pleasure, Tim."

The news program cut to commercial and Spencer lost all interest in the television. His stomach grumbled. He hadn't eaten since noon yesterday and he felt dizzy and lightheaded.

Spencer went back to his car, threw the black backpack in the back seat, and then grabbed his guitar case. He walked to the subway, where there was a lot of foot traffic, took the guitar out of the case, threw the case on the ground, with the top open, so that maybe people would throw change in it, and then started playing.

"Oh, I lost my job at the grocery store — because of my stupid laser eyes," Spencer sang as he strummed the guitar.

"This guy said — 'Hey, Spencer, I bet you can't hit the can on the top of that stack of cans with your shitty laser eyes. I'll bet you 50 dollars, and cut off my *left nut*. You can't hit that can with your laser eyes, Spencer — because you *totally suck*!"

An old lady tossed a few pennies into Spencer's guitar case as she walked by, without turning her head to look at him.

"Thank you ma'am," Spencer said, tilting an imaginary hat with the hand which held the guitar pick, in solute of her. Then, he went back to singing the song. "So I told that guy, *fucker I can so hit that can*...because I'm a *total schmuck*!"

Spencer stopped singing for a moment to play a brief

guitar solo interlude. A guy in a fedora chuckled at his lame joke and threw a quarter in the guitar case as he walked by.

"Thank you, sir," Spencer said and he began singing again. "So then I shot lasers out of my eyes and missed the stupid can that he was pointing to. Instead I hit the wall behind it and blew a huge freaking hole in the *wall*. So I got fired. That's right I got fired. My laser eyes got me fired–Just like they got me fired at *the mall* — at Burger Boy, at the ticket booth, at the movie theater at the parking garage and at the *mess hall*!"

Spencer stopped singing for a moment to play another brief instrumental and then broke into his refrain:

"So please won't you lend me some money. Please people, I'm starving to death. I haven't had a decent meal, since my mom kicked me out, please I promise that I won't buy meth. Please lend me some money. I'm starving to death. Some day I will be a famous rock star but right now I am starving to death!"

Spencer paused again to play an instrumental. This time he really got into it, tilting his head down toward his guitar so that his shaggy, black hair fell over one eye. A woman in a business suit tossed two dollars into Spencer's guitar case, and a man in a Hawaiian shirt, dragging a rolling suitcase tossed in a couple of quarters.

"Thank you, folks," Spencer said and then he began to sing again. "So then I was in my apartment and my roommate, Kalvin, was all like, 'See that mosquito over there? I dare you to zap it with your laser eyes!' And I said: 'No way, I won't zap it with my laser eyes!' and he said 'You're a *pussy* if you don't zap it with your laser eyes!' so I said 'Yea, alright, I'll do it. *Yea, alright I'll do it!* Yea, alright I'll do it!' So then I shot lasers out of my eyes, missed the mosquito he was pointing to, and blew up the TV instead. His girlfriend was so mad. So he told her it was *my idea*. Which is why she threw me out on my ass, and that's what *I'm doin' here*."

Spencer strummed his guitar and interjected

sensuously from behind a curtain of displaced hair: "*Also*, I didn't pay the rent."

Spencer tossed his head back, forcing the hair out of his face and started singing again: "So please won't you lend me some money. Please people, I'm starving to death. I haven't had a decent meal, since my mom kicked me out. Please I promise that I won't buy meth. Please lend me some money. I'm starving to death. Some day I will be a famous rock star but right now I am starving to death! Death! *Pain!* Death!...It isn't pretty people. Can you spare a sandwich?"

Spencer strummed a final chord on his guitar dramatically and then put his arm out to signal the end of the song. There were a few scattered applauders, but mostly he was met with complete and total apathy. A plump older woman, dressed in young people's clothes, booed him and threw an empty, greasy sandwich rapper into his guitar case like it was a waste paper basket.

"..Oh, boo yourself," Spencer grumbled, crossing his arms defensively.

A teenager with profuse pimples and a buzz cut clapped slowly. He was wearing a red and white striped shirt, a pair of baggy jeans, and an expression that suggested sinister intent.

"Good song, friend," the teenager said and he stopped clapping.

"Thank you," said Spencer.

The teenager dug his hand into the pocket of his jeans and pulled out a candy bar, which he handed to Spencer.

"Oh my God, thank you so much," blurted out Spencer gratefully. He grabbed the candy bar, pulled off the rapper, and shoved it in his mouth.

"My name's Jason Walker," the kid said.

"Spencer Tuckerson," said Spencer through a mouth full of candy bar. He put his hand out for the kid to shake. The kid looked at his hand disdainfully for a moment and then shook it.

Spencer stuck his hand in the pocket of his black jeans and pulled out a business card.

"Call if you ever need a band. We do birthday parties, bar mitzvahs, whatever. Play gigs were ever we can get them," said Spencer.

"Uh huh," murmured Jason incredulously, staring down at the card in his hand. He stuck the card in his pocket and then looked back up at Spencer. "That song you were just singing, was it a true story?"

"Yea," said Spencer, "Well, sort of. Just a little bit of improv, venting about my life."

"So you really have laser eyes?" Jason asked.

"Uh huh," confirmed Spencer.

"Shit, man, then why are you sing-begging for meals? Why not just use what you've got to get what you want? That's what other folks with superpowers do," said Jason.

"Laser eyes kind of aren't good for anything," said Spencer.

"Uhhh...yes they *are*. They can blow holes in walls and probably kill people," said Jason.

"Uh...so can explosives and guns. What's your point?" said Spencer.

"My point is why not use that to get money?" said Jason.

"What you mean like with a sideshow?" asked Spencer, confused.

"No I mean like...doing villain stuff, you know," said Jason.

"Heheheheh...naw, naw dude. That's illegal," chuckled Spencer dismissively. He shook his head and then slouched over his guitar to tune it.

Jason shook his head. Then, he took a yellow notepad and a pen out of his pocket, scribbled something on the note with the pen, and then stuck the note to Spencer's forehead quickly. Spencer's eyes got big and went unfocused.

"Think about it," Jason said. "Consider your options."

With those words, Jason quickly grabbed the money out of Spencer's guitar case, shoved it in his pockets, and fled.

Chapter 12:
The Ghost of a Smile

"Hey, girl."

"Viola, Hi," Harriet said, picking up her cell phone with one hand and putting it to her ear. She gripped the white leather wheel of her red convertible with the other hand and drove over the suspension bridge, which lead into the city. Her long black hair was in a ponytail, and was blown behind her as she sped down the road.

"Benji got out of the hospital yesterday," Viola told her, "I think Lilly's really happy about that. They're hanging out like a couple now and junk."

"So they're a couple now?" Harriet asked rather indifferently.

"Sort of. Unofficially," said Viola, "They're both so shy and really just perfect for each other. I've never seen Lilly so happy but she deserves that, you know. She's had a really hard life. Her parents died when she was really young, you know. And she's been depressed a lot lately. But I think that Benji makes her happy. I saw her smile yesterday... and I haven't seen that in such a long time. I really hope it works out between those two."

"That's nice," said Harriet, "What about you and Stuart?"

"We're not a couple," replied Viola flatly.

"That's not what I meant," said Harriet, "I was talking about that one time, when he didn't show up for Sexy Super Friends club and you were acting like you had just had a big fight with him or something."

"Oh..haha...that was nothing," Viola chuckled, "He just got this crazy idea like you were evil or something and told me that I should drop you from the team. So, I was all like: 'I've known Harriet longer than anybody and blah blah blah, go screw yourself.'"

"Wow. Thanks for sticking up for me, I guess," said

Harriet a little unsurely. If she was being totally honest with herself, the radiation from that accident had probably made her *a little bit* evil. Or had it just made her sadistic? Sadistic? *Evil?* Semantics aside, were those two words really mutually exclusive things?

"Listen, my father's memorial's going to be in a few days. I would really love it if you could come," said Harriet.

"Oh, sure. I'll be there," said Viola excitedly. She knew from experience that any event held in association with the Ross family was bound to be extravagant to the point absurdity.

"Tell the team they're invited too," said Harriet.

"Ok."

"I'll send you all formal invitations. It's an RSVP event," said Harriet. She was really dreading the memorial and hoped that some of her friends might show up to make it less boring, impersonal, and obligatory.

"Yea. Can't wait. I will be there or be square."

"Be round."

"That's my plan."

"Bye."

"Ok. Bye."

Chapter 13:
EAR MUTILATOR Cuts a Record Deal

That evening, Spencer drove to Devin's apartment. The band had met with the talent agent from Headless records yesterday, while Spencer was interviewing for a new job as a waiter at a local restaurant. Spencer had hated missing the interview with the record company but there was still a chance that they would pass up EAR MUTILATOR for the record deal and he needed to get serious about replacing his old day job. Begging for crumbs was starting to get embarrassing.

Spencer was happy though, because there was a chance, albeit a very slim one, that all of his hopes and dreams were about to see their fruition and that everything he had worked and sacrificed for was about to be his. The guys had news for him and Kalvin had told him over the phone that he really aught to hear it in person. Spencer took this as a good sign because if the band was turned down, Kalvin probably would have just told him about it right then and there.

Spencer parallel parked his shitty, dented, red Honda a few blocks away from Devin's apartment building, and then got out of the car and walked there with a grin on his face. He stuck his hands in his pockets and whistled. There was hope for his career as a musician yet, and nothing could have made him happier.

Spencer walked into the apartment building, and was surprised to find the band waiting for him in the lobby. They looked cheerful, which was a good sign.

"Oh, hi guys," Spencer said, still grinning. "Why are you all out here in the lobby?"

"Because the last thing I need is ol' Spanky Fuckerson blasting my apartment to shit with his laser eyes," said Devin rather coldly.

"I thought we agreed that you're not going to call me that anymore," complained Spencer combatively, but despite his aggressive stance and tone, it remained clear that he was trying to hide the involuntary hurt in his voice with a bit of forced bravado.

"Except everyone calls you that behind your back anyway, don't they?" grumbled Devin.

Kalvin shook his head.

"Come on, man. We talked about this," Kalvin pleaded quietly. "Be nice."

"Fine. You tell him, then," said Devin.

"...So....we didn't get the record deal?" Spencer speculated uncertainly.

"Uh...no...um....actually..." Kalvin replied haltingly.

Danny cleared his throat and spoke in Kalvin's place.

"There's good news and bad news," he said.

"....Yea?" replied Spencer cautiously.

"The good news is EAR MUTILATOR got the record deal," said Danny.

"Heheheh...*yea*! Alright!" Spencer celebrated, punching the air. He couldn't believe what he was hearing. This had to be the happiest day of his life.

Danny and Kalvin seemed to be made uncomfortable by Spencer's display of joy. Devin groaned and rolled his eyes.

"Bad news is that you're no longer EAR MUTILATOR's base player," Danny finished quickly.

The grin slipped off of Spencer's face.

"...Huh?"

"Headless Records has a base player set up for us. A guy who's been in the industry for awhile," said Devin, and then he added bluntly: "They don't want *you*."

Spencer looked down at his feet. His eyes began to glow red and he bit his lip.

"...Why not," Spencer asked quietly.

"They just wanted someone with more experience playing base," said Kalvin in what he hoped was a comforting tone.

"I play lots of instruments," murmured Spencer. "Not just base."

"I'm really sorry this didn't work out for you, buddy. Just try not to get all laser eyes, ok?" said Kalvin, he reached out cautiously and patted Spencer on the shoulder.

Spencer wrapped his arms around himself and slouched defensively. The crimson glow radiating from his eyes grew brighter.

"O...ok," he stuttered involuntarily.

"I understand if you want your guitar back," said Danny as the red electric guitar he played had once been Spencer's.

"...You keep it," replied Spencer quietly, closing his eyes. The red glow was still visible through his eyelids.

Spencer turned around and walked toward the door of the apartment lobby. He kept his eyes shut so that he wouldn't loose control and laser something that he might have to pay for.

"OW!"

Spencer walked face first into the wall a few inches to the left of the door to the lobby. His eyes shot open and red beams of light shot out of them, blasting a man sized hole in the wall.

Spencer sniffled as involuntary tears trickled from his still glowing eyes. He darted through the man-sized hole created by the laser blast and back to his car, where he broke down completely. Spencer was not a dignified crier, like the heroes of dramatic movies, who weep a single tear quietly and look cool while they do it. He whimpered and bawled like an infant, slamming his forehead down on the wheel of his car and accidentally beeping the horn. The last thing he wanted to do was call up his mother in tears and beg her to let him move back in. But what other choice did he have? He was never going to be a rock star...and he was *so hungry*.

Spencer wiped his face off with the back of his hand, grabbed his cell phone and dialed his mother's number.

While he waited for her to pick up, he rehearsed what he would say to her in his head: ....*Mom , I...no...no...instead I should say... Mother....I...*

Spencer's mother answered the phone.

"...Hello?" she said.

"...waaaahhaaahaaaaa.....*Mommy!*" Spencer bawled.

"Spencer?"

"....I want to go hooome," Spencer moaned between sobs.

"You have a lot of nerve, calling me up like this after you told me to *get fucked* and ran off to the city to be a big rock star," Spencer's mother growled.

"...I-I'm sorry....I was wrong....Please let me come back home. Please," Spencer wept.

"How's it going, Spencer? Are you rich and famous yet?" Spencer's mother asked sarcastically.

"....No.....I was wrong....just please let me move back in...please, I'm so hungry," Spencer wept.

"Absolutely not. You got to stay in my house 18 years rent free already. I've done my job, you ungrateful brat," said Spencer's mother.

"...Please....I'll p-pay rent....I'll even pay on time. I'll pay extra rent. I'll cut off my nut sack and throw it in with the rent if that's what it takes!"

"No. Absolutely not. Your damn laser eyes have already cost me a fortune. Do you think I'm made of money? This problem you're having, whatever it is, is not my problem. You're 19 years old now. You figure it out," spat Spencer's mother viciously and then she hung up.

Spencer let his cell phone slip out of his hand and hit the floor of the car. Then, he put his face in his hands and cried some more. This had been exactly the response from his mother that he had been expecting. It made him angry to think that he had been stupid enough to expect something different.

"This s-sucks...." Spencer sniffled. And then he began

talking to himself rather neurotically. "...Everybody always treats me like shit even though I've never done anything to them," Spencer's eyes began to glow again. He gritted his teeth and wrapped his arms around himself. "....That fucking asshole, Devin....my fucking asshole mother....All I ever do is be nice to people and be a chill laid back guy," Spencer's eyes grew brighter and he started to tremble with rage. "....but the problem is I lay back and let people walk on my face...but not anymore. No. Not any fucking more. The old Spanky Fuckerson is dead. The new...guy whose name I haven't come up with yet...has been born. That guy doesn't care what's wrong or right, what's bad or good, what's legal or not legal. Man, I can't wait to be that guy."

Spencer took a deep breath and wiped the tears off of his face with the back of his hand. He grinned, thinking about what it might be like to be a super criminal.

"Heheheh...I'm going to do whatever I want to do and take whatever I want to have," Spencer said happily, his grin broadening. An image of Justice Bitch in her tight leather midriff shirt and short pants flashed in his brain, her expression stern; reprimanding; *sinister*. "...and I want you, *Justice Bitch*."

Spencer grabbed the steering wheel of his shitty, red honda with both hands and cackled like a hyena: ".....heheheh...heheheh...HEHEH*HEEHHEEH*!"

His eyes glowed with a greater intensity and his grin stretched wide. Fueled by a new optimism, a new goal, and a new purpose, Spencer began devising a scheme to lure out The Justice Bitch.

Chapter 14:
The Public Memorial Service

On the day of her father's memorial service, Harriet wore a floor-length, black gown with short sleeves, and a neckline that showed a sliver of her shoulders. The outfit was simple, elegant, and classy; exactly the sort thing that a person like her was expected to wear to an event like this memorial. Harriet slipped on a pair of black heels and a black onyx choker to complete the outfit. She facetted her hair in neat bun behind her ears, and then spritzed it with hairspray to ensure that it stay in place. When she was done with that, she took a step backward and stared at herself in the mirror. The grim scowl of a person she did not recognize stared back.

Harriet wanted to look sad, yet, for some reason, she just could not force herself to look this way. She didn't feel sad. She felt pissed off. The memorial service was a formality and a social obligation. She did not want to attend this event. She wanted to morn her father in her own way....by pretending that he had never existed to begin with.

Harriet walked into a large closet and grabbed an old-fashioned lady's hat and black veil from a shelf full of hats. She put it on her head so that the veil obscured her face. Harriet walked back out in front of the mirror and looked at herself again. Only her chin and frowning, painted lips were visible beneath the black lace veil. She nodded at her reflection solemnly. The veil, she decided, was the perfect tool for masking her socially deplorable apathy.

The memorial service was held at Platinum Arches Country Club, where Harriet's father had spent much of his free time. Renting the place out had been far from cheap, but Harriet's father had told her on several occasions that he had wanted his memorial service to be held at the Platinum Arches Country Club.

Harriet groaned as she handed her invitation to the limo driver, and the limo driver handed her invitation to the man at the front gate, who wore a white security guard's uniform and cap. The man looked at the invitation, nodded, and then pushed a button on a remote control he was holding, causing the gate to open slowly. The late William Fredrick Ross was high-maintenance even from beyond the grave.

Harriet's limo rolled down the wide pathway, which lead up to the entrance of the country club, past fountains, elaborate topiary, and wandering memorial goers in black, formal attire. They held glasses of Champaign and gathered in circles, speaking to each other excitedly. Some of these people were friends of Harriet's father, wealthy men with old money and pretty, plastic wives. Others were white-uniformed caterers and employees of the country club.

Harriet's limo stopped in front of the steep marble steps, which led to the entrance of the country club. Her driver stopped the limo, came around to her door, and opened it. Harriet stepped out of the limo. Then, she ascended the steps. Once at the top, another man in a tuxedo pulled the large, intricately-carved, mahogany doors open for her, and she stepped inside.

A violinist stood on an elevated platform near the center of the room and played a haunting melody. She was skinny and pretty like the carvings of leaves engraved in the stone walls around her, and she wore an ankle-length, black skirt with a white, button-down blouse. An odd thought occurred to Harriet: *Should I have hired that young goth-looking fellow to play this event? He did seem pretty eager to play a gig somewhere.* Harriet snorted and cackled at her own stupidity. That miscreant play at William Fredrick Ross's memorial? She could practically hear her father dry-heaving in his grave.

An older woman with dark blond hair, in a short black dress, and six-inch high stiletto heels, turned in her direction. This was William Fredrick Ross's first wife, Barbara.

"Is something funny, Harriet?" Barbara asked, unamused.

"Oh no, *no*," Harriet answered her apologetically. "I

was just thinking about something funny. Which is not this. This memorial event is not funny."

Harriet walked toward one of several catered tables covered in white tablecloths. The tables were lined with tall, clear vases filled with arrangements of white lilies, and, more importantly, a generous assortment of delicious snacks. The snacks were what Harriet was interested in. She found a stack of plates, grabbed the one on top, and started piling it high with baby sausage rolls, cheese-stuffed pastry dough, and honey barbeque chicken wings.

Viola approached her with a plate piled high with vegetable lasagna and parmesan cheese rolls. She wore a broad-rimmed, black hat tied with a black ribbon and an ankle-length, short, black dress, with a puffy fringe.

"Harriet, hi!" Viola greeted her cheerfully.

"Viola. So glad you could make it," replied Harriet with a socially appropriate degree of somberness.

"I'm sorry for your loss," whispered Lilly.

Harriet jumped backward, startled by Lilly's sudden appearance. She had not noticed her standing there, next to Viola.

"William Ross was always such a cool guy. I'm sure the world will miss him," said Viola.

"Thank you," replied Harriet flatly. She did not know what else to say.

"Guy, guys! She's over here!" Viola called into the crowd of memorial attendees dressed in black.

Benjamin and Stuart emerged from the crowd, and walked toward the refreshment table, waving politely. Both men wore black tuxedos. Benjamin, whose aura stank of its usual corruption, wore a black bowtie. Stuart was tieless and his yellow-blond hair was slicked back with a lot of gel.

"Harriet," Stuart greeted as he approached.

Benjamin's eyes lit up when he noticed the vast array of decadent snacks on the refreshment tables and, for a time, he ignored Harriet entirely.

"Oh my God. This is the nicest party I've ever been to," Benjamin said. He grabbed a plate and started stacking slabs of beef Wellington onto it.

"I'm so glad you guys could make it," said Harriet.

"We're glad to be here," said a morbidly obese guy, wearing saggy, ripped jeans and a visibly ketchup-stained, white t-shirt. Then, he belched loudly.

Harriet stared at the man incredulously for a moment and then a vein started to throb in her forehead. She looked back in Viola's direction.

"Uh....Viola...." Harriet murmured, attempting to keep her voice even. "Who is *this*?"

"This," announced Viola cheerfully. "Is my new friend, Finsveld."

Finsveld scratched his ass with one hand and grabbed a piece of Beef Wellington with the other.

"Hey whatsup. I'm Finsveld," he said in a low-pitched monotone, before jamming the piece of Beef Wellington into his mouth and chewing slowly.

"Well, he wasn't invited," Harriet pointed out crossly.

"Nah, he's my plus one," said Viola, putting an arm around Finsveld's shoulders.

"You don't get a plus one," fumed Harriet.

"Relax, girl," Viola said, grinning. "He's the newest member of the team. Has the power to change the clothes that people are wearing at will. Which will really come in handy incase we have to change into our costumes fast. You know, incase of a surprise villain encounter."

"Ok, fine. He can stay," conceded Harriet begrudgingly, "But he has to obey the dress code just like everyone else."

"Yo, Finsveld, change your outfit. Show a little respect," shouted Benjamin through a mouthful of gravy and mashed potatoes.

Finsveld snapped his fingers and his baggy jeans and stained t-shirt were replaced by a chicken mascot costume with a giant foam chicken head.

"Oh hoho....classic Finsveld," Viola chuckled.

"Make him change again," Harriet grumbled.

"Sorry, Har, Finsveld does pretty much whatever he wants to do," said Viola, shrugging.

"Finsveld is a free spirit," interjected Finsveld in his low-pitched monotone and then he shoved a piece of chocolate cake in his mouth and walked away.

"Great," said Harriet, crossing her arms. "You got anymore surprise guests for me? How about Fuck Man, the man with the power to turn his shit into strings of asparagus, while wearing a string bikini? Or Loud Disruptive Dinging Noise Man, the man with the power to disrupt any conversation by making dinging noises with the tiny urine hole at the end of his penis for hours on end."

"Both of those mans declined my invitation to join the team," Viola said, feigning ignorance of Harriet's sarcasm. Fuck Man and Loud Disruptive Dinging Noise Man were both real radiation altered citizens, who lived in Propopolous City. "Plus I'm pretty sure that Fuck Man's a villain now."

The violinist on the stage finished playing and bowed. A scattered audience of memorial attendees clapped politely and she stepped down from the stage. A fat, bald speaker walked onto the stage and took the microphone.

"At this time, may the guests please be seated as we begin the ceremony?"

Harriet sat in one of the seats and endured the litany of speakers and celebratory recollections of her father with gruff indifference, mercifully masked by the black veil of her old-fashioned hat. Her father had been a mostly secular man. This memorial ceremony was just a bothersome social obligation. Harriet derived no comfort from it. But people would have had things to say if there hadn't been one.

Bored, Harriet glanced over at Viola and Stuart (who were mumbling quietly to each other about something), and then over at Lilly and Benjamin. Lilly had her arm around

Benjamin and was playing with a strand of his curly auburn hair. Perhaps they were a couple officially now. Either way, however, Harriet gave exactly zero fucks. Present also was Harriet's father's first wife, Barbara, and her two sons; high ranking manor staff; a young, dark-haired limo driver, wearing dark sunglasses; and Reynolds the butler. Finsveld was nowhere to be seen; probably still stuffing his face at the refreshment table.

Harriet's cell phone rang. She answered. Several guests glared at her but she ignored them.

"What?"

"It's your financial advisor, Gary," a man's voice replied.

"Not now, Gary. I'm in the middle of something," snipped Harriet angrily.

"This is important, Miss Ross. Super Annoyo is suing you for his broken jaw on the grounds that *you are* Justice Bitch."

"Me? Justice Bitch? Ridiculous horseshit. "Super Annoyo can't prove a damn thing," growled Harriet bluntly. Then she hung up on him.

"At this time, I will step down and leave the mic open for anyone who would like to say a few words in memory of the late William Fredrick Ross," the fat, bald man announced. He then stepped away from the mic and walked off of the stage.

A man walked up to the stage and took the microphone. He wore a black track suit with a long black cloak (that looked like it had once belonged to a cheep vampire costume from the Halloween store) and a black plastic mask, which covered the top half of his face.

The crowd murmured, confused by the presence of this oddly dressed fellow. None of them were quite sure who he was or what he was doing here.

"Hey," the man said. His voice was that of a young man and it was one that Harriet thought that she recognized.

"William wassisname Ross was...*like*....super cool and stuff. He was super nice...maybe. He always showered everyday and he probably loved babies. But not, like, in a creepy way, just, like, platonic love of babies. He was so awesome...he had a collection of pens....and, like, he'd share a pen with you if you asked him. I think. I don't know. And when he screwed a beautiful lady he would probably always wear a condom if she asked..."

Harriet stood up.

"Shut up and get off of the stage," she shouted angrily.

"Why don't you come up here and make me?" the man shouted back and then he continued his eulogy somberly. "Unless she was an ugly lady, then he would just poke holes in the condom and laugh at her behind her back. He had many ugly children that way."

The stranger was alluding to the tabloid rumors of Harriet's father's sexual deviance and promiscuity. Beneath her black veil, Harriet's carefully painted features contorted with rage. Baseless and condescending accusations spread by her father's political adversaries were hardly a respectful or appropriate topic for this event.

"He was also known for his generosity and his kindness. He was so generous that, during his life, he donated almost nothing to charity. And he was so kind, that...instead of paying contractors for contributing to his company, he had them killed by goons in black masks."

"That's not true! You *shut the fuck up*!" Harriet blurted out. She stormed up to the stage, intent on ripping the microphone out of the oddly dressed fellow's hand. Just as her fingers were about to close around the microphone stand, however, the man wrapped his arms around her and forcibly pulled her toward him. With her super strength, she could have easily ripped him off of her and thrown him across the room. However, she couldn't do that and reveal that she was Justice Bitch in front of so many people. If she wanted to not be sued by Super Annoyo, she couldn't let everyone in this room know that she was Justice Bitch. Especially not first wife, Barbara. That bitch had always hated her and would testify on the behalf of Super Annoyo in an instant if given the opportunity.

The masked man pulled Harriet to his chest with one arm and gripped the stand of the microphone with the other.

"Turn out your pockets and give me everything you've got! Money, wallets, credit cards, *everything*! Or the girl dies!" the man shouted and his eyes began to glow red. He shot a pair of lasers out of his eyes and hit a massive ice sculpture of a weeping angel, on the center of a round table, which was positioned at the center of the room. The statue shattered into pieces and shards of jagged ice flew through the air. People screamed, got out of their seats, and covered their heads and faces protectively.

"Heheheheh...." the man chuckled, apparently very amused by his audience's reaction to this display of power. "I am *Death Laser*! Heheheheh....*Fear me!*"

Chapter 15:
The Sexy Rad Super Pals vs. Death Laser

Death Laser's gloved hand clutched Harriet tightly to his chest and she felt his tall, skinny body pressed up against hers; the hard muscles in his arms encircling her waist; the bristles of his five o'clock shadow grazing the skin on her neck. He smelled like disappointment and cheap cologne.

Harriet was not sure what she should do. She did not like pretending to be powerless while this weirdo laughed maniacally, and ruined what would have otherwise been a perfectly uneventful, albeit highly expensive, nuisance of an evening. Beneath her thick, black veil, Harriet's face assumed a thoroughly pissed-off expression.

Death Laser's aura felt slightly tinged but definitely not as corrupted as the aura of a killer. In the days following her father's death, during the lowest point of her deep, dark depression, Harriet had visited a prison to hyperventilate creepily while she stared at death row inmates. While doing this, she had imagined what it might feel like to cut each inmate's testicles off with a pair of dull scissors. This was something that she had contemplated through the haze of a post-radiation madness, before she had discovered a more productive outlet for the sadistic urges produced by her altered brain. The experience, however, had taught her something about her aura sensing abilities. For during her visits to death row, Harriet had discovered that she could tell a killer from a non-killer. To her, it seemed that the aura of a killer had a distinctive twinge to it, which non-killers lacked. Death Laser lacked the killer's twinge, so he *probably* wasn't going to kill her. But then again, how reliable were Harriet's aura sensing abilities? She hadn't had many opportunities to test their accuracy just yet.

"Yea...just uh....put your money in that pile right there. Yea. Ok. *Hey!* No escaping!" Death Laser instructed the crowd. A few people had stuck their money and wallets in the pile that was growing at Death Laser's feet. However, others kept their money and ran for the exits. Seeing that Death Laser hadn't shot the first few brave escapees, more people were gathering the courage to keep their money and run.

Harriet observed the fleeing funeral guests and Death Laser's extreme reluctance to shoot them with amusement. It seemed that her aura sensing abilities were correct in this instance. This guy wasn't a killer. So she probably had nothing to worry about. Someone would call the police. She would be rescued. He would be arrested and this whole stupid thing would be over with.

Unless....

"Stop right there!" Viola shouted, emerging from the door, which led off to the lady's restroom, in full costume.

Stuart, Benjamin, Lilly, and Finsveld jumped out from behind a row of potted plants and stood behind her. Stuart, Benjamin, and Lilly were all in full costume but Finsveld just wore a stained t-shirt and a pair of baggy pants with the fly pulled all the way down. In his left hand, he held a greasy burrito, which he shoved into his mouth and started chewing.

"We are the Sexy Rad Super Pals!" Viola announced, pointing upward at the ceiling for some reason.

"You seem to be short one member tonight, Sexy Dumb Something Friends," said Death Laser. "Where, pray tell, is Justice Bitch?"

"When, pray tell, did you become a British guy stroking a bald cat?" Viola shouted back.

"Huh?" Spencer replied confusedly.

"She means pick a persona and stick with it!" shouted Stuart.

"Nobody says 'pray tell' anymore, buddy," said Benjamin.

"Oh yea, well...uh....your hair is stupid," said Death Laser because he couldn't think of a better retort.

"Your brain is stupid!" shouted Benjamin back.

"Oh yea, well...uuumm...*shut up!*" shouted Death Laser unsurely.

"Enough witty banter! *Let's fight!*" Viola declared, putting her fists up.

Viola, Stuart, and Benjamin charged at Death Laser with their fists raised. Lilly vanished and reappeared behind Death Laser, kicked the back of his shin hard, and then disappeared again before he had the chance to turn around. Death Laser grimaced and directed his glowing eyes at the top of Harriet's head. He held her out in front of him like a shield as Viola, Stuart, and Benjamin grew closer to him.

"Come any closer and Ms. Ross is 'gonna get a laser through her skull!" Death laser warned. Harriet, Stuart, and Benjamin fell back cautiously. In the distance, Harriet spotted Finsveld empty what remained of the buffet's raw oysters onto a plate already piled high with cheese roles.

"Finsveld is indifferent," Finsveld confirmed bluntly.

Lilly reappeared on the chandelier overhead, and sat there, cross-legged, staring down at the top of Death Laser's head.

"Ok..." said Viola to Death Laser cautiously. She put her hands up to show him that she was unarmed. "What are your demands?"

"He's bluffing!" Harriet shouted in frustration.

"I want an escort to the parking lot. Keep the cops off my trail long enough for me to escape and you can have her back," said Death Laser.

"He's full of shit!" Harriet shouted. "Kick his ass already!"

Lilly vanished and reappeared by Benjamin's side. She leaned into his ear and whispered: "Believe her. She knows what she's talking about."

Benjamin's eyes flashed green, and the long snack table grew a lopsided face. Then, the resulting monster charged at Death Laser, like a rampant centipede, on many twisted table legs. Plates, food, white lilies, and clear vases were thrown everywhere. Remaining funeral guests fled hazardous glass projectiles as they flew from the back of the living table, covering their faces and heads protectively with their arms as they darted toward the exits. Death Laser yelped when he saw the massive, hideous thing heading strait for him, let go of Harriet, and began running.

Death Laser darted quickly across the room, his long, thin legs easily outrunning the table monster's many short and twisted-up crippled ones. But then, Lilly vanished and appeared a few inches in front of him. She stuck out her leg and he tripped over it, falling face first onto the floor. In an instant, the table monster was on top of him; its large, razor-toothed mouth opened wide and dripped large rivulets of saliva onto the back of his head. Death Laser struggled under the weight of the monster's twisted legs and managed to turn onto his back. His eyes lit up red and then ejected a pair of laser beams, which blasted a large hole in the face of the beast. Green slime oozed from the beast's lopsided forehead, and its many legs collapsed underneath of it as it fell down dead. Death Laser pushed the thing off of him and then struggled to his feet.

Viola jumped into the air and kicked Death Laser in the face, tearing his left cheek with one razor sharp talon. He yelled, staggering backward, and clutching his bloody face. Stuart grabbed him by the shoulders and shook him.

"Now you're going to jail," Stuart announced.

Death Laser struggled to free himself from Stuart's grip. But Stuart had super strength and could have held onto a thrashing African elephant without much effort. Confident that this weak, skinny villain had exactly zero chance of pulling free from his grip, Stuart threw his head back and laughed triumphantly.

Death Laser pulled his leg back and kneed Stuart in the crotch. Stuart let out a high pitched yelp and grabbed his own spandex clad groin, falling to his knees. Death Laser fled in the direction of the men's room.

"Get him!" Viola shouted.

Viola and Benjamin chased after Death Laser but he easily outran them both. Lilly appeared in front of him to impede his path, but he easily pushed her out of the way and disappeared into the men's room.

Benjamin and Viola darted into the men's room after him. Lilly followed slowly, shaking her head with disdain. Harriet watched the door for a few moments and then the three reemerged, looking confused and frustrated.

"He's gone!" Viola announced to the crowd.

"Must have escaped through the window," Stuart offered as a possible explanation.

The remaining funeral guests chattered nervously amongst themselves. Some of them emerged from behind the vases of large, decorative, potted plants, where they had been huddled to avoid being skewered by a stray laser, or bowled over by the massive, drooling table centipede. Women bolted barefoot for the exits, carrying black heels in their well manicured hands. The patter of men's formal loafers accompanied the squeak of woman's soles, across the smooth marble floor, as many of the remaining guests exited the building in droves. Perhaps these people were afraid that Death Laser was there, in the country club, curled up in a stall in the men's room, or hiding behind a large potted plant, nursing his wounds with baited breath while patiently planning his reappearance.

First wife, Barbara, however, did not leave. She crossed her arms impatiently and tapped her foot, surveying the mess with a venomous glare. Barbara's eyes locked on Harriet and she marched over to her, stepping over the fallen white lilies and piles of broken glass, which lay in her immediate path.

"*You*," she hissed, pointing a shaking finger in Harriet's direction.

"What, bitch, you wanna' fight?" Harriet said, her eyes narrowing in irritation. As combative as her father's first wife could be, she was still having a difficult time accepting that *anyone* would want to pick a fight here and now, in the aftermath of that ridiculous Death Laser situation.

"You did this," hissed Barbara, still pointing. "You did this, *Harriet*. When you invited those super freaks to what should have been a private affair!"

"The Super Something or Other Sexy Action Buds?" Harriet inquired.

"Yes them," fumed Barbara, "And the young man with the laser eyes too. They've ruined the funeral — and made a mockery of your father's memory! Harriet, I have never been more *disgusted* in my *entire life!*"

"Ok, I didn't invite Death Laser, ok," explained Harriet crossly, "And FYI, even if I *did* invite him, it's none of your goddamn business because *I paid for the memorial* so I can invite anyone that I want to. I can invite Fuck Man and Captain Jizz Face to the party if I want to. Because its *my* party, Barbara. And *I* get to decide who's invited to it. Not *you.*"

"You vulgar little whore," Barbara whispered darkly.

"Oh and guess what," said Harriet, pointing a finger in Barbara's direction. "You're only here because I was nice enough to let you have an invitation, *Barbara*. So suck on that."

"You act like that money is yours to do with whatever you want!" Barbara shouted bitterly, her face getting very red.

"Yes, actually, because my father left it to me in his will."

"Well, I've got news for you, *Harriet*. Your father wrote lots of wills, and I'm willing to bet *my life* that yours is not the most recent one!" Barbara shouted.

"Ooh, I'm *so* scared," Harriet mocked, "What are you gonna' do? Forge a fake will. Don't worry, bitch. My lawyers'll shoot it down fast."

"Well, you better get your lawyers ready," said Barbara. "Because they're about to be my lawyer's soon."

"Sure. Whatever help's you sleep at night," said

Harriet.

"You're father left his most recent will in a locked travel safe so that it wouldn't be discovered and destroyed," Barbara blathered, "Probably because he knew that if you read it. You would rip it up and shove *your will* in everybody's face instead."

"That's just stupid. Why wouldn't he just give the will to his lawyer?" said Harriet.

"The-a-lawyer-he uh…he must have…*SHUT UP*! I'm leaving this train wreck, but don't think I won't be back. One way or another I'm going to get what's mine, and there's nothing that you can do about it!"

Barbara turned and stormed out, her black stiletto heals, clinking like tiny daggers as they stabbed the marble floor below her.

"Well? Is that It?" Harriet shouted, turning 360 degrees to survey the remaining people in the room. "Any more *vultures* come to *pick my father's carcass clean!*"

Remaining funeral guests stared at her like she was something diseased and said nothing.

Viola emerged from the lady's restroom dressed in her funeral attire again.

"What was all of that about?" she asked Harriet, looking confused.

"My father's first wife, Barbara," said Harriet, "She's a an old, gold-digging whore and she thinks she should get everything just because she was married to my father first. Says she's got some secret will that says she gets everything but she can't get it out of 'the locked safe' that my father put it in so that I wouldn't get my grubby little paws on it before he died."

"She's insane," agreed Viola comfortingly.

"I know, right?"

"But it is a little strange that your dad left everything to you and not your mom," said Viola a little hesitantly.

"What's strange about it?" said Harriet, "They're

separated. She lives in California with the beautiful male model that she bought; didn't even bother to show up for the funeral. He felt slighted. Can you blame him?"

"Hmm...and who were those two guys that Barbara showed up with? ...Your brothers?" Viola replied hesitantly.

"They're Barbara's sons but they're not related to me. She had them in a previous marriage."

"But did your dad...*like them* at all?"

"What are you trying to say?" Harriet murmured caustically.

"Nothing, *nothing*," said Viola unsurely, shaking her head. "I'm sure that you have nothing to worry about."

Chapter 16:
Barbara and the Safe

Barbara stomped out of the building and into the courtyard, where white-uniformed employees of the establishment trimmed topiary bushes and swept winding cobblestone pathways. The sky overhead was now dark and the police had arrived. The lights on the top of their squad cars flashed read and blue, casting an eerie, alternating glow over the fountain were Barbara's two sons sat, awaiting her return.

"Roland!" Barbara shouted caustically, addressing the elder of her two sons.

Roland stood abruptly and smoothed his black suit jacket with both hands. He was about thirty-years-old, auburn haired, and square jawed.

"Yes, mother," he replied.

"Have you found a way of getting into that safe yet?" Barbara barked caustically.

"Mother, we've talked about this. I've tried everything. The safe still won't open."

"Everything? Are you sure?" Barbara snipped impatiently.

"Mother, why are we talking about this now?" Roland asked, sounding exhausted.

"Sledge hammer?" Barbara asked.

"Yes."

"Blow torch?"

"Yes."

"How about trying different lock combinations at random?"

"We did that for hours!" Barbara's younger son, Vincent, chimed in, sounding exasperated. He was fair haired and as slender as his brother was broad shouldered.

"I didn't ask you," hissed Barbara disdainfully.

"Yes," replied Roland at length, after it became clear

that his mother would not accept Vincent's reply as the official answer.

"What about crushing it in a pressurized chamber?" Barbara asked.

Roland rolled his eyes and shook his head.

"Ok, *one*, where am I supposed to get a pressurized chamber, and, *two*, that would destroy everything inside," replied Roland in an exasperated whisper, "and *THREE*, can we please not talk about this with all of these *cops* buzzing around."

"Its not illegal to claim something that already rightfully belongs to you!" Barbara shouted, sounding very offended by the insinuation.

"No, of course not," said Roland calmly. "But if you keep screaming like a maniac one of those cops might come over here and start talking to us. Do you want that?"

"No, no, of course not," replied Barbara and she lowered her voice. "I just can't let the skank daughter of that little trophy wife slut think that she's won for another minute. It's killing me Roland. Just, *killing* me."

"Mother," interrupted Vincent quietly.

"What is it, Vincent?" Barbara asked, still sounding slightly offended.

Vincent pointed in the direction of a nearby fountain, which featured a nude statue of the Greek god, Poseidon, clutching a trident and spewing a stream of water from his open mouth. A man wearing black slacks and an inside out black t-shirt was perched on the edge of the fountain, pulling coins out of it with his hands and then shoving the coins into the pockets of his now soggy trousers. Barbara recognized the man's shaggy black hair and goatee as belonging to Death Laser.

Barbara walked over to him and her two sons followed.

"You," Barbara accused, and Death Laser turned his head in her direction to acknowledge her.

"Me?" Death Laser replied, pointing to himself and then

shrugging as though confused.

"You're Death Laser," Barbara accused.

"Nope," said Death Laser and then he resumed pulling coins out of the fountain, while looking very unconcerned.

"I should call some of those cops over here and have you dragged off to prison," hissed Barbara dangerously.

"Oh, I'm not too worried about that," said Death Laser, without looking up from the fountain. He reached deep down into the water and pulled out a quarter, then jammed the dripping quarter into his pocket.

"Oh, and *why not?*" Barbara inquired skeptically.

"Because I can help you with your safe problem," said Death Laser, sticking his hand in the water again.

"Stop it. Stop doing that," said Barbara, very irritated by his nonchalance.

Death Laser pulled his hand out of the water and turned around to face her, still looking unconcerned. A few dozen feet to his left, a police officer was talking to a white-uniformed grounds keeper, and taking notes on a tiny pad with a pen, while he nodded boredly.

"My powers make getting stuff out of other stuff really easy," said Death Laser, jabbing himself in the chest with his thumb proudly. "I could open your safe for you, no sweat."

"Oh yea, well if you can open safes, then why are you stealing money out of a fountain instead of stealing it out of a safe?" chimed in Vincent sarcastically.

Death Laser dropped the coins in his hands and slammed his palms against his forehead.

"Oh man, I'm such a frickin' idiot! I didn't even think of that!" he moaned shaking his head.

"And don't you still have pockets full of people's money that you stole from the funeral?" Vincent said, narrowing his eyes.

"Naw, I dropped it all when The Ultra Cool Action Something or Others beat the crap out of me," said Death Laser, raising his head slightly, so that the bangs of his shaggy hair fell back and the slice in his cheek from Hawkette's talon was left visible.

Barbara grinned.

"Oh, you poor thing," she crooned, still grinning rather sinisterly. "How about a bit of honest work, son? Open my safe for me and I'll give you a hundred dollars."

"500 dollars," Death Laser corrected quickly.

"Alright 400," Barbara groaned.

"Deal," Death Laser said and he stuck out his hand for her to shake.

Barbara looked at him disdainfully for a moment and then, with some reluctance, shook his hand.

"Alright, we have a deal." Barbara agreed.

Chapter 17:
Your New Best Friend, Finsveld

The next night, Finsveld attended Hawkette's weekly Sexy Rad Super Pals meeting. He wore a pair of loose jeans with a non-functioning crotch zipper and a ketchup-stained, sleeveless, white shirt. Finsveld had a lot of clothes but usually lacked the energy to throw them into the washing machine. When he wanted to wear clean clothes he usually just bought new ones and dumped them on top of a pile in his apartment next to empty soda cans, indispensable cardboard boxes filled with miscellaneous items, and rotting sandwiches.

The Sexy Rad Super Pals were sitting in their usual booth, near the front window of the diner. Viola sat next to Stuart and across from Lilly and Benjamin. She didn't notice Finsveld enter the diner at first, as she was preoccupied with folding her paper napkin into a triangle and flicking it across the table at Benjamin's face.

"Gooaal!" she shouted happily as the paper triangle hit him square in the forehead, bounced off and landed back on the table.

"Yea...you got me," said Benjamin.

"Oh hello, Finsveld!" Viola greeted, noticing Finsveld for the first time. "Welcome. Sit down. Sit next to me."

Stuart and Viola slid over on the seat towards the wall and Finsveld sat down. The seat creaked under the weight of his rotund body.

"You remember my friend Finsveld, right?" said Viola.

"Hello," said Stuart to Finsveld.

"Hi," said Benjamin.

"Welcome," whispered Lilly quietly.

"Mmn....Finsveld..." Finsveld mumbled.

"An't that cute. Finsveld says his own name a lot," said Viola. "Kind of like a Pokémon."

"Finsveld was cursed by an old gypsy woman to always talk this way," said Finsveld.

"Uh...yea..." mumbled Lilly quietly.

"I guess I can get used to that," interjected Stuart weakly.

"That's the best," said Benjamin, "I just love that kind of crap. You know the kind of crap that people do in cartoons but would never actually do in real life, like continually referring to themselves in the third person. I find that tolerable and not at all incredibly, unbearably, mind-numbingly irritating."

"Excellent," said Viola, as always, feigning oblivious to sarcasm. "Then I'm sure we'll all be great pals."

"Yea, says Finsveld, sure, whatever toots," said Finsveld, and then he belched loudly. "Finsveld has to go piss like a race horse. Because I'm Finsnveld."

Finsveld stood up and then added: "Mm...yup. *Finsveld.*"

And then he walked away.

"Uh listen, Viola," Stuart mumbled timidly.

"Yes?" Viola answered.

"Me, Benji, and Lilly were talking and..." Stuart began.

"And *what*?" Viola interrupted.

"And we think that maybe it would be a good idea to start being more selective about who we let onto the team," finished Benjamin more aggressively. "You know with maybe some interviews, psychological tests, background checks, or you know, knowing who they are for more than like two minutes before we tell them all of our secrets and personal identities."

"Why, Benjamin, if I didn't know any better, I would say that you have a problem with Finsveld," said Viola, narrowing her eyes with distain.

"He's kind of right, Viola, I don't trust half of the people you drag off of the street to join the team," said Stuart, "Particularly not that Justice Bitch character. I think she might actually be out of her mind."

"Who, Harriet? She's just weird. She's totally harmless.

You're being paranoid," said Viola, waving her hand dismissively.

"No, Stuart's right. Harriet's creepy as hell...Though she is still *rich* so we should keep her around just incase she decides to offer the team a donation from her father's foundation," said Benjamin.

"Don't be a money grubbing whore, Benjamin," argued Viola crossly, "Harriet's my friend, ok? She could be your friend too if you gave her a chance."

"Ok, fine, you've known Harriet for awhile, and you swear she's not crazy. I'll respect that. Maybe you know better than me," said Benjamin, "But what about Finsveld?"

"What about Finsveld?" Viola repeated, "Finsveld's the best."

"...Viola, how long have you known Finsveld?" Lilly whispered timidly.

"I met him a few days ago," said Viola, "Why?"

"Its not that we have anything against your new friend," offered Stuart comfortingly, "We're just not sure if we're comfortable with you giving out our secret identities to strangers, that's all."

"Finsveld is not a stranger, you guys," said Viola, "Finsveld, is Finsveld, ok. And if you all suck it up and just give him a chance, he's going to be all of your best friends. You'll all sleep with a picture of him under your pillow, and build a shrine to him out of dried macaronis for Valentines Day, because *that* is how much he'll mean to you in the end."

"...Uh...I don't know, Viola," whispered Lilly timidly.

"He'll be a Sexy Rad Super Pal," said Viola, "Just you wait and see."

"Quite frankly I don't think he's sexy enough," whispered Lilly.

"Well, sexy is more about the way that you feel," disputed Viola.

"That's just like what somebody un-sexy would say," said Benjamin.

"Are you accusing me of being *un-sexy*?" Viola replied angrily.

"Uhh..." Benjamin replied, timidly.

"Because I could un-sexy you right off of the team, if that's the case. Don't make me choose between you and Finsveld," snapped Viola aggressively.

Finsveld returned to the table and sat down next to Viola.

"There's no toilet paper in there," Finsveld informed them bluntly. His monotone made it difficult to tell whether or not he intended this statement as a joke.

"See, he's delightful," argued Viola, as though this argument was ironclad.

The entrance of the diner creaked open and Harriet stepped inside. She was dressed in black healed boots, a black knee-length pencil skirt, and a half tucked-in black button down shirt. Her hair was black and disheveled, frizzed from the California humidity with a sloppy part.

Harriet walked over to the table where the Sexy Rad Super Pals sat and joined them. Her expression was strange, far away, in some sadistic, lust-drunk fantasy. A moment passed, during which, The Sexy Rad Super Friends stared at her. She seemed obvious to their cautious and guarded expressions. The clock on the brick wall behind them, ticked slowly. Harriet opened her painted mouth and said with fever: "So, who are we going after tonight?"

Everyone at the table, with the exception of Viola and Finsveld, stared at her with alarm. If her demeanor were anymore predatory it would have reached the point of obscenity.

"Yea, ok so first..." Viola began.

"No, first," Harriet interrupted quickly. "I need to bust some skulls or my heart is going to explode."

"Alright, so let's get straight to the point," Viola corrected herself, "Lilly, what intel have you gathered for us?"

"The Frenchman is back in town," Lilly whispered

forebodingly, "I've been doing some spying at a villain bar called The Black Hatchet. And word on the street is...Frenchman's working on a computer virus. He's got a couple of other villains to invest their stolen money on it."

"Who are they? Do you know?" Stuart asked.

"Yes, actually," Lilly whispered in reply, "They go by the names Fuck Man and Captain Jizz Face."

"Wait? Those guys are real?" Harriet interjected, "I mean...I've heard of them before....but thought they were just like...a big joke or something."

"No, they're real," whispered Lilly, "They got their start in the underbelly of the adult film industry, materializing stuff out of their assholes and transforming people into cum piles."

"Shit," Harriet swore.

"If those fuckers are funding it than it must be something really terrible," said Benjamin with a shutter and then he asked cautiously: "What is it? Do you know?"

"Some kind of computer virus, I believe," Lilly whispered informatively, "It'll take every computer in the city down and then the Frenchman will turn around and charge everyone for the antivirus software to remove it, effectively ransoming the city for millions."

"Nobody saw you, right? Nobody knows that you know this?" Viola asked.

"No. I was invisible when I heard this. It's probably legit," Lilly whispered.

"Hmn....Finsveld knows where The Frenchman's apartment is," said Finsveld.

"What! How?" Benjamin interjected incredulously.

"Finsveld delivered a pizza to his apartment a couple of weeks ago," said Finsveld. "Yup, Finsveld ate part of the pizza before I got there and when The Frenchman checked the box before he paid for the pizza...and Finsveld didn't think he would check, while Finsveld was still standing there. They never check while Finsveld is still standing there. I mean...the old gypsy woman did...but Finsveld's point is. Usually they never check the pizza box that Finsveld is holding. Anyway, he said something like: "Captain Jizz face! Turn this fat fuck, Finsveld, into a pile of cum! But like...Finsveld heard that he was talking a really fake sounding French accent. So Finsveld threw the pizza in his face and ran."

"Hahaha...that's awesome," laughed Viola. "Do you still remember the address?"

Finsveld wrote and address on a napkin and slid it over to Viola. Viola picked the napkin up and read it.

"Alright, then! Sexy Rad Super Pals! Let's rock 'n roll!" Viola celebrated, punching the air.

Finsveld snapped his fingers and the Sexy Rad Super friend's clothes were replaced by their costumes. Finsveld remained in his t-shirt and jeans.

"Finsveld's not going back there," he said, and a terrified expression contorted his features briefly. He shook his head as though the emotion were a fly that could be frightened away by a sudden movement. Then, the expression was gone. "Finsveld wishes you good luck."

...

Viola, Harriet, Stuart, Lilly, and Benjamin entered the Frenchman's apartment building. They tiptoed past the sleeping doorman, piled into the elevator and hit the button marked 15 on the elevator's inner wall. There was an old woman standing in the elevator who stared at the oddly dressed group with a disapproving scowl and said nothing. She got out of the elevator on the 15th floor and hobbled away. The Sexy Rad Super Pals moved in the opposite direction, toward The Frenchman's apartment.

"This is it," said Viola quietly, "15th floor. Apartment 29-B."

They all stared at the plastic plaque on the door, at the end of the hallway, which was inscribed: 29-B.

Then, the floor fell out from underneath of them and with much screaming and flailing of limbs, they plummeted straight down.

Chapter 18:
The Adventures of Fuck Man and Captain Jizz Face

"Eh, mister Fuck Man, and ehhh mister, ahhh how you say, Capitan Jizz Face?" said a man with a thick and very unconvincing French accent, wearing a pink, floral-pattered, silk robe. This was The Frenchman, a man with the supernatural ability to speak in an unconvincing French accent pretty much all of the time and without any effort at all. He had dark blond hair, which was parted directly down the middle and a dark blond mustache to match.

"Yes," replied a man wearing a woman's green string bikini and a green mask, which covered his scalp and the top half of his face. This was Fuck Man, the man with the supernatural ability to transform his own feces into nearly any conceivable object (including weapons or explosives) before ejecting it form his anus.

"De Fuckputer it azzz beeen, how you say, destroyed," said The Frenchman.

"Destroyed!" Fuck Man repeated, nonplused. He threw his arms up into the air in exasperation. "How can this be? Does *Captain Jizz Face* know about this?"

Captain Jizz Face walked into the room. He wore a full body, white spandex suit which also covered the entirety of his face head and neck. The letters C, J, and F were embroidered on his chest in off white.

"Well, I do now," said Captain Jizz Face.

"The Something or Other What'ch Ma Call it Friendz, dey are surely behind it!" said The Frenchman. "Now our plan to destroy the city, eet ees ruined, ruined I say! Fuck Man dis' is terrible! I spent more than twenty whole minutes coming up with dat evil plan!"

"Forget your evil plan!" Captain Jizz face announced angrily, "Without The Fuckputer, how am I supposed to look at Internet porn?"

"You, *shut up!*" said The Frenchman, pointing an

accusatory finger in the direction of Captain Jizz Face. "When ah agreed to dis evil alliance I did not know that you villains would be, how you say, stupid and useless assholes! Ah do everything! All you stupid idiots do is look at internet porn and turn my furniture into splooge wid your magic powers!"

"Hey don't look at me, that was Captain Jizz Face," said Fuck Man.

"You, *shut up*," spat The Frenchman disgustedly.

The Frenchman's apartment/secret laboratory, was tastefully decorated, with dark-stained, hardwood floors, intricate, dark-stained molding, and sea foam green walls covered in collectible plates, which featured a vast array of Norman Rockwell Paintings.

The Frenchman walked past a red velvet ottoman, and a large puddle of frothy white semen that used to be a Victorian style red velvet sofa, to his computer desk.

"Luckily the regular-puter survived," said The Frenchman, tilting the screen of his computer toward Fuck Man and Captian Jizz Face so that they could see it clearly. Fuck Man and Captain Jizz Face walked closer to the computer, and leaned over The Frenchman's head to see the video on the screen.

The Sexy Rad Super Pals were being recorded on live video feed, in a small, metal-walled room. They stood around a large, tall computer shaped like a penis and testicles, smashing it to pieces with fists and sledge hammers. Apparently some of them were equip with sledge hammers for the occasion.

"Do you see dat?" said The Frenchman, pointing to The Sexy Rad Super Pals as they pulled the fuckputer's circuit boards apart and started stomping on them. "The fuckputer is ruined! Now we will have to build a new one before destroying all of the city's computers with de Super Fuckputer Virus!"

"Well whose idea was it to store the Fuckputer under the trap door, huh? I told you anyone who falls through it could just hack the thing to pieces," said Fuck Man.

"And I told *you* to disable the trap door until we could steal a better place to hide le Fuckputer!" The Frenchman screamed back, pulling at his short locks with both hands in exasperation.

For the express purpose of being an asshole, Captain Jizz Face, chose that moment to reach out and tap a row of bubbling test tubes sitting next to The Frenchman's computer with his middle finger, transforming them into a frothy puddle of semen. The semen dripped off of the table and onto the floor, forming a sticky puddle at The Frenchman's feet, and soiling his brown loafers. The Frenchman didn't seem to notice, however, he was too busy explaining his evil backup plan.

"However, dat is ok," said the Frenchman. He picked up a metal box with a red button on it, and turned his computer chair toward his ridiculously dressed companions. "Because I hauve a, how you say, a *backup plan*." The Frenchman pushed the red button on the metal box with his thumb. A loud clicking noise echoed from the computer. The Frenchman flipped a switch on the metal box that he was holding, and then opened a latch at one end of the box, revealing a speaker, which he then held up to his mouth and spoke into: "Now you are trapped, Super Something Don't Care Buddies!"

"Huh?" Viola's voice murmured through the computer's speaker.

"Oh shit, just what I needed today," grumbled Harriet, "Now I'm going to be late for the reading of the will."

"Don't worry, we should be out of here in no time," said Stuart. Then, he ran to the edge of the metal walled room with his fists raised and started punching the walls. They dented slightly but refused to break. Blood trickled from his large fists but he continued punching at the wall.

"In a few moments," said The Frenchman, "I will release a toxic nerve gas, into the fuckputer chamber, and den ah will be, how you say, slowly killing you *dead*! Mwaha*hahahaha*!"

"Crap, he's gonna' kill us!" shouted Benjamin, "Stuart, punch harder!"

"I'm punching as hard as I can! It's not working!"

A quiet, still, girl with white-blond hair vanished from the screen.

"Where did she go?" Fuck Man asked, as he noticed the girl's sudden absence.

"Who?" inquired Captain Jizz Face.

"The girl with the white hair. She's gone." said Fuck Man.

Lilly reappeared, sitting cross-legged on top of the computer that the three men were staring at.

"Gaagh!" the three men shouted in unison, jumping backward.

Lilly, didn't react. She stared at them, her eyes distant; ice blue and unblinking. The three men stared back at her, for a moment, trying to register what had just happened. Lilly reached out slowly, her tiny white fingers closing around the metal box in The Frenchman's hand, then, snatched it away from him and disappeared again.

"Who's the stupid useless asshole now?" said Fuck Man, narrowing his eyes at The Frenchman. "It's you, Frenchman. The stupid and useless asshole is *you*."

"Well ah still did more for diss operation than either of you idiots!" said The Frenchman in his own defense. "I can wait for those Super Justice Which-ma-call-eets to starve to death down there, if that's what it takes to get mah revenge!"

Lilly reappeared at the other end of the room. The three men turned in her direction, then, darted after her. She vanished and reappeared at the other end of the room before they were able to reach her.

"Fuck Man, Captain Jizz Face," she whispered, "The Frenchman doesn't appreciate you or your unique skills."

"She's right!" complained Captain Jizz Face, "The Frenchman doesn't appreciate us *or* our unique skills!"

Captain Jizz Face touched The Frenchman's red leather ottoman with his middle finger, turning it into another puddle of white ooze.

"Sockreblu!" the Frenchman exclaimed observing the place where his leather ottoman used to be with disgust and horror. "Do you have any idea how much that cost, you imbecile?"

Fuck Man reached behind himself and pulled a piece of asparagus out of his ass, then chucked it at The Frenchman's head. The asparagus bounced off of the Frenchman's wincing face and landed on the floor rather uselessly.

"Appreciate our unique skills, damn it!" Fuck Man shouted.

"Never, *never*! I bring you here because you invest your stolen money in the production of The Fuckputer! Not because I want semen and ass asparagus, how you say, *thrown all over mah apartment like ay x-rated film!*"

Lilly disappeared and then reappeared in front of The Frenchman's computer. She watched the screen, as Harriet and Stuart pounded on one of the metal walls, which were now covered in fist sized pits and valleys.

"Ok, I think the metal's thinner now," said Harriet to Viola. "Try cutting it."

"Ok," said Viola.

She jumped into the air, extending one of her taloned feet outward, and slicing deep gashes in the metal wall.

"It's working! Keep going!" goaded Benjamin.

"Enough of dis sheet! Get dee Ghost Gal! She 'as dee Fuckputer Room Control Device!" exclaimed The Frenchman.

"Right!" shouted Fuck Man.

"Let's kill 'er!" shouted Captain Jizz Face.

Fuck Man and Captain Jizz Face raced toward Lilly. But the moment they were close enough to touch her, she vanished again and reappeared at the other end of the room.

"I'm not the real enemy here," whispered Lilly.

Fuck Man and Captain Jizz Face split up and ran to

either side of the room. Lilly vanished and reappeared on a chandelier at the center of the tastefully decorated room, just as Captain Jizz Face was about to reach out and touch her arm with his middle finger, turning her into a goopy puddle of frothy pus.

Lilly put her hands out in front of her and wiggled her fingers mockingly as Fuck Man and Captain Jizz face began piling up what remained of The Frenchman's furniture to try and reach her.

"Oooh...distraction....ooooh!" she mocked breathily.

"Great bloody ass-reaming baguettes!" The Frenchman swore, "The Super Something Rat People! Dey 'ave escaped!"

Fuck man and Captain Jizz face turned in the direction of the Frenchman's computer and the live video feed of the Fuckputer Room. Pieces of metal debris littered the room's floor and there was a large, human-sized, hole ripped into one of the room's metal walls. The Sexy Rad Super Pals were nowhere to be seen.

Lilly vanished from the top of the chandelier and reappeared on The Frenchman's computer desk, with her arms and legs wrapped around his desktop computer. Her tiny white fingers clutched every flash drive that The Frenchman owned.

"Thanks for the tech, boys," she whispered. And then she winked and vanished along with the computer and all of the flash drives.

For hours, The Frenchman, Fuck Man, and Captain Jizz Face searched the apartment building as well as the apartment building's basement, which contained a trap door, leading to The Frenchman's secret underground lab. But the ghost girl was nowhere to be found. She was gone now and with The Frenchman's computer and flash drives, she had access to all of their secrets.

Chapter 19:
The Rightful Property of Barbara

The limousine where Barbara, Roland, Vincent, and Spencer were sitting rolled past tall buildings and crowds of pedestrians stopped at crosswalks.

Barbara's first two husbands had been millionaires, and each of them had given her both a son and a very large divorce settlement. Consequentially, Barbara had both very expensive tastes and the money to satisfy them. The inside of the limousine she was riding in had a square of inward-facing, red, velvet seats, and a tinted sound proof window, to separate herself from the limo driver at times when it was not necessary to give him instructions.

As Spencer had promised, his powers made removing William Fredrick Ross' will from Barbara's locked safe quick and simple. Spencer grinned and handed the will to Barbara who snatched the thing out of his hand eagerly.

Barbara stared down at the envelope. It was sealed shut with a glob of red wax that had the initials *WR* pressed into it. The words: "Penned by William Fredrick Ross in the Year 2015. To be opened in the event of his death," were written in a swirling, black-inked calligraphy beneath the seal.

"Well, aren't you going to open it?" Spencer asked after a few moments.

"No I'll leave it sealed until the lawyer reads it. That way that awful little trollop won't be able to claim that I tampered with it," said Barbara, clenching her fist self-righteously as she imagined her step daughter, Harriet, spending her, *Barbara's*, x-husband's money in ways which she did not approve. She imagined Harriet purchasing a mink shawl and a string of black pearls that aught to have belonged to her, *Barbara*. Then, she pictured Harriet buying a Jacuzzi (the rightful property of Barbara), before inviting Fuck Man, Captain Jizz Face, The Human Turd Muncher and Finsveld over for a naked Jacuzzi party/Satan worship orgy, during which they shot pictures of Barbara and her two son's on William Fredric Ross's mantel place with rifles that should have been Barbara's.

"Mother, you could just open the envelope and then re-melt the wax with a candle, so that no one can tell that you opened it," said Roland after awhile, when it became clear that his mother would not stop staring angrily into space without his prompting.

Barbara was snapped out of her daydream. She turned her head in the direction of her eldest son and barked: "That would make me just as bad as *her*! I'll let the lawyer open it. Let the true will of the Great William Fredric Ross be known!"

"Doesn't it strike you as the slightest bit odd that he kept this will locked in a safe and that he told only the butler where it was and that it should be opened in the event of his death?" said Roland, sounding a bit concerned.

"Heh. Weird," commented Spencer.

"There's nothing *weird* about it. I was the one and only true love of his life. He wanted to make sure that *I* received the inheritance that that nasty little daughter of his would have fought to deny me!" Barbara informed them rather dramatically, banging her fist against the velvet lined limo seat for dramatic effect.

Spencer had had quite enough of this.

"So uh...when am I going to get my money?"

"Your what, honey?" Barbara asked innocently.

"The 400 dollars you promised me for opening the safe."

"Ugh," Barbara groaned. "Fine. You miscreant."

Barbara took a hundred dollar bill out of her black sequin change purse and handed it to Spencer.

"Where's the rest of it," Spencer asked, his eyes narrowing with agitation.

"Take it and be happy with it, you little ingrate," said Barbara. "I'd drive you straight to the police station and have them arrest you, but I don't think that there's a prison that could hold you, anyway. So what would be the point?"

"You promised 400 dollars," Spencer complained crossly, his dark brows furrowing with agitation. "We had a deal."

"We did, did we?"

"Yea, we did. I open your safe for you and you give me 400 dollars."

"400 dollars, huh?" Barbara said.

"Yes."

"And you don't want 100 dollars?" Barbara said.

"No."

Barbara ripped the hundred dollar bill in half and then threw the pieces up into the air.

"Well, now you get *nothing*, brat." she growled.

Spencer gritted his teeth and fought back a pair of angry lasers building in his eyes. The sudden and unexpected destruction of the money that would have funded his next meal, stung him in a manner most unpleasant. Still, he was not prepared to walk out of his arrangement with Barbara *completely* empty handed.

"Ok. *Fine.* I'll take nothing," said Spencer, sounding exasperated. "But could you do me a favor?"

"What?"

Spencer stuck a hand into the pocket of his black jeans and pulled out a folded piece of paper.

"Will you give this letter to Harriet for me," he asked, "I want her to know that I was responsible for her undoing."

Barbara chuckled.

"You hate her too, then?" she asked rhetorically. "Makes sense to me. She is so *horrible*."

"Just make sure she gets that, ok?" said Spencer.

Barbara unfolded the piece of paper and read it quickly. A smirk curled her painted lips and broadened slowly as her eyes scanned the page.

"Do you like it?" Spencer asked unsurely, when he noticed the way that Barbara was beaming at his letter.

"Like it?" Barbara said, still smirking. "I wish that I could cross your name out and write mine on the bottom of it."

"Thanks," said Spencer, "But please don't do that."

"No. Of course not," said Barbara.

"So you'll give it to her, then?" Spencer asked.

"Sure thing, scamp," said Barbara, sounding much more fond of Spencer than she had been before discovering that they shared a common enemy in Harriet. She reached an arm out and mussed Spencer's shaggy black hair as though he were one of her own sons. "Now get out of my car."

Chapter 20:
The Reading of the Will

Harriet arrived to the reading of her father's will late that evening. Her hair was a tangled mess, her makeup was smeared, and her socks didn't match. One sock was black and ankle length and the other was a gray tube sock with a white stripe down the side. The battle against The Frenchman and his associates had dragged on for much longer than she would have liked and she hadn't had much time to slough off her hero costume and put on something culturally appropriate for the will reading. She noticed the socks problem after she was already in her car and on the way to the lawyer's office. Then, she shrugged and mumbled:

"What difference does it make?" to herself as she parked in the lot outside of the lawyer's office, stepped out of her car, and slammed the door shut behind her. *Why bother to look nice for a bunch of fat greedy vultures hoping to snatch away a piece of my fortune?* she thought.

The lawyer's parking lot was full of expensive cars belonging to friends and relatives of the late William Fredrick Ross. Harriet passed a few limousines, a candy apple red Lamborghini, a black Hennessy Venom GT, and an electric blue Ferrari with a back license plate which read: "RICHR THN U." She spotted Reynolds the butler as he emerged from a black Lexus and slammed the door shut behind him. He wore a black tuxedo and a grim expression.

"Reynolds, hello," Harriet greeted politely, though, in truth, she was a bit irritated that he had bothered to show up to the reading of the will. How many acquaintances of her father, she wondered, would turn up, hoping to snag a handout?

"Harriet, how are you?" Reynolds replied.

"Good, good," said Harriet, "How have you been?"

"I've been coping," Reynolds replied grimly.

Harriet and Reynolds entered the lawyer's office to see

a number of relatives and acquaintances, sitting around the lawyer's desk in wooden chairs. They wore black formal clothing and dour, mournful expressions that suggested they were grieving, even though the vast majority of these people had rarely if ever visited William Fredrick Ross when he was alive. There were a handful of people there that Harriet didn't even recognize.

Harriet sat down in an empty chair next to a rotund, white-haired woman whom she had never seen before in her life.

"Hello," the rotund, white-haired woman said to Harriet.

"Hello," Harriet replied.

"I'm William Fredrick Ross's great aunt Roberta," the rotund, white-haired woman informed Harriet proudly.

"Uh huh," said Harriet, staring at the empty desk were the lawyer was supposed to be.

"William and I were always so close," Roberta bragged, "We used to spend a lot of time together, walking through the gardens, eating watermelon slices in the summer. He will be missed."

"Yup," Harriet said, still staring at the empty desk where the lawyer was supposed to be. She knew for a fact that her father was not at all fond of watermelon.

"He used to say that *I* was his very favorite great aunt," Roberta bragged.

"Hey, good for you, lady," said Harriet, still staring at the empty desk where the lawyer was supposed to be. She had never, *in her life*, heard her father mention a "Great Aunt Roberta." Not even once.

"Say, who are you?" Roberta inquired of Harriet conversationally.

"I'm a rodeo clown from the circus," said Harriet, without taking her eyes off of the empty desk where the lawyer was supposed to be. "Where William Fredrick Ross spent much of his free time."

"Is that so?" Roberta inquired curiously, "How did you and William meet?"

"He came to one of my performances at the rodeo," said Harriet.

"The rodeo, really? I had no idea that William was interested in that sort of thing," said Roberta, intrigued by this new piece of information.

"Oh, yes," lied Harriet, "He used to come to all of my performances. He liked seeing the horses, and the cows, and the bulls...but mostly the bulls. Those were his favorite, or so he used to tell me."

"But I thought you said that you were from the circus," interjected Roberta, sounding confused.

"Oh, yes," lied Harriet, "William convinced me that I should take my rodeo act to the circus. So I did. I just took all of those cows and bulls with me into the circus tent and it worked out just great. I even won an award. It was made of gold and everything. After that, we set a pile of hundred dollar bills on fire and danced around it to celebrate."

A tall, middle-aged man in a black tuxedo, whom Harriet had never seen before in her life, stood up and turned in her direction.

"With all do respect, ma'am," the man said angrily, "This is a private Will Reading for family members and close friends of William Fredrick Ross only. Not for rodeo clowns, or circus clowns, or whatever you are. You should leave."

"Nope. I'm staying," said Harriet, crossing her arms defiantly. She directed her gaze back at the empty desk where the lawyer was supposed to be, wondering how he had the nerve to be even later to and give even less fucks about this tiresome formality than her. "And the rest of the clowns from my circus troop will be showing up soon, so you better get more chairs."

Barbara, Roland, and Vincent entered the lawyer's office.

"Oh, and there they are now," Harriet announced.

"Harriet," Barbara greeted, smirking.

"Barbara," Harriet parroted back. She stood up and walked over to Barbara and her two sons.

"I have something for you," Barbara said and she held out the folded piece of paper that Spencer had given her for Harriet to take. "Death Laser left it at the country club for you."

"Thanks," said Harriet. She took the piece of paper out of Barbara's outstretched hands. Then, nodded at Roland and Vincent in greeting and returned to her seat.

Harriet glanced up at the desk where the lawyer was supposed to be. He still wasn't there. She looked down at the folded piece of paper that Barbara had given her. Then, unfolded it. There was a short letter written on the piece of paper in a scratchy, lopsided hand writing. The letter read:

Dearest Harriet,

I want you to know that I am aware of your secret and that the will, which will be read this evening, would have remained lost and unread if not for my intervention. Whatever happens as a result of this, is because of me — because my hatred for you is intense and unyielding.

In the spirit of good sportsmanship, I'll give you a hint as to where I will strike next, should you desire revenge. Here's your hint: I'm going to rob the convenience store on the corner of Washington and 3rd Street at 4:00 p.m. on Saturday the 22nd. I am telling you this because I am extremely confident that there is nothing that you or anyone else can do to stop me. Especially not Justice Bitch. Because she sucks. And is super lame.

You may doubt my abilities as a villain, now. However, I trust that, in time, you will see me as the threat to your way of life that I truly am.

And we will be mortal enemies locked in an eternal combat.

Your Nemesis,

Death Laser.

Harriet folded the letter back up and stuffed it into her purse.

"Pht," She scoffed in amusement, rolling her eye, "'*My nemesis.*' In his dreams."

The lawyer, a portly, balding man in a black suit and tie, entered the room. He sat down behind his desk, opened one of the top drawers, and removed an envelope containing a will from it, placing it down on the desk in front of him.

"Sorry about the delay. There was a lot of traffic on the way here. Anyway, let's begin," said the lawyer.

"Wait, *wait!*" Barbara shouted, standing up and waving her will, the newer one, in the air. "There is a more recent will. This one was written in 2015 by William Fredrick Ross! I have it here!"

Harriet watched in disbelief as Barbara sprinted over to the lawyer, holding a new envelope. Was there really a new will, naming Barbara her father's heir? Was Death Laser really the person responsible for the new will's sudden appearance? Was it a forgery? Or had the old man simply gone mad before the accident, the way Harriet felt herself going mad right now?

The lawyer opened both envelopes, checked the dates and signatures on both documents, and then nodded.

"Yes, I believe this is the more recent document," the lawyer said. Then, he picked Barbara's will up and began to read it: "Being of sound mind and in the presence of witnesses, I hereby bequeath my estate as follows: To my estranged wife, Kathleen Ross, who despite her many flaws, was good at keeping secrets, albeit, at a price, I leave my mother's diamond necklace and earrings, in hopes that she will return to Propopolous City in order to retrieve them and, in doing so, be reunited with Harriet during these troubling times."

The lawyer cleared his throat and continued reading:

"To my step sons Roland Vanderbilt and Vincent DuPont, who, for a time, were as dear to me as my own children, I leave 100,000 dollars worth of stock in the Ross Foundation *each*, in hopes that they will benefit from the company's rising popularity in the future."

Roland and Vincent murmured to each other and shrugged indifferently.

"It's not bad," whispered Roland to his brother.

"It's better than nothing," whispered Vincent back.

"It's good. It's a good sign," whispered Roland.

Barbara's smirked broadened and she glared at the back of Harriet's head (Harriet was sitting in the front row of chairs and Barbara was sitting close to the back).

"To my first wife, Barbara Propopolous," The lawyer continued. Barbara straightened up in her chair when she heard her name and her heart began to beat fast with anticipation.

"The love of my life and my friend and confidant, during a time when those closest to me had forsaken me, I leave the entirety of my esteem, because it is a word that looks and sounds a little bit like estate, and she will be fooled into thinking that I have left her my estate when she reads this for the first time."

The smirk slipped off of Barbara's face, and was replaced by an expression of open-mouthed shock and outrage.

"Especially since," the lawyer continued. "When I was alive, even after our divorce, I made a point of telling her that I would leave her everything I owned after I was dead, as a sort of joke. What made it funny was that whenever I said it she would always believe me no matter how thickly I laid it on. Poor Barbara. She was never very smart."

Barbara's pencil-thin, silver eyebrows pulled taunt with rage and her face got very red. Harriet grinned and stifled a snort of derisive laughter. How could she have let Barbara make her believe that her father would give her, his ex-wife, the estate? The idea was really rather absurd when she thought about it. Perhaps it had just been her crazy new brain making her extra paranoid.

"To my daughter, Harriet Ross," the Lawyer continued.

This is it, Harriet thought. *He's going to leave me the rest of the estate and this stupid formality can be done with.*

"I leave the sum of 500,000 dollars, as well as 100,000 dollars worth of stock in the Ross Foundation and the black Lamborghini."

Harriet's face contorted into an expression of open-mouthed disbelief, not at all unlike the one that Barbara had worn only a moment ago.

"In hopes that she will use these resources to build herself a life," the Lawyer finished. He cleared his throat and then began reading again: "To my butler, and the *true* love of my life, Reynolds Sanderland, who was, in confidence, my lover and my dearest friend." A symphony of hushed, disapproving murmurs flared up suddenly and then died down as the family members in attendance waited with baited breath for the will's much anticipated conclusion. "I leave the entirety of my estate, with the exception of those things previously stated as being bequeathed to others. In the estate is included all remaining properties, finances, stocks, and executive privileges over The Ross Foundation. Any person who contests this shall forfeit his legacy."

Harriet sat there in front of the lawyer's desk, paralyzed by shock; her eyes dilated and unblinking; her mouth wide open. Never had she suspected that her father was having a secret affair with Reynolds the butler. All around her, friends, relatives, and acquaintances of the late William Fredrick Ross were voicing their shock and disbelief in shrill, frantic, judgmental, and sometimes even jealous tones. Their inane babble filled the room, and drowned out the lawyer's voice as he read what remained of the will, which was, from the words that Harriet could gather, a brief confession of love written to Reynolds the butler by her father before he died. The sea of background noise felt a world away. Harriet glanced at Barbara and her two sons. The first wife stood abruptly, dignity forgotten as she yelled and cursed her misfortune. In the seat next to her, Harriet caught Roberta and the man who had told her to leave, whose name she did not know and did not care to know, blathering their lament. Then, she glanced at Reynolds, sitting near the back of the audience; his bald head bowed; silent tears dripping down his wrinkled face as the lawyer finished reading. There was true anguish there in that crinkled expression mixed with a profound yet bitter joy.

Chapter 21:
The Nemesis

In a strange way, Harriet supposed this made sense. That must have been why the most recent will had been locked tightly in that safe. It had been to keep her father's secret hidden until after his death, so that all of these people that were ranting and gossiping to each other right now would just leave him alone. And yet still, she felt so cheated. How could she have known so little about her father? How could this man that she had dismissed for years as annoying, overly meddling *help* have meant more to him than she did? And more importantly — what was she supposed to do now that she wasn't fabulously wealthy anymore, but merely, reasonably well off? Would she have to work now? Not just for pleasure, but because she had to? Where would she live? How would she plan for an uncertain future? And most importantly, if she wasn't a wealthy, carefree heiress, who wore pretty dresses to fancy parties, smiled for interviews, and scoffed openly at the worries and cares of lesser mortals, then who was she?

"I don't even know who I am anymore," Harriet moaned, putting her hands over her forehead.

In the sea of babble and confusion which surrounded her, however, this comment went ignored.

"Let's go, boys!" Barbara yelled angrily, after having grilled the lawyer for several minutes about the legality of the will. "Your stepfather's in hell with all of the other homosexuals now!"

Harriet rose out of her seat and locked eyes with Barbara.

"Shut the fuck up, *you stupid whore*," Harriet said to her.

"How *dare* you speak to me that way," Barbara hissed. "Do you *know* how much more *money* I have than you?"

Harriet sat back down.

"My God. She's right," she murmured to herself,

realizing this for the first time.

Harriet dug the crumpled letter from Death Laser out of her pocket and read it again. Her eyes lingered for a few moments on the last line:

And we will be mortal enemies locked in an eternal combat.
Your Nemeses,
Death Laser.

"Yea, you wish, buddy," said Harriet, folding the letter back up and shoving it in her pocket.

This was her father's betrayal and not Death Laser's. Even if Death Laser had played some small role in seeing the revised will found, she would not give him the satisfaction of acknowledging him as her nemesis. That would be exactly what that weirdo wanted her to do.

Later that night, Harriet met up with the rest of the Sexy Rad Super Pals at the restaurant. They all sat down at their usual booth, near the front window, ordered dinner from the disgruntled waitress, and then began politely complimenting Viola on her new hairstyle. She had grown it out slightly, replacing the bubble gum pink peach fuzz with short, acid green dreads.

At first, Harriet said nothing about her current financial crisis. The other team members had never been as wealthy as she once was and would not understand. Plus, she strongly suspected that they had been hoping for a donation from The Ross Foundation to fund their hero team this entire time.

Harriet drank her coffee and listened to the other team members converse excitedly. Stuart hinted a few times that the operation would go a lot more smoothly if the team had a jet and a secret headquarters. Harriet picked at the green beans on her plate and tried to ignore him.

"Serious business team," Viola announced, "Crunchy Toast Muncher has been traveling from museum to museum in the city, turning art into toast and then consuming it for pleasure. "Already, three of the city's major museums have been targeted and completely cleaned out."

"Well, there goes my museum curetting job," groaned Harriet without looking up from her plate.

"I thought you quit that job," said Viola.

"Well, now I want it back," replied Harriet angrily. To avoid talking to Reynolds tonight, she was planning to rent a hotel room to sleep in. She would drive back to the mansion and pick up her clothes and personal effects tomorrow. The mashed potatoes in her plate reminded her of what she wanted to do to Death Laser's face with her fist. She picked up a little paper cup by the side of her plate and poured some gravy on it. The gravy was his blood.

Benjamin slapped a newspaper on the table and pointed to the headline.

"I heard also that The Frenchman has rebuilt his lab in downtown Ackerston," he said, "He may be up to no good again. Maybe we should check it out just to be safe. Keep a little casual surveillance on him."

"He can't do anything without his files," whispered Lilly, "I destroyed them all so it'll be years before he gets the Super Fuckputer Virus running again, whether other villains back him financially or not."

"What makes you think you got all of his files?" argued Stuart.

"Well, I'm pretty sure," Lilly whispered uncertainly.

Viola glanced at Harriet, who was staring down at her plate, stabbing her mashed potatoes with her fork aggressively.

"Are you alright, Harriet?" she asked, sounding concerned, "You seem a little...*off* tonight. I mean, more so than usual."

"I'm fine," Harriet said quickly, looking up from her plate for the first time in several minutes. "I was just thinking that we should be going after this Death Laser guy, that's all. What's his secret identity? *Huh?* Where is he hiding?"

"Somebody's smitten," Viola postulated. She smirked knowingly and Harriet glared at her.

"I am not *smitten*," said Harriet angrily, her face flushing slightly. "I just want to kill this guy. That's all."

"I thought I said no killing," reminded Viola.

"Right. No killing. Ok. What I meant was that I want to beat his ass up and throw him in jail," said Harriet, "I think he knows my secret identity, Viola. He wrote that he 'knows my secret' in the stupid hate letter he sent to me. Do you know what that means? Super Annoyo is trying to sue me for assault! If his lawyers find out I'm Justice Bitch, I'm completely and utterly *screwed*."

"Why are you freaking out? Aren't you super rich anyway?" said Benjamin.

Harriet glared at him.

"For your information, *Benjamin*," growled Harriet. She didn't much care for the stink of Benjamin's aura tonight. "Thanks to Death Laser, I'm no longer rich. Now I'm only *reasonably well off*."

"I wish I was reasonably well off," Benjamin sighed.

Harriet told the rest of the team what happened at the reading of the will and Death Laser's role in it.

"— And thanks to Death Laser knowing what my secret identity is," Harriet finished, "I've had to spend some of the money I've got left keeping my lawyer on retainer incase the Super Annoyo lawsuit becomes an issue."

"Hey, don't worry about finding a place to stay, girl. Stuart and I've been looking for a third roommate anyway. You can stay with us until you get back on your feet," said Viola.

"*Viola—*" Stuart complained.

Viola pushed a finger to his lips to shush him.

"Sh. It'll be great," Viola assured him. "We'll each pay one third of the rent instead of half and then we can hang out in the afternoon and be buddies."

"*Viola—*" Stuart began again, glancing over at Harriet who was now glowering while she violated the mound of mashed potatoes on her plate with a butter knife.

"Yaay–buddies!" Viola interrupted, with a tone of forced cheerfulness, quickly drowning out Stuart's complaint.

"Thanks, Viola," said Harriet, "I appreciate it."

"So, this Death Laser guy..." Viola inquired, grinning. "Is he your *nemesis*?"

"I told you I don't have a nemesis," said Harriet.

"Every hero has to have a nemesis," said Viola.

"What about you? Wasn't Super Annoyo your nemesis? Don't you need a new nemesis now that he's in jail?" said Harriet in annoyance.

"That's not how the nemesis relationship works. He took a dump on my lasagna, remember? Whether he's in jail or not, he's still my nemesis, at least until a bigger grudge comes along and knocks him out as the frontrunner. I'm not really a grudge kind of person, but you just kind of have to have a nemesis anyway. That's just what heroes do. Its how we roll," said Viola.

"Ok, fine, if I concede that Death Laser is officially my nemesis, then can we just go after him?"

"Well, he has to commit a crime first," said Viola.

"He pretty much just announced that he's about to do a bunch of crime stuff," said Harriet.

"I really think that Crunchy Toast Muncher is a bigger threat right now," Lilly interjected meekly. Her comment was ignored.

"I've got an idea," said Benjamin, "How about we split up for the night? That way we can patrol the final gallery that Mega Toast Muncher hasn't devoured yet, keep tabs on The Frenchman, *and* stalk Harriet's crush all at the same time."

"He's not my crush, you ass. He's my nemesis. And he wasn't even that 5 minutes ago before Viola forced me to call him that," said Harriet crossly.

"Yea, whatever," said Benjamin.

"It's a good idea," agreed Viola, "Alright, so how about...me, Stuart, and Benji wait for Mega Toast Muncher at the art museum, Lilly does surveillance on the Frenchman, and Harriet stalks her bae."

"He is *not* my *bae*," Harriet interjected crossly.

"If he's not your bae, then don't stalk him," said Benjamin, smirking.

"I'm not stalking him because he's my bae...whatever the hell *that* means. I'm stalking him because he's a criminal under surveillance. How is that different than Lilly stalking The Frenchman?"

"It's different because you like him," said Benjamin, still smirking.

"And how do you know that Lilly doesn't like the Frenchman? Huh? How do you know she doesn't keep a picture of him under her pillow at night while she dreams about his stupid mustache?"

"I promise I don't do that," whispered Lilly, shaking her head and putting her hands up in her defense.

"Don't drag Lilly into this, ok," said Benjamin, "She's a saint."

"Alright team, enough chatter! Let's move out!" Viola announced.

She put her hand in the middle of the table and everybody put one of their hands down on top of hers.

"Sexy Rad Super Pals!" Viola began.

"Let's rock and roll!" the other team members finished, pulling their hands back off of the table.

Chapter 22:
The Robbery

Spencer slouched forward and stuck his hands in the pockets of his jeans as he walked, whistling the melody to a quick paced and optimistic song. He had bandaged the part of his face that had been sliced open by Hawkette's talon with a rectangle of gauze and some medical tape. The injury still stung, but in a way that he was learning to enjoy.

Spencer was pretty sure that Harriet and Justice Bitch were the same person. They looked like the same person. They sounded like the same person. They were probably the same person. Right? *Right?* They had to be. *And even if I'm wrong*, Spencer thought, *they're still both hot.*

Spencer found his shitty red Honda, parked near the corner of an intersection. He removed a few coins that he'd fished out of the fountain at the country club from his pocket and fed the meter that he was parked next to with them. Then, he pulled his car keys out of the other pocket, unlocked the car, and sat down in the driver's seat, pulling the door closed behind him. Spencer removed the piece of gauze from his face, and observed the bloody vertical stripe under his eye in the driver's side mirror. He grinned and pressed on the injury with his thumb nail to make it hurt more.

"Agh!" he yelled, still grinning. Then, he dug his thumbnail into a place near the edge of the slice which was shallow and scabbed over. His grin broadened. Perhaps this injury would leave him with a cool villainous scar.

Spencer put the same dirty bandage back on over the slice and secured it with a couple of fresh strands of medical tape. He had a whole roll of medical tape still, but only one piece of gauze left. So this was the best he could do at the moment as far as changing the bandage.

Spencer pulled a black mask on, and then put on the plastic Halloween Dracula cape he'd worn to the country club.

"Ok," he said, glancing at himself in the driver's side

mirror of the car. "Time to do some high profile stealing of stuff. You ready, Spence? Ok."

He grinned nervously at himself in the driver's side mirror and then jumped out of the car.

If Harriet was in fact, Justice Bitch, then she would have gotten his letter, and with it the less than subtle hint that he was going to rob this convenience store at exactly this time and place. She would be waiting for him inside of that convenience store, he imagined, tight leather midriff shirt against her large breasts and muscular flat stomach as she stood there amongst the bags of potatoes chips and sugary beverages; hands on hips; jaw clamped tight; trembling with boiling-hot sexual rage. Spencer practically skipped past the corner street sign that marked the intersection of Washington and 3rd street, delighted by this sultry mental image. Pretty soon, he anticipated, that Justice Bitch was about to have her hands *all over him.*

Spencer strolled into the convenience store. A bell rang and a pair of electronic doors slid open to admit him. He walked up to the young Indian guy at the counter and stared at him for a moment, his eyes glowing red.

"Can I help you?" the man behind the counter inquired of Spencer politely.

The corona of red light radiating from Spencer's eyes grew brighter.

"I am Death Laser," Spencer announced.

"...*Ok,*" the man behind the counter replied unsurely. "You're Laser Man. I got it."

"That's Death Laser, the bringer of chaos; the destroyer of cities and of minds. Haven't heard of me? Well you're about to. Remember my name is Death Laser. That's D-E-A-T-H-L-A-S-E-R. *Death Laser,*" Spencer confirmed, spelling it out, just so there could be no mistake. "Remember that name. Maybe, write it down. It's Death Laser."

"Good for you, kid," the cashier groaned in annoyance.

"So, like, if any sexy, tight-leather-wearing lady, comes

in here, looking for Death Laser, or is maybe hiding somewhere in the store, waiting for Death Laser to make an appearance. Tell her that Death Laser was here."

"I don't understand," said the man behind the counter, "Is this supposed to be a joke?"

Spencer threw his head backward and cackled insanely.

"A joke," Spencer laughed, "A *joke*? I am Death Laser! *Death Laser* is no joke! Heheheh…heh…I should reduce your store to a smoldering ruin for such an insinuation!....Because I'm *Death Laser*."

"Sir, are you going to buy something or just keep telling me your name over and over again?"

A pair of red laser beams shot from Spencer's eyes and shattered the bullet proof glass window behind the cashier's head. The cashier shouted and jumped out of the way of a glass projectile. His eyes grew wide and his body grew tense as he glanced over at Spencer, whose eyes began to glow red again.

"Put all of the money in that register into one of those plastic bags over there!" Spencer shouted.

The cashier grabbed a clear plastic grocery bag from behind the counter, opened the cash register, and began feverishly stuffing money into it.

"Slower!" Spencer ordered, afraid that the robbery would be over with too quickly and that Justice Bitch would miss it. "What is this like a race or something?"

A look of confusion twisted the cashier's face and he slowed down.

"Hey, *hey*, man! *Slower!* Slower than that!" Spencer instructed.

The cashier's face contorted with an expression of utter bewilderment and he slowed down even more. Spencer glanced over at the door, expecting to see Justice Bitch standing there, but saw only the silhouette of his shitty, red Honda parked a few blocks away against the darkening sky. Justice Bitch was nowhere to be seen.

"Hey! What are you doing?" barked Spencer at the man behind the counter. "You know what, why don't you just....you know, put those bills in there one at a time. And then, like, put the change in there one coin at a time.....but you know what....just put the change in there first—*and START WITH THE PENNIES!*"

"Sir, have you *lost your mind*?" the cashier murmured incredulously.

"Just do it!"

The cashier shrugged and then started picking the pennies out of the cash register one at a time, then dropping them slowly into the plastic bag.

"Is this going to take much longer?" said a curly-haired old woman in a pink knit sweater, clutching a cantaloupe. She had gotten behind Spencer in line, during his conversation with the cashier. "I really want to buy this cantaloupe."

Spencer stared at the old woman for a few minutes, waiting for her to leave. The red light disappeared from his eyes as twenty or so seconds passed and he grew impatient with her continued presence.

"Ok, fine. You first," Spencer sighed and he stepped out of the old woman's way.

The old woman walked up to the cashier, paid for her cantaloupe and left. Spencer turned his head back toward the cashier, and his eyes began to glow again.

"Alright, keep putting the money in the bag!" Spencer shouted.

The cashier started shoving money from the cash register into the bag.

"Hey-HEY! Not too fast!" said Spencer, glancing back at the door. Justice Bitch still wasn't there.

"Uh....what the fuck are you doing?" a woman murmured darkly. Hers was a voice that Spencer recognized. Smooth and rich. Like hot chocolate.

"What's it to you, lady?" replied Spencer in irritation. He turned around and saw Justice Bitch, waiting in line behind him; her eyes narrowed in agitation.

"This robbery has been going on for almost ten minutes now," Justice Bitch informed him caustically. "Aren't you afraid that the police will get here before you decide to leave?"

"Pphht. Cops don't scare me," scoffed Spencer, crossing his arms with distain. "My powers make it super easy to break out of prison. Probably."

"Is that so?" Justice Bitch replied skeptically.

"You bet your sweet tits it is," said Spencer, assuming what he judged to be a villainous stance, with his feet set wide apart and his head tilted downward; his glowing red eyes staring upward into Justice Bitch's cold brown ones.

"You know, I should really have just let the police deal with you," said Justice Bitch, "But you're just *so* irritating that I thought I should stop you myself."

"Heheheheh...heh...that was your mistake, Justice Bitch. You're no match for me!" Spencer announced dramatically.

Justice Bitch shook her head with distain.

"But then I saw..." Justice Bitch motioned toward the cashier behind the counter who was still slowly dropping pennies into an almost empty plastic bag. "....Whatever *this* is....and I realized something."

"...Realized what?" Spencer interjected. "That we will be mortal enemies to the bitter end? Locked in a ceaseless, unending battle?"

"I realized," said Justice Bitch, shaking her head. "That you're only doing this crap to get attention. So sure I could fight you and end this whole thing right now. But that's exactly what you want, isn't it? It's the whole reason why you're doing this."

"What's a matter, Justice Bitch? Afraid to fight me?"

"Not at all," replied Justice Bitch evenly. She realized now that the best way to get revenge on this pitiful 'nemesis' of hers was to ignore him completely. "It's just that I don't care."

In the distance, a police siren could be heard. Flashing red and blue lights lit up the glass wall behind the cashier as a few police cars pulled up.

"Look at that. The police are here," Justice Bitch noted indifferently. She walked around Spencer, who was staring at her quietly, mouth agape. Then she grabbed a tube of lip balm from a display in front of the cash register, paid the man behind the counter with cash, and exited the store without looking back.

Chapter 23:
Trust

Benjamin was the first to arrive at the diner that evening. He ordered some coffee and a plate of French fries and was eating them when Harriet arrived.

"Hello," Harriet greeted Benjamin and she sat down.

"You're here early," said Benjamin and he dipped one of his French fries in a paper tube of ketchup on his plate, then, stuffed it into his mouth.

"So are you," said Harriet not altogether hiding the irritation in her voice. She did not know Benjamin very well and did not feel very comfortable having to speak to him without Viola as a mediator.

"I'm always early," said Benjamin.

"Noted."

Benjamin picked another French fry out of his plate, dipped it in the ketchup, and then stuffed it in his mouth.

"So how did you fare with your nemesis last night?" he inquired conversationally.

"Eh…I think I'm going to choose a better nemesis. This guy's just a punk petty thief," said Harriet, "My new policy is just to ignore him."

"So you're just going to forget about the way that he fucked with your father's will reading?" Benjamin inquired indifferently.

"Eh….that wasn't really him, was it? That was my father distributing his money the way he wanted to distribute it," said Harriet, "How'd it go with Crunchy Toast Muncher last night?"

"Crunchy Toast Muncher was a no show," said Benjamin, "So the whole thing just turned into a fieldtrip to the art museum."

"Oh," said Harriet who considered her self a person of wealth and taste with an appreciation of fine art. "I'm sorry I missed that."

"But if you want your museum curetting job back there is still one art museum left in the city…for the time being," said Benjamin, "Who knows. Crunchy Toast Muncher's still on the loose, so he might be back to eat the exhibits any day."

"Right," said Harriet.

There was a long awkward pause during which Benjamin paid extra attention to the fries on his plate as he ate them. Harriet stared off into space.

The chubby blond waitress walked over to their table.

"You want somthin', sweetie," she asked Harriet gruffly.

"Uh…coffee? Maybe one of those sausage bagels."

"Coffee and sausage bagels it is," the waitress said and then she scribbled it on her notepad and walked away.

"Harriet can I ask you a personal question," Benjamin inquired.

"Sure."

"What's *wrong with you,* anyway?"

"*What?*" Harriet replied darkly. She did not at all like that question or the way he had asked it. So snide and suspicious.

"There's something about you, Harriet. You just creep me the fuck out," said Benjamin bluntly. He ignored the growing scowl on Harriet's face and continued to pick at the fries on his plate as though he had just made a comment about the weather.

Harriet gritted her teeth, her eyes narrowing dangerously. With some difficulty she resisted the urge to jump over the table and pummel Benjamin's face into bloody pulp.

"*Really,*" she hissed almost imperceptibly, her voice quivering with bottled rage. "How so?"

"Oh…I don't know…" said Benjamin, feigning innocence. "Like how you're all creepy and quiet unless you have something to say about murdering people or beating them up. Or how you're always glaring at me like you want to

reach over the table and rip my face off. I mean, maybe you're
just a harmless eccentric like Viola seems to think you are.
She trusts you, you know. But then again, Viola trusts
everyone. That's her fatal flaw" said Benjamin and his
strange, acid green eyes glinted dangerously beneath the light
of an overhead lamp. The lamp flickered momentarily, and,
for a time, his face was hidden in shadow. "I'm just saying.
Why should *I* trust you?"

"Why should *I* trust *you*?" Harriet replied coldly. Was
Benjamin secretly a threat to the team? Was this why
Benjamin's aura stank of corruption? Had Harriet's initial
impression of him as a mellow, passive, harmless guy been
false? Had her aura sensing ability known something that her
common sense could not fathom about this stranger whom
she knew so very little about?

"I think you better leave, Harriet," said Benjamin
evenly, and then his eyebrows drew together in a look of
aggressive distain. "Nobody wants you here."

The waitress returned to their table with a plate of
Harriet's food and a cup of coffee on a tray. Harriet was silent
and glared at Benjamin as the waitress placed the food down
in front of her. The waitress, sensing a tension that she was
not altogether comfortable with was silent as she placed the
coffee down in front of Harriet and then hurried away.
Harriet waited for her to leave and then spoke once more.

"Sorry, *Benjamin*," Harriet hissed quietly, her voice
dripping with disgust as she uttered his name. "I'm not going
anywhere."

The bell over the entrance to the diner jingled and
Viola, Stuart, and Lilly stepped inside.

"Hey, guys!" Viola greeted them cheerfully. She
waved at them and then sat down in the booth next to
Benjamin. "I was just telling Lilly how super stoked I am that
Harriet's going to be roommates with me and Stuart. Right,
Stuart?"

"Uh...yea," agreed Stuart timidly. "*Super stoked.*"

Lilly sat down in the booth next to Harriet and nodded silently. Stuart sat down next to Lilly and across from Viola.

"This is going to be so much fun!" exclaimed Viola excitedly, "We can stay up late watching chick flicks. Talking about boys. Just like in high school. It'll be so much fun."

"Yea, I can't wait," agreed Harriet, though in truth the part of herself that enjoyed watching chick flicks and talking about boys was now struggling to continue its strangled existence beneath the torrent of sadistic rage that was her post-accident brain chemistry.

"At least now we'll have a roommate who can pay the rent," said Stuart, "Not like Homeless Joe."

"Hey, Homeless Joe was a treasure," said Viola a little defensively, "He might not have paid the rent but he enriched our lives in ways that you couldn't even have imagined. Not everything's about money, Stuart."

"Uh…right," agreed Stuart reluctantly.

"What happened to Homeless Joe?" Harriet asked curiously.

"Anyway, let's get down the business, team," said Stuart, changing the topic quickly. "How did each of you fare on your individual missions last night? Lilly?"

"The Frenchman spent the night watching TV," whispered Lilly, "So nothing to report there."

"And as you've all probably heard," said Viola, "Crunchy Toast Muncher didn't show up at the art museum last night."

"Must have decided to keep that one in business," said Benjamin.

"But why?" Viola mused.

"I don't know…maybe he decided he likes art," said Benjamin unsurely.

"Or maybe it was a distraction and he was actually somewhere else last night," said Viola.

"Maybe….no never mind…forget I said anything,"

whispered Lilly quietly.

"Harriet? What about you?" Stuart asked.

"Me?" Harriet mused.

"Yea, did you stop Death Laser's robbery?" Stuart asked.

"Uh...yea actually. But it wasn't really very difficult. I just called the police and had them take care of it," said Harriet.

"He didn't put up a fight?" Stuart inquired with some surprise.

"Uh...no. When the police came, I heard he just kind of went with them," said Harriet, "I'm revoking his status as my nemesis he's not really a real villain, just kind of a fool."

"A fool in love maybe," said Viola.

"Viola, I swear to god," Harriet growled in exasperation.

"That's why he keeps showing up to rob things but never leaves with any money," said Viola, grinning. "He's not doing it for the money. He's doing it for the chance to meet you."

"Sure he is," said Harriet sarcastically, crossing her arms.

"I'm just sayin'," said Viola, her grin broadening. "Nobody with superpowers sucks that hard at being a villain unless they're trying to suck at it."

"Yes, yes, you're very perceptive," said Harriet dismissively, "He must be a crappy villain on purpose. You've figured it out."

"I'm serious Harriet," said Viola, still grinning. "I think this Death Laser guy just has a big crush on you."

Harriet groaned.

"That can't possibly be what's happening here," she said, "Probably he's just a stupid attention seeker who wants to be famous or something."

Viola shrugged.

"Maybe you're right," she said.

"Uh...guys?" Lilly murmured.

Harriet, Viola, Benjamin, and Stuart glanced in Lilly's direction. She had a newspaper in her hands and was reading it. Harriet blinked and tried to remember if she had seen Lilly holding a newspaper earlier. Then, decided that she didn't care. Everything that Lilly did was so easy to ignore.

Lilly turned the newspaper toward the group, and pointed to the headline of a story cramped into the bottom left corner of one of the newspaper's inner pages.

Stuart took the newspaper out of Lilly's hands and began to read it.

"Crazy Laser Face Robs Local Convenience Store," Stuart read, "A masked man with the ability to shoot lasers out of his eyes held up a local convenience store last night. Store owner, Aabheer Sharma (32), told reporters that the masked man called himself 'Crazy Laser Face.' 'He destroyed my bullet proof store front with his laser eyes and then told me to empty the register. But luckily the police arrived in time to stop him from escaping with any money,' says Sharma. Crazy Laser Face was arrested but managed to escape police custody before being unmasked."

"Looks like the media is taking him semi-seriously," said Benjamin.

"The media is idiotic," said Harriet, "The more seriously it takes him, the more he's going to do crap like this."

"There's more," said Stuart and he continued reading. "Police reported that before Crazy Laser Face's escape, he divulged a detailed plan to rob a Maxwell Bank on Third Street at 3:15 on January 13th. Police deputy, Samuel Robberts (41) told reporters: "I asked him why he was telling me things [about his planned robbery] and he just laughed maniacally and said that the police and The Justice Bitch would be powerless to stop him whether they knew he was going to be there or not."

Stuart put the paper down. There was silence for a

moment.

"Well," said Harriet, "I certainly won't be there."

"Oh come on, Harriet, why not?" Viola moaned, "It's *so* Romanic."

"No," said Harriet, "No way. And you guys aren't going to be there either. I've fed this man's dilution for long enough. If it's really me and not money he's after, then he's bound to tire himself out and give up at some point."

"Aw, Harriet, you've resisted your instinct to punch face without just cause," said Viola, "I'm so proud of you."

"See," said Harriet, glaring at Benjamin. "I have self control."

"So, lets assume that your theory that Crazy Laser Face is going on a crime spree, not because he's trying to make money but because he wants to meet *you,* is, let's say, ridiculous, self-absorbed bullshit," said Benjamin, "Does that mean that based on that assumption, you're just going to let this wacko...wreck things and steal whatever he wants?"

"Crazy Laser Face or Death Laser or whoever he is, is too low caliber a criminal for us to bother with," said Harriet, "Let the police handle it."

"But if the police could handle it, wouldn't he be in custody right now?" Benjamin challenged.

"I'm sure they'll get him next time," said Harriet dismissively.

"Yea, what she said," said Viola, matching Harriet's dismissive tone. "Anyway, guys we've got a more important fish to fry. Lady Gorge is in town."

The team was quiet for a moment. All of them (excluding Harriet) grew tense.

"What?" Harriet asked, "Who's Lady Gorge?"

"Miz Mayhem," Viola explained, calling the villainess by a more popular alias this time.

"Ooh...,"said Harriet, as the seriousness of how dangerous this person was finally hit her. "Oh. Ok. I get why you all got quiet now. I'm going to sit this one out. I don't want to mess with someone who's got powers like hers."

Lady Gorge, or Miz Mayhem as she was more often called, had been making the papers and the news for years. She ate candy and junk food pretty much nonstop but still managed to be skinny because she had the power to transfer her fat to other people by touching them.

"She's the lady who should be fat but isn't because she keeps making other people fat instead," said Harriet so that the other team members wouldn't think that she was completely ignorant.

"Not just that, but she can absorb other people's fat," said Viola.

"And she can touch someone young and transfer years of her life to them, making them older, and herself younger. That's how she's stayed young for so long. Nobody actually knows how old she really is," said Stuart.

"I've seen her touch an old man, absorb his years until he was an embryo, and then turn around and touch a young man until he was so old that he crumbled into dust," said Benjamin quietly, "And she can do the same thing with appearances, infestations, and diseases. She can take what you've got and give you what you don't want. Lady Gorge is *no joke.*"

"Well she's back in town," said Viola, "And probably up to no good. I say we watch her."

"Seconded," agreed Benjamin, "If she's anything like she was five years ago, when she was trolling around my high school, looking for naive young guys to suck the life out of...yea, I'd say the city's safer with her dead."

"As much as I hate to agree with you," said Harriet, "I don't think I can argue with that logic. Let's crush this bitch flat before she has a chance to do any real damage."

"Guys, guys, *hello,*" interjected Viola, waving her hands a bit to get their attention. "Lady Gorge hasn't done any crimes in a little over two years. The word is, she's reformed.

Watching her is just a precaution."

"*Reformed*," scoffed Benjamin, "Do you really believe that?"

"I'll believe it until I have reason to believe otherwise," said Viola sternly, "So if any of you wind up killing that woman, you better have a damn good reason."

"Fair enough," said Harriet.

"Ok," said Benjamin, "For you, Viola."

The bell over the front door of the diner jingled and Finsveld walked in. Today, he was wearing a pair of ripped jeans and a ketchup-stained white t-shirt with a hole in it. He walked over to their table. Then, belched and scratched his testicles.

"Finsveld is late," Finsveld announced.

The Sexy Rad Super Pals finished their meal. Then, walked out to the parking lot. Finsveld snapped his fingers. Harriet's, Viola's, Stuart's, Benjamin's and Lilly's clothes disappeared and were replaced by their hero costumes in an instant.

"Well, I've done what I do," said Finsveld, turning toward the group and adding: "Good luck, guys."

Finsveld turned around and started walking away.

"Are you sure you wouldn't like to come with us?" Viola called after him.

"Nah...Finsveld's got, like, TV to watch and stuff," said Finsveld and then he turned and walked away.

"Alright guys!" announced Viola energetically and then she made a fist with her yellow-gloved hand and held it out in front of her. "Sexy Rad Super Pals!"

Harriet, Lilly, Benjamin, and Stuart put their hands on top of Viola's

"*Let's rock and roll!*" they all chanted and then they took their hands out of the pile.

Chapter 24:
A Day in the Life of Miz Mayhem

Miz Mayhem was known by only some as "Lady Gorge" and by almost no one as Bernice Walden. She was over two hundred years old, and pretty much everyone who had known her by her real name was now long dead. It was a sort of anonymity that mortal villains could never hope to achieve, and for years Miz Mayhem had enjoyed this anonymity immensely. She had been a villain without a name, and therefore a villain who could never be truly unmasked. How strange it was to write the words "Bernice Walden" on a name tag and then stick the words on her own left shoulder for others to read; how surreal. Bernice felt like she was standing outside of herself as she did this; as though she were watching a stranger from a distance. A stranger named Bernice Walden.

She opened a chocolate bar and chomped down on it for comfort, quickly devouring it in its entirety. Then, pulled a second candy bar from the pocket of her fir-lined silk robe, unwrapped it and chomped down on it again. Bernice was a pretty, curvy woman, with blue eyes and long, wavy, blond hair. Having been raised in a different time period, she was more comfortable wearing long gowns and robes than modern clothing. Today she was wearing her favorite fur-lined salmon-pink robe, a long, power blue dress, long, white, silk gloves, and a pair of white heels.

Bernice walked over to the circle of chairs at the center of the room and sat down in one of them. She watched as other people sat down in the chairs all around her. These people were all ex-villains but they looked like ordinary, unremarkable people in standard, modern clothing. All of them wore name tags.

"Welcome, *welcome*," a man in a tweed suit greeted them. He wore glasses and had short, conservatively styled, brown hair, which was parted to the side and flecked with grey. The stubble on his chin was grey and his tie was a deep blackish-purple. "I am Dr. Gordeau. You may call me Dr. G."

"Hello, Dr. G," a few of the people in the group greeted in return.

Gordeau sat down in the last empty chair of the circle, between Bernice and a man with a nose ring and a shaved head. He smiled affably and then continued:

"This is the ex-superpowered cons support group, so, if you're here for the 'Marriage Maintenance' workshop with Dr. Samson you want sweet 258-A. This is sweet 258-B. People often make that mistake."

Several people, including the man with the shaved head and nose ring got up and left the room.

"It's two doors down on your left," Gordeau informed the couples as they walked away. "There's a closet and fire escape between this room and that one, so people often get confused."

Now four or five people remained in the group. Gordeau glanced around at them all and smiled affably.

"Let's begin with an ice breaker. We'll go around the circle counter clockwise and I want each of you to tell me who you are and why you are here today," said Gordeau and he turned toward Bernice. "You begin, Ms. Walden."

"Ah…yes…well…," Bernice stumbled, "I am Miz Mayhem…well, I was Miz Mayhem and I'm here today because I'm very old. I've lost my reason to live, and I'm very tired of living….You see, I was exposed to the radiation a long, long time ago and when that happened, I attained the ability to touch someone and take something of theirs or give them something of mine."

"I don't think I understand what you mean," said Gordeau.

"Give me your hand," Bernice said. Then, she pulled her long glove off and held a bare hand out for Gordeau to shake.

Gordeau stared at her hand unsurely for a moment; a

look of genuine fear betrayed his professional mask. Then, he
put his hand in hers and shook it. The grey in Gordeau's hair
shifted to auburn. The lines around his mouth, forehead, and
eyes softened. While at the same time, lines of grey snaked
down Bernice's blond curls, her smooth skin sank, and
crinkled around her mouth and eyes. Bernice let go of
Gordeau's hand. The other members of the group gasped in
amazement. A middle-aged woman with a perm clapped as
though this were a magic trick.

"There. Now you're ten years younger," Bernice said
to the counselor. "And I am ten years older. That's the way it
works."

"I don't feel younger," said Gordeau curiously,
touching his face with the palm of his hand to see if he could
notice a difference. "Do I look younger?"

The members of the group nodded their affirmation.
There were a few scattered "yea"s and a polite "You look
good."

"This is the way I kept myself young for so many
years," explained Bernice, "I sucked the life out of the young
and gave them my old age. I sucked the health out of the
healthy and gave them my diseases. I gave them my cataracts;
my extra weight; my injuries. This hair isn't mine either, the
color, I mean. I stole the color from a girl in 1947 and gave her
my brown hair in its place," Bernice paused and pointed at
her own eyes with the index and middle finger of one hand.
"This eye color isn't mine either. I took it from my sister, and
my visual acuity, I took that from someone who was a very
talented marksman, that is, before I blinded him. For years I
was content to live this way. I found a man that I loved, made
him look the way I wanted him to, and then, made him an
immortal by transferring the life force of others onto him. Ah,
yes…we were married after that, and lived happily together
for many years. Unfortunately, however, my precious love
still wasn't indestructible. He was killed in a car accident two
years ago and that's why I'm here today. I'd like to make my

peace with god; give something back to the community, so that I can finally die…the way that nature intended."

"That's a beautiful sentiment, Bernice. But I believe that suicide is not the answer," said Gordeau, "An individual with your skills and experience could be a very valuable asset to society. Have you considered being a mentor for at-risk superpowered youth?"

"No. But perhaps I'll consider it. Only for a short time, though" said Bernice quietly, "I've been so very lonely since Stefan died."

"Have you tried internet dating? There's some really great dating sites for radiation-altered singles."

"Ah, yes, well….I'm the kind of woman who loves only one man in my lifetime. These 21st century men, with all of their fancy do-dads and thing-a-ma-whats-its," she waved her hands around in the air to expose the pretentious absurdity of "do-dads and thing-a-ma-whats-its." What she was really talking about were cell phones and flash drives.

The counselor nodded.

"They're just not the same," continued Bernice, "and *the internet,* I don't like it. I have never owned a computer and I never plan to own one."

"Thank you for sharing, Bernice," said Gordeau, turning toward the man sitting to Bernice's right. He had a mustache and was mostly bald. "Mr. Domingo, please tell the group who you are and why you are here to day."

Bernice listened with no small degree of boredom to the poverty, childhood trauma, and substance abuse related tales of other ex-villains in the group. To entertain herself, she pulled a gigantic bag of ruffled sour cream and onion potato chips from her purse, and began shoving fistfuls of the crunchy yellow flakes into her open mouth.

"Mr. Walker?" the counselor inquired of a pimple-faced kid with a swollen black eye and a busted lip. The name tag on his chest read: "Jason Walker."

"No comment," the kid replied darkly, and crossed his

arms.

"Will you please share with the group who you are and why you are here today?" Gordeau asked.

The kid glared at Gordeau and was silent.

"Uh...ok, then. You don't have to share anything that you're uncomfortable sharing," said Gordeau. Then, he turned to the person to Jason's right, a fat, balding man with wire-framed glasses.

"Mr. Conroy, please. Tell the group who you are and why you are here today," Gordeau said.

The group continued for an hour and a half. Each ex-con (excluding Jason Walker) shared their former secret identities, their supernatural abilities, their criminal pasts, and their varying reasons for coming to the group that day. The fluorescent lights overhead flickered. There was a discussion, and then a useless activity that involved each ex-villain writing his or her feelings down on a piece of paper and then ripping the paper into pieces before throwing it into the air like confetti. Jason did not participate in this activity but instead, crossed his arms and rolled his eyes when the counselor proposed it. The fluorescent lights overhead flickered again.

"Well, that concludes our group for this week," said Gordeau to the group. "I hope to see you again next week, when we'll be discussing deep breathing and healthy outlets for negative emotions."

The group rose from their seats and dispersed. Jason walked over to Bernice, still scowling.

"Have you noticed the lights flickering in this room?" Jason inquired of her darkly.

"Yes, now that you mention it. I have," replied Bernice.

"It's the ghost girl," explained Jason morosely, "Her presence creates electrical disturbances."

"Do you think that Ghost Gal is spying on the ex-superpowered cons support group?" Bernice murmured.

"I *know* she is," said Jason bluntly. He put his middle

finger up and brandished it at the drop ceiling, where he imagined Ghost Gal was probably hiding, invisible and perched on the edge of a suspicious missing ceiling panel, staring down at the group.

"I know you're there, bitch," Jason growled at the missing ceiling panel. Jason put his middle finger down and turned back toward Bernice.

"Listen, Mrs. Walden," said Jason, assuming a more business like tone. "I'm not here to share my feelings or whatever."

"Then, what are you here for?"

"I'm here because this crap is court ordered, but actually..." Jason said and then he began whispering so that Ghost Gal wouldn't hear him, "I'm also here because I want to team up with some other high powered villains and take down The Sexy Action Pals."

"Oh, no, *no*. Those Sexy Action Clowns have taken enough of my time, good day sir," said Bernice and she began to walk away.

Jason got between her and the door and she glared at him, crossing her arms and waiting for him to move.

"Listen, Mayhem. I didn't sit here and listen to all of these loser's stupid sob stories for an hour and a half to be turned down by the only villain in the room that would be a real credit to my team."

"*Your* team? Ah ha ha...don't make me laugh," said Bernice.

"Together, *with our combined powers*, you and I...and maybe a few select others....We would be an *unstoppable* force. We could rule this city," said Jason.

"Yes, well....I'm not like that anymore," said Bernice. Then, she stepped around him and walked through the door into the hallway. Jason followed her.

"I think you'll change your mind, Bernice," he said as she speed walked down one of the hallways, turned left, and then disappeared from sight. "I can be very *persuasive!*"

Chapter 25:
The Rise of Death Laser

"Fernando! I love you!" the beautiful actress on the television announced rather artificially. Her dewy, amber locks were blown by a sudden breeze, while at the same time, the gentle ocean waves crashed against her bare feet.

"Anastasia!" a muscular, handsome man with dark skin cried as he ran across the sand and toward the beautiful woman. He had a deep sensual voice and a Spanish accent. The screen cut to the sun sinking low in an orange sky and then back to the face of the beautiful actress.

The handsome actor ran up to her and put his arms around her.

"I thought you were going to marry Douglas!" he said, sounding as though he were reading the lines off of a piece of paper as he spoke them.

"I couldn't!" exclaimed the beautiful actress, very artificially. "I was thinking about *you* the whole time!"

"Oh *Anastasia!*"

"Oh *Fernando!*"

The beautiful actress began making out with the handsome actor. The camera zoomed out on the beach and the setting sun so that the actors were now a silhouette against the backdrop. Slow, sad music began to play. The screen went black and the credits rolled.

"That...*was beautiful*," said Viola, wiping a tear from her eye.

"Eh," said Harriet indifferently and she shrugged.

The two of them were sitting on the couch in the living room of what was now Viola, Harriet, and Stuart's apartment. It was an old, brown couch with a tweed texture and a pattern of green and red Chinese dragons printed on it. The room itself was dressed in a grey and white stripped wall paper and was badly lit. An old-fashioned-looking hanging lamp overhead, swung from a copper chain, and cast the couch below in an eerie orange light. A few open cardboard boxes filled with surplus masks and costumes from the party store that Viola ran during the day reflected the blue and purple lights of a couple of lava lamps on a nearby table.

"Is it over yet?" Stuart's voice groaned from the adjacent kitchen.

"Ooh… *Street Car Love Story* is on after this," said Viola to Harriet, ignoring Stuart entirely. "That's the story of two rival gang members who fall in love."

"Yea, I've seen it," said Harriet, "Doesn't everybody die at the end?"

"Yea, but *first*, they fall in love," said Viola.

Stuart walked from the kitchen into the living room. He had a beer in his hand, which he snapped open as he walked. It made a brief fizzing noise, and then he lifted the beer up to his lips and drank from it, before sitting down on the couch next to Viola. He reached for the remote.

"No!" Viola complained and she leaned backwards, holding the remote away from him.

"Yes," said Stuart, reaching across Viola and grabbing for the remote.

"No."

"Yes."

"Get away!"

"You said that if I made dinner, I could have the remote for an hour and a half," Stuart reminded Viola crossly.

"Yea, *well*…I say a lot of things," said Viola dismissively, "Harriet's the *new* roommate. Let her decide."

"Hey, hey, hey, *whoa*. Don't drag *me* into this," said Harriet quickly, putting her hands up in supplication.

"*Oh*, ok, I see how it is. You're siding with *him* now," said Viola.

"I *am* not."

"Harriet, you seem like a reasonable person," said Stuart to Harriet in an even voice. "Don't you think we should vote on what gets played on the only TV in the house tonight?"

"Um...," Harriet murmured unsurely.

"Well, I never said that this apartment was a *democracy*," said Viola crossly.

"No, it's a dictatorship," said Stuart.

"You're damn right it is," said Viola, poking Stuart in the chest with one of her painted pink nails.

"Viola, I pay just as much rent as you do," growled Stuart angrily. "Give me the remote."

"You can't have it."

"Fine. Fine, *whatever*. Forget about me ever cooking again," groaned Stuart in exasperation.

Now Harriet *had* to say something. Stuart had gone to culinary school and by day he worked as a chef in a fancy restaurant. During his time in the military, he had worked as a cook as well, and, as a result, he had years of culinary experience that Harriet could really taste in the meals he prepared. That night, he had prepared the most tender and delicious roast pork that Harriet had tasted in several years. It was the kind of meal that Harriet was accustomed to but could no longer afford now that she was not fabulously wealthy but merely, reasonably well off.

"You know what, guys..." said Harriet, grabbing the remote out of Viola's hand. Stuart's threat to stop cooking was enough to make her side with him in this argument.

"Hey!" Viola complained.

"Let's just watch the news, ok?" said Harriet and she changed the channel to the news.

"*Yes*. Finally! Thank you, Harriet," sighed Stuart with relief. The thought of being forced to endure another romance movie was giving him a headache.

"Alright. *Fine*," Conceded Viola a bit reluctantly. "You are the new roommate after all, so I guess tonight's really all about you."

An old man news anchor, with neatly parted grey hair, who wore a dark blue suit with a white button down shirt and a black tie, appeared on the screen. To his right was a pretty, blond, female co-anchor with a lot of makeup on.

"Tonight's top story," the news anchor announced in a deep, articulate voice. "A mysterious masked man who calls himself 'Death Laser' has broken into a Rosswell Bank in Propopolous city and emptied its vaults. Police, who had received warning from the villain about where and when he would strike next after the villain's last robbery, were at the scene before he arrived. Yet somehow, the masked man was able to slip past them and run off with millions of dollars worth of stolen money. Leaving *everyone,* scratching their heads, *wondering: How* did he do it? Here to talk about Death Laser's latest robbery today is expert criminologist, Daniel Wilton."

The camera cut to a black table with a clear glass top were three people sat in tall black chairs. The camera zoomed in on the face of a middle-aged man with a long sharp nose and a pair of ears that stuck out like an elephant. He was wearing a black suit.

"Author of *Super Security Measures: The Does and Don'ts of Villain Proofing Banks, Museums, and Private Residences,* Temere Williams," the news anchor introduced.

The camera cut to a close up of the man sitting next to Daniel Wilton, Temere Williams. He was a middle-aged, dark-skinned man with a shaved head and a beard who wore a dark blue suit.

"And, Psychologist Stephanie Ragnoff," the news anchor introduced.

The camera cut to a close up of the woman sitting next to Temere Williams, Stephanie Ragnoff. She was an older woman with short grey hair, red lipstick and a pair of wire-framed glasses, who wore a sleeveless, white dress.

"Oh boy," said Harriet rolling her eyes at the television. "This is *really* going to go to Death Laser's head. They've got a whole *panel* of fancy assholes talking about him now."

"Shh…," Viola shushed Harriet, "Let the fancy assholes

talk, Harriet. This is their show. Not yours."

The discussion about Death Laser's robbery went on for some time, and, as the panel of experts talked, the screen periodically cut to blurry security camera footage of Death Laser's robbery, followed by a flash of red light and static.

"You see, the bank should have invested in titanium enforced security cameras," Temere Williams said, "They're resistant to the lasers produced by most varieties of radiation-altered criminals."

"I disagree," said Stephanie Ragnoff. "Why should the banks have to spend hundreds of thousands of dollars on enhanced security features, when the issue here is really with our mental health system? These mentally ill people aren't getting the treatment they need and that's the real issue here."

"But do you really believe that Death Laser is mentally ill?" said Daniel Wilton. "He was able to escape successfully with a pretty lucid and well thought out plan. And after years of experience working in the criminal justice system, I have to point out that confused, poorly thought out schemes are usually the telltale sign of mental illness. Eccentric behavior is not, in itself, proof of it."

"Have you seen footage of Death Laser?" argued Stephanie Ragnoff, "He's clearly mentally ill."

"I disagree."

"Whether or not he's mentally ill is really irrelevant," said Temere Williams, "Proper security measures would have prevented the robbery. And they're really much more cost effective than you might think."

"I can't believe they're still talking," groaned Harriet.

"Looks like they're taking your nemesis seriously, Harriet," said Viola.

"I told you, he's not my nemesis," said Harriet as she watched the blurry footage of Death Laser breaking into the bank for what must have been the 15th time. "He sucks too much to be my nemesis."

"I don't know, Harriet," said Stuart, "He's getting more

news coverage than we ever did. Looks like he might be for real this time."

"The media blows things out of proportion," said Harriet, "I'm not getting involved."

"The police don't even know how he keeps escaping," said Stuart.

"The police are idiots," said Harriet, "But I'm sure they'll still figure it out soon and then Death Laser will go to jail and this whole stupid media circus can end."

A week passed, during which Harriet moved her stuff into the empty room of Viola and Stuart's apartment. There was already a bed here, a single bed with a black and white striped comforter, positioned beneath an oval mirror in a bamboo frame. There was also a box window that looked out on the brick wall of a nearby apartment building and over the narrow alleyway below.

By day, Harriet applied for jobs, periodically visiting an art museum or a gallery for an interview. By night, Harriet dawned her hero costume and joined the Sexy Rad Super Pals on their patrols. Lilly, whose powers made her very good at spying on people, rarely joined them. Instead she kept track of Crunchy Toast Muncher, The Frenchman, and Lady Gorge, who were, for the time being, dormant. Every evening she would report back to the group with some extremely uninteresting new information about the person that she had been stalking that night.

"The French Man's been watching a lot of old movies lately," Lilly whispered one evening, after reconvening with the group in Viola and Stuart's apartment. "He's not really very motivated these days…Lady Gorge made a new breakthrough in group tonight. She feels the need to be the constant center of attention because of a feeling of abandonment due to her absent father…Crunchy Toast Muncher…is still hiding. I looked in all of his usual haunts…but I still couldn't find him."

Every night, after Lilly and Benjamin left the

apartment. Harriet sat down in front of the television and watched the news. Death Laser was being talked about nonstop by every local media outlet every day. Apparently, he had started robbing a major bank in Propopolous City every afternoon at exactly 12:13 p.m. The police were always left clueless, wondering how he had managed to get in and out of the vaults without their notice. Death Laser left videos for the police in the vaults he emptied. In these videos, he bragged about how easy it was to steal things, and made fun of how stupid he felt the police were.

Another week passed. Harriet got a curetting job at the last remaining art museum in the city. By day, she lead a guided tour through a Jackson Pollock exhibit, all the while, keeping an eye out for Crunchy Toast Mucher, who might have, at any time, reappeared to transform and devour the exhibits. By night, she watched the news. Death Laser's latest video for the cops was usually a headline and clips of it were shown as Death Laser's specialized panel of fancy assholes: Daniel Whats-his-face, Temere So-in-so and Stephanie Who-gives-a-crap, debated the video's significance or lack there of.

"Play the clip, Jim," the old man news anchor instructed of a man offstage.

The screen cut to a blurry video of Death Laser, who usually wore a long black cape and black plastic mask that covered most of his face. His eyes burned like the tips of lit cigarettes beneath his mask and he cackled insanely. Then, he spread his arms wide and motioned toward the stacks of hundred dollar bills piled up in the vault behind him, grinning.

"See all of this money," Death Laser bragged obnoxiously. "It's totally mine now. Do you know why?" Death Laser paused for a moment as though waiting for an audience to reply and then answered his own question: "Because cops suck and I'm *amazing*. And do you know who else can kiss my ass?" Death Laser paused again as though listening for an audience response. "*The Justice Bitch.* Why do you think she hasn't shown up to any of my robberies, huh? Clearly, it's because she's *afraid* to fight me. It's beca–"

The video clip was stopped short, though clearly Death Laser's full rant went on for longer than that.

"He has a really strange obsession with The Justice Bitch, don't you think?" the self-proclaimed expert criminologist postulated.

"Yes, I believe he's mentioned her multiple times before as his nemesis," agreed Stephanie Ragnoff.

"I believe that's irrelevant," said Temere Williams. "This young man making an ass of himself in these videos, should be taken as a reminder that we need better security in our banks, to match a changing world where a growing number of radiation-altered citizens, whether we like it or not, are living among us."

Harriet groaned and turned off the television. She was *not* going to let Death Laser get to her. She was *not* going to acknowledge him as her nemesis.

Stuart walked into the living room, glanced over at Harriet on the couch, and then glanced over at the television.

"You're watching this again," he observed.

"Yea, what's it to you?"

"Far be it from me to get involved in this kind of crap, but it seems like this Death Laser guy is really getting under your skin," said Stuart, sitting down on the couch next the Harriet.

"Don't be ridiculous," said Harriet, not turning her head to look at Stuart but rather continuing to stare at the TV. "He's not my problem. I'm not getting involved."

"Well, if reverse psychology's his game, then he's certainly playing *you*."

"Do you really think that he's playing me?"

"Think about it," said Stuart, "He told you, in so many words that he *wanted* to fight you, right? That he didn't really even want the money. But what if….and hear me out here….*what if*, in reality, he said that because he really *doesn't* want to fight you or any of us for that matter. What if his first couple of botched robberies were just part of his strategy…to convince you that you shouldn't get involved?"

"How could he possibly know that would work?" Harriet said.

"I dunno. Its just a theory," said Stuart.

Viola walked into the living room from an adjacent hallway.

"He's right, Harriet," she said, "This not wanting to get involved thing. It's not like you. Seriously, Harriet, *why are you doing this?*"

"Ah…I don't know. This whole downward transition into the upper middle class has been taking up a lot of my energy, I guess."

"Breaking news!" the blond female co-anchor announced from the television. "Death Laser and his henchmen have taken over The Ross Manor!"

"That *son of a bitch!*" Harriet screamed, standing up quickly. She glared at the TV like she wished it would explode and balled her hands into fists.

The screen of the television cut to a blurry video of Death Laser sitting behind a large and intricately carved mahogany desk, Harriet's father's desk. Bright sunlight shined through the glass wall behind him; a glass wall which looked out over a distant Propopolous City skyline. This was certainly Harriet's father's office. Death Laser grinned and spun around a couple of times in Harriet's father's black leather computer chair, then, put both of his muddy shoes up on the desk and crossed his arms, as he faced the camera, still grinning. He was wearing one of Harriet's father's suits, a grey one with a red tie.

"Hey, this is a pretty sweet crib," Death Laser commented cheerfully. By the way he spoke, Harriet thought that he might have been talking to a second person in the room, off screen. "I think I'm going to make this my *evil lair!*"

Death Laser paused for a moment to cackle

triumphantly, before adding sarcastically:

"Gee, I sure hope *Harriet Ross* doesn't mind!" Spencer took his feet off of the desk and spun around in the chair again.

"Hehehehe*heheh*...heh...heh..." he cackled mockingly and then the video cut out.

"That *son-of-a-bitch*!" Harriet screamed again. The thought of that buffoon living in her father's house was really too much for her to bear. She smashed her fist down on a little wooden table near the entrance to the hallway and the piece of furniture was cracked in two. Then, she slammed a foot against the floor and the boards underneath crumbled with a startling *bang*, creating a hole that went through to the apartment underneath.

Harriet drew a shaking hand over her red face and wiped the sweat from her forehead, breathing heavy.

"I'm so sorry, Viola," she apologized, "I promise I'll pay for the damages."

"Don't sweat it," said Viola cheerfully, "I'll just take it out of your security deposit. I'm pretty used to my apartment getting destroyed by superpowers by this point anyway."

Harriet crossed her arms and began pacing the room, with a furious scowl plastered across her face.

Stuart stooped down so that his mouth was level with Viola's ear.

"Get her *out of here* before she destroys something else," Stuart whispered gruffly.

Viola nodded.

"Uh...Harriet, let's get out of here...get some lunch, go shopping or something?" Viola suggested timidly. Harriet did not respond.

"That greasy little *peace of shit* is *a dead man*!" Harriet screamed as she continued to pace the floor. Her manicured nails shot to her dark, disheveled hair and she tore at it madly. A trickle of blood spilled out over her forehead.

"Does this mean...we're going after Death Laser,

finally?" Stuart said with some degree of irritation.

"Fine! Yes, yes we are!" Harriet yelled. She sat back down on the couch and crossed her arms, breathing in and out slowly in an attempt to calm herself down.

The apartment was quiet for a moment. Viola and Stuart stared at Harriet with apprehension as her breathing slowed and the redness faded from her face.

"But I'm the one who gets to kill him," Harriet murmured quietly. She pictured herself strangling Death Laser until the crimson lights faded from his eyes and almost smiled. She did not smile, however. Instead, the corners of her mouth twitched neurotically and so did the lower lid of her left eye. "You got that?"

Chapter 26:
Stand by your Financial Advisor

During her lunch break, Harriet usually went into the museum's employee break room. Here there were a couple of soda machines and a generous assortment of store-bought Danishes in plastic pouches, sitting on a silver tray at the center of a long, wooden table.

Harriet sat down at the table and grabbed a Danish. Her cell phone rang. She retrieved it from her purse, tapped the "answer" button on the screen, and put it up to her ear.

"Hello?"

"Hello, Harriet? This is Gary, your financial advisor," the voice on the other end of the phone informed her earnestly.

"Get lost, Gary," murmured Harriet grimly, pulling the plastic package of her store bought Danish open with a dry *pop*. "I can't afford you anymore."

"No, actually, I'm calling because of the lawsuit," said Gary, "Super Annoyo's friends keep sending me literally thousands of junk emails with the tag line: Fuck You Gary Goldstien. I didn't open any of them because I felt that they must contain a computer virus of some kind. But then he started having his pals leave threatening messages on my answering machine. I changed my number so many times, Harriet. You have no idea. Super Annoyo's followers started a fake profile of me on every social media site you can imagine where they have me saying stuff like I've got aids and I'm a Nazi..."

"Are you a Nazi?" Harriet interjected callously. She crossed her legs and took a bite out of the Danish she was holding. It was cold and stale. The yellow "lemon" filling was more like a gelatinous chemical sugar mush.

"Harriet, *I'm Jewish*," Gary replied with exasperation.

"A Jewish Nazi. How unoriginal," said Harriet drolly. She glanced over at a painting of bare trees at the edge of a snowy lake, which hung above the mini-fridge in the break room.

"And I don't have aids either," said Gary defensively.

"Really? Have you checked?" Harriet teased.

"This is serious, Harriet. I'm losing clients. My fiancé broke up with me. It's all because he thinks I still work for you."

"So sue him for defamation of character," said Harriet, "You are a lawyer, aren't you?"

"I've already begun the process, yes," said Gary, "But I don't think that suing him is going to get his supporters to leave me alone. Since he's not attacking me directly, it'll be hard to prove that he has anything to do with it."

"You can do it, Gary. I have faith in you," said Harriet conversationally, "Show those trolls whose boss. Hey, has Super Annoyo set up a fake social media page for me yet?"

"No...I don't think so, not *yet* anyway. I think he's afraid of you. That's why I'm calling actually," said Gary, "I think I'd like to help you shoot down Super Annoyo's lawsuit, maybe countersue for pain and suffering."

"I told you, Gary. I can't afford you," said Harriet.

"I'll work for free," said Gary.

"I don't think I'd like to be thought of as a charity case, Gary. I can still pay you something."

"No, Harriet. I insist. His people started Photoshopping my head onto gay porn. This just got personal," said Gary.

"Really, Gary. I never took you for the *revenge* type," said Harriet, crossing her legs and holding her cell phone up to her ear with her shoulder as she used both of her hands to peel a piece off of the unspectacular Danish and put it in her mouth.

"Well, you know. This is also business," said Gary, "This is bound to be a high profile case. I could use the notoriety."

"Considering who your father is, do you really need

it?"

"Well…I'd also be helping a friend."

Harriet threw her head back and laughed.

"It's cute that you think we're friends," she said rather ambiguously, and she grinned, imagining the look of distraught confusion on Gary's face as he wondered exactly what she meant by that. Gary was not Harriet's friend. He was the son of one of Harriet's father's friends. However, the way Gary talked sometimes made her wonder if maybe he saw their relationship in a different way than her.

"Uh…"

"But don't you worry about a thing. I'll be sure to stop by that prison and put the fear of God back in Super Annoyo," Harriet said.

"You better not do that, Harriet. If you threaten him, he could use it against you in court," Gary warned.

"Ok, Jesus, fine. I'll stay away from Super Annoyo," Harriet complained with some annoyance. Then, she added affectionately: "Still, I think its time he learned, when you fuck with my financial adviser. You fuck with me."

Chapter 27:
Trauma

Gordeau pushed the bridge of his glasses up with his index finger. Then, he put on a forced, professional smile and motioned toward his circle of clients with his hands.

"I want to thank everyone who participated last week for sharing their thoughts and feelings openly and honestly," said Gordeau, "I know that it can take courage to trust others, but remember. This is a safe place. Nothing that you share with me or the group will leave this room."

Jason rolled his eyes and groaned, then, glanced up at that suspicious missing ceiling tile. Ghost Gal was surely still up there. Probably even taking notes or recording the super ex-cons with a tape recorder.

"Last week, we talked about what makes us angry and what anger feels like to us," said Gordeau, "So, this week, I thought we'd talk about how we deal with anger. Let's begin with Bernice. Bernice, how do you deal with anger?"

"I hurt people," said Bernice bluntly. Jason noticed that the furrows in her skin and the grey streaks in her hair were gone this week. Her breasts were also a bit larger.
She must have sucked ten years and two braw sizes out of some woman that pissed her off, Jason thought. *Reformed, my ass.*

"Thank you for sharing, Bernice," said Gordeau, "Ted?"

A bald man with a beer belly sitting next to Bernice replied:

"I buy things that I can't afford. Like this one time, I was really mad because my wife was talking about leaving me, so I bought a huge flat screen television with money that I stole from girl scouts."

"Girl scouts?" Gordeau reflected curiously.

"Yea, it's like whenever I see girls scouts selling cookies, I grab the table that the cookies are on and—"

Jason lost interest in what Ted was saying and stopped

listening. Gordeau
was wearing a purple suit today, and it made Jason think of
something that he had seen before.

Others spoke. Jason did not listen to what they had to
say. Instead he stared at Gordeau and tried to figure out who
exactly the man reminded him of.

"Jason?" Gordeau inquired after awhile.

"Huh?" Jason murmured, having been unexpectedly
jarred out of deep contemplation.

"How do you deal with anger?" Gordeau said,
reminding Jason of the question.

"You're Trauma, aren't you?" accused Jason bluntly.

"Excuse me?"

"Trauma, the super criminal who incapacitates people
by making them relive a flashback of their worst trauma in
vivid detail. You wear a mask that looks like an inkblot psych
exam and your costume is purple and covered in red inkblots.
It's you, isn't it?" said Jason.

The room was quiet for a moment. The members of the
group stared at Gordeau, waiting for him to confirm or deny
this startling accusation.

"Well, yes," conceded Gordeau a bit nervously. It had
never been his intention to share this with the group. "But
that was a long time ago."

"Really? So, you're a criminal too?" Jason pointed out
rhetorically.

"Well, yes. But villainy is a young man's game."

"You look young enough to me, there. Dr. G," Jason
challenged, alluding to the ten years that Bernice had taken off
of Gordeau's face in the first session.

"I'm—"

"But let me guess," interrupted Jason sarcastically,
"You're not like that anymore? Is that what you were going to
say?"

"Jason, you never did tell us who you are or why you
are here," said Gordeau, attempting to change the subject.

"We're not talking about me, here. We're talking about you," said Jason, becoming visibly agitated by the hypocrisy of Gordeau's reluctance to disclose personal information.

Gordeau nodded calmly.

"The ability I got from the radiation gave me an insight into the deepest emotional pains of others. And it's true that when I was younger, I used that ability for evil. I tortured my enemies with their own personal demons until they were powerless to stop me."

Gordeau cleared his throat and continued.

"But my ability was not inherently evil only what I chose to do with it. In time, I found that revisiting the traumas of the past can help individuals work through pain and gain a healthy, productive understanding of themselves and the events that made them who they are. After a time, the effects of the radiation made me see that my true calling was as a councilor."

Gordeau was quiet for a moment. The members of the group (excluding Jason who rolled his eyes and crossed his arms defensively) clapped. The older woman with the perm wiped a tear from her eye and said: "Dr. Gordeau, you're an inspiration. When I look at you, I see me!"

Jason groaned, annoyed that his ploy to make the group hate Gordeau had not worked.

The applause died down.

"Jason, you never told us what effect the radiation had on you," Gordeau inquired in a calm, affable voice.

"You want to know what my power is?"

"Yes."

"My power is that I can turn things into stone by touching them," Jason lied to shut Gordeau up.

"Thank you for sharing, Jason," said Gordeau. "For our next activity, I'd like you all to take out a piece of paper and a pen or a pencil. I want you to write a short letter to yourself or draw a picture. Tell yourself what's good about your power and how you can use it to be a source of strength to the community instead of a force for chaos and destruction. When we're done, I want you to pass your papers to the left so that everyone here can read what you have written and so that you can read what everyone else has written."

Jason grinned evilly. This was exactly the kind of opportunity he had been waiting for.

"For instance, Bernice could use her power to help obese people loose weight, and people who are underweight, like, say, for instance, *the starving*, gain just enough to be healthy," Gordeau offered for an example. "Think about what *you* could do."

Jason pulled a spiral notebook from the backpack that he had brought with him, which had been open on the floor in front of his chair. He opened the notebook and wrote the following words:

"You will read every word on this paper and obey the instructions assigned to you without exception. Bernice Walden and Nathaniel Gordeau, you will join my super villain team, which I, Jayson Walker, will be the leader of. Anyone in this group who is not Bernice Walden, Nathaniel Gordeau or myself, who reads this will be a meal for The Crunchy Toast Muncher, after I utter the trigger word. Please note that the trigger word is "Beef Wellington." You will all write your names and phone numbers on this piece of paper when it is passed to you, so that I can call you when it's time for you to hear the trigger word."

Jason put his pen down and ripped the piece of paper from his notebook. Then, still grinning, passed it to the left.

What followed was not witnessed by Lilly. Who, as fate would have it, was not present that day.

Chapter 28:
Enter: The League of Evildoers

That evening, Jason, Bernice, and Gordeau put on their villain costumes and drove to The Ross Manor, which was a large, Victorian-style castle on the edge of a cliff overlooking the city. Jason was wearing his Richard Nixon mask and a parking cone on his head with a t-shirt and jeans. Bernice was wearing a long, fir-lined, pink velvet robe, white heels, a few strings of white pearls around her neck, and a white pearl broach. She had on a white and pink Mardi Gras mask with a number of white, pink, and black feathers coming off the sides of it. Gordeau, who was driving, was wearing a purple tuxedo with a red bowtie, a matching purple top hat with a red band and a monocle on a silver chain. His mask was white and covered in a pattern of red splotches, which resembled both a splatter of blood and the contours of a psychological inkblot test.

"This death Laser fellow lives in The Ross Manor now, is that right?" Gordeau asked.

"Yes," said Jason with some degree of irritation as he believed that this should have been obvious.

"And you want him to join The League of Evil Doers?" Gordeau asked.

"Yes," said Jason.

"But not the rest of the super ex-cons group?" asked Gordeau.

"No. Their powers suck too much. I only want villains with good powers on my team."

"I'm sorry but don't laser eyes technically count as a power that sucks?" interjected Bernice from the back seat. "I mean you could accomplish the same thing by having one man who owns a gun on your team."

"As far as I'm concerned, Death Laser has the best superpower of all," said Jason and he paused for dramatic effect before continuing: "*Money.* The best superpower is *money,*" Jason concluded, "After Death Laser agrees to fund our project, we'll be unstoppable."

Gordeau turned left at a coffee shop on the corner and began driving up a steep and narrow incline. As he drove, posh little department stores and restaurants thinned and then relented entirely.

"Why ask Death Laser for money? He's only rich because he's been robbing banks. I do prefer to rob my own banks, Jason," said Bernice with some degree of irritation. "This is all very contradictory to my nature."

"Death Laser's already emptied every bank vault in the city," said Jason.

"You behave as though there's only one city in the world, darling," said Bernice patronizingly.

"Oh yea, well I'm the team leader so we're doing it my way," snipped Jason with irritation. He stared out the window at a steep incline of green, manicured grass being tussled by a powerful breeze. "I don't want to waste time robbing banks when I should be taking over the world."

Bernice shook her head and tutted.

"I remember when I was like you," she said.

Gordeau's car reached a high, arched gate formed from an elegant interlocking pattern of steel spirals. Two guards, wearing black ski masks and black slacks with black polo shirts, stood at either side of the gate, holding black machine guns. A few feet to the left, a trio of black-uniformed grounds keepers were in the process of painting the stone wall surrounding the manor black.

Gordeau rolled down the driver's side window and spoke to one of the guards:

"Eh, excuse me?"

The guard walked over to the window and peered in at the three villains.

"Uh, yea, hello," the guard said.

"We're here to speak with Death Laser," said Gordeau.

"Yea...sorry our boss is kind of an idiot, so I have to

ask everyone who comes up here this question. Right. Um. Here it goes. *Is Justice Bitch with you?"* the guard asked with the tone of a man in a mascot costume who must begrudgingly recite his theme park's corny catchphrase.

"No," answered Gordeau truthfully. Beneath his red splatter mask, he raised an eyebrow in derision.

"I'm sorry but Death Laser does not wish to speak with anybody at this time," said the guard quickly, "Please leave."

"Trauma, do your thing," instructed Jason boredly.

"Right," said Gordeau. He curled the fingers on his left hand and a ball of black mist gathered in his palm. Before the guard knew what was happening, Gordeau hurled the mist at the guard's face and it poured into his head through his nose holes and open mouth.

"Oh no...oh no....oh *God!*" the guard screamed. His eyes clamped shut and he dropped to his knees, trembling. His eyelids twitched and he began to whimper as though he were dreaming. "D...don't touch me! Stay away!"

The other guard ran toward the car. He was a bit chubbier than the first one.

"Hey! What's going on over here!" he demanded.

"Miz Mayhem," Jason instructed, smirking maliciously.

Bernice got out of the car and walked over to the guard who was still standing, while the other guard fell to the ground and began flailing around like his body was being beaten by an invisible bat. Bernice reached out and touched the remaining guard's bare forearm with the palm of her hand.

"....Hahahahah!" she cackled maliciously as the guard screamed and fell to his knees. His body began to shrivel and deflate, while at the same time, beneath the robe, Bernice's body began expanding like a balloon. In an instant, Bernice became a rotund woman with a double chin, floppy drumstick arms, and a large, round belly. The guard crumbled to the ground, dead. He now resembled a horrific skeleton covered in floppy, loose skin. The grounds keepers dropped their paint rollers and ran screaming.

Jason got out of the car and walked over to the guard who was still alive and flailing around on the ground, screaming in pain. He waited for a few minutes and the man grew still. Then, he opened his eyes and rose to his feet, hyperventilating.

"What the hell did you do to me!" he screamed and he raised his rifle high, prepared to shoot Jason pointblank in the face.

Jason took a parking ticket with the words "You will open the gate and let us in" printed on it, and quickly stuck it to the guard's forehead. The guard's eyes dilated and his hands loosened on the gun.

"Uh…let me just…open the gate for you," the guard murmured robotically. Then, he turned and walked toward a keypad built into the wall, to the right of the gate. He entered a few letters and numbers into the pad. Then, hit the enter key. The metal doors of the gate swung open.

The League of Evil Doers got back into Gordeau's car and began driving down the cobblestone road, past blindingly green, carpet-like lawn, fields of paper whites, topiary bushes shaped like dollar bills, and a large golden statue of William Fredrick Ross. The statue was positioned before the front of the entrance to the manor. It stood at the center of a circle of grass, contained with in a cul-de-sac of cobblestone driveway. In the statue, William Fredrick Ross was portrayed as a handsome older man with a thick head of hair who wore a three piece suit. He stood tall and confident with his legs spread apart and his chin resting on the fist of one hand. His eyebrows were drawn together as though in deep contemplation.

Gordeau parked his blue sports car behind a black limousine and a large, shiny, black truck with massive wheels and flames airbrushed onto the sides of it. The League of Evildoers got out of Gordeau's car and walked up the steep marble steps to the mansion's entrance, an arched, white-marble-framed, mahogany door. Jason reached out a hand and rang the doorbell.

Another black-uniformed henchman wearing a black ski mask opened the door.

"Is Justice Bitch with you?" the henchman inquired of them dutifully.

"Yes," lied Jason with a groan.

The henchman glanced at Bernice who stared back at him with a raised eyebrow and a smirk.

"Yes, that's me, darling" she lied, fluffing her hair with the palm of her hand.

"Come right this way," said the henchman.

The League of Evildoers followed Death Laser's henchman into The Ross Manor. There were white marble floors here, roman-style pillars, and a pair of grand winding staircases, which led up to the second floor. The place was noisy and swarming with construction workers. The buzz of drills, pounding of hammers, and clanking of nail guns reverberated off of the high ceiling as gruff-voiced construction workers shouted to be heard above the chaos. In places, the white marble roman pillars had already been replaced by gleaming onyx pillars engraved with screaming skulls.

"Yea, sorry about the noise," said Death Laser's henchman as he led the League of Evildoers around a pile of displaced dark wood floor panels and toward one of the winding staircases. "Death Laser is having the place remodeled."

Death Laser's henchman led The League of Evil Doers up the steps and to a row of doors on the second floor.

"The second door on your left is Death Laser's study," said the henchman, "That's were he usually is."

"Thank you," said Gordeau.

The henchman nodded and then turned and walked down the steps again.

The League of Evil Doers walked over to the second

door on the left side. Jason pushed the door open and walked through it. Gordeau and Bernice followed.

Death Laser's study, which was really William Fredrick Ross's study, as it was still, for the most part, decorated to William Fredrick Ross's taste, had a dark hardwood floor and a high stained glass ceiling that let in a lot of red and blue colored light. The walls were lined with tall dark wood bookcases, filled with books in old fashioned bindings. In the middle of the room was a large dark wood desk with a black computer chair positioned behind it. Death Laser was in partial costume, wearing his long black cape and black mask with a pair of loose grey jeans and an emo band shirt. He was sitting on a large black beanbag chair, on the floor, in front of a massive flat screen television.

"Hello? Death Laser?" Jason addressed him.

Death Laser's eyes were glued to the television screen. His black-finger-nailed hands gripped a console controller.

"Yea, what?" he said without turning his head to look at them, and then, as an after thought he added. "Oh, yeah and before I forget, I'm out of caviar so I guess go get some more. Like, ten cans more....I frickin'...*love* that stuff."

"*Death Laser!*" Bernice barked with irritation.

And the sound of a stern female voice made Death Laser jump. He paused his game and stood up, turning toward them with a randy grin on his face. The grin slipped away as his eyes landed on a pudgy Bernice, and he realized that she must have been the one speaking to him.

"Oh, *damn it*. You're not her," he pouted with frustration. He shook off his disappointment quickly and put on a professional demeanor in its place: "So what can I do for you fine folks?"

"*We*...are the League of Evildoers," said Jason very seriously. He posed villainously with his legs spread apart and his hands balled into fists. Bernice and Gordeau, who were standing on either side of him posed as well, Gordeau with his index fingers on his temples and Bernice with her hands on her hips and one leg bent. The three held their poses for about four seconds and then dropped them.

"We'd like to have you as a member," Jason said.

Death Laser chuckled.

"Thanks, but I'm doing pretty well on my own," he said.

"We have a plan to take over the world," said Jason.

"And with your financial backing, you can make that plan a reality," said Gordeau, attempting to sell the offer with a bit of patronizing enthusiasm. "So, what'd'ya say, kid? You could own one fourth of the world!"

"Yea, no thanks," said Death Laser, "I'm pretty happy with what I've got here."

"Don't you want to rule the pitiful normals like a god?" Bernice asked, "That has always been *my* dream."

"Ruling the world doesn't really interest me," said Death Laser, sticking his hands in the pockets of his jeans and slouching a bit.

"Why the hell not?" said Jason, already frustrated.

"Eh, too much responsibility, I guess," Death Laser shrugged. "I'm not interested. Go away."

Death Laser sat back down in the bean bag chair, grabbed the consol controller, and started playing his game again.

"Join my team, you freakin' douche bag!" Jason exclaimed with irritation after several long seconds of being ignored by Death Laser. Death Laser did not respond to his outburst and continued to play the game.

"The Jaywalker, let me handle this," said Gordeau, stepping forward.

The sound of a gun being fired rang out from the large flat screen television set as Death Laser blasted the heads off of several eye-less, skin-less demons, running towards his in-game avatar.

"Death Laser," Gordeau said, "There must be something we can do for you in exchange for your financial backing. We are very talented and dangerous villains: Trauma, Miz Mayhem, and The Jaywalker. Perhaps you've heard of us?"

"Yea," said Death Laser. He paused the game again, stood up, and walked over to the desk. "You guys are really evil and kill people and stuff...and my nemesis, Justice Bitch. I can't have her get distracted by your murder and mayhem. We are bitter foes enraptured in an eternal struggle of good and evil, her and I."

"Uh...what the fuck?" Jason murmured incredulously.

"Bound by fate, our destinies will be forever entwined," said Death Laser dramatically, sitting down at the edge of the desk and shaking his fist at the sky.

"Right..." murmured Jason incredulously, raising an eyebrow.

"So yea, I do actually have a request for you guys and if you do it, I can give you...How much do you need?" Death Laser asked.

"50 million dollars," said Jason.

"Ok," agreed Death Laser. "But in return, I want you to promise that whatever illegal things you do....you always make sure that everyone knows that the person who's actually behind it is me and that it was actually my idea."

"Uh...*what?*" Jason murmured and with some effort, resisted the urge to add: "you fucking dumb-ass."

"If anyone asks, or I guess even if they don't ask, you tell them that whatever bad stuff you're doing is actually my idea. And I don't even care what it is. I don't even want to know," said Death Laser, "Just make sure everyone knows that the most dangerous villain in the city is definitely me. Do that and you can definitely have as much money as you want," said Death Laser.

"So let me get this straight," said Jason. "You'll give us as much money as we want and all we have to do is go around telling people that our crimes are *your* fault? And you don't want to rule the world or make a profit on your investment or anything. You just want everyone to know that our crimes were *your* fault. Can I ask you a question, Death Laser?"

"Yea, sure. Anything," said Death Laser pleasantly.

"Were you dropped on your *head*?"

Gordeau and Bernice flinched as though expecting Death Laser to get angry and revoke his offer.

Death Laser chuckled.

"Yea, knowing *my* mother. *Probably.*" he said, grinning.

Death Laser stuck a black-finger-nailed hand out for Jason to shake and Jason shook it eagerly.

"Pleasure doing business with you," Death Laser said.

Jason let go of Death Laser's hand and crossed his arms disdainfully.

Death Laser cackled, and tilted his head so that his eyes were masked in shadow. Now he no longer had to worry about other villains out villaining him by doing things that he was afraid to do, like kill people or mutilate them irreparably. Now he would get credit for all of it and therefore would never be outdone. That way, Justice Bitch would know that he was a *serious* villain and would never dream of upgrading to a more dangerous nemesis.

Chapter 29:
Sexy Rad Super Pals vs. The League of Evildoers

"The superpowered ex-con support group has stopped meeting," Lilly whispered very seriously to the other Sexy Rad Super Pals as they were eating dinner that evening.

"What do you think that means?" Benjamin replied quietly.

"I think it means that something must have gone awry," murmured Lilly almost imperceptibly.

"You don't think they started an evil team, do you?" Stuart asked.

"Yea, I think that's probably what's going on here," confirmed Benjamin.

"Sweet we've finally got an evil team to fight!" exclaimed Viola excitedly. She stood up and slammed her fists down on the table in front of her, grinning big. "We're finally real Heroes, playing in the big leagues! We might even start getting some news coverage if this thing plays out well."

"Unfortunately, the news only seems to care about our star player," interjected Benjamin coldly. He stirred his coffee with a straw and glared across the table at Harriet, with such noxious veracity that he might have been willing her head to explode.

"Yea, sorry, I wasn't aware that this was about being famous, *Benjamin*," Harriet replied scathingly.

"Well...ah haha...its not," chuckled Viola, attempting to deescalate the tension between the two of them. "It's just that you know...it's always been my dream to do this professionally...and the party store hasn't been doing too well lately. Notoriety helps."

"You can get paid to do hero stuff?" Harriet asked.

"Sure people hire heroes to handle their personal problems all of the time," said Viola.

"Isn't that...kind of like...*being a mercenary*?" Harriet asked.

"...Nah, girl, it's nothing like that at all," said Viola confidently, "Heroes for hire have *superpowers*....and *wear spandex*. Anyway, we need a strategy to come out on top against this evil team. Lilly, do you have any idea who they are or where they might be assembling?"

Lilly stared down into the bowl of soup in front of her, and then glanced across the table at Viola.

"You act as though I have weirdly specific knowledge about everything," Lilly whispered.

"Well, don't you, though, Ghost Gal? Your powers were made for reconnaissance," said Viola.

"She has a point," said Stuart to Lilly. "You have a better chance of finding them than any of us."

Lilly sighed. "Fine," she said quietly, "I'll go around and see about what all of the disbanded group members are up to."

Lilly disappeared from sight.

"So...now, what do the rest of us do?" Benjamin asked, picking up his coffee and lifting it up to his parted lips.

Harriet was quiet for a moment as she contemplated. The others discussed recent villain activity in the area, and argued about which villain they should track that night. Harriet tuned the conversation out. She could not stop thinking about that smirking idiot, Death Laser, sitting in her father's chair with his mud-crusted, black boots up on her father's desk. The image was stuck in her mind, reasserting itself when she tried to think of something else. It stabbed at her heaving chest like frozen daggers. It was as though Death Laser had his hands around her throat and was squeezing her windpipe shut so that she could not breathe.

"Uh...Harriet?" Viola asked after awhile. She had noticed a look of homicidal rage come over Harriet's face as she was speaking. "Are you, ok?"

"Yea. Fabulous. Never better," huffed Harriet in reply.

The chubby waitress returned to their table and put a plate of food down in front of each of them.

"Hey, weren't there five of you here a minute ago?" the waitress asked, noticing Lily's empty seat. She stared at the fifth plate on her tray, looking confused. Perhaps she had imagined the fifth person.

"Just box it up. I'll bring it to her later," said Benjamin.

The waitress nodded and walked away.

"Hey, so...what were we talking about?" Viola asked, grabbing a hand full of French fries out of her plate and shoving them into her mouth.

"Crunchy Toast Muncher took a vacation to the Bahamas and we can't afford to go there, so tracking him is out tonight," recapped Benjamin, "And Harriet's *boyfriend* living in The Ross Manor doesn't bother me any, so we can ignore that crap."

"Really, *boyfriend*?" Harriet repeated with disgust. "Do you *want* to get punched?"

"Go ahead. Try it. Go. I could take you any day, bitch," said Benjamin, standing up abruptly. His eyes began to glow a bright acid green.

Viola stood up as well, and put her arms around Benjamin's shoulders, saying: "Hey, hey, hey, whoa, no infighting, ok? I'm sure she was only kidding."

Benjamin exhaled slowly and then sat back down. Viola sat down as well and then focused her attention on the fries in her plate once more.

The Sexy Rad Super Friends continued their meal for a few minutes, that was, until their conversation was punctuated by the sound of a nearby television:

"Breaking news!" a female newscaster's voice announced very seriously. Harriet lifted her head to stare in the direction of the flat screen television on the wall above the bar of the diner.

The female newscaster continued to talk: "A group of powerful villains, calling themselves 'The League of Evil Doers' has somehow gained possession of a very expensive looking giant doomsday machine and is currently using it to wreak havoc upon the city! Channel 66's own Harold Peabody is on the scene! Harold?"

The screen cut to a tubby middle-aged man in a suit, holding a microphone. Behind him, people were screaming and fleeing in droves. A distant building collapsed into rubble. The whirl of police, fire trucks, and ambulance sirens nearly drowned out the male newscaster's voice as he spoke.

"Karen, I'm standing here a few blocks away from where the chaos is taking place," the male newscaster said.

Viola stood up so quickly that she nearly jumped out of her seat.

"All right! That's all I need to hear!" she exclaimed.

She balled her hand into a fist and held it out over the table.

"Sexy Rad Super Pals—" She pronounced enthusiastically.

The other members of the team all put their hands on top of hers.

"—Let's rock 'n roll!" they all said together.

Chapter 30:
Mega Death Bot

The Sexy Rad Super Pals sprinted toward the block of the city where the League of Evildoers' "doomsday machine" had been wreaking havoc. As they ran, twisted street signs, fleeing pedestrians, and busted up buildings with broken windows became more prevalent. Viola and Stuart jumped into the air as they ran and began flying forward, quickly leaving Harriet and Benjamin far in the distance. Then, Benjamin tapped a traffic light with the back of his hand as he was running. The traffic light grew a few twisted faces from its circular, plastic, light coverings and its long metal pole detached itself from the ground, and slithered along toward the source of the danger. The living traffic night now resembled a monstrous serpent. Benjamin hopped on the traffic light serpent's back and it shot off into the distance. Now, Harriet found herself running alone.

The Jaywalker, dawning his orange parking cone hat and Richard Nixon mask, stood atop a large, humanoid robot and cackled madly. The robot was covered in gleaming chrome and its circular eyes were a pair of massive red LED lights.

The Jaywalker held a megaphone up to his mouth and cackled some more. Then said: "We are the League of Evil Doers. Bow to us, you lousy normals. We're about to really *fuck shit up!*"

Miz Mayhem emerged from a hatch where the back of the robot met the base of its neck. She climbed up to where The Jaywalker was standing and whispered something in his ear.

"Oh right...I almost forgot..." The Jaywalker murmured. He put the megaphone back up to his lips and shouted: "I should also mention that this giant robot has been generously provided by our sponsor, Death Laser!"

The name "Death Laser" made Harriet twitch.

"That shithead who's been living in my house is behind this?" she murmured under her breath and then she sprinted forward, her feet pounding crater-shaped holes in the sidewalk. Fleeing pedestrians screamed and swerved out of her path to avoid being crushed by her.

Harriet felt her long, messed-up, black hair be swept backward as she ran. The world was a nearly invisible blur as she shot forward, her feet barely touching the ground. She could not help but grin a bit. This was the fastest she had ever run.

The Jaywalker shouted into the megaphone: "We are superhumans capable of unleashing unspeakable horrors upon your families and homes. Give us your money or prepare to be irreparably fucked."

The robot's massive feet crashed against the road, creating fissures in the pavement. Then, the robot balled his hand into a fist and struck the side of a building. A large crater was left in the building's brick surface, laying bare the scattered innards of several apartments.

"This is your warning. You will worship us like gods or be irreparably fucked. Hand over your government to us and you will be spared," the Jaywalker muttered into the microphone. His voice carried the flat business-like tone of an automated storm warning or a public service announcement.

Stuart flew toward the massive robot, his red cape racing behind him, intent on punching The Jaywalker square in his Richard Nixon mask.

"Eat shit, Nixon!" Stuart yelled as he was mere inches away from ramming his fist into the Jaywalker's face.

The robot swung its massive fist and it collided with Stuart's entire body, sending him flying backward across the city. His arms and legs flopped limply as he plummeted face-first and hit the pavement a few blocks away.

Viola shot downward, her taloned feet clicking against the cracked pavement as she landed. She stared down at Stuart who was bloody and bruised.

"Stuart?" Viola murmured, sounding concerned. Due to the nature of Stuart's superstrength it was rare to see him appear in anyway injured.

"I'm ok," Stuart said, standing up slowly. Bits of cement were sticking to his tattered and bloodstained spandex suit. "Listen Viola, you can't fight that thing. If it hits you like it just hit me, it'll kill you."

"I'm fast," said Viola. "I can dodge it."

She turned and started to walk away. Stuart reached out and grabbed her by one of her wrists. Viola spun around quickly, and tried to wrench her arm out of Stuart's superhuman grip.

"Let go, you psycho!" Viola shouted, tugging at her arm violently. Stuart's grip did not loosen, however.

"Viola, please. We're out of our league here," Stuart pleaded.

Benjamin arrived at the foot of the massive robot as it stomped awkwardly forward and threw another punch at the side of another building, crushing dozens of square windows in metal frames. The sound of shattering glass and squealing metal filled the air, and then shards of glass fell against the robot's chrome body, making a sound like a sudden downpour as they formed scattered piles at the robot's feet. The Jaywalker shielded his masked face with his hands as the waterfall of glass poured down over him.

"Goddamn it, Trauma!" the Jaywalker swore over the megaphone. "Are you trying to kill me?"

"Well, I told you not to stand on the damn thing's neck," Trauma's voice echoed from inside The Jaywalker's head.

"Whatever, asshole, this looks cooler and besides, how else are people supposed to know *who I am*?" The Jaywalker muttered indignantly and then he added a: "Hey wait, you're telepathic?" as an afterthought.

"Yes, actually, I am," said Trauma, "Back in the day, I used this power to convince my victims that they were going crazy, and mutter things like 'Your parents never loved you' and 'You should kill yourself.' Pretty nasty stuff really but I have to admit, it was *incredibly fun*."

The robot stomped forward, kicking a serpent-like living traffic light, and a snarling park bench with a dripping, lopsided mouth, flat against the side of a building. Then, the robot continued to meander forward, unencumbered.

"Looking back, it seems communicating telepathically with people to psychologically torture them was a bit immature," Trauma's voice continued in the Jaywalker's head. "And using this ability to guide people during flashback therapy was a much more satisfying application of the ability. Do you know why, Jay?"

The Jaywalker did not answer.

"Because I was using my ability to help people. It is much more difficult to help people than it is to hurt them. It takes more skill; offers more challenge; more satisfaction; more pride."

"Shut the fuck up, Trauma. I could tell you to kill yourself right now and you would immediately do it, because you would have to. Because I fucking own you," The Jaywalker thought angrily.

"Just try to think about what I said, Jay," Trauma's voice told him.

"Fucker, if I see or hear you in my head again. I'm going to make you electrocute yourself," The Jaywalker thought violently.

"Uh...right...ok...I won't bother you about it again," Trauma's voice answered.

Harriet reached the foot of the giant robot and then quickly climbed up its leg. She kept expecting one of its metal hands to swat her away but this did not happen. Instead, the robot kept meandering forward, swinging its arms more or less randomly as it walked. Harriet took a deep breath, and then quickly scaled the robot's thigh, ass, and back, reaching one of the robot's wide, chrome shoulders as quickly as she could. She straightened up and held her arms out so that she could balance as the massive robot lurched forward.

The Jaywalker was standing just a dozen or so feet away from her, holding on to the robot by its chrome neck. Beneath the Richard Nixon mask, she saw that his eyes were still swollen and purple from their last encounter. She watched as their bruised lids narrowed with agitation. He did not turn toward her or acknowledge her presence. Something must have been distracting him.

The memory of what Viola had said about not killing villains wrung in Harriet's mind.

"*No killing! If you try to kill anybody again, you're off the team, got that?*" she heard Viola say inside her brain. For some reason, the memory of Viola's voice had sounded distorted…almost like… a deep-voiced, 40-year-old man poorly impersonating a woman, but Harriet did not see why this should be important.

She nodded, quietly conceding that she would attempt to take The Jaywalker down without excessive force.

"That's right, flee, flee you lousy normals," The Jaywalker murmured over the loud speaker. A swarm of pedestrians shrieked and scattered to avoid the robot's vast, kicking legs. A few cars screeched and skid. One of them slammed into the side of a building and burst into flame. Harriet heard the man inside of the car shriek and squeal as he was burned alive.

She crept quietly closer to The Jaywalker, withdrawing a pair of handcuffs from the front pocket of her leather shorts. She was inches away from him now. All she had to do was jump on top of him and cuff his hands behind his back.

The Jaywalker turned around quickly and slapped a yellow note to Harriet's forehead. In the next instant, she was unconscious and plummeting head-first toward the pavement.

Chapter 31:
Who's in Charge?

The next morning, Spencer dressed himself in one of William Fredrick Ross's suits, a black one with white pinstripes and a white bow tie. He brushed his shaggy black hair out of his eyes and then put some jell on a comb and swiped it back.

As he was walking from William Fredrick Ross's bedroom to his office, Spencer caught his reflection in one of the newly installed, black onyx pillars. He paused in front of the pillar, grinned, and winked at himself, pointing to his reflection with both hands:

"Lookin' rich today, Mr. Ross," he said. And then he answered himself: "Hey, thanks, Mr. Ross."

Spencer went back to William Fredrick Ross's office and sat down behind the desk. He grabbed his black acoustic guitar, which was leaning off of the side of the desk, and then began to strum it, putting his feet up on the desk as he did so.

"Oh...people are dead, people are dead," he sang experimentally. The melody was one of ironic cheerfulness. "Lots and lots of people are dead! George Washington is dead. Michael Jackson is dead. Everyone who was alive in the 17 hundreds is dead! Seriously who the fuck cares?"

Spencer pushed a button on the intercom sitting on the desk. Then, picked up the bulky, old-fashioned phone attached to it and said: "Hey, Vince, can you bring me some more of that caviar and white truffles. I'm frickin' starving up here. Hey, thanks a bunch, man."

Spencer put the phone back down on the intercom and resumed strumming his guitar.

"People are dead, people are dead!" he sang, "Seriously, what's a few more? My dad is dead. I deserve to be dead. Seriously, what's seventeen more?"

There was a knock on the door. Spencer put his guitar down and took his feet off the table.

"Come in," he said.

The door creaked open and Jason, Bernice, and Gordeau all walked into the room.

"You wanted to see us, Mr. Tuckerson?" Gordeau inquired politely.

"Uh yeah, I did," said Spencer, looking a bit nervous. "Uh, this is....this is kind of hard to say....and its kind of my fault a little bit....I sort of...misled you in a way. But sorry, I think this is for the best."

"What are you talking about?" Bernice asked.

"Yeah...sorry...this is kind of hard for me. I've never fired anyone before," Spencer said messing with his hands a bit. He looked away from them and then back, staring them down, determined to go through with the firing process.

"You can't be serious," Jason grumbled, crossing his arms.

"With all due respect, Mr. Tuckerson, I don't understand what we did wrong," said Gordeau, "Did we not do exactly the kind of thing that you told us we should do?"

"Uh...yeah... that's kind of my fault like fifty percent....forty percent....maybe twenty percent...no ten percent...no definitely twenty percent. This is definitely twenty percent my fault..." Spencer babbled, shaking his head. He looked a bit ashamed. Jason glared at him and silently told him to go fuck himself.

"Mr. Tuckerson," Gordeau interrupted.

Spencer put up a hand up to silence him: "Quiet. I'm firing you."

"Why?" Bernice asked, a bit distraught. She was not accustomed to being fired from things.

"Ok, so I was watching the news and um...yeah...so seventeen people were killed during your rampage with the giant robot that The Ross Foundation funded. And I know that I probably gave you the impression that bystander fatalities are ok...and I might have even said it, but I don't know I guess....maybe they're not. I mean...they had like...a memorial for the people on TV and stuff...and it was really sad, you know. Like, some of those people were little kids. Their parents were on TV crying and it was really sad...and also you killed one of my guards the first time you broke in here. So yeah, you guy's are fired. Sorry. I'm revoking your funding," Spencer finished awkwardly, scratching his head.

The room was quiet for a moment. Jason glared at Spencer and said nothing, breathing hard.

"Yea...soo....revoking your funding..." Spencer said again, after it became apparent that they were not about to leave.

"To fuck you are!" Jason spat viciously, "You can have that money back when you pry it out of my cold, dead hands, you stupid goddamn retard."

"Yea, I'm revoking it so...I guess. Give it back?" Spencer said, cautiously. He was beginning to see that there was a problem here.

"Yea, too late. You all ready gave it too us. So guess what? You're not getting it back," said Jason.

Spencer stood up and slammed his hands down on the desk, glaring at Jason.

"Fine then, my henchmen and your henchmen are just going to have to go to war!" Spencer yelled. His eyes began to glow red.

"What you think I'm afraid of some pansy fucker who doesn't even want to kill anybody? Bring. It. On. I will mop the floor with your metrosexual ass!" Jason yelled back.

Spencer shook his head and blinked a few times. The red lights faded from his eyes.

"Ok, so maybe firing you was a bit *harsh*..." Spencer said, biting his lip nervously as he fought back the anger swirling inside of him with well practiced finesse. Too much negative emotion and he was liable to loose control of his laser eyes. "Maybe instead you can just agree...to keep the civilian casualties to a minimum?"

"Hey, fuck you, Death Laser, I'll kill who I want to

when I want to. You got that? I didn't become a super criminal so that I could take orders from some douche-bag emo fuckboy!" Jason yelled. He busted out a yellow note pad and a pencil from the front pocket of his jeans, then, wrote something quickly. When he was done, he ripped the top note off of the pad and rose from his chair. Bernice and Gordeau followed his lead and rose from their chairs as well.

One of Spencer's black-uniformed henchmen entered the room, holding a silver tray filled with jars of caviar, sliced white truffles, and French baguettes. As Jason was leaving, he quickly slapped his scribbled-on note square to the henchman's forehead. The henchman dropped the silver tray, withdrew the gun from his belt, and shot himself in the head, with swift, unnerving efficiency. The clatter of the tray followed by the hallow bang that splattered the man's brains echoed throughout the grand, high-ceilinged room. Spencer heard the door to William Fredrick Ross's office slam shut. The League of Evildoers had gone and Spencer was left staring open-mouthed at the mess of bloody skull fragments and slimy, stringy, brain chunks that were scattered around the headless corpse of his fallen henchman. Spencer's eyes began to glow red as they welled up with tears, and then, overcome by a wave of intense nausea, he lurched forward and vomited a gloppy mixture of caviar and stomach acid onto William Fredrick Ross's 700 dollar black formal loafers.

Chapter 32:
Evil Plans

Jason exited The Ross Manor. Bernice and Gordeau trailed close behind. Jason crossed his arms and scowled as he walked past rows of dollar-bill-shaped topiary and the large, golden statue of William Fredric Ross. A few of Death Laser's black-uniformed henchmen spotted the trio and scattered, avoiding eye contact.

"What's the matter, Jason. I've never seen you kill someone with one of your yellow sticky-majigs before," Bernice asked after awhile.

"Like I said, if I feel like killing people, I'm going to kill people. And besides, I had to show that emo fuckboy over there who's boss. He thinks he can fire *me*? Nobody fires The Jaywalker! I have freaking *mind control powers!*"

"But, Jason, you had a chance to kill The Justice Bitch and get her out of our way once and for all. Why did you not kill her like you did Death Laser's henchman?" Bernice asked with some distress.

"Justice Bitch is not a threat to people with powers like ours, she's just a dumb bruit. Not that I'm not going to kill her, I plan to. Its just she's really famous and people *think* that she's a big deal so I don't want some other villain like Laser Fucker claiming credit for her death. I've got to make sure that there are news cameras pointed at me when I kill her so that people will know that it was me; so that everyone knows what a heinous motherfucker I am," Jason explained.

"I don't want to make you mad or anything but out of curiosity, I just have to ask: Do you have a specific goal in mind?" Gordeau asked.

"Yea, I told you. I'm going to own this city and rule the normals," said Jason.

"Right. That's not what I meant, Jason. In counseling, we learn to teach our clients to use SMART goals," said Gordeau.

"Are you saying my goals are DUMB? Because, if that's what you're saying, then I can easily arrange for you to go jump off a 50 story building," said Jason.

"No, Jason, it's an acronym."

"*Fuck* you."

"An abbreviation," Gordeau explained incase he had not been clear. "The letters stand for things. Your goals have to be specific, measurable–"

Jason interrupted Gordeau: "Yea, enough of your psychobabble *bullshit*. You want to hear my plan? Here's my plan. I'm going to kidnap the mayor and his staff...you know like anybody who has any kind of power in this city, and I'm going to command them to be my slaves or something. Crime is going to be legal. There'll be complete chaos."

"That's not a very well thought out plan. How could we possibly profit from that?" Bernice muttered to Gordeau.

It's still better than destroying random buildings with the Mega Death Bot. Like we were before, Gordeau's voice replied inside of Bernice's head.

This is just great, Bernice thought sarcastically in Gordeau's direction. *Why haven't we always followed the orders of a sixteen-year-old boy?*

Gordeau stared back at her and answered telepathically: *I keep trying to get in his head but all I can do is talk to him. I can't get in his memories. If I could get in his memories maybe I could torture him with them until he freed us.*

"Also, my other plan involves the Crunchy Toast Muncher," said Jason, smirking evilly. "So as soon as he gets back from his tropical vacation, I'll be luring him with quite the sacrifice."

Gordeau and Bernice glanced at each other, each raising an eyebrow. What exactly was Jason planning?

Chapter 33:
Roommate Exile

Harriet opened her eyes slowly. The ceiling was blurry, but she still recognized Viola's old-fashioned wall paper pattern and the tiffany ceiling lamp that hung above the couch.

"That is it. You're out of here! Pack all of your shit up! I want you out!" she heard Viola yell.

"You can't do this to me, Viola, I pay rent!" Stuart yelled back.

Their voices sounded distant, muffled. Harriet sat up slowly and felt the adhesive of the yellow note square attached to her forehead. Then, she yanked it off and read the sloppy pencil writing on it: *You will become unconscious for 4 hours.* She shrugged and put the note down on the coffee table. The Jaywalker had probably written a few of these in advance incase he was suddenly attacked.

"I could have gotten them, Stuart! They got away with it because of you!" Viola yelled. Harriet heard something crash. The noise seemed to indicate that Viola had just thrown something at Stuart's head.

Harriet sat up and blinked a few times. The room came into sharper focus.

"Fine! Whatever! I don't want to live here anyway!" Stuart yelled back.

Viola, was holding an arm full of miscellaneous items that looked like they belonged to Stuart, men's clothing, sneakers, a big plastic alarm clock, pictures of Stuart with friends and family. Harriet groaned and rubbed her aching head. She had a feeling she knew what was about to happen next.

"Good! Never come back!" Viola yelled, wrenching the front door open and throwing the miscellaneous pile of Stuart's possessions out into the hallway.

"What do you really hope to accomplish, Viola, huh?

Can you tell me that? Do you really want to kill yourself trying to fight these shitheads?" Stuart ranted.

"I'm a *hero*, ass-wipe, that's what I do!"

"You want to die doing this shit? Fine. Forget you. I hope you fucking die!"

"I hope *you* fucking die! Get the fuck out of my apartment and never come back!"

"Yea, don't worry! I'm never coming back!" Stuart yelled then he stomped through the front door and slammed it behind him.

Viola kicked the closed door with her foot and its sharp talons left deep slices in the varnished wood.

"You better fucking not!" she yelled after him.

The apartment was quiet now. The only noise that could be heard was the distant whirl of the dishwasher in the kitchen and the buzz of a window air conditioner. A few moments past during which Viola stood very still and stared at the door.

"...Viola?" Harriet inquired, standing up and walking towards her.

Viola hung her head and wept quietly.

"Oh...*Harriet!*" she murmured, "I can't believe he's gone!"

"What the hell happened?" Harriet asked, genuinely confused.

Viola walked over to the kitchen and sat down at one end of the round, white kitchen table.

"He wants me to retire from hero-ing," Viola muttered angrily, "Says that my power's not strong enough to go up against Death Laser and The League of Evildoers. Shows how much he knows. My power is the fucking best. Shit. Now Benji and Finsveld are the only two boys left on the team. We need more boys or no one will take us seriously. Just...just *wow*...I can't believe he's gone."

"I thought you said you two weren't a couple," Harriet said, walking over to the kitchen cabinet. She opened the cabinet and withdrew a mug with a bunch of pastel-colored, wide-eyed, cartoon kittens on it, then filled it with hot water in the sink.

"We weren't...but I always felt like we were going to be. We were almost there...I think. I mean, I don't know what his problem was. Maybe he's gay. Maybe he's just not into black chicks. I don't know..."

Harriet grabbed a tea bag from the drawer that she knew Viola kept teabags in and dunked the bag in her mug of hot water a few times. Then, she placed the mug down in front of Viola. Viola picked the mug off of the table blew on it and took a slow, cautious sip.

"Forget him, Viola. He's not worth it," Harriet said. She sat down at the opposite end of the table and watched Viola fiddle with the string on her teabag.

"Thanks, Harriet. You're a good friend."

The buzz of the window air conditioner grew louder and more rampant. The clock on the wall above the T.V. in the living room ticked slowly.

"Hey...you don't need him, anyway. There are plenty of guys out there." Harriet said.

"Yea..." Viola replied quietly. "Yea, you're right. I don't need him. He was dragging me down. I mean...by this point it's pretty safe to say that nothing was going to happen with him, anyway. So what am I doing, right? I mean, he was such a dick anyway telling me that my friends are no good. He was always talking about how you might be secretly evil. He even had this pretty fucked-up theory for awhile that you might be secretly working with Death Laser. Talk about paranoid, right?"

"Yea, Stuart was fucked in the head. Good riddance, I say," Harriet groaned. She hated the idea that anyone could believe that she would team up with the jackass who had stolen her fortune from her.

"Yea...he was....I still kind of miss him, though," Viola sighed, blowing on her tea again.

"Hey, didn't Danny Plaxman give you his number when we went to see Ear Mutilator that time?" Harriet asked.

"Yea," Viola replied quietly.

"So why don't you give him a call?" Harriet asked.

"I don't know, Harriet...I mean....he's a semi-successful rock star right now. Do you really think he wants to hang out with a nobody like me?"

"Hey, you're no nobody, you're Hawkette, leader of The Mega Cool Hottie Friends," said Harriet.

"Sexy Rad Super Pals," Viola corrected.

"Exactly," said Harriet, "What you just said. And also, so like...he's a member of a semi-successful rock band. You're the owner of a semi-successful costume shop. You two should get together. Make something happen. I mean. Why the hell not? It's not like you to be all mopey like this and what girl doesn't want to go down on a rock star? Live a little."

Viola laughed, and in her mind's eye, she pictured the look on Stuart's face as he spotted her walking down the street hand and hand with one of EAR MUTILATOR's guitarists. She grinned, remembering every romantic comedy she had ever watched. By the tenets of romantic comedy logic, scoring Danny Plaxman as her boyfriend was sure to make Stuart jealous.

"You're right, Harriet," said Viola. She opened her purse and plunged her hand into it. "I'm going to call him now."

Viola shuffled her hand around in her purse, until her fingers closed around the folded piece of paper that Danny Plaxman had signed during her and Harriet's encounter with Ear Mutilator at The Hornet's Nest. She pulled the piece of paper out and flipped it over, revealing the phone number he had scribbled on it. Viola stared at the number for a few moments.

"Do it. Call him," Harriet goaded.

"Alright, alright, hold your freakin' horses, girl. I'm working up to it," said Viola.

"Viola walked over to the kitchen counter, where her cell phone was resting and unplugged it from its charger chord. Then she picked it up, and texted: "Hey, whats up Danny? I don't know if you remember me. We met at the Hornet's Nest right before Super Annoyo hijacked the city. Let's hang out some time, ok?" to Danny Plaxman's cell number.

"There," said Harriet, "Don't you feel better?"

"Yea, you know what, I do," said Viola, touching her short green dreads with the tips of her long, glossy, green fingernails. "Danny Plaxman's pretty hot, don't you think?" She smiled big and then added: "I dig dudes with crazy hair."

Chapter 34:
Death Laser's Revenge

Spencer was a little bit worried about The League of Evil Doers as well as the increasingly obvious fact that he could not control them. However, when he thought about it too much he started to panic, and when he started to panic, his eyes began to glow crimson as he felt himself start to lose control of his lasers. At times like this, he tried to think about something funny or pleasant to calm himself down. This usually worked but on the occasions when it failed, Spencer pinched the palms of his hands until they bled, or knocked his head a few times against the hardwood surface of William Fredric Ross's desk. Over the years, Spencer had found that hurting himself physically was the most effective way to fight back emotion-linked involuntary eye lasers.

Spencer found himself thinking about his poor decapitated henchman, feeling sad about it and, then feeling afraid that The Jaywalker would do a similar thing to him next. Silently, he ordered himself to stop feeling but this did not really work. He pinched the palm of his right hand and forced a grin. Then, turned on the old-fashioned radio on William Fredrick Ross's desk, and tuned it to his favorite alternative rock station.

He leaned back in his chair and listened to it for a few minutes, thinking about Justice Bitch. His grin broadened.

"She has to be pretty pissed at me right now," Spencer said to himself confidently. "Heheheheheh....heh....She can't ignore me forever."

"We've got new music from EAR MUTILATOR! This is blowing up the charts! Are you ready for this! We're playing it for you—*now*!"

Spencer's hand moved toward the radio to turn it off. Acknowledging that EAR MUTILATOR was a huge success without him invariably led to destructive eye laser incidents.

"This one is called 'Everybody Hates You, Spanky

Fuckerson'!" the radio host announced.

This song is about me, isn't it? Spencer thought with a mixture of curiosity and bitterness. Spencer put his hand down and left the radio on, letting the song play. His eyes began to glow crimson and he began repeatedly smacking his forehead against the surface of the desk, to keep control of them.

There was a quick base line, drums and then electric guitars. Devin's scratchy voice assaulted Spencer's ears. It was incompetent in a way that only someone who had taken years of voice lessons could detect and the second that Spencer heard it, he was reminded of how much he could not *fucking stand* Devin.

"There's this di-ldo...That we have to put up with. He thinks he's so fuckin' cool. He thinks he's so fuckin' chill! But he's not cool, and he's not chill."

The band members all shouted together: "He's a fucking dildo!"

"And he thinks that everybody likes him, but everybody hates him — he's a fucking cu–unt," Devin sang and then his voice accelerated slightly. "Spanky Fuckerson, you're such a poser, I'd like to run you over with a big. Bulldozer."

"*Hey!*" all of the band members shouted in unison.

"Everybody hates you, Spanky Fuckerson! You piss me off so much I don't know. Where. To. be. Gin. Every time I turn around, and see you there, I want to pull out alla'of'my hair. I want to tell you — that nobody likes you*!* No one — *no one!* You should probably *kill yourself!*"

An electric guitar solo began to play. Spencer stood up and walked across the room, Devin's voice ringing in his ears.

"The Jaywalker was right about you, Spencer," Spencer muttered to himself. "You are a fucking pansy...so are you a super criminal or aren't you? Make. Them. *Pay.*"

Spencer punched the tall, ornately carved, wooden door of William Fredrick Ross's office and a pair of red laser beams shot out of his eyes, blasting a man-sized crater in it.

"Oh-*oh*, everybody hates you, Spanky Fuckerson!" Devin's voice sang.

"Yeah! Yeah! *Yeah!*" the other band members chanted.

Spencer stepped through the hole in the door and out into a red marble hallway lined with black onyx pillars. Each one was covered in a jumbled pattern of screaming skull carvings.

"You piss me off so much I don't know. Where. To. be. Gin!" Devin sang.

Spencer walked down one of the two winding stairways, leading to the foyer of The Ross Manor. The stairways, which had been carved mahogany with a runner of white carpets originally, were now carpeted crimson red, and had black onyx railings topped with carvings of screaming skulls.

"Spanky, don't you see—that you could *never*. Be. Like me! Nobody cares that you took *voice lessons*. Don't tell me again that you can play the harpsichord, you fuckin' ding dong. Nobody thinks you're cool. Go back to the fucking marching band!" Devin's voice shouted tauntingly and then he began to laugh and laugh both hysterically and derisively, until his scratchy guffaws were drowned out by an aggressive crescendo of electric guitars.

...

Harriet sat in the passenger seat of Viola's van, watching people zip by and entertaining herself by seeing what she could sense about them by taking in their auras.

Viola turned right and the van swerved, tires screeching, the bird-shaped air freshener around her rearview mirror flew sideways. It began to rain. Harriet looked out through the window and up at the overcast sky, which was almost the same grey as the towering skyscrapers that threatened to block it out.

"So did Danny Plaxman text you back?" Harriet asked Viola.

"No," Viola replied a little bitterly, "It's driving me

crazy."

Lilly appeared, suddenly, sitting cross-legged on a box of brightly-colored costumes in the back of the van. She was wearing a baggy white t-shirt and a pair of white jeans.

"Where are you guys going?" She whispered.

Both Viola and Harriet jumped in their seats.

"Lilly! God, you have to not scare me like that when I'm driving!" Viola exclaimed.

"Sorry," Lilly whispered, "I just thought you might like to know. I've found out where the League of Evildoer's secret headquarters is. They have an underwater lair a few hundred miles south of Sunbeam Beach."

Harriet sighed and said wistfully: "I had a view of Sunbeam Beach from my bedroom window when I was growing up. Not the public part. The private part...that my father owned. There were never any people on it. Except for that one time that some fat people wandered on to it...and my father had them chased off of the property with attack dogs, and then sued them for trespassing."

"Oh, ok," Lilly whispered, "So, where are we going, again?"

"The costume shop," Viola said, "It's getting close to Halloween, so I'm holding an event to try and attract more customers.

"Oh...what kind of an event?" Lilly inquired breathily.

Viola's cell phone rang and she unplugged it from the phone jack in her car, staring down at the screen.

"A canceled one," Viola said, dropping the phone again. She slammed her foot down on the gas and accelerated. "Just got a text from Danny Plaxman. The band's in trouble."

...

Viola's van pulled into the parking lot of a tall building with the words: "HEADLESS RECORDS INC." printed above its entrance in large, bold, silver, capital letters.

Viola parked sloppily, and then jumped out of the car, ripping her clothes off quickly to reveal her hero costume underneath. Then, she threw the clothes back into the van and put her pink pleather mask on, slamming the driver's side door behind her. Harriet and Lilly emerged from the van and followed her to the door. All three of them were now in full costume.

"Does anyone besides me find it weird that he called us and not the police?" Harriet mused, noticing the disturbing lack of police sirens.

"Weird," Lilly murmured breathily, "But *flattering*."

The three women entered the building. It was strangely empty and quiet. Their footsteps echoed against the marble floor as they trudged through a large, high-ceilinged lobby, the walls of which were lined with records.

"There are people here," Harriet said quietly, "I can sense them. I think they're being held captive in the rooms."

"Wild. How can you tell?" Viola murmured in reply.

"I don't know. I can just tell," Harriet whispered.

"Do you think that means the band's being held captive?" whispered Lilly.

Harriet found a flight of stairs and, sensing that unlike the elevator, it was free of people, she headed toward it.

"This way!" She whispered to Viola and Lilly quickly. "Hurry!"

Viola darted toward the stairway and Lilly vanished, reappearing a few dozen feet behind Harriet, halfway up the first flight of steps.

Harriet heard the elevator chime. The elevator door opened and a dozen people emerged. Most of them were dressed in business attire but Harriet also spotted a guy with a shaved head, baggy pants, and a lot of gold chains around his neck that she recognized as a popular R&B singer. There was also a young woman with very blond hair and a silver sequin tank top who might have been there to record a pop album. The group of people looked afraid and they were followed by a few men wearing, black slacks, black polo shirts, and black ski-masks. Each of the masked men was holding a black pistol at the group of hostages that walked in front of them.

"Just cooperate, please," one of the masked men instructed them calmly, "If you cooperate, you will not be harmed."

Harriet could sense that the masked man was telling the truth. She began to ascend the first flight of stairs.

"Wait, Harriet! We have to save those people!" Viola whispered aggressively.

Harriet turned back around and whispered quickly: "No, Viola. Those people aren't the ones in danger."

"Is this your aura sensing thing again?" Lilly whispered more quietly than usual.

"Trust me, I know what I'm talking about," Harriet whispered calmly.

Viola nodded and began to ascend the steps. The three women ran up the first flight of steps. As they moved, Harriet could feel the presence of intense fear, and then of an individual she had encountered before, one that she thought she recognized. The presence of these things grew more powerful as she ran.

The three women reached the next flight of steps, and then the final flight of steps. Harriet could sense the presence of her adversary grow stronger still.

"He's on the roof," Harriet said.

"Got it," Lilly murmured very seriously.

She disappeared and then reappeared between Harriet and Viola as they ran, grabbing each of them by the forearm. Then, the three of them disappeared, reappearing on the roof of the building.

Harriet blinked a few times and staggered forward, struggling to quickly orient herself. The world was a spinning, nauseous blur.

"Shh..." Lilly whispered, "I still don't think they know we're here."

"Can you please *warn* me the next time you're going to do something like that?" Viola murmured with frustration.

"Sorry. It was taking too long," Lilly whispered in reply.

The nauseous feeling was fading slowly and the world was growing still again. Harriet was left with a pounding headache. She steadied herself against the side of a brick structure, observing her surroundings. They were on the roof now. The sky overhead was a rolling blanket of dusty rain clouds. The floor beneath her black leather boots was a smooth, grey slab of stone. The brick wall she had been leaning against, it seemed, belonged to a tiny square structure, with a door in it, presumably leading to the levels below. Viola was staggering around like a drunk, flailing her arms to keep her balance. Lilly was standing still and quiet, alert and completely unaffected by vertigo.

Harriet blinked a few times. Her headache dulled. Her vision cleared. She could see now, the thing which Lilly had been looking at with such attentiveness. Kalvin Pierce, Devin Forress, Danny Plaxman, and a fourth man that Harriet did not recognize, were gagged with duct tape and tied to rolling office chairs. Each office chair was perched precariously close to the edge of the building and tied at one end to a curved metal ventilation pipe sticking out of the center of the roof. Death Laser stood at the center of the group of men, smirking evilly, his eyes glowing red as thunder struck in the distance and it began to rain. A sudden breeze moved his long black cape and shaggy, disheveled hair.

"Hehehehehehe..." Death Laser cackled, as he stood there, silhouetted against the darkening sky, waiting patiently for Harriet and Viola to regain their balance.

"*You!*" Harriet growled, when she could finally see him.

She stormed up to him glaring, noticing as she did so that the quality of his costume had improved greatly. His mask, pants, and cape were now studded black leather. His shirt was white with the letters DL written on them in red capital letters and the sleeves sloppily ripped off.

"Hehehehehe..." Death Laser cackled again as he

watched her approach, his grin broadening. A dull blush crept over his pale cheeks.

"I should have known it was *you*," Harriet growled.

"You're too late, Justice Bitch!" Death Laser announced dramatically. "They're all going to die...after I find the scissors that I was going to cut the ropes that they're tied to the building with. And then, after that, after I get around to it, I guess. I'd like to watch them suffer for as long as possible, basically. And what worse way to suffer than to know you're about to *die!* Heheheheh...Hahhahhahheheheh....."

"Wait? Did you just say that you *lost* the scissors that you were going to cut the ropes with?" Lilly whispered incredulously.

Death Laser put a hand up to his ear.

"What's that, dear? You'll have to speak up!" Death Laser called back mockingly.

"She said you're stupid!" Viola called back, staggering forward. She was still severely nauseous from being transported.

"Nuh uh...you're just jealous of how smart and great I am!" Death Laser called back, "I can afford to misplace the scissors because there's no possible way you could stop me! That's just how great I am and how much you suck by comparison!"

"Enough of the witty banter," Harriet muttered sarcastically. She was now only a few inches away from where Death Laser stood. She poked him in the chest with her index finger and he flinched away, still grinning. *"Let's end this."*

Death Laser cackled nervously, and then took a step backward. His grin never flickered.

"No," Death Laser said, his eyes growing brighter and more crimson by the second. "Let's *begin.*"

A pair of laser beams shot out of Death Laser's eyes, and, even though Harriet was standing a mere four or five inches away, he still managed to miss badly. The lasers flew right over Harriet's head and hit the brick structure with the door in it, exploding it to bits of twisted up support beam and rubble. Viola darted toward Death Laser and jumped into the air, her sharp talons aimed at his face. Death Laser covered his already talon-scarred face with his arms and ducked, before darting quickly to the other end of the building. Harriet ran after him. Viola darted toward the bound men, who were still perched precariously near the edge of the building. Lilly disappeared and reappeared next to the new band member. He looked about thirty or so, with an attractive face and youthful, punk-influenced clothing, a nose piercing, and a black Mohawk.

As Harriet gained on the fleeing Death Laser, the villain turned around quickly and shot a pair of laser beams at her. Again, he missed badly, hitting the window of a distant building, which shattered into a thousand glistening shards and littered the city below.

Viola pulled the gag off of Danny Plaxman and then started sawing through his ropes with her foot talons. Lilly spotted the pair of scissors that Death Laser had misplaced, lying next to a pile of smoldering rubble. They were warped slightly from the blast but probably still usable. She vanished, reappeared next to the scissors, picked them up, and then vanished and reappeared next to the new band member again. She pulled the gag off of him, and then started to saw through the ropes which bound him, using the dull edge of Death Laser's warped scissors.

Death Laser shot another pair of Lasers in Harriet's general direction. They glided a few dozen feet to the right of her head and hit a distant billboard, blasting a hole in the face of a grinning model with bindingly white teeth, holding a tube of "Super Clean Ultra White Tooth Paste."

Harriet screamed and launched herself at Death Laser, fists raised, prepared to pummel him bloody for everything he had stolen from her. Death Laser Stepped quickly to the side and then darted away.

Harriet slowed to a stop, clutching her aching side and breathing heavy. Long sprints were not her strong suit. Death Laser's grin broadened as he realized this, and he slowed to a casual stroll, making it to the edge of the building as Harriet struggled to catch her breath. He withdrew a cell phone from one of the pockets of his leather pants, and then tossed it over the side. He gave the now untied Danny Plaxman the middle finger with one leather, finger-less-gloved hand, and then shouted viciously: *"Fuck you,* Danny!"

"...*You*...you sent that text, didn't you?" Harriet accused between gasps.

Death Laser chuckled evilly and then shoved his hands into one of the pockets of his leather pants, withdrawing a fist full of photographs. He held up one for Harriet to see. It was a picture of her sixteen-year-old self on one of her father's yachts, wearing sunglasses, a large wicker sun hat, and a floral print designer sundress. The late William Fredrick Ross was standing next to her, wearing a three-piece suit and holding a martini. Both Ross's wore similarly pissed off, disinterested expressions and stood with their arms crossed, not looking at each other.

"Since I own almost all of your family photographs, now, I thought I'd share some with you!" Death Laser taunted.

"Give that back, asshole! I don't have that many pictures of my father!" Harriet shouted, before sprinting at Death Laser again.

Death Laser threw the picture over the edge of the building, and then shot a pair of lasers at it as it was falling, somehow managing to hit it dead in the center with each blast.

Harriet's screamed and tackled Death Laser, knocking him onto the ground. He giggled stupidly and blushed, the red lights fading from his brown eyes as he stared up at her. She was now straddling him with her muscular thighs. She sensed his growing arousal not only in his expression but also by his shifting aura. She knew then and there that he was very close to getting a boner and this, more than anything that he had done or said that day, enraged her. She grabbed him by his shoulders and slammed his head roughly against the cement, but not so roughly that he could hope to sue her the way that Super Annoyo was trying to. Blood poured out from underneath of his head, staining the cement underneath with smears of crimson. He was still grinning in that idiotic, lust-drunk way.

"Hehheheheh...heh....hurts *so good*," he boasted.

"Yeah! Let's see how good it hurts, when I SMASH YOUR HEAD OPEN and punch your brain into bloody mush!" Harriet screamed pulling back her fist high.

Viola sprinted over to her.

"Harriet, no! You can't kill him!" Viola shouted, "We have to take him to prison!"

Harriet stood up slowly, but kept her boot on Death Laser's throat, pressed against his Adam's apple. She took a deep breath and closed her eyes.

"You're right," she said quietly.

She took her foot off of Death Laser's neck and he lay on the ground for a few minutes, breathing heavy and rubbing the deep boot-shaped bruise on his throat with both hands. Before he could sit up, Harriet slammed her boot down on his chest, pinning him to the ground.

"So what do we do now?" Harriet asked darkly, looking up from the villain pinned beneath her foot and back at Viola.

Viola shrugged.

"Take him to prison, I guess," she said.

"Uh...guys..." Lilly whispered. She was ignored.

"Prison. Pst. Prison is too good for these people," Harriet growled, crossing her arms and rolling her eyes. "Maybe we could just throw this clown over the side of the building and pretend like it was an accident."

"Harriet, no!" Viola said, shaking her head rapidly. "We're heroes — we can't do that kind of thing!"

"Uh guys..." Lilly whispered.

Viola put up a hand to silence her.

"Not now, Lilly," she said, "Harriet, what is it with you and killing people? How many times do we have to have this conversation? Have I not made it clear that Sexy Rad Super Pals don't kill people?"

"Yea, but that's the thing. *Why*?" Harriet said, putting her hands on her hips. "Have you seen crime statistics? Most super villains break out of prison after the first two months. Is there even a *point* to putting super criminals in prison?"

"Guys..." Lilly whispered a third time.

This time both Harriet and Viola turned their heads in her direction and shouted: "*What!*"

"Death Laser is gone," Lilly murmured bluntly.

Both Harriet and Viola glanced down at the place where Death Laser had been, under the sole of Harriet's boot. Death Laser was gone and Harriet's boot was on the floor.

"Son of a bitch!" Harriet yelled in exasperation, stomping her foot down on the floor several times.

Chapter 35:
Trauma vs. Harriet

That night, Harriet dreamt of her father. He was sitting on a square, white couch in the very white and very minimalist living room of The Ross Manor. The glass wall behind him let in a lot of bright sunlight and a view of the distant Sun Beam Beach. He was wearing a black tuxedo with white pinstripes, a white bow tie, and a fedora.

"Harriet, welcome! Come, join me please. Let's talk as we always have," William Fredrick Ross said, beckoning her towards him.

Harriet raised an eyebrow.

"Father, you don't sound like yourself," she said, "And when have we ever...*talked*?"

Cautiously, Harriet approached the man. There was something very suspicious about this man, something very unlike her father. As she drew closer, it became increasingly obvious who, in fact, this man was. She could sense his aura clearly now.

Harriet sat down next to the man and stared at him, frowning and narrowing her eyes. Her father's face stared back at her, crinkled and pale. His hair was grey and slicked backward as it had been for as long as she could remember. His eyes were the appropriate shade of pale blue. However, there was a different consciousness lurking behind those eyes, one that Harriet had felt before.

"Hello, Trauma," Harriet said quietly. She turned her head away from Trauma and stared at a row of white lilies in clear vases on a white shelf on the opposite wall.

"Trauma? Who's that? I am William Fredrick Ross," Trauma replied a little hopelessly.

"Call yourself whatever you want, Trauma," said Harriet. "I know it's you."

The room was quiet for a moment. Harriet stared at the wall in front of her.

"So you can incept people's dreams, can you?" Harriet inquired casually, continuing to stare at the wall in front of her.

"Yes," Trauma replied quietly, "With some limitations."

"What limitations?" Harriet asked.

"Ah. A true villain never throws down his deck and reveals all of his cards to brag about which one's he's holding," Trauma said, leaning back against the couch and staring up at the ceiling.

"You haven't met a lot of villains," Harriet replied with a small amount of sarcasm, and an image of her buffoon nemesis standing on the roof of Headless Records, invaded her mind's eye.

"With all due respect, Miss Ross, I've met quite a few," replied Trauma with a knowing smile.

"So I've heard that your main power is jumping into someone's brain and forcing them to relive the worst experiences of their lives," said Harriet conversationally, "So, out of curiosity. How's that working out for you?"

Trauma shrugged.

"Not well, actually."

"Yea, I figured."

"I've been searching your brain all night and I haven't found a single emotional memory. Or rather, the kind of emotional memory that I'm looking for. I'm curious. What's your secret? How are you fighting me off so well?"

"Well, at the risk of throwing down my cards, let's say...I don't always feel emotions the way that other people do. I never have. I don't know how well I hide it, but secretly, I might actually be a sociopath," Harriet said.

"Oh?" Trauma replied quietly, "A sociopath? What makes you think that?"

"People tend to think that the way I've been acting is because of the accident...but the truth is...I've always kind of been this way. And the truth is, it has nothing to do with my memories or my past. I was never abused, or neglected, or bullied, or unpopular even. I've lived a charmed life and yet, I'm still unhappy. I was *born* fucked in the head. My personality is a mental deformity," Harriet said, "Shit. Why am I telling you this, anyway?"

"Because you want to, I imagine," said Trauma.

"You want to know the truth about me, Trauma?" Harriet inquired.

"Might as well, since I made the trip."

"The truth is that I'm lonely. I feel even lonelier when I'm with other people. The only emotion I feel is anger. And I suppose, blood lust. At any point when I don't feel either of those two things, I don't feel anything at all. So you're a psychiatrist, aren't you? Can you tell me, Trauma.....what's wrong with me?" Harriet asked, quietly.

Trauma stared pensively into the distance and did not reply.

"Was I born without a soul? Is everyone like this secretly but just a better actor than I am? Why is it impossible for me to genuinely give a shit about *anyone*?" Harriet said, her voice growing louder and more frantic as she spoke.

Trauma turned his head in her direction and stared into her eyes.

"I don't think you're being entirely honest with yourself, Harriet," he said.

"And who am I with out my money, anyway? Am I even anyone at all? I'm just this big hallow, empty—" Harriet punched the couch with her fist as hard as she could, and the white leather was punctured by a smoldering saucer-sized crater. "*Nothing!* I'm nothing. I'm like air with a face. I don't know…do you think I should seek counseling or something?"

"I like you, Harriet. So I'm going to let you in on a little industry secret," Trauma said. He was quiet for a moment. Harriet heard Reynolds the butler's feet tapping against tile in the kitchen as he prepared a meal. "Therapy doesn't work. It's just another scam that *bad* people use to make *lots* of money."

    "Yea I guess that makes sense," sighed Harriet, "Hey, Trauma?"

    "Yes, Harriet?"

    "You won't tell anyone what I said, will you?"

    "Let me tell you something else, Harriet," Trauma said, standing up and removing the black fedora from his grey head, with one swift, elegant motion. "If you trust a stranger to keep your secrets confidential, then *you're a fool.*"

Chapter 36:
The Wall

The next day, Trauma went to speak to Death Laser in William Fredrick Ross's office.

When Trauma arrived, Death Laser was sitting behind a desk with a note pad, scribbling something and muttering to himself. His feet were on the desk, his hair was messed up, and he was wearing one of William Fredrick Ross's white button-down shirts over a pair of his own black skull-print boxer shorts.

Trauma cleared his throat and then inquired politely: "Mr. Tuckerson?"

Death Laser flinched and took his feet off of the table quickly, dropping the notebook on the table.

"Shit, you're here already?" he said.

"Ah, yes, Mr. Tuckerson. You told me to report back to you at 10 a.m. Don't you remember?" Trauma informed him patiently.

"Uh...yeah that's right."

Death Laser smoothed back his disheveled hair and then folded his hands awkwardly.

"I entered the mind of Justice Bitch last night, as per your instructions, Mr. Tuckerson."

"Yea?" Death Laser replied, his face lighting up, figuratively. Not literally. His eyes remained brown and unlit. "What did you find?"

"Nothing you would be interested in," Trauma said, "Unfortunately, it seems that the resiliency she got from the radiation makes her highly resistant to deep mind infiltration. I only saw what she allowed me to see."

"Aw, that's too bad," Death Laser said, sounding a bit disappointed. He moved to put his hands in the pockets of his slacks but then remembered that he wasn't wearing pants and gave up on it. "I was hoping to learn the details of her emotional weaknesses so that I could better exploit them."

"Right. Though, while I was in there I did happen to bump into her consciousness. She spoke to me briefly before the morning."

"What did she say?" Spencer replied, perking up a bit.

"A bunch of nonsense about how she's a sociopath and doesn't feel anything, but really, Mr. Tuckerson, I'm more concerned about you."

"Me?"

"With all due respect, Mr. Tuckerson, I'm worried about you."

"No you're not," Death Laser corrected indifferently. Trauma was known for luring his enemies into a false sense of security by feigning friendliness.

"Well you've got me there. *I'm not.* Even so, it might be wise for you to sort out your priorities. Maybe do something about that mess inside your head. I can't help but feel that you're doing this for the wrong reasons."

"Is there a right reason to be a super criminal?"

Trauma shrugged and said: "You've got me there. Anyway, do us all a favor and get your priorities straight. I can't have this League of Evildoers thing tarnish my legacy. If I'm going to be a part of it, I'd like to see it have more direction."

"Wait a minute have you been... *inside my head*?" Spencer blurted out a bit indignantly. This breach of privacy was a violation.

"It's what I do."

"What did you see?" Spencer asked cautiously, color rising in his face.

"*Everything.*"

Death Laser fell silent. A sick panic flooded him and a sly smirk twisted what he could see of Trauma's face beneath the ink splotch mask as this happened. At that moment, it finally hit him how dangerous Trauma really was and how little control he really had over this overpowered henchman.

"I saw quite a lot of fucked-up things while I was

wandering your mind, Spencer. But for our purposes, as business partners, I'm only really concerned about one fucked-up thing in particular. This childish crush you have on The Justice Bitch. Its time to leave it behind you," said Trauma.

"Hey. It is not a *childish* crush," Spencer interjected defensively. He crossed his arms and muttered quietly: "It's a very *mature* crush."

"All crushes are childish, Spencer. I used to feel the same way about my ex-wife," disclosed Trauma. "She was a hero too, you know. Fire Freak was her moniker. I was obsessed with her as a young man, but after some time we ran out of things to say to each other and when that happened, I decided once and for all....that it was time for her to go. I made her relive a day from her past when a school yard bully forced her to eat dirt again, and again, and again, and again. For days, and weeks, and months: again, and again, and again, and again. I hardly paused to let her eat and sleep. I had a goal in mind, you see—I wanted her to kill herself and I whispered it in her mind every night before the four or so hours that I let her sleep. And always, I whispered the same thing: 'The only way to escape is to die.'"

"Holy shit," Spencer muttered, his heartbeat growing faster by the second. "Hey, you uh...you wouldn't do s-something like that to me, would you? I mean...we're friends, right?"

"We're business partners. But anyway, back to the story," Trauma continued. "Firebrand held out for longer than I would have liked. A lot longer. But *everyone* has their limit and if I am relentless enough, I will inevitably push them to their breaking point. Firebrand hung herself and do you know what I did, while she was hanging herself?"

"Try to stop her?"

Trauma chuckled sarcastically and then said without humor. "You're adorable. *No.* I got inside her mind and laughed, and laughed, and laughed while I felt her consciousness fade from existence, never giving her a moment of peace until her very last breath. It was the only way to be sure that she was dead."

"God, you must have hated her," Death Laser murmured.

"Yes, Spencer, I did. But you see my point is, when I was a young man, like you are now, I had felt that I was in love with her. Love can seem like the most beautiful thing in this world, for a short time, when you're naïve and riding high on the deceptive brain chemistry or youth. But the illusion of love is mortal, and not only is it mortal but it has the lifespan and significance of a goldfish, or a small rat. As for me and Fire Freak, our relationship went the way that they all do—as the years dragged on, my love for her grew old and died...then, it started to rot; to smell; to draw in the maggots and the flies. What had once seemed beautiful and pure was now terrifying and ugly; a vulgar and scathing parody of what I had once held sacred. And I hated her for it. Oh God, how I hated her for it...for, you see, Spencer, that's what hatred *is*. *Hatred* is the festering corpse of love. By killing her I was effectively tossing that corpse into its grave. Where it belonged."

"That's, wow...why would you..." Spencer murmured. His fear of Trauma prevented him from completing the sentence: *...do that, you fucking psycho*. However, he suspected by the furrowing of Trauma's brows and the deepening of his frown lines that the sadistic therapist had heard it anyway.

"Don't look at me like that. It is natural to be repulsed by something dead," Trauma said very seriously. "Anyway, I guess my point is. Don't throw your life away for some meaningless, pretty woman that you're just going to want to *kill* later. If she's about to hurt or kill you, you shoot a laser beam at her face and blast her fucking head off. Don't let her stand on your neck. I'm telling you this because I like you, kid. You remind me of me," Trauma cleared his throat. "But perhaps I'm projecting a bit."

"Uh...wow....well....I'm going to go wrap my head in

tinfoil and stare at a wall for a few hours so...I guess...*bye*..."

Trauma, chuckled: "I assure you, Mr. Tuckerson. Tinfoil will do nothing to stop *me*. If you want to protect that fucked-up little nightmare machine you call a brain, then the only way to do it is to stay on my good side. Make sure that I like you, Mr. Tuckerson, because the moment that I don't like you, you're in *big* trouble. That being said, I would very much appreciate five hundred thousand dollars, I've been wasting so much time doing things for Jaywalker and the League of Evildoers that I lost my job and my rent is due so..."

"Yea, of course. Anything you want. No problem."

Trauma stood up, walked over to Spencer, and shook his hand.

"Thank you very much, Mr. Tuckerson," Trauma said, "And I hope you'll consider what I said."

Chapter 37:
Captain Lawsuit

Gary Goldstein was a man in his early thirties with wide shoulders, a serious, square face and thick, neatly-parted, slightly wavy, auburn hair. Today, he wore a black suit with a dark blue tie and carried a brown leather briefcase.

"Harriet," he greeted as he spotted his childhood acquaintance, Harriet Ross. The two had agreed to meet at the art museum where Harriet worked as a curator. She looked a little bit different than he remembered; slightly more muscled; slightly less cheerful. Her hair was black now and so were her clothes and her long, false fingernails. *She must still be grieving her father,* Gary assumed dismissively. It did not cross his mind that the effects of the radiation might have contributed to this change in her.

"Hello, Gary," Harriet greeted him boredly. Her black heels clinked across the marble floor of the art museum lobby as she walked over to him. "I don't suppose you're here for the tour?"

"Uh, no actually, I'm not," said Gary, "I have news about Super Annoyo's assault lawsuit. I wanted to tell you in person."

"...*And?*" Harriet inquired after a long silence.

"I don't think he has a leg to stand on. In the state of California, it's illegal for a hero to inflict permanent or semi-permanent/severe injury upon a villain, unless their life or the lives of others are under direct and immediate threat. Broken bones definitely fall under the law's definition of 'semi-permanent/severe.' So, the prosecution will argue that you broke his jaw even though the video evidence suggested that Super Annoyo had already surrendered at that point."

"He didn't *surrender*. He was trying to *extort me,*" Harriet interrupted angrily. "Which is what *I'll* say. *However,* in the video that was recorded of the incident, he stated that it was not his intention to hurt you or anyone else in the room. This might move the jury to see this incident from his perspective. Whether or not he was telling the truth is a matter of speculation. The fact that he had that infant with him, I think, will ruin his case. Even though he had put the child down, it was still in his possession and therefore, in danger. Additionally, the child's mother was killed by the madness that he inflicted upon her with his mass mind control ability, making him her indirect murderer."

"*Direct* murderer," Harriet interrupted bitterly.

"*Semantics.* My point is that the fact that the child's mother is dead may move the court to see the situation from your perspective. Super Annoyo's not exactly a popular guy. He did mass mind control the entire city and I think more people are terrified of him than give a crap about his human rights."

"Human rights," Harriet scoffed, rolling her eyes. "Can you believe this PC garbage? It's as though the government *wants* us to be overrun with super criminals."

"It is what it is, Harriet," sighed Gary, "As heroes we are beholden to the law."

Harriet laughed.

"You say that like you're a hero too, Gary," she said.

"Well, in away, I am," Gary said, grinning. "I may not have *superpowers*, but that doesn't mean I'm not a *super powerful* Wall Street lawyer."

"Oh I see what you did there. You used words to mean other words and made a not funny pun with it," said Harriet, grinning. Where as an ordinary person would have considered Gary's wealth and accomplishments impressive, by Harriet's grand estimation, he was only a reasonably well off *peasant*. "Lousy normal," she added, quoting The Jaywalker. The museum lobby was quiet for a moment and then they both looked at each other and laughed.

"So how has that hero team you hang out with been doing?" Gary asked.

"Not good, actually. We're down one member. Which

means we only have two guys now and one of them is barely even a hero. He just helps us change our outfits fast. My friend seems to think that we need to replace the guy that left with another male or we won't be taken seriously, which proves she's deluded because we weren't taken seriously when we had *three* males," Harriet joked, "Maybe four's the tipping point?"

"Well, tell your friend that I'd like to volunteer my services as the honorary sixth member," said Gary. He dug a business card out of his pocket and handed it to Harriet.

Harriet took the card and looked at it.

"I'm having déjà vu," she said.

"Take me with you on your missions and I can advise you against things that you could be held legally responsible for. I may not have superpowers but I could be invaluable in a fight," he said and then he grinned and added. "Just call me...*Captain Lawsuit.*"

"Captain Lawsuit, huh?" Harriet repeated with mock incredulity. "I wasn't aware that you were a captain of anything. Anyway, I'll pass your information along to my friend. You should expect a call."

After this exchange, Harriet and Gary walked around the art museum for a few hours, remembering old times, when they had both been children and had played around the dollar-sign-shaped topiary that encircled The Ross Manor. The gardens surrounding the place were extravagant and stretched for what seemed like miles. Harriet thought of them, and a spasm of rage surged through her body like a bolt of electricity. One way or another she was going to take that property back.

Chapter 38:
Concerning the Senseless Yuletide Tragedy

It was December in the city and Spencer wandered The Ross Manor aimlessly, with his hands in his pockets, whistling, and trying very hard not to think too much about the past. One of his higher ranking henchmen had taken it upon himself to decorate the foyer and the two grand staircases at the manor's entranceway for Christmas. There was now a large, lighted Christmas tree at the center of the foyer. Tinsel and twinkling strings of lights had been woven around the railings of both massive, winding, black staircases. It made the whole place look considerably less imposing, which bothered Spencer, but not as much as the memories of the past that this festive image summoned.

Spencer could remember a time when he used to like Christmas. It had been before his accidental exposure to the radiation and before the emergence of his supernatural abilities, when he had been a small child, small enough to believe the lies that adults tell children at Christmas. He remembered his mother, at a time when she had been alive in her heart; free of the hatred and grief that Spencer would come to associate with her as an older woman.

Around this time of year, she used to sing Christmas Songs while she baked gingerbread men for Spencer and his two younger brothers. She wove strands of tinsel into her dark hair and told stories about flying reindeer and magic Christmas elves. She had been a different person back then, as yet un-maimed by senseless tragedy.

When Spencer thought about this version of his mother, he could not help but remember his father also. Spencer's father had been a gentle, patient man, a middle school music teacher, and really the best father that Spencer could have asked for...but that was before it all....*went to hell*. Spencer tried to think of something else but this strategy failed him. A wave of misery crashed over the young villain and his eyes began to glow crimson. He blinked the lights away quickly and shook his head.

Gordeau entered The Ross Manor from the front entrance way. He was wearing his purple villain costume and ink splotch mask. Spencer could see the man's mouth under the mask, grinning with sadistic glee. He must have known what mental anguish was gnawing at Spencer's subconscious. Or maybe Gordeau was just cheerful about the holiday and the large amount of money that Spencer had recently given him. Spencer couldn't be sure which it was. He was not a mind reader, unlike Gordeau.

"Mr. Tuckerson," Gordeau greeted him.

"Trauma," Spencer greeted in reply, "Hey, how's it hangin', man?"

"*Adequately,*" Gordeau replied humorlessly, "I can tell by what you're thinking that these Christmas decorations are making you miserable. Why not just order your underlings to take them down?"

"I don't know...the henchmen have formed a committee or something where sometimes they do different stuff for holidays to improve workplace morale. They all seem to be enjoying it," Spencer shrugged. He usually just let his henchmen do whatever they wanted.

"Well, are you the boss or aren't you? If you hate it, make them take it down," said Gordeau.

"Meh. I wouldn't want to ruin everybody's fun by being a triggered little bitch," he said, shrugging again.

"Because you hate Christmas?"

"I *really* fucking do," Spencer admitted, "But that's kind of, like, super lame and cliché and stuff—and nobody's business but my own, so don't read my mind, man."

"Sorry."

"Hey, don't even worry about it."

"Before I forget, I came to tell you that the Crunchy Toast Muncher is returning from his vacation today. The Jaywalker is planning to recruit him to The League of

Evildoers," Gordeau said.

"Sweet. He may be a little fucker but that kid works really hard, doesn't he?" Spencer said.

"He's motivated. To say the least," conceded Gordeau.

"Well, that's perfect. The only famous artwork he hasn't eaten yet in Propopolous city is in the museum where The Justice Bitch works. After he eats the museum empty, The Justice Bitch will be completely ruined! And lo, she will acknowledge my destructive power! *Heheheheheh...heh*!"

"Yes, yes, your destructive power. How will you bring about her ruin, oh dark one?" Gordeau replied with some sarcasm.

"After the museum is empty, she'll be out of a job. And then her Christmas will be, *you know*...it'll suck! Best plan ever." Spencer expounded excitedly. "After we hit the art museum, Crunchy Toast Muncher and me can go fuck up the merchandise at the outlet malls so that there isn't anything to buy!"

"Yea, good luck with that. There's *a lot* of things to buy," Gordeau interrupted.

Spencer ignored him and continued talking: "Then, I guess if we steal a bunch of stuff before everything is destroyed, so that if people want to buy stuff for Christmas, they'll have to buy it from us for a redonkulous price. Then, I guess I've stolen a shit ton of money already. So I'll just pile all of the money I made up into a big pile. Call the news. Tell them I'm going to donate it to charity...and then instead set it *on fire*. Heheheheh...heheheh...heh..." Spencer cackled and then he added as an after thought: "That'll be funny."

Bernice entered the foyer from a room at the top of the stairway. Today she was curvy and small-waisted. She wore a long, antique-looking gown that had probably been fashioned for a renaissance fair and a wide-brimmed green hat adorned with a long white feather.

"I couldn't help but overhear your conversation, gents," she said, green skirts gliding behind her as she slinked down the stairway. "So, allow me to key you in on a little century-old wisdom: a monkey makes everything funnier."

"Um, what?" Spencer inquired.

"A monkey makes everything funnier," Bernice repeated very matter-of-factly.

"So, what are you suggesting?" Spencer asked.

"Well, I should think what I'm suggesting is rather obvious, lad. I'm suggesting that after we set the charity money on fire, we release a bunch of screaming monkeys, just to hammer in the fact of how clever and amusing we are. I assure you, Mr. Tuckerson, when the monkeys are through, this information will be lost on no one," Bernice said.

Spencer could not tell if she was being sincere or employing some kind of old-timey sarcasm but did not exactly care. He loved the idea.

"I like the way you think," he said to Bernice.

"You better get to work robbing that zoo, then," said Bernice.

Spencer grinned. The image of pandemonium Bernice had in mind appealed to him greatly. However, there was still something missing, something even more extreme that would send the city spiraling into a panic, effectively disrupting the lives of everyone who lived there.

"I have an even better idea," he said and then his eyes began to glow and he laughed and laughed until he was out of breath.

...

Gary was present and the next meeting of the Sexy Rad Super Pals, which did not surprise Harriet at all, since he had called Viola and asked to join the team as an unofficial 6th member the night before. Viola had quickly informed him that she would make him an *official* member.

"The next meeting's going to be at the costume shop. No, the one on 10th street. That's right, Maskie's Halloween," Harriet had heard her tell Gary over the phone. Then, Viola had hung up the phone before turning in Harriet's direction and shouting excitedly: "Captain Lawsuit just joined the team!"

"It's a Christmas miracle," Harriet had added dryly.

That night, Harriet knocked on the front door of the costume shop. It clicked unlocked and she stepped inside. Rows of rubber monster masks lined the mesh shelves. A colorful assortment of costumes hung from clothing racks. Foam manikin heads with brightly-colored wigs lined the shelves behind the deserted cash register.

As Harriet walked, a rubber zombie with a motion sensor in it sprang to life and growled menacingly. Startled by the sudden noise, Harriet tackled the man-sized rubber doll and ripped its head off. Harriet glanced down at the rubber head in her hand and swore. Sparks flew from the loose wires hanging off of the doll's metal tube of a severed neck. She dropped it and swore again. She needed to be more careful not to succumb to her violent instincts.

Harriet walked to the back of the store. Here there was a door, which lead to a storage room in the basement of the building. She thought about the now headless, man-sized zombie doll; about its sparking, severed head, gripped between her slender hands. She imagined blood dripping from the doll's neck and the plastic zombie face replaced by the flesh face of Super Annoyo.

"Nope...no. Don't think about that," Harriet muttered to herself, "Gary will take care of that."

Harriet opened the door at the back of the room and descended a steep stairway to the storage area in the basement. Here there were piles of cardboard boxes, presumably filled with merchandise for the shop. The walls were covered in posters depicting models in Halloween costumes as they carried plastic candy buckets and posing artificially. The ceiling was lit by a few light bulbs hanging from loose wires.

"Harriet!" Viola's voice called. "Harriet, over here!"

Harriet followed Viola's voice to a clearing in the stacks of boxes. Here a circle of different colored bean bag chairs was set up. Gary was sitting in a yellow bean bag chair. Lilly and Benjamin were sitting together in a larger, red, bean bag chair, with their fingers laced together, staring into each other's eyes. The rest of the beanbag chairs were empty. Viola was sitting in a lawn chair, which physically elevated her above the other members of the group. This was likely on purpose to remind everyone of her superior rank.

Harriet sat down in a dark blue beanbag chair next to Gary. Then, Viola introduced Gary to the group:

"Yea, so this is Captain Lawsuit," Viola announced happily, "He's the newest member of our team. So, please, give him a warm welcome."

The group exchanged greetings and each member introduced themselves briefly, providing their hero names and their powers for Gary's information.

"Well, I'm not really a superhuman," said Gary, "I'm just a lawyer with a personal score to settle against Super Annoyo."

"A personal score. Please elaborate," Viola goaded. She loved a good nemesis story.

Gary told the Sexy Rad Super Pals about Super Annoyo's supporters' personal attacks and slander against him.

"He says it's because he saw pictures of me with Harriet in college. He was crazy when I went to confront him in prison and foaming from his broken jaw. Wrote it down on a piece of paper because he can't talk. He said something like: 'I can tell by the way that she's looking at you in that picture that you're her friend. By hurting you, I can hurt her'."

"Everyone's swooping in to steal my nemesis. First Harriet, and now you," complained Viola.

"Maybe you need a better nemesis," said Benjamin, "Super Annoyo has got so many personal grudges against people. I don't even think he remembers *you* anymore."

"Benji, I love you," said Viola with some agitation, "But sometimes you've just got to learn to respect a gal's relationship with her nemesis."

There was a flat screen television on the wall, behind Viola's head, surrounded by Halloween posters. The television was on mute and Harriet watched as the news lady switched from perky to horrified, as the picture of Labrador retriever puppies in a large cardboard whelping box was replaced by footage of a burning city.

"Turn the TV on," Harriet murmured seriously.

Viola grabbed the remote from the arm of her lawn chair, stood up, turned around, and un-muted the TV.

"It's pandemonium here at the Main Street Shopping Center, Steve," the news lady announced. A loud crashing noise, followed by Spencer's awkward cackle, echoed behind her and she jumped, glancing behind her. An elephant blew air through its trunk as it galloped through the mall, past palm trees that were alternatively either on fire or covered in screaming monkeys. Shoppers screamed and ran to avoid being trampled by the stampeding elephant.

Then, Miz Mayhem sprang up behind the news lady and yelled out: "Surprise!"

The news lady shrieked as Miz Mayhem embraced her, quickly absorbing a couple decades of her life, so that she devolved into a thrashing ten-year-old in too-large clothing. Miz Mayhem, now lined and grey, dragged the news lady away from the camera and shouted: "That's enough, dear! Death Laser's got something to say!"

Death Laser's voice came over the mall intercom: "People of Propopolous City!"

The Jaywalker sprinted toward the screen. The camera man panicked and toppled the camera. It landed on its side, so that the burning mall was now sideways. Off in the distance, the camera man screamed like he was about to be ripped apart, and then fell strangely silent.

"Heheheheheheh...heh...." Spencer's voice echoed. "As

you know, the Ross Foundation is a charitable organization. Since I've taken over the organization from William Fredrick Ross's successor, Reynolds Sanderland, through military force, the money that was donated to the Ross Foundation has been, so far, untouched. However, tonight…that's about to change. All of the money that was donated to this organization, currently not in use, is going to be burned in a gigantic pile. Tonight! At The Main Street Shopping Center! Aaaaaat 6 o'clock! Don't miss it! It's going to be quite the fireworks show! And Justice Bitch, don't you miss it! Hehehehehehehehehehehe...heh.....heh..."

Harriet stood up and clenched her fists. Then, raised her face toward the ceiling and yelled: "You fucking SON-OF-A-BITCH!"

Chapter 39:
Charity Burn

The Sexy Rad Super Pals arrived at The Main Street Shopping Center, this time, accompanied by Gary. Who, as per Viola's insistence, was wearing a hero costume of his own. It was really more of a plastic mask and red cape over his existing tan three-piece suit than a costume, but these modifications seemed to satisfy Viola.

The news man standing outside the shopping center announced to the cameras: "It appears that a band of heroes is braving the chaos! Will they succeed where the Propopolous city police have failed? Only time will tell!"

A wall of police officers in riot gear surrounded the shopping center. As Harriet sprinted past them, however, she noticed that they were all in a zombie-like trance. Their eyes were wide and unblinking; their arms limp at their sides. Many of them had dropped their guns and nightsticks. Some had merely collapsed like inanimate dolls.

"This looks like the Jaywalker's work," said Benjamin, "He must have sent them a mass email or something."

"Careful team," instructed Viola, "Jaywalker is a powerful mind control user. Don't read anything you see lying on the floor or taped to a wall, on a television screen or on your phone. That's how he gets you."

The Sexy Rad Super Pals entered the building. Rows of palm trees spaced throughout the interior were either on fire or covered in screeching wild animals. A giraffe strode by and snatched a leaf off of a decorative plant on the top floor.

"Is this what he's doing with my father's money? Purchasing wildlife to unleash on the streets?" Harriet muttered incredulously.

Spencer's cackle rang over the store's intercom.

"Yea, keep laughing, you piece of shit! I can't wait to smack that smirk off of your stupid face!" Harriet yelled.

"Hehehehheheheh....you're hot when you're angry..."

Spencer's voice cackled in reply.

Harriet yelled and sprinted forward. Rage curled her hands into fists and sent her feet flying against the floor of the shopping center, cracking the marble with her furious footfalls.

"Harriet, Harriet, watch it! You could be held accountable for any property damage that the cameras can prove in civil court!" Gary called after her.

Hearing this, Harriet strode with less force, so that the floor would not continue to fissure.

"Thanks, Gary!" Harriet shouted back.

A few lions ran out of the shoe store and launched themselves at Benjamin but before they could pin him down and rip him open, Lilly jumped between Benjamin and the lions, wrapped her arms around the man and disappeared with him.

"Fuck...where'd they poof off to?" Viola swore. She jumped into the air and started gliding toward the ceiling window, searching for her missing friends. A bizarre thought invaded her mind: the night her grandmother died, in the hospital, after having fought for over a year against the ravages of intestinal cancer. It was vivid now, as though she were reliving it. And then, the strength of the delusion became so powerful that she lost track of where she was and what she was doing. The old woman was so frail and thin as she gasped her last breath. Viola plummeted out of the sky and hit the second floor of the mall, collapsing into a convulsing heap as the fantasy consumed her. Trauma laughed menacingly as he emerged from behind a shelf, in the book store, and then strolled away, past an inert Viola and into the adjacent coffee shop, very satisfied by his work.

Now, Harriet was running by herself. She glanced back and saw Gary sprinting after her but he was far in the distance. Benjamin was nowhere to be seen but his presence could be felt in a pair of sentient palm tree monsters which seemed to have uprooted themselves and were now running with her as well. Wherever Benjamin was hiding, he must have been zapping stuff and bringing it to life as soldiers that would fight blindly on his behalf.

Harriet spotted Death Laser at the center of the mall, with his shaggy black hair and his stupid shit-eating grin. Even through the black mask that covered the top half of his face, she could tell that the villain could not have been more delighted to see her running towards him. This lack of fear was infuriating. She could sense his aura as she approached him. It glowed with a sort of confused arousal. His grin broadened. She sensed his blush beneath the mask.

One of Benjamin's palm tree beasts reached Death Laser before Harriet did and swung itself like a giant fist toward the top of his head. Spencer jumped out of the way and shot a pair of laser beams out of his eyes, blasting the beast to pieces of shredded trunk. The second tree beast approached quickly but before it was within ten feet of him, Death Laser unleashed another pair of crimson laser beams from his eyes and shot that one to shreds too.

"Heheheheh....Justice Bitch. We meet again at last!" Death Laser cackled, throwing back his head and striking what he judged to be a villainous pose, with his hands on his hips and his legs spread apart. Then he broke the pose and slouched forward, so that his shaggy black hair slid forward and covered one of his eyes. He held out a detonator for Harriet to see.

"Hehhehheh...Is that a stick of dynamite in my pocket, or is my wiener just happy to see you?" he chuckled. Harriet noticed now that the large pile of money that Death Laser was standing next to was wired with explosives.

"Yea, laugh it up, Einstein. If you detonate those explosives, you'll be blowing yourself up too." Harriet growled.

"So what, huh? I might just be feeling a little suicidal today. Care to take that chance, darlin'?" Death Laser replied, still grinning.

"You're not going to blow yourself up. You're full of shit," said Harriet.

"At 6 o'clock it all goes up in flames, baby!" Death Laser announced dramatically.

"Harriet, be careful! This guy might just be crazy enough to kill us all, himself included!" Gary yelled.

Death Laser turned toward Gary, and, for the first time, his mischievous grin quickly sank into an irritated scowl.

"Who the fuck is *he*?" Death Laser growled.

"Oh, yea.... I'm uh... *Captain Lawsuit*. I just follow The Trendy Awesome Guys around and provide them with legal advice," Gary replied unsurely.

Death Laser spun around, grabbed a wad of charity money from the pile, and then shot a pair of laser beams at it, setting the wad of cash a blaze.

"You know what? Don't fucking care," said Death Laser, waving a hand dismissively. "Jaywalker, destroy him!"

The Jaywalker emerged from a nearby store, breathing heavy through his Richard Nixon mask.

"Thought you'd never ask," The Jaywalker replied in a voice both dripping with malice and distorted by the rubber mask.

"Gary! Don't read anything he shows you!" Harriet warned.

The Jaywalker ripped a yellow notepad from his breast pocket and scribbled something on it with a pen. Then, he sprinted toward Gary, holding the note out so that the sticky side would attach to his clothes. Gary dodged out of the way and aimed a kick at The Jaywalker's side, knocking him to the ground. The Jaywalker straitened up slowly, and then charged at Gary a second time. Now the two men were fighting, dodging each other's rapid blows, skidding around the floor of the mall as each one aimed to knock the other on his ass.

"Hey, *hey*! Justice Bitch! Eyes over here!" Death Laser shouted to get her attention. Harriet turned around and looked at him. The villain was still holding the wad of smoldering bills. "I'm going to drop this and set the whole pile on fire. Then, the money that should have gone to the widows and orphans or whatever will just be *ash*!"

Harriet sprinted forward and tried to grab the smoking wad of money out of Death Laser's fingerless-glove-clad hand.

Death Laser cackled and pulled his hand away.

"Too slow," he teased with a smirk.

Harriet yelled and then sprinted toward him, fists raised. Death Laser was faster than her, even though his long, skinny legs slid across the marble floor as he stumbled away clumsily. She could not seem to catch him, no matter how infuriatingly close he seemed to be, and by making her chase him around in circles, he found, it was easy to tire her out. Harriet began to hyperventilate as she slowed to a crawl.

"Fight me, you coward!" she huffed, clutching her side, which ached from the long sprint.

"Mn...nuh uh. Wouldn't want to hurt you," Death Laser teased.

"Oh, please," Harriet muttered, "Like that's what you're worried about. You'll never get away with this, Death Laser!"

"Heheheheh....what you gonna' do about it? Throw me over those beautiful thighs of yours and give me a superpowered spanking?" Death Laser cackled, smirking. She could sense his blush beneath the mask and it enraged her.

"How about instead I break both of your legs!" she yelled, launching herself at him again.

He dodged her blow and then tried to kick her legs out from under her but the kick failed to penetrate her iron defense. It was only an annoyance, like being flicked by an index finger. Harriet aimed a punch at his face and he quickly ducked to avoid it. Then she screamed and tackled him, pinning him beneath her supernatural weight.

Death Laser giggled nervously and she could feel his heart beating rapidly against her leather-clad chest. His face was only a few inches from her own, staring up at her. He could have easily shot a pair of laser beams out of his eyes and blasted her head off, but instead, he closed his eyes and opened his mouth slightly as though perhaps hoping that she would lower her face and press her lips against his.

"...What are you going to do now?" he murmured nervously, his already pounding heartbeat increased slightly and his grin spread wide. "Are you going to put the *handcuffs* on me before you send me to jail? Heheheh..."

"Yea, *probably,* you fucking creep," Harriet replied humorlessly.

"But when you let me up, I'm going to run away and you'll never catch me again," Death Laser pointed out innocently.

"No," said Harriet, trying to ignore the growing stiffness in Death Laser's crotch. He was right about one thing, if she let him up, it would probably be impossible to catch him again. "You're going to roll over and let me cuff you, then, I'm taking you to prison where you belong."

"What if I don't wanna?"

"Then, I guess I'll have to fucking force you, won't I," Harriet muttered with irritation.

"Yeah....punish me or I'll never learn."

"Shut the fuck up," Harriet snapped angrily, then, she stood up grabbing him with one arm and rolling him onto his stomach, before withdrawing a pair of handcuffs from her pocket and cuffing his hands behind his back.

"Yes, ma'am," he murmured dreamily, his voice muffled slightly by the shopping center floor.

Harriet felt a tap on her shoulder. She flinched and glanced to her left.

"Hello, Harriet," Gordeau murmured darkly. A flash of smoke emerged from his palms and then Harriet's vision was consumed by it. The last thing she saw before being dragged into the realm of Gordeau's fantasy, was Death Laser as he cackled and set the pile of charity money ablaze with a beam of crimson light. The pyramid-shaped cash pile burned like a flaming Christmas tree. Then, the smoke from it set off the fire alarms and the sprinklers.

Chapter 40:
The Accident

"You are, in fact, the center of the universe and every narcissistic thought that you have ever had is completely justified," Gordeau's voice whispered soothingly. The sound of the fire alarm was getting farther and farther away. Harriet could no longer feel the cold, smooth shopping center floor, beneath her immobile body.

"Thank you Gordeau, I've always felt that that was true, secretly," Harriet whispered back sleepily. "You must be better at reading my mind than you pretend you are. Kudos to you on not throwing down your deck to brag about what cards you're holding."

"Sleep, Harriet. Sleep," Grodeau's voice goaded.

"Hm...okey dokey, then," Harriet replied dreamily.

She was now in one of her father's old limousines, the one with the red leather interior and built-in hot tub. Her father sat across from her. His eyes were ice blue, his grey hair slicked back and plastered beneath a grey, pin-striped fedora. In his right hand he held a half empty martini glass and in his left hand he held an olive on a toothpick.

"Father, if you drink many more of those before your press conference, I'm afraid you'll be drunk," Harriet said. It felt as though she were saying this for the first time, though of course she was not.

Harriet's father bit the olive off of the toothpick, and then dropped the toothpick back in the martini glass, stirring it absentmindedly.

"That's absurd, Harriet. Everyone knows that I don't get drunk. I only get tipsy and besides it's all just a bunch of blah, blah, blah, blah, blah. Everyone will love what I say regardless. So, really, why does it matter if I've been drinking or not? Loosen up! Reynold's fetch Harriet a drink so that she can loosen up!" Harriet's father shouted cheerfully.

The aging butler nodded his head quietly and then

obeyed, strolling over to the minibar at the back of the limousine and mixing Harriet a martini. Through one-way glass, Harriet watched cars and skyscrapers roll by. Reynolds returned and handed her the martini.

"Thank you, Reynolds," Harriet said. Reynolds nodded quietly and then returned to his seat.

"Do you know why I'm so rich, Harriet?" Harriet's father asked.

"No, father, why are you so rich?" Harriet replied stiffly. She raised the martini to her parted lips and sipped it slowly, watching skyscrapers and angry pedestrians roll by through the one-way glass.

"Because my father was rich and when he died, he left everything that he had to me. God knows, I'm not smart enough to get this rich on my own. I mean... Ross Foundation, Stosh Foundation, I don't even know what that mess is about! What does it even do?"

Harriet shrugged.

"How the fuck should I know?"

Harriet's father laughed and said: "Honestly, I couldn't tell you either."

"Sir, the Ross Foundation is..." Reynolds began.

Harriet's father put a hand up to silence him.

"Quiet, Reynolds. Can't you see we're having a moment here?" he said. Then, he lifted his martini glass in Harriet's direction. "Here's to not giving a fuck."

Harriet tapped her martini glass against his with a sharp *clink*.

"To not giving a fuck," Harriet repeated gruffly and then they both drank.

Harriet's father lowered his glass, and said fondly:

"Harriet, my girl, you are, in fact, the center of the universe and every narcissistic thought you have ever had is completely justified."

"Tell me something I don't know," replied Harriet dryly.

"You're not like me, Harriet. You could make it on your own if you had to," said Harriet's father. "In fact, I'm sure th-"

The screeching of brakes filled Harriet's ears. The glass behind her father's head collapsed inward and she raised both arms to shield her face from the spray. The car was knocked onto its side and then began to roll. Harriet screamed. Shards of safety glass were suck under her eyelids. Her eyes watered as she failed to blink them away, bits of the martini glass cut into her forearms and the palms of her hands, sticking there like tiny daggers.

Then, everything was still and quiet. Harriet opened her eyes slowly. The car was up-side-down and she was hanging from her seatbelt, bleach blond hair dangling beneath her. She looked at her hands and saw blood but also something different, a luminous green liquid that was burning her skin like a blanket of bees. The liquid made her feel...different some how, strange and exhilarated. She released the clasp on her seatbelt and tumbled to the ground with a clumsy *plop*, into a puddle of more green liquid mixed with blood, colored alcohol from the bar, and shards of broken glass. Her ears were ringing. A bloody Reynolds was yelling but she could not hear him. She was in shock. She stood up slowly and observed the huge tankard marked "toxic radiation" now turned on its side; barrels of green fluid rolled every which way. Many were open and leaking.

"Harriet, he's dead!" Reynolds screamed when, at long last, Harriet's hearing had returned to her.

"What?"

"Harriet, it's Will!" Reynolds sobbed angrily, "He's dead! He's fucking *dead*!"

Harriet sprinted over to where Reynolds was standing and stared down at the shredded corpse of her father. His neck was snapped left. The left side of his face was ripped off. His eyes were open and empty.

"Fuck," Harriet swore in disbelief and then she dropped

to her knees before the corpse. A pair of tears cut tracks in the green slime that covered her face.

Chapter 41:
Trap House

Harriet opened her eyes slowly. Her face was wet with tears. She wiped them off with the back of her hand and sat up quickly, realizing for the first time that she was in a bed. It was a round bed with a black comforter on it. The mattress was comfortable and probably expensive. The thread count of the sheets was very fine.

Harriet stood up and stumbled across the black carpet, feeling depressed, disoriented, and increasingly furious. Her father was dead and she loved him. She loved her father. Why did that therapist fucker have to come along and remind her that she loved her father? She had been doing such a good job of forgetting. Remembering was pain.

"Fucker, I don't love anything," she growled under her breath as though speaking to an absent Gordeau.

Harriet stumbled over to a mirror by the bed and saw that she was still dressed in her hero costume.

"I give zero fucks about all human beings and don't you forget it," she added as she looked at her reflection in the mirror. As her vision returned to her, she noticed that the mirror frame was made of stone and had several screaming skulls carved into it.

"What the fuck?" Harriet murmured when she was finally conscious enough to notice how stupidly this room was decorated. The black carpets, high stone arches, and stained glass windows, filled by depictions of smirking demons torturing souls in hell, were tasteless and lacked subtlety. Clearly, a villain with too much money lived here.

Harriet walked to the edge of the strangely familiar room and tried the steel handle of the antique door, leading out. It was locked.

A voice came over the intercom, through a speaker in the ceiling.

"Hehehehheh....Did you sleep well? Now you're dead,

Justice Bitch. In about thirty minutes, the floor of this room is timed to drop out. When that happens, you'll drop into a pool of rabid piranhas and be ripped to shreds! And if you're not dead within the first five minutes of that, the pool will fill with boiling hot acid and you'll be melted to the bone! Or cooked! You know, *whatever*!"

"Hey, asshole, if you wanted to kill me, then why didn't you just blow my head off when I was unconscious instead of transporting me to this overly convoluted trap that I can easily escape from?"

"Uh...because I have a room with a floor that drops out and a pool with piranhas and boiling acid in it?"

"Right, ok, I guess that makes sense," said Harriet calmly and then she added with an incensed shriek: "If you're a fucking—*IDIOT*!"

"Heheheheh...try to escape, just try! You'll never do it! My plan is too good!" Death Laser laughed and then the intercom clicked off.

Harriet groaned and then walked over to the door of the room, grabbed its iron handle with one hand, and with one swift, violent motion, ripped the door off of its hinges before stepping through it.

The hallway looked familiar. It was ribbed with high, skull-engraved, onyx arches. Harriet glanced down at the floor and saw that it was a checkerboard of black and red marble. None of these things looked familiar, yet, Harriet was sure that she had seen this hallway before. She stared at the hallway incredulously for a few moments, as she worked to reverse engineer Death Laser's redecorating in her mind. She pictured pure white walls, white marble floors, and clear vases filled with white flowers, by a large window, facing her father's private beach. *Shit*, she thought with no small amount of annoyance, *this is The Ross Manor isn't it? Reynolds would die if he saw what Death Laser and his home improvement goons have done to the place.*

Harriet crept quietly down the hallway, alert and

poised to strike should Death Laser's henchmen descend upon her. She spotted the round window, which had once filled this space with light. It was now darkened by a pattern of black and red checkered stained glass.

Harriet kept walking. The door at the end of the hallway led to another hallway. Harriet started jogging. The door at the end of the next hallway led to yet another identical hallway. Harriet broke into a sprint. The door at the end of the third hallway led to a fourth identical hallway. She dashed to check every door in the fourth hallway but each door seemed to lead to yet another identical hallway. She collapsed onto the marble floor hyperventilating and then swore.

Death Laser's voice came through a speaker in the ceiling, thick with amusement:

"Congratulations, Justice Bitch, you've escaped my piranhas and acid trap! However, the whole manor is now a trap! All of the hallways and rooms turn 360 degrees and also move up and down like frickin' elevators! So you can run forever, but you'll just be running in circles, unless I let you escape. Did it cost a shit ton of money? Yes. But it was worth it to see the look on your face. Hehehehehe....*yes*! Look at you! You're trapped like a rat!"

"Death Laser! I'm going to find you and ring your stupid neck!" Harriet yelled.

Death Laser chuckled in sarcastic reply: "Oh noo....I'm in trouble now. I guess I'm the cheese at the end of this maze. You know, because you're the rat. Are you impressed by my analogies?"

"*Fuck you*," Harriet spat, "Fuck you and fuck your analogies."

The sound of a guitar being strummed came over the loud speaker. Then, to Harriet's chagrin, Death Laser cleared his throat as though preparing to sing. Harriet started frantically checking the doors, desperate to find a way out before Death Laser could start singing. Surely, the man's shrill, mind-splitting squalls would give her a migraine to rival the ones induced by Super Annoyo.

"She's trapped like a rat, trapped like a rat, Justice Bitch is trapped like a rat. She thinks that she can punch her way out of here, but I'm not very worried about that." Death Laser sang, strumming his guitar. Harriet was surprised to observe that Death Laser sang with the professional competence of someone who had been trained to sing and practiced often. When he was talking, he spoke with the scratchy ignorance of a burnt out Californian with too much time on his hands, but when he was *singing*, his voice was, in a word, *angelic*.

"Trapped like a rat, trapped like a rat, Justice Bitch is trapped like a rat. She's trying to smash her way out of my trap, but I'm not very worried about that! Because last night, while she was knocked out, I went ahead and set off the bombs. That's right, last night—the mall—*burned the fuck down*. And then fire spread, yes the fire spread—to the whole—*mother fucking town*." Death Laser sang. Harriet groaned and rolled her eyes, she could tell that he was making this song up as he went along.

"You suck at song writing!" Harriet yelled.

"This is improv, baby!" Death Laser shouted back cheerfully, and then he continued to strum the guitar and sing. "Now the mall's ash, no it wasn't pretty. Your pals couldn't stop me, I own this damn ci-ity!"

"Ever hear of a refrain!" Harriet shouted with frustration as she tried yet another door that lead to no where.

"Oh, I've heard of refrains," Spencer replied sardonically and then he immerged from behind the door at the far end of the hallway, strummed the black acoustic guitar he was holding and sang: "Harriet Ross, how much do you cost? I'd throw you my last fucking dollar. Harriet Ross, if you're really the boss! Won't you drag me around by my collar?"

"Enough bullshit. What did you do with the Sexy Action Which-ma-kalit Schmucks?" Harriet murmured, eyeing

Death Laser cautiously as he approached. His eyes began to glow red.

"The Sexy Action Something-or-other Dudes are all dead. They exploded or something," said Death Laser shrugging.

"Bullshit," said Harriet, pointing at Death Laser accusingly. She could sense the lie in his aura. "I don't believe you."

"Yea, I like killed them all or whatever. Blew their heads off with my laser eyes. And they were all like: 'No, nooo please don't kill us. You're awesome and we're super lame!' But then, I was all like: 'Fuck it, I'm gonna' kill you all anyway. Because I'm a stone cold psycho.' Are you mad?" Death Laser inquired nonchalantly. "You're mad. I can tell."

"You know what? That's it. You're going to jail this time." Harriet growled. She reached out a hand to grab him but he darted away. She sprinted after him, but her foot caught a trip wire and then the floor dropped out from underneath of her. She screamed as her body plummeted straight down into the pool of swarming piranhas below.

Chapter 42:
Piranha Tank

Harriet hit the water with a splash. The piranhas converged on her immediately, gathering in a great swarm of brown, flailing fins. They sunk their teeth into her flesh, but due to her super resiliency attribute, never managed to leave more than a superficial wound. She swam forward blindly, punching piranhas out of her path as she moved. They were hungry and repeatedly soared back toward her like magnets, despite the fact that they had not yet managed to draw blood.

I have to get out of here, Harriet thought. *And soon or this whole tank might fill with boiling acid like Death Laser said.*

Harriet swam forward frantically, kicking piranhas off of her legs with the heels of her boots. She moved slowly, as though sloshing through a thick quicksand. Exhausted by the weight of the flailing piranhas tangled in her hair and clothes, Harriet feared she may collapse and drown.

"Holy shit! He threw a girl down here!" a deep, scratchy voice bellowed.

Harriet swam in the direction of the voice.

"Here! Over here!" the voice yelled, "This way! Keep going! You're almost there!"

Harriet reached the side of the tank and slapped a palm down on the flat smooth surface beside it. A man grabbed her by the hand and tried to help pull her up as she struggled to her feet.

Hyperventilating, Harriet recognized the owner of the voice that had called to her during her struggle against the piranhas, as the lead guitarist of EAR MUTILATOR, Devin Forress.

Devin Forress was a platinum blond and sexy in the way that only rock musicians in their early twenties can be sexy, with straight, skinny legs, and muscled shoulders. His aura did not glow with the same sort of cocky nonchalance that Harriet might have attributed to him before, however.

Instead, he projected a demeanor of being simultaneously forlorn and enraged. His clothes were torn and his short blond hair was disheveled. His fingers were bandaged and bloody.

"You're Devin Forress," Harriet observed.

"And you're Justice Bitch," Devin replied.

"Shit. What are you doing here?" Harriet asked with genuine curiosity.

"Yeah...After your fight with Death Laser on the roof of Headless Records, he just went ahead and had one of his henchmen buy the company outright. Then, he appointed Spencer Tuckerson of all people to run it. So, one day, ol' Fuckerson comes into my recording studio, interrupts my goddamn recording, in his fucking pretentious three-piece suit to tell me and the band that he owns Headless Records now. And I'm like: 'What the fuck? Spanky Fuckerson owns Headless Records, now?' And he laughs in his stupid fucking way you know: 'Heh heh heh heh...' Then, he tells me that my singing is shit and that he's going to fire me and replace me with a different lead singer. So I say: 'Oh let me guess, Fuckerson, that singer is you, right?' And he says: 'No. But the replacement I've picked out is still definitely an improvement. Then, that shithead calls a couple of zoo keepers into the room with a gorilla and sits there for thirty minutes while the gorilla shrieks into the microphone. So the lead singer of EAR MUTILATOR is a fucking gorilla now, right? And I say: 'Nice job, shithead, you ruined a perfectly good band just to make a shitty reference to a Warren Zevon song.' Then, Spanky, because he's a dick-head, swears up and down that he doesn't know what I'm talking about and that he *genuinely* believes the gorilla is a better musician than me. And he says: 'Since we've known each other for such a long time, I'm not even going to fire you. I'll just give you a different job where you won't have to embarrass yourself with your shitty singing.' So, then, he throws me down here and puts me in charge of feeding Death Laser's goddamn piranhas."

"Well," Harriet shrugged, "On the bright side. At least you're still employed."

"Yeah, easy for you to say. Look at my fucking hands!" Devin waved his bloody bandaged fingers in Harriet's face furiously. "I went from being a fucking rock star, to getting my fingers snagged by goddamn piranhas when I throw them feeder fish. This is Fuckerson's revenge...because I managed to get him kicked out of the band. But I'll get him back for this one day, you'll see. I would have shoved his head in a toilet years ago if it wasn't for Plaxman."

"Plaxman?" Harriet inquired.

"Yea," said Devin. He pulled a silver, skull-shaped lighter and a packet of cigarettes out of the pocket of his torn jeans, stuck a cigarette in his mouth, and then lit it. "Plaxman met Spanky in juvie when they were both about 10-years-old, so they were tight for a long time."

"Oh," said Harriet, "So you guys all met each other when you were kids?"

"Yea, me, Plaxman, and Kalvin met in high school, which is when we started the band. Plaxman was always cool but, then, when we started the band, he started dragging his dingus friend, Fuckerson, along with him to practice. Spanky dip-shit Fuckerson, that marching band, voice lessons, socially retarded, *ass stain* of a human being. I knew that he was trouble from the beginning."

"So how do you think he knows Death Laser?" Harriet inquired.

"To fuck if I know," Devin shrugged, taking a long drag from his cigarette.

"You don't think that maybe..."

"No way."

"They could be the same person?" Harriet finished.

"Huh....no wait. Fuckerson did have the laser eye thing going on. Huh....yeah, guess I get high too often to notice this kind of stuff. But you know there's a lot of people with radiation powers in the city and Fuckerson's a mega dork. He could never make this whole super criminal thing work for him so well. So, yea, maybe not." Devin took a drag from his cigarette. "Some stuff is just a mystery, you know?"

"Uh huh...well, I never gave much thought to it either," said Harriet, "But now that I think about it, it does kind of make sense. I mean they look and sound kind of alike and have the same power and the same grudges, and apparently work together for some reason. I mean, it has to be him. Right?"

"Jesus, some people just aren't comfortable with ambiguity," Devin muttered, exhaling a puff of smoke. "Fuckerson could just be Death Laser's nephew or something."

"Yea, I guess that's a possibility. Or maybe..."

"Maybe."

"...He's an evil clone or something," finished Harriet.

"Exactly, every time you turn on the news, everything you ever hear about is just Death Laser and evil clones. It's like....what about other stuff, you know? What about the stock market?"

"Exactly," agreed Harriet absentmindedly, "*The stock market.*"

"Fuck, I hate this place," Devin said, exhaling a puff of smoke.

"I thought you said you work here?" Harriet asked.

"Yea, technically I do but then the door that leads down here got stuck and Fuckerson, because he's a dick-head, swore up and down that he couldn't figure out how to open it. He's not fooling me, though. I know he locked me down here as part of his revenge. So uh...are you going to save me or whatever?"

"Uh...yea, sure. We should both be able to get out of here safely," said Harriet, "So when does the acid fill the tank?"

"Huh?"

"Death Laser said that the tank fills with boiling acid or

something like that," said Harriet.

"Oh, yeah, he would say something like that. He's full of shit, though. He loves these goddamn piranhas and filling the tank with acid would kill them. Every once in awhile he throws a burger down here, just so that I don't starve and can keep pH testing the water."

"Alright then," said Harriet, "Where's this door you say won't open."

"Oh, yeah," said Devin. He walked to the edge of the room where the platform they were standing on met the wall. There was the faint outline of a door here and an empty hole where, presumably, a handle used to be. "This is it."

Harriet walked over to the door, dug her fingers around its faint edges, and then pried it open with one violent tug.

Harriet and Devin exited the piranha room and entered a narrow metal stairway, leading up to the upper floors. Devin sucked in air loudly as he took a drag from his cigarette.

"Sh..." Harriet said quietly, "Don't make any noise. If he thinks we're still in the piranha room he won't change the hallways and we can just escape."

"*What*?" Devin muttered quietly. Then he shook his head and said: "Ok, whatever." Devin dropped his cigarette and snuffed it out with the heel of his sneaker. "Get me the fuck out of here, already."

The two of them crept quietly up the steps.

The voices of a couple of henchmen could be heard, conversing in the room above:

"—But Death Laser said..." a husky voiced henchman muttered unsurely.

"Who cares *what* Death Laser said. Everyone knows that Jaywalker is the real boss around here," a henchman with a think New York accent replied.

"He gave us an order."

"And so did Jaywalker. He'll be taking over soon, but

you didn't hear that from me. Anyway, when Jaywalker's ready to take the reigns, he'll want Death Laser put down quick and clean," said the man with the New York accent.

"No way. He'll want to make a spectacle of it, really make the guy suffer first."

The henchmen's voices grew more distant as they walked further away. Both of these men were killers. Harriet could sense it. Harriet felt their auras fade as they moved out of range.

She opened the door at the top of the steps and stepped out into the hallway. Devin followed.

Harriet's cell phone rang. She froze and then fumbled for it in her pocket. Startled to find that Death Laser hadn't thought to take it from her while she was under Gordeau's spell, her hands closed around it and she attempted to silence it quickly, accidentally pushing the "answer" button.

Devin shot her a look of hateful look of incredulity as she lifted the phone to her ear and answered the call.

"Harriet, it's Gary. Are you, ok? You disappeared after the fight at the shopping center."

Harriet and Devin scurried down the hallway quickly. The two henchmen had heard them and were quietly turning around and doubling back to investigate the disturbance. Harriet could sense this. Devin could not. But there was no point in alerting him. The information might only make him panic.

"Yeah, I'm fine, Gary. This is not a good time," said Harriet. She and Devin reached the door at the end of the hallway.

"Oh, sorry, just thought you should know, the district attorney is dropping the Super Annoyo criminal case against you. They seem to think that he can't prove you did it. The civil case is still on though. The burden of proof in civil court is not as steep and there's little danger of being unmasked during the legal proceedings."

"Thanks, Gary. We can talk about this later, ok? Bye,"

Harriet said and hung up the phone. She could sense the henchmen drawing closer. Devin opened the door at the end of the hallway and sprinted through it. Harriet followed him. This time, the hallway opened into, not another hallway, but a foyer with a pair of curling onyx staircases and a tall Christmas tree at the center of it.

"Oh, thank god" Harriet sighed, observing that this was not another turning trick hallway but rather, a new room with a door that led to the outside. "He must not have realized we got out."

Spotting his escape route, Devin sprinted down the nearest staircase and bolted through the door, into the courtyard. In the next instant, he had vanished from sight, without so much as a "thank you" or a "goodbye."

"Well," Harriet muttered as she stared at the empty space where the handsome musician had been standing only a moment ago. "So much for getting lucky."

It was then that the panel underneath of her feet collapsed and she fell through the floor again.

Chapter 43:
Observation Room

Harriet landed on a pile of pillows, on the floor of a secret room, inside of the stairway. The narrow room was lit on all sides by the screens of security monitors. Live footage from various rooms of the manor played before her eyes in every direction. A man in a computer chair sat in front of the screens. Harriet rose to her feet and approached him cautiously.

The chair turned toward her slowly, and she was confronted by a grinning Death Laser.

"What do you just have trap doors everywhere, now?" Harriet muttered incredulously.

"Yeah, pretty much," said Death Laser.

"And I suppose you think it's ok to keep Devin Forress locked in a room with a bunch of Piranhas and hardly any food for god knows how long?" said Harriet crossly, putting her hands on her hips. The grin slipped off of Death Laser's face.

"Well, in my defense," Death Laser said. "He *is* an asshole."

"Why did you bring me here, huh?" Harriet asked crossly.

"Because we're mortal enemies locked in an eternal battle of good and evil. We were supposed to fight. Why won't you try to beat the crap out of me the way you did Super Annoyo and The Jaywalker, huh? Why won't you fight me for real?" Death Laser inquired with a note of genuine distress.

"Because if I punch you, you'll probably start crying and then run to a lawyer," Harriet groaned.

"Will not."

"Will too times infinity."

"Agh...damn it. You just jumped right to the times infinity one," Death Laser grumbled, scratching the back of his head with one fingerless-gloved hand.

"You better not have felt me up while I was unconscious," Harriet muttered suspiciously.

"Nah, that's not my style. Wouldn't be very sporting of me," Death Laser replied with a shrug. She could sense that he was probably telling the truth.

Harriet reached into the inner pocket of her jacket and felt for her handcuffs. They were missing.

Death Laser pulled the handcuffs out of the pocket of his slacks and raised and eyebrow: "Looking for these?"

"Ugh," Harriet groaned.

"If you want them back, you'll have to fight me for them," Death Laser said, his mischievous grin returning. Then, he grabbed his slacks by the waste band and dropped the handcuffs down the front of them. "Whoops, where could they be hiding? I guess you'll just have to pat me down and find out."

"Goddamn it. I hate you," Harriet muttered. She was not about to reach down Death Laser's pants to get those handcuffs, and if she tried to restrain him with her bare hands, she would probably just end up hurting him, and then he would just turn around and sue her for assault.

She walked to the edge of the room and, rather than searching for the hidden door, simply reached out with both hands and tore a hole in the drywall large enough to step through. Death Laser watched with amazement as huge chucks of drywall were flung across the room and, in the next instant, Harriet had disappeared from sight.

Chapter 44:
The League of American Heroes

Harriet strolled around the empty art museum, thinking about the day before. Death Laser still had her handcuffs. She would have to buy a new pair, a better pair, one that her nemesis could not Houdini his way out of the next time she tried to drag him off to prison.

Harriet straightened a crooked painting on the wall, near a statue of a muscular, nude Roman soldier holding a spear and a shield. There was a typo in the description of the statue, an extra lowercase s on the front of the artist's name. Spotting it, Harriet swore and removed the description from the plastic plaque at the base of the statue, then, went to her desk to type up another one.

As she was doing this, she thought about the old butler, Reynolds Sanderland. Where was he living now and how had Death Laser wrestled her father's property away from him? Had Death Laser's hired goons simply dragged the old man out and then changed all of the locks? Or had they murdered him and buried him somewhere where no one would find the body? Harriet could not be sure. She had not spoken to Reynolds since the reading of her father's will and was not exactly sure how to contact him. She did not know his cell number, and had never thought to ask for it.

Harriet picked up her cell phone and called Gary.

"Gary Goldstein, personal injury lawyer," Gary answered robotically.

"Garry, it's me, Harriet."

"Harriet, hi."

"Do you have Reynolds Sanderland's contact information?"

"I don't think so but I'll look around."

"Thanks, Gary."

"No problem."

...

That night, there was a Sexy Rad Super Pals meeting scheduled. Harriet and Viola drove to the costume shop in Viola's van. It was getting close to Christmas and Viola was wearing a frumpy sweater with Rudolf embroidered on the front of it, despite the warm and humid California weather.

"So what happened to you guys after Gordeau shot me down?" Viola asked, staring at the road in front of her as the van rolled up a steep incline.

"I'm not really sure, Gordeau got me too eventually. I almost had Death Laser, and then Gordeau snuck up behind me and snapped me into one of his vivid flashbacks. When I woke up, I was at The Ross Manor."

"The Ross Manor, huh? Death Laser's Ross Manor?"

"Yup. He had the whole place decked out like the dumbest haunted castle. I'm talking skulls, demons, everything in black. It's like he was worried that I might forget that I was in an evil lair or something."

"For real?" Viola laughed, "I don't imagine your dad would like that at all."

"He wouldn't and neither do I," said Harriet, "Word on the street is Death Laser stole the place from Reynolds Sanderland with 'military force.'"

"Shit," Viola swore, sounding impressed. "So what happened next?"

"Convoluted traps. He turned the mansion into a trick house with moving rooms and piranhas in the basement. Had Devin Forress imprisoned next to the tank. So, I helped him escape."

"Hey, who do you think is the hottest member of EAR MUTILATOR, Harriet? Danny, Devin, or Kalvin?"

"I don't know. They're all hot," replied Harriet, "If I had to choose between them, I'd probably pick Devin."

"I'd go for that Spencer Tuckerson. He was the cutest one, with his big ol' brown eyes and whatnot," said Viola.

"Shouldn't you like Danny, because he's technically the one you're seeing?"

"Yea, well, he's pretty hot too. I mean, seriously, they're *all* hot," said Viola.

"California boys, am I right?" Harriet sighed.

"Ya' gotta' love those California boys," Viola agreed. "So what happened next?"

"I don't know. We fought, I guess. He's kind of hard to catch."

"Yea, I saw him on the roof of Headless Records. He runs fast. I mean, not super fast, just kind of normal fast. No offence, girl, but you run kind of normal slow to normal average speed. I mean....sometimes you make holes in the ground with your feet but that doesn't really make you run faster," said Viola.

"Yea, I guess that's true," said Harriet, "Anyway, after you got knocked out, during the battle at the mall, I tried to hit him a couple of times, and usually I can get them if they come at me, but this guy tends to keep his distance just enough so that he's impossible to hit. And then, as I'm trying to hit him, I realize: 'What the hell am I doing? If I use physical force again, I'll probably just get another lawsuit handed to me.'"

"Yea, sometimes you've got to just ignore that risk. Avoiding personal injury suits is kind of what the secret identity thing is about," said Viola.

"I know, I know...but...with the whole Super Annoyo trying to prove I'm Justice Bitch in civil court thing...I just can't risk complicating that right now. And I was thinking: 'Hey, I'm strong. I don't even really need to hit him. I can just push him down, handcuff him, and carry him to prison. No violence necessary.'"

"Kind of weird that you just decided to be nonviolent all of a sudden," said Viola, "What happened to miss punch face first and ask questions later?"

"Oh, she's still there. Just laying low at the moment,"

said Harriet, with some irritation. She could tell what Viola's was about to suggest by the teasing tone of her voice.

"You know what I think?" Viola inquired with a smirk.

"No. Viola, what do you think?" Harriet groaned even though she knew exactly what Viola thought.

"I think that you didn't hurt him....because you *like* him," said Viola, grinning.

"You're a jerk," Harriet groaned, "And *no*. Honestly the guy is driving me insane and intimidating him doesn't work because he's a *masochist*, so threatening him just turns him on. Between *that* and the threat of more lawsuits, and the fact that he's faster than me, and the fact that if I did hit him, he'd probably just *like it*...trying to fight him is like trying to strangle your shadow. I mean you can *try*, but it won't work and you'll just look like a fucking fool while you're doing it."

"Oh man, I think you're over thinking this, Harriet," said Viola, shaking her head with a grin. "I cut Death Laser's face at the funeral, remember?"

"Yeah."

"And, judging by the way he grabbed at his face and yelled, I'm going to hazard a guess that he didn't like *that* at all. No one's a masochist 100%."

"Huh...I guess you're right. It's like what Stuart said."

"Don't fucking talk to me about Stuart. He's dead to me," Viola muttered. Her mood darkened considerably when Stuart's name was mentioned.

"*So*....what you just said made me think of what that guy we used to live with who's dead now said," Harriet tried again, framing the thought so that Stuart's name would not be mentioned again. "Maybe Death Laser's doing a reverse psychology thing...telling me he wants to fight because *really*...that's the last thing he wants."

"...*Maybe*," Viola mused, "Or *maybe*...he's just got a big masochist crush on you."

"Jesus, Viola. You watch too many romantic comedies," Harriet groaned.

...

The meeting of the Sexy Rad Super Pals went the way it usually did, with Lilly repeating rumors she had heard at The Black Hatchet and Viola shouting "Sexy Rad Super Pals...Let's rock 'n roll!"

The team dawned their costumes and then patrolled the streets for a few hours. However, they encountered no crimes. What they encountered instead was Stuart, in his patriotic cape and spandex, followed by three or four other costumed heroes.

"Viola? What are you doing here?" Stuart asked when he saw her.

"Same thing as you. Patrolling the streets," Viola replied crossly, "Who are those jokers? Your new pals?"

"This is my new team," Stuart replied humorlessly.

"I'm Stars and Stripes," said a muscular, spandex clad man with a large white star embroidered across his red spandex chest.

"I'm Lady Liberty," said a green spandex clad woman with a green plastic mask and a green spiky head band.

"And I'm Flago," bellowed a deep-voiced man wearing a sandwich board with an American flag on it."

"Together we are—" Stuart began dramatically and then the other three chimed in: "The League of American Heroes!"

"Ugh. Whatever," Viola groaned and rolled her eyes. She started walking away and Benjamin, Lilly, Finsveld, Garyand Harriet followed her.

"Why don't you go home, citizens? It's far too dangerous for superhumans with low level powers such as yourselves to be out here, let the *professionals* handle this!" Stars and Stripes called after than as they walked away.

"Viola they're challenging our cred," Lilly whispered meekly, "Should we fight them?"

"Whatever," Viola groaned and she kept walking. "It's

just Stuart and a bunch of his stupid army buddies. They'll get knocked down by the first villain that rolls by."

"Hey, we heard that!" Flago called after her.

"*Good!* I hope you heard it!" Viola yelled back.

The sky grew darker as the sun sank low over the horizon. Viola stormed into a nearby convenience store and then stormed out with a slushy. Harriet watched her down the whole thing in five or six rapid gulps, then, toss the empty container down to be skewered by her talons.

"Well...tonight has been a bust," said Harriet.

"Yeah....Finsveld is bored," added Finsveld.

"Well, you know what, *Finsveld?* Not everything always has to be about *you*, ok?" Viola snapped.

"Jesus, Viola, what the hell's wrong with you tonight?" Benjamin interjected.

"You know what, nothing," said Viola, "I don't know why I'm getting so worked up about this...I mean....it's just Stuart and his stupid army buddies. They're not a threat to us....right? I mean...it's clear who has the superior team. *Me*. Obviously."

"We shouldn't pick a fight with them anyway," said Benjamin, "I mean, we're all fighting to keep Propolous City safe, right? So, we should all support each other."

"Yea, I guess you're right," conceded Viola begrudgingly.

Chapter 45: Heroes, Villains, and the State of California

The next day, Harriet drove to the art museum. There was a big exhibition scheduled to begin at 1:00 p.m. that afternoon and it was her job to make sure that the display was set out properly. For the occasion, she had purchased wine, cheese, crackers, fruit, plastic cups, and paper plates with the museum's catering budget. She carried several shopping bags with her as she unlocked the front door of the museum with her work key and stepped inside. Mr. Samson, another museum curator who she worked with, greeted her as she entered.

"Good morning, Harriet," he said.

"Good morning, Mr. Samson."

Mr. Samson was an older man with thinning grey hair, who wore a sweater vest and a bowtie over black slacks and a polo shirt. He picked a painting off of a nearby table and hung it on the wall above a plaque which read: "Screaming Death by Vigo Von Crucible." The painting was an abstract piece, in which a man, distorted hideously by cubism, devoured the limbs of a screaming, bloody woman.

"Huh..." Harriet murmured as she observed the painting. Vigo Von Crucible was known for his disturbing abstract paintings, which often featured people being ripped apart and consumed.

Harriet walked passed several more of Von Crucible's gruesome paintings, to a plastic fold-out table. She then dropped the shopping bags onto it and started laying out the refreshments. As she was setting out the bottles of wine, she felt a tap on her shoulder. Harriet flinched and spun around quickly. A tall, skinny man in his forties with wavy, dirty-blond hair and a pair of large round glasses confronted her. She recognized the face immediately, as it belonged to a photo from the display.

"Vigo Von Crucible!" Harriet gasped with surprise, "I

wasn't expecting to see you here so early!"

"Yes, well, when I was a boy in Germany," Von Crucible replied with much intensity and in a thick German accent. "My mother always said that the early bird get's dee toast and the late bird gets dee *nothing*."

"Uh...ok then," said Harriet unsurely. Von Crucible's unnecessary intensity was making her uneasy.

"But then again, she would know," said Von Crucible and Harriet watched nervously as he removed a piece of toast from one of the pockets of his too-tight denim jacket and raised it slowly to his lined face. He took a bite out of the toast and it crunched loudly. He swallowed, and then, he finished his sentence: "Dee dirty bitch."

"Hahaha...*yeah*..." Harriet replied nervously. She wasn't sure how else to react to this bewildering statement.

Von Crucible nodded politely, bit into the piece of toast a second time, and then wandered away.

At 1 o'clock, the exhibition started. Guests filed into the room to pick away at the refreshment table as Von Crucible spoke to them about his work. The crowd gathered around the eccentric man, and stared at him as he motioned dramatically with his hands and spoke with unnecessary intensity about his childhood in Germany. According to him, to be alone was to "starve." To be with others was "to eat cat shit out of a dying cat's litter box." Mothers were "spongy." Grouchy old men were "dry and tasteless." Beautiful young women were "delicious, juicy delicacies dat get stuck between your teeth." Von Crucible was freakishly entertaining, like the large painting of the man with the bloody gash of a mouth sitting on top of a pile of screaming human heads, which hung behind him. Guests looked at the man, as though he was, himself, a disturbing painting. They crowded around him in a circle, entranced by his pretentious nonsense and elegant crazy talk.

Harriet was left by herself, standing next to the refreshment table with a glass of wine in her hand. She could feel her black heels slowly sinking into the floor. Von Crucible paused in the middle of a rant about his mother and Harriet was momentarily fooled into thinking that he was about to stop talking.

"—Dee dirty bitch! She was *stringy*, like dee insides of a rotting pumpkin!"

"Ugh," Harriet groaned with distain as Von Crucible started talking again. It was getting later in the afternoon and Von Crucible *still* showed no signs of slowing down or shutting up.

Gary walked into the room, wearing a black suit with a blue tie for the occasion. His auburn hair was parted down the side and gelled conservatively.

"Gary, you made it," Harriet said when she saw him.

"Yea, I got out of a hearing early and thought I'd stop by," Gary said. He motioned in the direction of the ranting artist, now surrounded by a thick crowd of curious museum goers. "Who's the artist?"

"Vigo Von Crucible," Harriet shrugged, "He has demons in his past or whatever."

"Oh, wow, did you meet him? What's he like?" Gary asked.

"Well, he's an artist, you know," Harriet said, "So, *you know*, crazy and kind of full of himself. Whatever puts those asses in seats, that's what I always say...but seriously, I was lucky to book Vigo. The man draws a crowd like a car accident," Harriet paused to sip at the glass of wine she was holding. "So, yeah, if he walks over here you're probably going to see me drop to my knees and kiss his ass....figuratively speaking."

Gary poured himself a glass of wine and then started piling cheese and crackers onto a paper plate.

"So, just out of curiosity...what happened after, you know...you got kidnapped by The League of Evildoers..." he asked quietly, so that he would not be overheard by Von Crucible or the museum guests.

"Nothing, I don't think," said Harriet, "I just busted out of Death Laser's lame-o trap and freed his hostage, you know the story."

"But he didn't try to touch you or anything?"

"Nah," Harriet replied dismissively.

"Thank God," Gary sighed, now oddly fixated on the piece of cheese on the end of his tooth pick. He was now spinning the hors d'oeuvre with his index finger and thumb and not looking at Harriet. "The way he was flirting with you at the shopping center really had me worried."

"Aw, really? You were worried about me?"

"Yea, a little bit."

"No, I don't think there's anything to worry about," said Harriet, "He only asks me to spank him every time I see him because he's a sexist creep. Not because he has a thing for me. He probably says that to all of the female heroes."

"Fun fact, it is technically legal for a hero to administer a non-consensual disciplinary spanking to a villain in the State of California," Gary informed her.

Harriet downed what remained of her wine and laughed: "Really? That is *seriously* fucked-up!"

"Yea, I guess it is," Gary laughed, "Its still in the books from like the 1930's, completely legal as long as you do it with an open hand and don't cause any permanent damage."

"Dee blood. It represents the bile that spews from the mouths of simpleton critics!" Von Crucible shouted angrily, waving his arms around like a mad man. His increased volume, effectively interrupted Harriet and Gary's conversation. "They do not understand! They taste like hypocrisy—LIKE BLOOD AND BILE!"

Harriet and Gary glanced over at the rabid artist, with blank expressions. Von Crucible's eye twitched and then Harriet snorted into her empty wine glass.

"Harriet shh..." Gary whispered quickly, "If he thinks you're laughing at him, you'll insult him."

"...Sorry," Harriet whispered back, grinning. "It's just

that, you know, he's coo-coo bananas..."

"Yeah...I know..."

"Hey, Gary?" Harriet asked.

"Yea?"

"You remember that one time, in college, when we dated for like five minutes?"

"Sure," Gary replied. He was a few years older than Harriet and had been near the end of his law school days during Harriet's freshman year of college. The summer after that, they had dated. Their relationship had not been a particularly passionate one, but rather, an alliance of convenience, which seemed to come with the unspoken understanding that they would both, eventually, move on to something else. At least that was the way that Harriet had seen it. Yet, now, after years of separation, Harriet was beginning to see Gary in a different way.

"You want to do that again?" Harriet asked, smiling at her old friend fondly. He reminded her of better days, of golfing and country clubs, private jets, and expensive wine. Not the rat piss she could afford with the museum catering budget. A sophisticated man like Gary knew as well as she did that the world had better things to offer.

"Yea, I was thinking about that actually....when we started talking again," said Gary.

"I could tell," said Harriet.

"I mean...I'm a little hesitant since just being your friend has gotten me in trouble with villains," said Gary, "And you can be a bit...."

"A bit *what*?" Harriet demanded angrily. Without meaning to she returned her wine glass to the catering table with too much force and it shattered.

Gary's eyes got big and he flinched away from her, adding quickly: "Nothing. Never mind."

"Yea, so...we're dating again?" Harriet asked.

"Yea...I guess we are," conceded Gary nervously. With a shaking hand, he lifted his wineglass to his parted lips and then swallowed.

Chapter 46:
Human Sacrifice

Before the exhibition closed, Vigo Von Crucible bid farewell to his audience with a sweeping bow and a gracious: "Stay *delicious*, my pot pies."

The museum goers filtered out of the room, looking confused but satisfied. A couple of old ladies in fancy dresses murmured: "...*pot pies*?" and then shrugged and made a beeline for the gift shop.

Von Crucible exited the museum and walked out onto the marble stairway, which led down to the parking lot. Staring out at the people as they returned to their cars, his green eyes bore much intensity.

Von Crucible removed a pipe from his pants pocket, poured some tobacco in it, and then lit it, puffing thoughtfully. Jason Walker emerged from the crowd and walked up to him. Seeing that the kid was dressed in a hoodie and baggy jeans, Von Crucible shrugged at him with distain as he approached.

"You are not dressed for this occasion," Von Crucible informed him, derisively.

Jason ignored the snobbish remark and said:

"Are you Von Crucible?"

"I am."

"I've got something for you to read," Jason said, removing the trap letter he had prepared from the pocket of his baggy jeans.

Von Crucible pushed the letter away:

"I don't read on my days off and I am not interested in what you are selling."

Jason sighed and returned the letter to his pocket.

"We all boil in butter, boy. We all pick the shreds from our teeth like so much walrus semen," Von Crucible informed him confusingly.

"Uh huh. Right...walrus semen...*anyway*, Word on the

street is, you know how to get a hold of the Crunchy Toast Muncher," said Jason, changing his tone from casual to businesslike.

"Who told you dat?" Von Crucible demanded.

"Some guys at The Black Hatchet," said Jason and then he lowered his voice so that a crowd of people exiting the museum would not overhear him. "They said that they hired Crunchy Toast Muncher to do a job for them and as payment, he requested a human sacrifice, which was arranged through you."

"Ridiculous conjecture. I know no thugs at The Black Hatchet. Tell me, boy, what were their names?"

"Sand Trap and The Human Parking Meter," Jason said.

"And wat else did they tell you?" Von Crucible inquired, exhaling a puff of smoke.

"Just that about 10 years ago you arranged to have a human sacrifice from them delivered to Crunchy Toast Muncher in exchange for a favor. They said that he used to roll with a villain called Vore Whore, who could make herself small, climb into her enemy's stomach and rip him open from the inside."

"Ah, yes, Vore Whore," Von Crucible said fondly, staring off into the distance as though recalling a plot essential flashback. "I remember her well. She tasted like the sun as it rises at dawn." Von Crucible lowered his pipe and turned his head in Jason's direction, gazing at him with a new fondness. "Are you a cop?"

"What?" Jason murmured. Though he knew that this question had probably been on Von Crucible's mind, he could not help but be slightly insulted by the insinuation. He put up his hands as though to push the idea away and said quickly: "No, no, of course not. I *hate* cops."

"Hahahehheh..." Von Crucible chuckled, "They are the sheet dat gets stuck to the heel of your boot, and then is tracked around the carpet."

"Exactly."

Von Crucible's green eyes bore into Jason's brown ones with bizarre intensity and the artist said in a hushed tone: "You were right dee first time, boy. I do, from time to time, arrange deals for dee Crunchy Toast Muncher. What are you offering?"

Jason grinned evilly and replied: "A whole super ex-con support group full of willing victims."

"Willing victims, you say?" Von Crucible replied, sounding impressed. He returned his pipe to his mouth and sucked in air. Then said: "He does pay extra for dee *willing* victims."

"Yea, well they're all suicidal people with a vore fetish," Jason lied. In truth he had hypnotized the support group to sacrifice themselves and act as though they were doing it willingly when he, Jason, gave them the command.

"Highly suspect."

"They met online on a weird website, you know, like perverts do," lied Jason with a straight face.

"Alright then," Von Crucible conceded, "I will inform dee toast man of your offer. How many?"

"Six."

"Very good, very good. And what favor do you require in exchange?"

"A job," said Jason.

Von Crucible nodded. And Jason envisioned, his enemy, The Justice Bitch, shrieking as her limbs where transformed into breadsticks and then consumed by a mad cannibal. It would be so easy to kill her after she was a limbless torso, so satisfying. Jason pictured himself slicing her head off in front of the news cameras. He pictured the look of horror on Death Laser's stupid face as the object of his obsession bled out, gasping her last *disgusting* squelch of a breath and the life faded from her eyes, her lungs slowing to a stop. Then, and only then would the world know the depths of Jason's brutality.

Chapter 47:
The Sanderland Complex

Harriet had been brought up to appreciate classical music, and her phone's ring tones reflected that. She heard a few chords of Mozart's Fourth Concerto play and then repeat a few times on an electronic sounding loop. She grabbed her phone out of her purse and answered it.

"It's Gary."

As she was walking past a newsstand, Harriet spotted a picture of EAR MUTILATOR, standing around a gorilla in a pink tutu on the cover of the Propopolous Times. She doubled back to take a closer look at it.

"Hi, Gary," Harriet said.

"Harriet, I was looking through a few of my old records and found Reynold Sanderland's contact information. Do you still want it?"

"Yeah."

Harriet walked over to the rack of Propopolous Times newspapers and narrowed her eyes at the image of EAR MUTILATOR. They were posed seductively around a gorilla in the pink tutu, as though having been given absurd instructions during a photo shoot. The gorilla was bearing its large, sharp teeth in a smile as though pleased to be considered a member of the band. It was holding a peeled banana in one of its paws.

"I've got his cell number and his home address," said Gary to Harriet over the phone.

"I'll take both, thanks."

Gary gave Harriet Reynolds's contact information and she wrote it down on the back of her hand.

"Thanks, Gary."

"No Problem."

"Bye."

"Bye."

Harriet hung up the phone and then dialed Reynolds'

number. The answering machine picked up. She groaned and hung up the phone again.

Harriet picked up a newspaper with EAR MUTILATOR and the gorilla on the front of it, stared at it for a few more seconds, and then opened it and read a few lines from the article:

"Since Devin Forress' vocals was replaced by Lulee The Gorilla's, sales of EAR MUTILATOR records have spiked. It seems EAR MUTILATOR is proving more profitable as an ironic novelty band," says the new owner of Headless Records and recently appointed CEO of The Ross Foundation, Spencer Tuckerson. "I mean, EAR MUTILATOR was always kind of a joke band, but I feel like the crap quality of Devin's singing was taking the joke just a little too far. Substituting that with Lulee's monkey screeches make the whole thing just tolerable enough for people to buy the records. So, overall, I feel that this was a smart choice on the part of the company."

Harriet snorted back a laugh as she imagined the gorilla screeches in place of Devin's singing. Increased sales of EAR MUTILATOR records were probably an unintended consequence of Spencer's childish vendetta against Devin and the rest of the group, but he was claiming credit for it as though it were something he planned. Harriet shrugged and thought: *Well...I guess, now I've got to buy it.* She paid the man at the magazine stand for the newspaper, and then folded the paper in half and stuck it in her purse.

"Wait...you look really familiar. Have I seen you some place before?" the newspaper salesman asked Harriet as she was clumsily shoving the newspaper into her cluttered purse. The newspaper ripped as though comprised of a single sheet of wax paper. She had forgotten her super strength and handled the thing with too much force.

"No, you must be mistaken," Harriet said to the newspaper salesman, "I've just got one of those faces, you know?"

She walked away from the newspaper stand and then

walked back and grabbed an EAR MUTILATOR CD with Lulee the Gorilla on it, muttering under her breath as she did so: *"Fuck me for doing this."* Then, she paid the new stand salesman for the CD and walked away.

...

In the kitchen of Viola's apartment, Harriet played the CD. It competed badly with the hum of the window air conditioner and the buzz of the avocado green, 70's refrigerator. The screech of the gorilla was more or less random and did not really match the drums and guitars that were its accompaniment. At first it was funny, but the joke wore off fast.

Viola walked into the kitchen, halfway through the first song and said: "Harriet, what the fuck is that crap?"

"I don't know, some EAR MUTILATOR shit. Can you believe that people buy this?"

"I can't believe that *you* bought this," Viola said.

"I don't believe I bought it either," said Harriet pensively, "Devin mentioned the gorilla when I found him in Death Laser's piranha room. I guess that put the idea in my head."

Viola opened the refrigerator and removed a beer, snapping the top open and sipping it slowly.

"Girl, you have *got* to get your shit together," she said.

"What the hell is that supposed to mean?"

Viola sat down in the kitchen chair opposite Harriet, leaned her elbows against the table, and said: "Come on, you know what I mean."

"I don't know what you mean."

"That guy you met that thought you were a prostitute, Spencer Tuckerson, he's obviously Death Laser. I mean, he's got the same hairstyle, the same goatee, the same build, *really* similar voice. *And*, Death Laser appointed Spencer Tuckerson the CEO of The Ross Foundation and the head of Headless

Records. Why the hell would he do that, if they weren't the same person?" said Viola.

Harriet shrugged and mumbled:

"I don't know. Maybe he's his nephew or something?"

"Harriet they're the *same* age—*and also the same guy*!" Viola blurted out with frustration. "I mean, on some level, you *must* understand that. That's why you bought that crap CD. It's because it's something *he* made."

"No...it can't be him," said Harriet, thinking of the night she had met Spencer Tuckerson with his greasy smile and spiked dog collar. The business card he had given her was still in her purse, next to her cell phone and a tube of red lipstick. She had been meaning to throw it away.

"Oh yeah, and why not?"

"It's his aura," said Harriet, "Death Laser's aura is dark, its angry....it's got that kind of twinge to it that makes me think...he must be capable of murder. Spencer Tuckerson's aura was different. He was....*he was....*"

"He was *what?*"

"He was *sweet*, ok? I can tell because of aura's I've sensed before, clean souls, you know like children, and charity workers, they have a sort of feel about them that I can't really describe....Jesus, how do I describe it? It's like trying to explain colors to someone who was born blind. So let's say...and I'm not saying this literally because this sense is not vision...let's say that Spencer's soul was *blue* the way that baby's souls are and that Death Laser's soul is *red* the way that death row inmates are."

"Uhhuh...but, like, what if auras change?" said Viola.

"How could it change so much in such a short amount of time?" Harriet argued.

"What if it doesn't take a lot for them to change? What if they change with your mood? What's my aura feel like right now?" Viola demanded.

"Your aura is always the same," said Harriet dismissively, "And so is everybody else's...at least as far as I can tell."

"Well, there's only one way to settle this," said Viola, grinning.

"Oh, yeah, and what's that?"

"You've still got that business card he gave you, right? So call him already and put an end to this mystery, junior detective. If they really aren't the same guy and the two of them are just working together, you should be able to get them to appear in the same place, at the same time."

"That'll never work," said Harriet dismissively, "Why in the world would the two appear in the same place, at the same time, just because Justice Bitch asked them to?

"Yea, *it won't work* because they're the *same guy*," Viola grumbled, frustrated by Harriet's reluctance to accept what she felt was a fairly obvious fact.

"Ok, fine," Harriet snapped with annoyance, "If it'll shut you up, I'll call him."

"Yay."

Harriet reached into her bag and withdrew both the business card and her cell phone. Just as she was prepared to start dialing the number, however, her cell phone rang. She picked it up and answered it.

"Is this Harriet?"

"Yes, it is. Who is this?"

"Reynolds Sanderland," replied the voice on the other end of the phone.

"Oh, hey Reynolds, it's so good to hear from you after all of this time. How have you been?" Harriet inquired.

"I've been coping. Listen, Harriet, I'm sorry that I haven't bothered to contact you before this point...it's just...I wasn't sure how you would take the news from the will reading," Reynolds' voice apologized haltingly.

"Oh, you mean the thing about how you and my father were secret lovers for years and he left my fortune to you instead of me. Completely over that, thanks," said Harriet with less sincerity than she had hoped to convey.

"Hm....yes well, anyway, now I'm returning your call."

"Right...well...thanks for that. It's been such a long time...and it's so unlike you to just fuck off to who knows where without saying anything at all. And what happened with Death Laser, anyway? How did he take over The Ross Manor?" Harriet asked.

"You know it's the strangest thing. I just left the manor for a few days to go visit New Zealand, and when I returned, all of the locks had been changed and a bunch of men in black masks were swarming the place.

"They did say on the news that Death Laser took over the property," Harriet said.

"Honestly, I don't know how he did it. It was so sudden that it was almost like a magic trick. I just left for a few days...and when I came back, your father's servants had all been replaced by Death Laser's henchmen. Who, of course, promptly demanded that I leave. So, here we are."

"I'm really sorry that happened to you, Reynolds...I mean...I've known you my whole life. You're like a father to me...I mean...in a way. We should get together sometime and have lunch or something."

"That um.... ok, Harriet."

Reynolds and Harriet arranged to meet. As she spoke with Reynolds, however, Harriet could not help but feel that there was something different about him; something suspiciously off kilter. He spoke to her with a strange formality that was, in her opinion at least, strangely rehearsed sounding. *No, I must be imagining it*, she thought. *He's exactly the same as he's always been.* The conversation concluded and Harriet hung up the phone.

Viola who was still sitting across the table from Harriet, drinking a beer asked: "*So*...who was that?"

"Reynolds Sanderland," Harriet said.

"Great," said Viola, "Now call Spencer Tuckerson."

"Crap," muttered Harriet, shaking her head. "I thought you would have forgotten about that by now."

"Yea, well, I didn't," said Viola, grinning, "Go ahead. Go. Call him. Tell him you need a band!"

"Um....I don't know. I mean he's kind of a big shot now. He probably doesn't even want to talk to me now that's he's Death Laser's right hand man," replied Harriet hesitantly.

"What's a matter? You too nervous to call him?" Viola teased.

"I most certainly *am not*," Harriet fumed. The assertion had struck a nerve.

"Or are you *afraid*?"

"You're such a bitch."

"You're just saying that," said Viola, grinning. "...because you're *afraid*."

Grumbling, Harriet pulled Spencer Tuckerson's business card out of her purse and dialed the number.

"There, I called him. Are you happy now?" Harriet grumbled to Viola.

"Yes."

A scratchy male voice came over the phone and murmured: "...*Hello*?"

Harriet froze, suddenly unable to speak.

"...*Hello?*" the male voice inquired again, sounding nervous and confused.

Harriet opened her mouth but no words came out.

"What are you doing?" Viola whispered, "Talk to him!"

"Is this Spencer Tuckerson?" Harriet asked in a voice that sounded a lot more pissed off than she had intended.

"Yea, this is Spencer. What's up?"

"I don't know what you think you're fucking doing working for Death Laser. What the hell's wrong with you, anyway?" Harriet blurted out at an unintentional volume. Then she added as an afterthought: "This is Harriet, by the way."

"...Oh...um....h-hi....Harriet," Spencer sputtered nervously.

"Well, answer my question," demanded Harriet.

"He threatened me," Spencer answered timidly, "I don't know why...probably because we're about the same height and build. I think he uses me as his public face to throw people off of his trail...so that they can't figure out his real identity so easily."

"...I guess that makes sense," Harriet muttered in reply, "But you still should have told him *no*."

"God...I don't know Harriet...he was talking about murdering my mom and brothers. I'm not strong, you know. I just find it easier to do whatever he says.

"Ok. Fine. Whatever. I guess that makes sense. Anyway, I'm calling because I need a band," Harriet lied.

This bit of information made Spencer perk up immediately: "Oh? Really? *Cool.*"

"Yea, so I was hoping that I could get you and Death Laser to play at the art museum."

"Weird and dumb request," Viola commented.

Harriet waved the comment off and ignored her.

"So how about it? You and Death Laser, you're both musicians, right? Play the art museum?"

"Um...he kind of doesn't do those kind of public appearances," said Spencer hesitantly. "But I do. I'll play at the art museum. I won't even charge anything. It's free. For my special lady."

"You mean your *special ed* lady," Viola groaned.

"Viola, shut up," Harriet whispered.

"Heheh..heh...."

"Great. Then I can expect to see you there?" Harriet inquired of Spencer.

"Yeah. Absolutely."

Harriet thought up a lie quickly. There was currently no event scheduled at the art museum but she could easily schedule one after the fact.

"There'll be an event at the art museum around 6 p.m. next Sunday. Can you make it?"

"Sure."

"Harriet, what are you doing?" Viola whispered.

Harriet ignored Spencer as he began rattling off a long list of musical instruments that he knew how to play and turned toward Viola, whispering: I'll invite him to perform and then challenge Death Laser to a duel at the same time and place. If one of them doesn't show up, I'll have to assume that they're the same person."

"Because both of them have been dying to get their hands on you," finished Viola.

"Exactly," whispered Harriet in reply. "*And*...if I take Gary and maybe make out with him a little bit in front of Spencer..."

"Harriet, you're talking crazy," Viola interjected quietly.

"If I do that...and Spencer really is Death Laser...it might provoke him into revealing his true identity."

"And by true identity, of course, you mean, the same guy but wearing a cape and a mask."

"Maybe. We'll see," whispered Harriet.

"....Harriet? I feel like you're ignoring me..." Spencer's voice murmured over the phone.

"No, no, of course not," said Harriet dismissively. "I definitely heard all of those things you just said. What were they again?"

"Uh...just....what kind of a performance were you looking for? I play the piano, the guitar, obviously, the drums, French horn, saxophone, flute, accordion, sitar, bagpipes, tuba, ukulele–"

Harriet strummed her fingers against the kitchen table as Spencer listed what must have been every instrument in existence and then rolled her eyes.

"Recorder, banjo, bongos, violin–"

"That's perfect Harriet interrupted, not sounding at all impressed. "Play the violin. Can you play classical?"

"Yes."

"Good. Show up on time. Play Mozart. Wear a tuxedo. I'll write you a nice check afterwards," Harriet informed him briskly.

"Heheheh...heh...ok," Spencer chuckled.

Harriet hung up the phone.

"You know it's always nice to say goodbye before you do that," said Viola.

"Yeah, yeah," Harriet muttered, waving a hand dismissively. "Hey, Viola, how do you challenge a villain to a duel?"

Viola stood up and walked back over to the fridge, opened it, looked inside, and then closed it again.

"Viola?"

"Um...you can do it. It's kind of an old tradition in this city. Benjamin knows about that kind of thing. Let me call him."

Viola grabbed her cell phone off of the kitchen counter and dialed Benjamin's number. She waited a few seconds and then said to Harriet: "Answering machine. Let me call Lilly."

Viola dialed Lilly's number.

"Hi, Lilly. It's Viola. Can I talk to you for a minute?"

Lilly appeared in the kitchen, a few inches in front of where Viola was standing. Her white hair floated around her like a halo for a moment and then drifted slowly down to her shoulders.

"What?" Lilly whispered.

Viola looked up from her phone and over at Lilly.

"How do you challenge a villain to a duel?" Viola asked.

"Oh, that's easy. You just go to a place they hang out and make an official announcement. In this city, The Black Hatchet is the place to do it. Just tell the bartender who you are, who you want to fight, and when, then he'll pass the message along to the guy you're looking for. It works because, if he doesn't show up, the other villains will think that it's because he's scared and he'll lose some of his villain cred on the street, or so I've heard," whispered Lilly.

Harriet stood up: "Oh my God, that's perfect!" she said,

grinning. "He'll have to show up. Lilly, where's the Black Hatchet? Can you take me there?"

"Yea, absolutely," Lilly whispered, "I go there with Benjamin all of the time."

"All of the time, huh? But he's not invisible like you, so how does *he* sneak around?" Harriet asked.

"He goes as his villain alter ego, Von Dali," whispered Lilly, the corners of her pale lips curling slightly.

"...*Huh*..." Harriet murmured suspiciously. She still did not trust Benjamin. Every time she saw him she was overcome by the stench of his rotting aura as it closed in around her. She also did not care for his personality much, or rather what little she knew of his personality; his suspicion of her; his haughty air of superiority.

"It's not a real alter ego, though. It's just Benjamin in a different costume," Lilly explained, still grinning. "We pretend sometimes. And also, it's good for being undercover."

Chapter 48:
The Black Hatchet

The next day, Harriet met Lilly and Benjamin outside of the art museum. Usually when she saw them, they were in their hero costumes, but today, they were wearing regular clothes. Lilly was dressed plainly with a white t-shirt and torn jeans. Her white hair was plaited into a long braid. Benjamin wore a loose black t-shirt, dark jeans, and a black backpack slung over one shoulder. He had his arm around Lilly who smiled up at him shyly from time to time. It was strange to Harriet, seeing the two this way. They looked like any ordinary couple as they walked up the marble steps, which lead up to the art museum's entrance.

Having just finished a long day of curating, Harriet was dressed formally in heels, a knee-length black shirt, and a white button-down blouse. She waved hello to Lilly and Benjamin. Then, they greeted her and Lilly whispered:

"If we're going to The Black Hatchet...then you can't wear clothes that people might recognize. Also, you should cover your face."

"Since you've been on TV so much, a simple mask probably won't be enough to stop them from recognizing you as Justice Bitch," said Benjamin. He spoke in the stilted, pragmatic way of a man being forced to do something against his wishes at the bequest of his girlfriend.

It's killing you that you can't say what you really think of me out loud. Isn't it, Benjamin? Harriet thought as the stench of Benjamin's corrupted aura enveloped her, drowning out all surrounding signals.

Benjamin took off his backpack and handed it to Harriet.

"Go into the restroom and change into this," he instructed in the same stilted, pragmatic tone. "It should protect your identity when we go in there."

Harriet went back into the art museum with the

backpack, entered a stall in the public restroom, and then unzipped the bag. There was a lot of black fabric smooshed inside. Harriet pulled the fabric out slowly, smoothed it out with her hands, and stared at it incredulously for a moment. The costume that Benjamin had provided her was a large black burka. Harriet put the burka over her head and squinted. Staring through the black mesh that now covered her eyes would take some getting used to.

The Black Hatchet was located in a narrow alley filled with trashcans. Its entrance was a narrow, rusty door that did not appear as though it should lead to any sort of a business or formal establishment. It was the kind of door that aught to have belonged to an aging crackhead's shithole of an apartment. Benjamin's car rolled to a stop outside the alleyway. Lilly vanished. Though Harriet could no longer see her, she could still sense her aura and Harriet knew that Lilly was still walking with them, though the ghostly woman remained invisible. Harriet exited the car, covered by the black burka.

Harriet glanced back at Benjamin, and, through a network of black mesh, saw that he wore no disguise. Instead, Benjamin approached the entrance of the shady establishment as himself. This made Harriet very suspicious.

Through the burka, Harriet watched Benjamin with distrust. Why did he not feel the need to protect his own identity? Why did he seem so comfortable showing his face in a place like this?

Benjamin walked up a short stretch of broken cement steps to the narrow, rusted door and knocked seven times. A flap in the door popped open and a pair of eyes peered out.

"What'da you want?" the eyes behind the door asked with the gruff voice of a husky goon.

"Money, blood, and booze," Benjamin replied robotically.

The door opened with a slow creak, revealing a dark and crowded room. As Harriet followed Benjamin and Lilly inside, a disorienting torrent of corrupt auras hit her like a tidal wave.

Inside, the walls were lined with dilapidated tables and mismatched chairs. A floor made of dirty and broken cement was littered by mostly male villains wearing cheap costumes, standing with beers in their hands, and yelling, or jeering at two men who fought in a cage at the center of the bar. Inside of the cage, a muscular man dressed as a shark, roared and charged at his opponent with superhuman speed. He lifted the plastic shark mask, opened his mouth, and shot a yellow laser beam at his opponent. The opponent, a skinny man, dressed in jeans, a t-shirt, and a blue and white luchador's mask, grabbed the laser beam out of the air. The laser's yellow light gathered in a growing ball between his hands and then he threw it back, blasting a hole in the shark man's grey tank top, leaving his muscular pecks burnt, bloody, and visible to the jeering crowd.

Benjamin maneuvered his way through the crowd and got to the back wall of the bar where there was a long counter. A skinny, scruffy man, wearing an eye patch, stood behind the counter, cleaning a glass with a dirty rag. The shelf behind him was covered in a chaotic array of alcoholic beverages, poisons, restraints, and devices of torture. Harriet surveyed the shelf curiously. There were a disturbing array of sharp metal things that she did not understand on display. They had price tags on them but she could not read them well through the mesh of the burka.

Benjamin slammed a fifty down on the table in front of the bartender.

"Put fifty on Shark Attack," he said.

The bartender took the fifty and said with fondness and respect:

"Hey, Von Dali, how's your dad doin' these days?"

"He's doing good. Just got back from a long vacation where he turned island natives into bread statues and then fed them to the seagulls."

The bartender laughed heartily.

"...Well, that sounds like your dad! Have a drink on me, and if you see Vore Whore...tell 'er she still owes me 50 bucks for The Human Parking Meter v. Snow Globe fight last Saturday."

"Yea, I'll let her know," said Benjamin, taking a beer from the bartender. He nudged Harriet with his shoulder and then whispered: "Tell him what you came for."

"Um...right....excuse me?" Harriet inquired of the bartender.

The bartender turned toward her as though seeing her for the first time.

"Allah akbar," the Bartender greeted with a condescending sneer.

"Don't mock my religion, you fucking dick," Harriet muttered in reply, "I came for two things. First, like some really good restraints. My nemesis is *ridiculous* when it comes to getting out of handcuffs, well....and also in every other way. Anyway, I need something better. Second, I want to officially challenge another villain to a fight."

"Whoa, whoa, whoa, slow down there, sweetheart. What was that first thing you wanted?"

"Restraints," Harriet repeated with a frustrated snarl. Being called "sweetheart" never failed to piss her off.

"I think I've got the thing you're looking for," the bartender said. He walked over to the shelf and picked something up, then, brought it over to the counter.

Harriet looked at the thing. It was a pair of thick, heavy manacles, connected by a short, solid bar.

"These are made of solid steel. They'll be useless against most types of super strength but any hero without super strength won't be able to get out of them, even if they're good at escaping from restraints," said the bartender. He pointed to a tiny metal flap in the restraints, which he unlocked with a key, underneath was a small computer screen, complete with a keyboard too miniscule to be manipulated by fingers. "To open it, you need both a key and a 24 digit access code that you have to dial with a tooth pick or a sharp pencil. Getting the code wrong will cause the restraints to administer a painful electric shock. Opening the hatch on the computer screen without getting the access code right within twenty minutes, will cause the hatch to close itself back up and relock. The wearer will then receive a painful electric shock. *And* since you're a friend of my pal, Von Dali, I'll throw in the ankle restraints for free."

"That's perfect," said Harriet. In her mind's eye she imagined Death Laser attempt to pick the lock on the wrist restraints and then get a surprise electric shock. The image filled her with more joy than she dare consciously acknowledge. "I'll take it."

The bartender grabbed a second pair of large, thick manacles, this one, connected by a longer steel chain and put them down on the counter. Harriet handed him a wad of money, then, slipped the restraints into the sleeve of her burka.

By now, Benjamin had wandered away. Harriet spotted him in the distance, yelling at the two superhumans in the cage as they continued to fight. He brandished the drink in his hand, laughing as, within the cage, Shark Attack charged at his skinny opponent, headfirst. The opponent was hit in the chest and he flew backwards against the bars of the cage, spitting up blood. Harriet could not help but feel that Benjamin looked more at home in this place than he ever had fighting along side Viola's rag tag band of vigilantes.

"So what was the other thing you wanted, again?" the bartender inquired of Harriet.

Harriet tore her gaze away from Benjamin and turned back toward the bartender.

"Right. So, I've heard that you can issue a challenge against another superhuman here," said Harriet to the bartender.

"Yup. In Propopolous, this is the place to do it," said

the Bartender, "Who are you and who do you wish to challenge?"

"My name....um.....uh..." Harriet fumbled for a moment, trying as she attempted to come up with a fake villain name. "...Is...is...*Lady Shade*...and I want to challenge Death Laser...at the art museum at 6 p.m. next Friday."

The bartender laughed.

"You can't be serious," he said.

"I am."

"Death Laser will destroy you. The last guy stupid enough to try and make a name for himself by challenging Death Laser got fucked up so bad that no body else wanted to try."

"*Really?*" Harriet responded, intrigued.

"But if you think you can do better, by all means, Lady Shade, it's your funeral. I'll make sure he gets the message right away," the Bartender said, and then he walked off to speak with a different customer.

"Lilly?" Harriet whispered as soon as the bartender was out of earshot.

"Yea?" Lilly whispered back. Though Harriet could not see her, she could sense her presence, a mere two feet or so from her left.

"Let's get out of here," Harriet said.

"Ok."

Chapter 49:
The Apple and the Tree

In the car, on the way back from The Black Hatchet, Harriet sat in the back seat and watched Lilly fiddle with the knobs on the radio and air conditioner. Every once in awhile, the ghostly wisp of a woman, paused to gaze over at Benjamin with a look of lust drunk admiration.

Harriet fiddled with the restraints that she had purchased from the villain bar. Then, she skimmed the instruction booklet that had come with it for information on how to program the 24 digit access code.

After awhile, Benjamin pulled over in a gas station parking lot. Lilly got out of the car to use the restroom. Now, Benjamin and Harriet were alone in the car. The awkward silence, which resulted, tempted Harriet to speak her mind.

"I knew there was something off about you," said Harriet to Benjamin suspiciously. Leaning the front half of her body into the space between the two front seats, she turned her head toward the driver's seat to stare him down. "Your father is The Crunchy Toast Muncher."

"That's right," answered Benjamin bluntly, narrowing his eyes with distaste. He glared back, unwilling to flinch away from her vicious stare.

"Does Viola know?"

"It's not a secret."

"Let me guess. Your alter ego's not an alter ego at all. Von Dali's your true identity and you're a double agent, working to undermine the super trendy action buds," Harriet accused. "Viola's too naïve to see it doesn't mean that I'm not. I bet you're just waiting for the perfect opportunity to betray Viola and The Hottie Action Squad and hand us all over to your pals down at the Black Hatchet."

"No actually, Von Dali *was* my true identity. And I would *never* betray Viola. She saw something in me when no one else could. She *saved* me," Benjamin responded, now sounding furious. "I keep my mouth shut around the other team members because I know they won't listen, but that doesn't mean that I don't know what a massive liability you really are. You want to know what I really think?"

"Not really."

"I think that you're a massive bitch. A vapid, self-absorbed, narcissist, with a violent hair trigger, and no redeeming qualities what-so-ever. You think you know everything, don't you? Well, guess what, you don't know *anything*. Because, guess what. I'd die before I let anyone hurt Viola.....*including you*. You think you know me? Well, guess what, bitch. You don't know me. You don't know anything about me. I'm done with that villain shit. I'm reformed."

"Eat shit and die," Harriet spat back.

"You should get out of here, Harriet. The team is really better off without you."

"You're just trying to get rid of me because you know that I'm the only one around who sees through all of your 'reformed' bullshit. But guess what, asshole? I'm watching you."

"And I'm watching *you*," Benjamin echoed back

The car was silent for a moment except for the buzz of the air conditioner. The image of an entire art museum transformed into rotting rectangles of bread invaded Harriet's mind. The image filled her with rage.

"...I knew it. I knew there was something wrong with you. Crunchy Toast Muncher is your father," Harriet said, after awhile, when at long last her anger became too intense to not express in words.

"No. Crunchy Toast Muncher *was* my father. He was also a violent, vindictive, abusive sociopath. As a form of punishment, he turned the family dog into a loaf of bred and then made me *eat* him. So yea, Crunchy Toast Muncher *was* my father. But I'm nothing like him."

"Well, you know what they say about the apple and the tree," Harriet mused darkly as Lilly appeared in the passenger seat of the car.

After Lilly's return, both Benjamin and Harriet fell silent, and as they always did in the presence of witnesses, pretended that there existed no conflict between them.

Chapter 50:
Museum Heist

The rest of the week passed without consequence. Harriet spent her days in the art museum, either curetting or bored and day dreaming of a time in her life when she had not been required to work. At times when the museum was empty and there was nothing left for her to do, she sat behind her desk and stared at the gilded, arched ceiling, remembering a time when she had gone to art auctions with her father, thoughtlessly bidding millions on master pieces to be displayed in the manor.

In the evenings, Harriet visited fancy restaurants, malls, and department stores with Gary. This invariably led to Harriet buying a lot of high-end clothes, shoes, makeup, handbags, soaps, and perfumes. Knowing that he would be rewarded with sex, Gary paid for everything with swift and predictable compliance.

After dinner and shopping, Harriet always brought Gary back to the guest room in Viola's apartment. Here, she would lay naked as Gary climbed on top of her and briskly crammed his genitals inside of hers. Gary was an intelligent, sensible, pragmatic man. However, he was in no way creative. He made love the way that he did everything else in his life: with swift and predictable efficiency. Gary had no kinks and preferred the missionary position. He did not like it when Harriet moved during sex because she had super strength and he was a normal human susceptible to being accidentally bruised and bloodied by her thrusting hips, grasping hands, and changing positions. So, Harriet got used to laying still like a doll and doing nothing. She closed her eyes and listened to him breathe, thinking about what she had recently purchased with his money. What shoes would go best with what dress? What dresses had not yet been accidentally ripped? Which shoes had not yet been accidentally snapped at the heels? Would she need new dresses and shoes to match her newest outfit? Should she wear the diamond necklace with the new outfit, or the pearls?

As her scheduled duel with Death Laser approached, Harriet arranged an event at the art museum to coincide with it. Maxwell Turbish, well known folk artist from Propopolous, agreed to make an appearance at the predetermined time. It had not been hard to get him to agree as, in life, Harriet's father had been a connoisseur of expensive art pieces and this had earned him many connections amongst Propopolous' artistic elite.

Harriet had posters printed to advertise the event. Later she purchased refreshments and wine, then, arranged them attractively on a table in the room where Turbish's new exhibit would be displayed. Afterwards, she called everyone she knew (except for Benjamin) and forcefully insisted that they come support the arts by attending this event.

The morning before the event, Harriet dressed herself in a black dress with large white buttons and a white waist sash. She paired the dress with white heels, pearl earrings, and a short pearl necklace, then, finished the ensemble with dark, red lipstick, black, smoky eye shadow, and a white ribbon in her hair. Finally satisfied with her appearance, Harriet left the apartment and made her way to the museum. She kept her hero costume folded up in her small, extremely expensive, black handbag, just incase it would be needed.

When she arrived at the art museum, Spencer was already there, sitting on the marble steps outside with his violin in his lap. He was wearing a tuxedo that looked strangely familiar and playing the instrumental from *The Devil went Down to Georgia*.

He stopped playing as Harriet approached him and his eyes got big, either from lust or from terror.

"Spencer," she said, "You're two hours early."

Spencer stood up awkwardly, fumbling with the bow of his violin as he did so.

"Heheheh...heh...*yea*," he chuckled with an awkward

sigh. Then, he blushed and added quickly. "But I uh-I-I could stay out here until you need me-if I'm bothering you."

Harriet thought about this for a moment. If Spencer was actually Death Laser's secret identity and she left him outside, then he could easily change into his costume, run inside, and then pretend like Death Laser had shoved Spencer into a river or something, thereby retaining the illusion that he was, in fact, two people.

Harriet sighed and said: "No, you're not bothering me, Spencer. Please, come inside."

Harriet unlocked the front door of the museum and stepped inside. Spencer followed her. She watched him carefully as he walked around the room, observing Turbish's paintings and sculptures with a mixture of whimsical delight and disgusted incredulity. He stood in front of the largest painting for a long time, and then, having determined what he thought of the collection, Spencer slouched, put his hands in the pockets of his black slacks, and said: "So this guy piles a bunch of hardened shit onto stands and then smears a bunch of shit onto canvases. And then...*sells it to rich people for millions of dollars?* Now *this guy* has got some *balls.*"

"These are guano paintings inspired by native African bowls and huts," Harriet corrected with irritation.

"This is literally crap," said Spencer, grinning.

"*You're* literally crap."

"No, I'm *figuratively* crap. The guano paintings are literally crap. Why are they worth money? Because some rich guy says they are?"

"*Yes,*" said Harriet, "So, shut up."

"Hey, I'm just kidding. I'm sure it's all great," said Spencer with a dismissive wave of his black-finger-nailed hand. Then, he wandered into another exhibit. Harriet followed him; determined to keep her eyes on him; determined to know, once and for all, if he was really Death Laser.

"You know, I painted a picture like that once when I

was like 4 years old with finger paints in preschool," Spencer said, as he stared at a canvas covered in sloppy green and red stripes.

"That's a priceless Jackson Pollock, you trailer trash ignoramus."

"Hey, the thingy underneath says he painted this with his penis. So if I were to whip my dick out and dunk it in some paint, and then smear it all over a canvas, would you give me a million dollars for it?"

"Your dick is not worth as much as Jackson Pollock's," Harriet said.

"Aw, darn."

Harriet glanced up at the clock on the wall, above her desk. The seconds ticked by and every second she spent alone with Spencer, waiting for the arrival of Death Laser, made her more and more nervous.

"But then if a took a crap and then let it harden into some type of a shape, could I sell that for a million dollars?" Spencer asked, squinting at the Jackson Pollock and then turning his head slightly.

"No, Spencer."

"*Well*, you are the expert on these types of things."

"But then–"

"Spencer, if you think that shit and dicks are funny, it's only because you're a fucking child."

"Because if I was an adult, I would think that shit and dicks are artistic," said Spencer.

"Exactly," said Harriet, "Now, you understand."

Harriet stormed back into the main exhibit, feeling one of her heels crack as she brought her foot down with too much force. She swore under her breath and then went to the locked drawer of her desk, where she kept extra shoes incase of an emergency. She fumbled clumsily through a pile of expensive heels and found a pair of unbroken white heels with little white bows on them, which she put on. Then, she dumped the broken heels in the drawer and slammed the door shut with too much force, causing the metal desk to fold in slightly. Harriet swore under her breath again.

"You ok?" Spencer asked her.

Harriet straightened up, and realizing that Spencer had been watching her, became alarmed.

"Yes, perfect."

"Do you always change your shoes, when you're at work?"

"I just thought about it and decided that these matched my outfit better," said Harriet.

"Heh heh heh..."

"What are *you* giggling at?"

"Nothing."

"I'm going to fix the refreshment table," said Harriet.

"Can I help?"

"No, that's fine. Just play with your violin or something while you wait," said Harriet. And then, as an after thought, she added: "Don't touch anything."

Harriet began laying out bricks of cheese and meat on tooth picks. Spencer leaned against a nearby wall and played a random melody on his violin. The melody became complicated and fast quickly and Harriet could tell that he was trying to impress her by demonstrating his skill. If she was being completely honest with herself, it was working.

"You're really good at that," Harriet said as she placed a couple of Champaign bottles on the refreshment table.

"Aw, thank you, Harriet," Spencer said. He arched an eyebrow, and then, increased the speed of his instrumental still.

There was a knock on the door. Harriet walked over to it and opened it. Gary was standing on the other side, wearing a grey, three-piece suit, a red tie, and a wooden expression.

"Gary," Harriet said, "*Finally*."

"Hello, Harriet," Gary greeted her.

Harriet pulled him inside.

"Dance with me," she said.

"Um...ok?" Gary muttered incredulously, "—*Woah!*"

Harriet pulled him along as Spencer played. Gary's initial reluctance to dance, prompted Harriet to lead, and soon her grip on Gary's hand grew so tight that he could not have pulled away from her if he wanted to.

"Listen, Harriet...." Gary murmured timidly.

Harriet stifled his words by pressing her lips against his and then forcing her tongue into his mouth. This made Spencer's instrumental grow more angry and rampant.

"Shut up and dance," Harriet whispered sensuously to Gary as she pulled him along like a rag doll.

As they danced, Spencer's instrumental grew angrier and angrier. People began to arrive for the event. Viola, Lilly, and a ketchup-stained Finsveld stood by one of the larger canvases, conversing with Mr. Samson, another employee of the museum. Harriet paid no attention to them. She was enraptured in the moment; staring into the reflective glare of Gary's large glasses. Soon, others joined the dance. As all of this was happening, Spencer's melody grew faster and faster and angrier and angrier.

"Harriet, *listen!*" Gary muttered in a desperate voice.

Harriet leaned in to silence him with another kiss but this time, Gary jerked his head away to avoid her.

There was an ugly squealing *snap* as Spencer drew the bow of his violin so hard that all of its strings broke at once.

"Uh...shit...all of the strings on my bow broke," Spencer announced to the growing crowd. "Let me just go back to my car and go get another one."

Spencer slouched and stomped out of the museum. The crowd applauded for him as he left.

After he was gone and the applause had died down, Gary said quickly:

"Listen, Harriet...um...uh...there's no easy way to say this..."

"*What?*" Harriet inquired impatiently.

"I just....I don't think we should date anymore."

"And *why the hell not*?" demanded Harriet with a mixture of outrage and incredulity. She released him from her grip and put her hands on her hips, glaring at him as he fumbled for words.

"It's just...you're really bossy...and you're always asking me to buy you stuff...and I have these bruises on my arms," Gary rolled up one of his sleeves to show her large, ugly, purple and black bruise that she had put there.

"I told you, that *wasn't on purpose*," Harriet said with some frustration.

"Yes, well, I know, Harriet but even so...it's a lot to deal with. I think I need to be with a woman who can't kick my ass, maybe someone less pushy; more agreeable. I'm sorry, Harriet, I'm just not that into you. I hope that we can still be friends," said Gary.

Harriet glanced around, in search of people she knew who might have witnessed the humiliation of Gary's rejection, but it seemed that The Sexy Rad Super Pals were no longer present at the exhibition. They must have gotten bored at some point during the long dance and left.

"Yea, of course," murmured Harriet awkwardly, she stumbled away, slightly dizzy from the long dance, and disoriented from the surprise rejection.

"I should probably leave," said Gary apologetically.

"Yeah, that's probably a good idea," said Harriet.

Harriet's eyes filled with tears and her vision blurred. She blinked the tears away, realizing as she did so that Gary had vanished into the crowd. Turbish had arrived and was now speaking to the crowd about his work. Harriet stood there politely with a drink in her hand and pretended to listen, with a fake smile plastered on her face. Though Gary had been very polite about the whole ending the relationship thing, she could not help but feel like discarded garbage.

"To me, *The Sun Rises*, represents a feeling of continuality, of community, and of being whole, but also of being broken, of being discontinuous, of being disconnected, of being dead and of being alive, of being awake or of a being in a deep dreamless sleep." Turbish said to the crowd of museum goers. He was a portly, middle-aged man, with a bald, shiny head and a moustache. A group of well dressed people had gathered in a circle around him, holding cheese cubes on tooth picks and plastic wine glasses full of Champaign. They watched him politely, as he spoke, sometimes breaking their gaze to drift around the exhibit, observing the guano paintings and statues.

Suddenly, the front entrance of the museum burst open and Death Laser stepped inside. His silhouette was tall and skinny, back lit against a flash of lightening. A sudden windstorm had kicked up, moving his black cape like a billowing flag, as a swarm of henchmen in black ski masks stormed into the building, holding rifles. The museum goers screamed. Hors d'oeuvres and plastic wine glasses where discarded on the floor as they fled.

A pair of masked henchmen cornered Turbish and a group of museum goers, near the edge of the exhibit, where a large guano statue of a man with erect genitalia doing a summersault was positioned. Harriet and a handful of other well dressed museum goers where driven against the opposite wall by four of five masked men, wielding pistols. Helpless to attack without revealing her superhuman ability, Harriet watched, with her back pressed against the wall, and a masked man pointing a gun in her face, as Death Laser strode to the center of the room, and toppled a guano statue of a horse with a carrot in its mouth, then, stepped atop the marble pedestal, where the art had previously been displayed. Having found for himself a suitable stage, Death Laser pronounced his intention:

"Hehehecheh...heh. I've come to do battle with a villain named Lady Shade, who was foolish enough to challenge me! Reveal yourself, Lady Shade, so that I might destroy you and then be on my way!"

Harriet inhaled deeply, and continued to watch Death Laser as he stood atop the marble pillar. Pieces of the guano statue he had displaced lay scattered in chunks along the white, marble floor. Seeing such a valuable piece of art be destroyed by Death Laser's wanton act of vandalism made Harriet furious. She breathed slowly and clenched her fists, determined not to rush out into the fray, and recklessly reveal herself as Justice Bitch.

"I'm *waiting*," Death Laser teased with a grin. Then, he stretched his arms wide out and said: "Here I am! Come and get me! I'll even give you one free punch!"

He waited for a moment and then said:

"Going once....going twice....still no? Well it seems she's decided not to show up. ...Well, anyways...since I made the trip....heheheheh...heh...heh. I guess I'll go ahead and steal something."

Death Laser leapt off of the pillar and walked over to a large canvas with different shades of brown and red streaked across it in large broad strokes. Harriet knew, from her background in fine art that this painting was *Sunset Forever Ending*. Largely considered Turbish's masterwork, *Sunset Forever Ending* was easily the most expensive painting in the collection.

"Hmm.....yup," said Death Laser as he leaned close to the painting, pretending to be examining it. He turned his head slightly and then said: "I'm gonna steal it."

With those words, Death Laser forcefully pulled the framed canvas off of the wall. It made a snapping noise and the frame cracked as he removed it, trailing pieces of wire. Painting in hand, Death Laser turned with a smirk and a twirl of his long black cape, then, exited the art museum. The masked henchmen followed in a line.

The henchmen who had been guarding the museum goers on Harriet's side of the room, retreated to the exit of the museum, along with Death Laser and the rest of his goons. Now unencumbered, Harriet bounded to the lady's room amidst a swarm of confused and frightened people, who were darting in various directions, trying to escape from the building, or dodging to find a hiding place incase of the villain's return. Harriet dodged into one of the stalls in the lady's room and quickly changed into her costume, then, ran back out into the chaos.

She ran out of the museum entrance and down the marble stairway, leading to the parking lot, just in time to see Death Laser carelessly toss the priceless painting into the backseat of a limousine. He stopped to turn around and flash Harriet both of his middle fingers, before disappearing into the back of the limousine himself. Harriet screamed and bounded toward the car, her fists clenched tightly in anticipation of ripping the mask off of Death Laser and then bloodying his stupid face.

The engine of the limousine kicked on and then it started to move as Harriet leapt onto the roof. With a loud *clank*, her powerful body dented the vehicle's metal roof with an impression of her knees and palms. The limousine accelerated, swerving around a corner in what was likely an attempt to knock Harriet off. Now the city was racing by in streaks of light and color. Harriet could feel herself sliding off.

With much force, Harriet dug her fingers into the metal roof of the vehicle. Her fingertips sank down as though moving against solid butter, and she hooked her nails underneath, latching on. The tires of the limousine squealed as it took another sharp turn. Harriet felt dizzy. The car turned again, as she clumsily ripped a chunk of the car's roof off and then jumped inside.

She stumbled and fell on her face, against the fine red carpet. Four or five masked henchmen gathered around her, raised their guns and then pointed them at her head as she struggled to rise to her feet. Harriet heard the click of safeties being released. Then, winced, in anticipation of having her head blown off. She heard Death Laser's voice as he strode toward her, but this time it was not jovial or teasing as she had come to expect. Instead, his voice was *angry*, as she had never heard it before:

"Lower the guns!...*Drop the fucking guns!*"

The henchmen hesitated, as Harriet stood and kept their guns aimed at her head, fearful that she might, at any moment, jump on them and rip their heads off.

"I said, *drop your fucking weapons!*" Death Laser shouted, "Back the fuck off!"

Slowly and with much reluctance, the henchmen lowered their guns and stepped backward.

"This is *my* fight," He said with a smirk, and then he ran at Harriet, with raised fists and glowing red eyes.

Harriet blocked his fists with her forearm. Though he hit her with his full power, she felt little more than an irritating tap. Given her superhuman strength, it would have been easy to overpower Death Laser and beat his face bloody until he surrendered, or simply reach out and nonchalantly snap all of his limps in half. He aimed a laser at her head and she dodged it, as she did so, thinking of Super Annoyo and his pending personal injury suit against her. Perhaps that was why Death Laser wanted to fight her himself. Perhaps he was fishing for a personal injury suit.

Death Laser shot another pair of crimson laser beams in her direction, she ducked to avoid them and they shot through the sound proof window, which separated the driver from the back seat of the limousine. The glass shattered and the driver screamed as one of the laser beams hit his right hand, instantly reducing his middle and index fingers to a bloody mush. The vehicle swerved, as the driver continued to shriek in agony. The second laser beam hit the windshield, radiating a wave of blinding spider web cracks. Then, the vehicle veered off of the road, and over a steep ledge into the ocean.

Chapter 51:
Crime and Punishment

The vehicle was sinking slowly, ocean water seeping in through the cracks in the doors. The masked driver was screaming and weeping as he held his bleeding, mutilated hand tightly. Death Laser seemed to have frozen as though from shock. His distraught expression irritated Harriet. Did he not know that something like this might happen?

"Nice going, *idiot!*" Harriet yelled at Death Laser in frustration. She gave him a shove that was little more than a tap of her palms against his shoulders and he stumbled backward. "Now, you're going to *kill us all!*"

"H...hariet...I..." Death Laser stuttered in response. Harriet ignored him and watched the henchmen struggle to open the doors of the vehicle. The water was up to her knees now.

"....Shit...shit...what now? What now?" Harriet murmured, glancing around the sinking limousine. She spotted several masked men, panicking and bumping into each other as they struggled to find an exit. "Right! Got to save the henchmen!"

Harriet sloshed across the limousine and punched out the safety glass with her fists, then, ripped off a pair of doors with both hands.

"Go, *go!* You can swim, right? Swim to shore!" she shouted at the henchmen.

Silently, the uninjured henchmen followed this instruction, exiting through the gaping hole in the side of the vehicle as it gushed water. It was sinking faster now, and the water was just above Harriet's waist.

Death Laser ripped his cape off and stumbled toward the injured henchman, who was still screaming and clutching his bloody hand.

"What the hell are you doing?" Harriet screamed at him, "He's done for! Leave him, or you're going to drown!"

Death Laser ignored Harriet and stumbled toward the injured henchman. Then, put an arm around his shoulders and dragged him toward the seeping hole that Harriet had torn in the side of the vehicle. Seeing how Death Laser struggled against the man's weight, Harriet sloshed forward, and picked the injured man up. He was quite large but she carried him easily. The water was closing in on her neck now. She sucked in air and ducked underwater, moving through the sinking hole in the side of the vehicle.

For awhile, she swam. Clutching the injured man with one arm, she moved, more or less blindly through the red water; salt stinging her eyes; waves splashing over her head. For an instant, she could see the blurry shore line in the distance. She closed her eyes and moved toward it, her left hand stretching in front of her as she moved, eager to touch land.

She gasped and choked as the water became more shallow; sand brushed her stomach. And she released the weeping, injured man. He crawled out onto the beach, choking and leaving a trail of blood behind him as he moved. Harriet stood and swiped a mop of soggy hair out of her face. Death Laser emerged from the water, damp clothes sticking to the contours of his skinny, muscled body.

"J...Justice Bitch!" he stammered between gasps as he stumbled toward her. His eyes began to glow crimson. "We're not done yet!"

"Oh, we are *done*, jack ass!" Harriet yelled, shooting him a vicious glare. "I am going to rip that mask off and take you to jail and *that* is *that*!"

Without warning, Death Laser reached out and snatched the mask off of Harriet's face. She screamed and grabbed for it but he was too fast. In an instant, he was clutching it in his hand and sprinting across the sand with it, toward the distant Ross mansion.

"Oh, yea, we'll see about that!" he yelled as he was running away.

William Fredrick Ross's private beach was dark and deserted, except for a bleeding henchman, stumbling toward the distant highway. Harriet was grateful for this, because otherwise, someone might have spotted her face as she was running after Death Laser, cursing and tripping over her damp feet. He was fast and she became tired quickly, slowing to a brisk walk, as she swore under her breath that she would strangle him dead.

She stomped past rows of topiary bushes shaped like hundred dollar bills, and what used to be a gold-plated statue of her father, now replaced by a silver statue of Death Laser, wearing the same clothes that her father's statue had worn, and standing in the same pose. Harriet paused to look at the statue for a moment and cursed as she did so, overcome with a profound rage. The absurd lengths that this ridiculous villain was willing to go just to provoke her, seemed to know no limits.

Determined to retrieve her mask before she walked back to the city, Harriet made her way up the steps leading to the manor's front entrance. Panting from exhaustion, she ripped the locks out of the manor's tall wooden doors, and then, pulled them open. She was surprised to find the entrance unguarded.

Cautiously, Harriet crept through the foyer. Her damp boots, squeaking against slick, black marble. She could sense Death Laser's aura burning all around her, bright and strong, it enveloped her, like the heat of a simmering furnace. From experience, Harriet knew that this could only mean one thing: Her enemy was very close, and stood waiting for her, poised to strike.

Harriet crept into one of the hallways. Her damp boots brushed red carpet as she move slowly, breathing heavy. Her heart was pounding in her chest. Her eyes were wide and bloodshot as they searched the dark corners of this enclosed space for a crouched figure in dark clothing. The intensity of Death Laser's aura grew as she moved down the hallway and this was how she knew that she was getting closer.

She reached the door at the end of the hallway, and turned the ivory skull of its handle slowly. The door creaked open and she stepped inside.

She entered the room. It was her father's library, vast and covered from wall to ceiling in tall bookshelves. This room looked much as it had when her father was alive, with old-fashioned green sofas and dark-stained end tables set against a dark-stained hardwood floor. There were steep and elaborately carved ladders reaching up to the tallest bookshelves. The stars and the waning moon shone through the glass panels in the high arched ceiling and the row of elaborate crystal chandeliers hanging from the ceiling's center pane were lit.

Harriet strode slowly through the room, noting with some satisfaction, that, unlike much of the rest of the manor, it bore no signs of its new inhabitant's personality. The books and the furniture were just as her father had left them. The fire place at the far end of the room, which was lit, remained unaltered with its dark wood, and elaborate carvings of ivy. She looked up slightly and cringed. The large painting of her father above the fireplace was now a painting of Death Laser, wearing his mask, and one of her father's grey, pin-striped suits.

"Ugh," Harriet groaned indignantly, as she was confronted by the insulting image. In the painting, Death Laser was smirking and sitting with his arms folded. The pose was, aside from the taunting malice in the expression, identical to the one that William Fredrick Ross had assumed in the painting that *should* have been there.

"Death Laser!" Harriet shouted.

She waited for a moment, scanning the room with her eyes. She could sense that he was close.

"Death Laser, I know your here!" she shouted with frustration. "Come out and fight me!"

She waited. The room was silent for a moment and then

a door beside the fireplace creaked open and Death Laser stepped out, holding Harriet's mask in one black-finger-nailed hand. His clothes and hair had dried considerably.

"Goddamn you're slow," he said as he stepped out in front of the tall flames of the fire place. His eyes burned like lit cigarettes beneath his mask. He pointed to his hair. "Look at this. My *hair dried* while I was waiting for you to get here."

"Yea, yea. Are you going to talk or are you going to fight?" Harriet muttered.

"Heheheheh...heh...Justice Bitch....they should call you Slow as my Ass Bitch," Death Laser chuckled.

"Yea, very fucking funny," Harriet muttered sarcastically, "But I'm not here to run a marathon, am I? I'm here to take you to prison."

"Yea, good luck with that," said Death Laser confidently. He leaned against one of the dark paneled walls of the room with one arm, and grinned flippantly, showing a lot of teeth.

Harriet ran at him, aiming to pin him to the wall and cuff his hands behind his back but he moved quickly and she hit the wall hard. The wood paneling cracked under the pressure of her supernatural weight.

Death Laser tapped her on the shoulder and she turned around quickly, bounding toward him. He yelled and ran toward the opposite end of the room, where he stood hyperventilating and clutching his side, in front of a wall of books. She ran at him, aiming to pin him against the shelf and put the handcuffs on him, but just as she was about to make contact, he dodged out of the way. She hit the wall and several shelves collapsed against her weight, sending an avalanche of books cascading down upon her.

"Heheheheh....Ms. Harriet Ross, ruining your own precious mansion," Death Laser taunted.

Pinned beneath a pile of books, Harriet stared up at the ceiling, hyperventilating and disoriented. She closed her eyes and drew in breath. As she did this, Death Laser quickly squatted, lowering the cleft of his ass toward her face, and farting loudly. Harriet choked and stood up abruptly, sending books flying as she bounded toward him, overcome by rage.

"Aaaaagh! *I'll kill you!*" Harriet yelled furiously and indignantly. All thoughts of being sued for assault had been pushed clean out of her mind.

She bounded toward him, extending a hand to wrench the mask off of his face. This time, she was successful in her endeavor, her fingers closed around the mask, and she quickly yanked it off, snapping the strings that held it to the back of his head.

The mask drifted to the ground, and she stood face to face, with a surprised and cornered looking, Spencer Tuckerson. She could tell that it had not been his intention to be unmasked, because his aura shifted and his face got very red.

"It's...it's *you!*" Harriet accused.

"Um...I thought you knew," Spencer murmured, without the mask, his demeanor was considerably more reserved. He must have felt exposed without it, because he shrank away from her, as though to conceal nudity. "I thought this was our thing. Are we not doing a thing?"

"You *lied* to me," Harriet accused.

Regaining his composure, Spencer grinned nervously and said: "Is it my fault that you were so easy to fool?"

Enraged by the realization that this *idiot* had tricked her into thinking that he was two different people, Harriet screamed and ran at him with her fists raised.

His eyes lit up red and he aimed a pair of Laser beams in her direction as she approached. She swerved left to avoid them and kept running at him. He dodged out of the way before she was able to make contact and fired a second pair of lasers, missing badly. The shots hit a chandelier overhead and it fell with a tinkling *crash.* Harriet ran at him a second time, and he blasted another pair of laser beams from his eyes. This time, however, she did not react quickly enough to avoid them. They hit her in the chest sending her sprawling backward. For the first time since the accident that had killed her father and left her irreparably mutated, Harriet felt pain. Blood squirted from her body as the lasers penetrated her skin like bullets.

"Harriet? *Harriet!*"

Death Laser's voice sounded far away. She heard his feet hit the floor hard as he sprinted toward where she lay. She was just cognizant enough to recognize that he was babbling apologetically. Harriet did not listen to him. She lay still and bleeding in a pile of burned books and broken glass. *Maybe*, she thought, *...if he thinks he's killed me. He'll retreat.*

"Harriet...Are you ok?" Death Laser warbled nervously, "Just...just move your foot or something if you're ok."

Harriet laid still. She could sense Death Laser moving close to her, staring down at the seeping injury that stained the black leather against her chest and right shoulder red. He moved closer. She could sense him. His feet were just a few inches to the left of her left calf.

Seizing this opportunity, Harriet swung her left leg and, without warning, knocked his feet out from under him. His body hit the ground with a *crash*, and then she leapt on top of him, quickly securing his wrists behind his back with the handcuffs. He tried to squirm away from her, but this act of defiance was as pointless as trying to crush a boulder. She withdrew the ankle restraints from the inside of her jacket and secured his legs with them.

She released him and he stumbled away from her with his wrists bound. She watched him stagger around, attempting to remove the handcuffs as he had somehow managed before. There was just enough chain between the ankle restraints to allow him to walk in short, awkward steps, yet in his panicked, desperate state, he seemed constantly ready to stumble and fall on his face. He pulled at the restraints a few times as though confident that he could break them or wriggle out of them. A look of alarm came over him, and he pulled at the restraints quickly and frantically, unable to break free.

"Ok...so you got me," Spencer said with a bit of forced jovialness. Harriet could sense the fear beneath the facade however. His heart was beating faster. His blood pressure was elevated. His aura felt heavy and dense. Spencer forced a flippant grin and said mockingly: "So what are you going to do now? Spank me as hard as you can?" Then, he blushed deeply and chuckled: "Hehehehheh...hehhehheh....heh...."

Harriet narrowed her eyes with incredulity and said: "No, actually, if I were to spank you *as hard as I can*, I would probably liquefy the fat in your ass cheeks, crush your tail bone to powder, and sever your spine, permanently paralyzing you from the waist down. Would you like that?"

"No."

"So...*yea*. I'm taking you to prison."

Hearing this, Spencer's eyes welled up with unshed tears. He dropped to his knees. Then, hung his head and murmured: "Harriet, please. Do you know what they do to guys like me in prison?"

"Fuck you up the ass, I imagine," replied Harriet with indifference.

Spencer hung his head and bit his lip, letting out a small sob and putting a hand over his cringing face.

"Oh, quit crying you big baby. You must have known that you were going to go to prison for all of this eventually."

"Please don't send me to prison....I just....just really wanted you to like me..." Spencer sniffled.

"Well, guess what? I *don't* like you. And guess what else? I'm never gonna like you. Never, never, never, never. *NEVER*," said Harriet crossing her arms and rolling her eyes up into her head. "Never."

"...I guess I deserve that," Spencer sniffled. "I just kind of thought that maybe you weren't catching me on purpose...but I guess I was wrong. I guess it's just because you're kind of gullible and suck at being a hero."

"What the fuck did you just say to me?" Harriet growled, narrowing her eyes.

"You're gullible and you suck," Spencer summarized.

"Keep talking like that and maybe *I will* give you a spanking," Harriet warned.

"It's kind of true though," said Spencer, cheering up slightly. "I mean it was pretty obvious who I was the whole time. I mean, I just had this really small piece of plastic covering the top half of my face. Heh...heh...and I made myself the CEO of Headless Records. That should have given it away. Also...I didn't do anything with my voice really. Come to think of it....you'd have to be a real idiot to not have figured it out."

"How fucking dare you."

"I have to call them as I see them."

"*You're* the idiot," Harriet growled angrily, "Did you really think you were going to get away with running around robbing banks, and causing pandemonium wherever you go? Huh? You could have died. Idiot."

"Yea, but I didn't," said Spencer, grinning. "Instead, I became the top villain in the city, and stole this sweet mansion filled with all kinds of great rich guy stuff. Got revenge on the people that wronged me. Got a shit ton of money. *And* had your father's statue bulldozed to put a statue of myself in its place. That was fun too."

"Oh you think you're so fucking smart, don't you?" Harriet seethed hatefully.

She thought of what Gary had said at Von Crucible's art exhibition: *Fun fact, it is technically legal for a hero to administer a non-consensual disciplinary spanking to a villain in the state of California. It's completely legal as long as you do it with an open hand and don't cause any permanent damage.*

"Well, yea, actually. I do. Man, I wasn't even going to do anything with that shit smear painting from the museum. I was just going to have it burned. But I guess it's at the bottom of the ocean now. So, I'll have to just burn something else. Maybe just like another huge pile of money...but probably like...I dunno...in front of orphans or something. It's a good plan for after I escape," Spencer blathered.

Harriet glared at him. The exasperating way that he kept purposely egging her on was making her *feel*...some kind of way. Spencer remained so bold despite being captured and at her mercy. She was enraged by the very idea of him, with his defiant grin, and flippant lack of respect for everything that she took seriously. Yet, this twinge that came over her stomach was not one of repulsion, and this heat that came over her body was not one of fury or of unadulterated hatred. She advanced on him like a hungry lioness stalking her prey and he smirked nervously, his eyes growing wide with apprehension.

"You know what..." Harriet muttered threateningly. Overcome by a bizarre mixture of anger and arousal, she grabbed Spencer by the back of his shirt collar and dragged him toward a green sofa chair near the fireplace. Its upholstery was scorched and blackened in places. Likely, collateral damage caused by Spencer's eye lasers. "Shut the fuck up and take your punishment."

Harriet plopped down in the chair and threw Spencer over her knees. His heart was beating fast again. His breathing quickened. The blood rushed to his face. Harriet raised her hand high, prepared to slap his bottom. But, then, she lowered her hand slowly and gently, as she thought about the potential implications of this. *I'm really freakishly strong. If I hit him too hard. I could seriously injure him*, she thought. Then, another thought occurred to her and she grinned. For safety, she would have to be able to see what kind of damage she was doing.

She gripped the waistband of Spencer's black slacks and pulled them down slowly. His heart rate picked up and his blush deepened as she curled her fingers around the waist band of his skull-print boxers and slipped them down over the curve of his upturned behind. Now, as Harriet sat there with a Spencer in facedown in her lap, she became aware of the contours of his wiener, resting against her leg and felt a rush of sexual arousal that she was not readily willing to consciously acknowledge. She stared down at his round, white, backside and resisted the urge to run her hand over its smooth arch. Instead, the raised her hand high and prepared to smack it.

Spencer let out an involuntary whimper and stammered: "T-this is embarrassing..."

"Good. You should be embarrassed," Harriet said, "Now, shut up."

She elevated her knee, so that his bare rump was humiliatingly arched. Then, brought her hand down against his bare butt in what was little more than a forceful pat. The light tap caused him to arch his back and cry out, as a purple bruise blossomed across pale skin.

"T-that hurt a lot more than I though it would," he gasped fearfully.

Harriet raised her hand and gave him another light smack.

"*Ow!*"

"Well, if it doesn't hurt, then it's not a punishment," said Harriet and then she whacked the underside of his behind with the palm of her hand, instantly reddening it with the force of the superpowered blow.

"*Ow!* Oh god...oh god...I think I learned my lesson...please stop," Spencer whimpered.

"Yea, I don't think you have," said Harriet administering another careful slap. Spencer whimpered and bucked his legs, clenching his teeth as he blushed hard. His bottom was getting red and sore fast.

"Ow! Please! Ow! I'll be good. Ow! I'll be good...I promise," Spencer whimpered. "Please, no more...*Ow!*"

"Beg and plead all you want," Harriet said, administering a sharp smack that made Spencer cry out and kick his legs. "You're still going to get such a spanking that you won't be able to sit your ass down again for the rest of your stupid life."

"...Ok....ok...I guess I deserve that. *Ow!*" Spencer cried out as his raised behind was struck again.

"Yea, you do," said Harriet, "Now shut up and think about what you've done, you fucking fool."

"...Y-yes ma'am..."

Spencer was quiet after that, except for the occasional involuntary gasp of pain. She aimed to strike him hard enough to make him sore without damaging the tailbone or spine. Not wanting to cause any permanent damage, she let up a bit when she saw that, in places, he was bruising severely. By this point, his cherry red behind, was sore to the touch, and he cried out when it was brushed against, let alone slapped. Seeing that this beating had effectively reduced Spencer to a limp, quivering huddle with butt cheeks like a pair of heated, red tomatoes. Harriet resolved to end the punishment.

"Did you learn your lesson?" Harriet growled, administering another sharp smack that made Spencer cry out in a warbly voice.

"Yes, yes...Ow! I'll be good! Ow! I promise I'll never be bad again! Just stop hitting me please!"

Harriet raised her hand high and brought it down against Spencer's bare bottom one final time. The slap made a loud noise and elicited a howl of pain.

"Alright, then, your punishment is over," said Harriet.

She pulled his pants and underwear back up over his badly beaten ass and he shuttered as the fabric brushed his skin.

"Does this mean...d-does this mean...that I don't have to go to prison?" Spencer warbled in a voice distorted by pain.

"Oh, you're still going to prison," said Harriet matter-of-factly. "You're just going with a sore ass."

"But...but I thought..." Spencer whimpered, his voice

breaking.

"Yea, well. I don't know what *you* were thinking. But *I* was thinking...that I was going to send you to prison with a sore ass," said Harriet.

"Oh..." Spencer murmured disappointedly. Given his recent experience, he now had trouble looking her in the eye. "Ok...I guess that's fair."

"Alright, then, let's go," Harriet groaned. She grabbed him by the elbow of one of his bound arms and led him toward the exit of the library. He did not resist, but rather, trudged along behind her, like a trained animal on a leash. She led him down the hallway and into the foyer, where a flat screen television on one of the walls was buzzing quietly in the background.

Harriet put her hand on the skull-shaped handle of the manor's front entrance and turned it slowly, not wanting to rip the door in half with too much careless forcefulness.

"I've never seen anything like this in my entire life!" a female newscaster remarked in the background with much forced peppiness.

The door creaked open and Harriet swore as she was confronted by a solid wall of snow.

Through her string of swears, and violent, tile shattering stomping, the news caster could still be heard: "Everyone here, Jim, is asking the same question. What the heck happened? A winter storm *this extreme* in *California*? On *the beach*?"

"It must be the work of some winter-themed villain," the voice of a male newscaster replied. "Perhaps Snowman Stan or Mr. Ice Bro."

With her free hand Harriet tried to dig through the wall of snow in front of her. But more snow kept falling down to replace the handfuls of snow that she had displaced. The snow was melting as it spilled into the foyer and soon, Harriet found herself, somehow both drenched in freezing water and no closer to her goal of digging through to the surface. She let go of Spencer's restraints and tried digging with both hands but this also was a futile endeavor. Once released, rather than running away, Spencer merely stood there and slouched, grinning with amusement as Harriet failed time and time again to make a dent in their ice prison.

"This is craziness, Susan! Unprecedented levels of snow everywhere, throughout Propopolous city! In some places, our helicopters have observed entire skyscrapers that have been buried completely by the snow! Luckily the buildings in Propopolous city have been designed to withstand extreme, superhuman-induced weather conditions! The same technology which allows submarines to explore the deepest reaches of the ocean is preventing these buildings from collapsing and protecting the people inside, reducing the number of fatalities we see each year from god class climate threats!" The male newscaster said. He stood in front of a green screen, which pictured vast mountains of snow, being filmed live by a cameraman in a helicopter.

"It's hard to believe that there's a city under that mess, Jim!"

Harriet turned away from the television and faced Spencer, with a scowl. He grinned back at her and arched an eyebrow.

"You did this," she growled, "Didn't you?"

Spencer shrugged and replied: "I swear, I didn't."

"Hey, but don't panic folks, we've got a team of heat and fire themed heroes, hard at work, melting and evaporating the massive snow piles. The way things are going, everything should be back to normal by tomorrow morning. Just in time for you all to go back to work and summer school, ha ha ha," the female newscaster announced with a forced fake sounding laugh. Her lipstick was just a little too red, and her blond bob had the unnatural glossiness of a boxed Barbie doll under strong fluorescent lights.

"Aw, mom, do we have'ta," Spencer groaned jokingly at the woman through the TV.

The footage from the news station's helicopter now showed a couple of masked men in red leotards flying around the city and shooting flames out of their mouths at the mountains of snow, evaporating them into vapor.

"Did you hear that, tomorrow, the snow's going to be melted," Harriet muttered in Spencer's direction. "And then, I'm taking you to jail."

Harriet grabbed the chain connecting Spencer's wrist restraints and walked him down the hallway again. Spencer shuffled along without resistance.

"Hey, where are we going?" He asked after awhile.

Harriet turned the corner and entered another long hallway.

"I've got to lock you up somewhere where you can't escape until tomorrow morning."

Harriet walked past the kitchen, where a staff of celebrated cooks used to prepare meals for herself and her father. It was now strangely empty, as was the rest of the house. This made Harriet wonder how and why Spencer had gotten rid of his Henchmen and staff before tonight.

Harriet walked into the kitchen, and found the room that she had been looking for, a small pantry stocked with cans, cooking utensils, and blocks of cheese.

Not wanting to accidentally injure him, Harriet shoved Spencer into the room, with a light tap of her palms on his shoulders, which sent him stumbling forward awkwardly.

"You can sleep here," she said coldly. He turned to face her and her eyes narrowed slowly into dangerous slits.

Spencer glanced down at the hard linoleum floor and asked: "I don't even get a pillow?"

"No."

"But, Harriet..."

"No."

"...I'm getting kind of hungry..."

"Well, you can forget about me feeding you," Harriet muttered, "You can just lay there on your red baboon ass all night and think about what you've done."

"You're *really mean*. You know that?"

"Oh, shut up," Harriet grumbled and then she slammed the door shut, before ripping a kitchen island out of the tile floor. It creaked as it was broken free and she lifted it over her head before setting it back down in front of the pantry door, locking it in place.

After that, Harriet trudged through the house, observing the familiar hallways and rooms. Though much of it had been made strange by the manor's new inhabitant, painted black and dense with skeletons and hellish imagery, the place still, somehow felt like home and she was glad to be back. She walked back to the room that had been her bedroom as a child, and then as an adult after she had returned from college. The room's white walls were now black, and the large arch-shaped window, which looked out over the Ross family's private beach, was now a stained-glass tapestry of smashed-faced demons torturing sinners in hell. She stopped in front of the window for a moment and snorted with derision as she observed the largest and reddest demon at the center of the window. It was skewering a naked man through the forehead of his screaming face. Through the clearest pieces of the glass tapestry, Harriet saw what appeared to be a wall of dark compacted snow. She turned and walked past the window, toward the bed. It was a king-sized canopy, the frame of which was carved from black onyx. The bed's sheets and curtains were a dark crimson color, and looked as though they had recently been washed and pressed.

Harriet kicked off her long, black boots, and then, removed her long black coat, which she folded and placed on the onyx cabinet. As she did this, she stared at herself in the circular mirror, which was built into the back of the cabinet. A grim-faced, wild-haired woman in black stared back at her. In that moment, she could not help but feel that she fit the scenery perfectly. The memory of her nemesis on the night that they had met flashed in her mind.

"But if I was a villain, you would spank me for free?"
He had said, the metal spikes of his black leather dog collar
glinting silver under the glowing streetlights.

"You're not a villain."

"Yea, but I could be."

Harriet lifted the crimson sheets of the bed and got
underneath of them, rolling onto her side. She sighed, the
corners of her mouth curling slightly.

I really showed that pervert. After that *beating, he'll never
want to be spanked again,* Harriet thought. And, with that
notion in mind, she closed her eyes and drifted off into a deep
and trouble-less sleep. Dreams of the accolades she would
receive after handing the notorious villain, Death Laser, over
to the authorities pleasured her until morning.

Chapter 52:
Winter Prison

Harriet opened her eyes slowly. She grinned, feeling strangely warm. As the fogginess of sleep waned, she grew still and her heart rate quickened. Something was off. She now noticed the weight of something against her body. Harriet glanced down and saw that this weight came from a man's muscled arm, draped over her side. This was undoubtedly Spencer's arm. The black-finger-nailed hand of which rested too close to the curve of her breast.

"Oh, goddamn it..." Harriet muttered. She pulled Spencer's arm off of her and rolled to face him. He grinned back at her mischievously and she noted with irritation that both of his arms were now free.

She narrowed her eyes and groaned: "How did you do it?"

"Heheheh....wouldn't you like to know?"

"Tell me."

Spencer reached into his pocket and withdrew Harriet's handcuffs. He held them up with one hand, and then moved his wrists toward both of the thick metal circlets, moving through them as his flesh made contact with the solid object. Harriet watched with amazement. Now that he was wearing the handcuffs again, he gave his wrists a tug, easily moving through them a second time, and pulling them off. To demonstrate the relative ease with which he was capable of this, he grinned and then moved through the cuffs again, putting them back on and then removing them again and again, several times in quick succession.

"I can move through solid objects. They call it 'phasing through' or being a 'wall phaser.' It makes robbing banks super easy. But yea, that's my secret power. It's never smart to tell your opponent everything that you're capable of. Always have a card up your sleeve," Spencer said, still grinning.

"Yea, your pal Gordeau said something like that," Harriet said and then something dawned on her. "Wait a minute....you could have escaped at anytime that you wanted to...and that must mean..."

"Heheheh...heh...."

"You *liked it*, didn't you?" Harriet groaned, now realizing that Spencer's cries of pain and please for mercy during the beating he had taken last night, must have been an obvious, stupid act.

"Believe it or not, I'm actually pretty tough."

"Let's see how tough you are when you go to prison," Harriet muttered.

"Yea, but, like, I can walk through walls...*soo*....that's *never* going to happen."

"Goddamn it."

"But it doesn't matter, anyway. I was bad, but you taught me a lesson, so now I'm good."

"That's the stupidest thing I've ever heard."

"Yea, but is it?"

"Yes," replied Harriet bluntly, "Unequivocally."

"I just needed some sense knocked into me. I swear, I'm a good guy now. I'm on your side," Spencer said.

Harriet sat up and smoothed her disheveled hair.

"Well, I guess, since you won't stay in prison, anyway..." Harriet stood up and walked over to the mirror built into the onyx cabinet at the opposite side of the room. She observed her smudged makeup and deflated hair with a shrug. Then finished her sentence: "Then, *whatever.*"

Harriet walked into the adjacent bathroom. Once comprised entirely of white marble, the large space was now overpoweringly red, with red marble floors and ruby encrusted faucets. The mirror on the wall above the sink, once mounted within an oval of polished gold, was now a held within the fanged mouth of a massive stone gargoyle. Seeing how the room had changed, Harriet muttered: "Oh Jesus fucking Christ." and turned on the faucet. She rinsed her

smudged face off in the sink, and smoothed down her
disheveled hair, frowning as Spencer entered the room.
Harriet stood up and wiped the smudged paint off of her face
with a moist towel.

"Well, this'll have to do until I can get back to my
makeup," Harriet said, staring at Spencer's reflection in the
mirror, with sticky, squinting eyes. "I don't suppose you have
any of that guyliner you wore at the Hornet's Nest lying
around here?"

She glanced back at Spencer who grinned at her for a
moment, showing a lot of teeth.

"You don't need makeup. You're Harriet Ross, 'the
most beautiful woman on planet Earth', according to May
2016's Pantheon Magazine," Spencer replied, sounding
dreamy and far away. He smiled the way that a fanboy who
doggedly obsesses over a celebrity smiles, while he gazes at a
poster of her in his bedroom.

"Oh please, my father paid that magazine to say that
about me."

"Even so," Spencer said, "It's still true."

"I'm going to the kitchens to have something prepared
for me, like old times, before I had to microwave waffles like a
raggedy peasant," Harriet said.

"Should I come with?" Spencer inquired hopefully.

"No."

"Harriet, I should probably point out that this isn't
officially your house at the moment. Technically, everyone
who works here, still works for me."

"So, what are you saying?"

"You could just run around smashing in henchman
skulls all day, and then try to bully them into making you a
sandwich, or, and this is the option I prefer, you could just
take me with you."

"You devious little..."

"Do you want to battle a hundred henchman who see
you as an intruder, or do you want to eat a quiet,

uninterrupted meal in peace as my guest? The choice is yours."

"I choose to kill the henchmen, thank you," Harriet replied with a snarl. Spotting a black plastic mask next to Death Laser's ripped black cape, by to the sink, Harriet grabbed the item and put it on to conceal her identity. It was not much different than the plastic mask that she usually wore, in fact, it was probably the same brand purchased from the same costume store franchise. An odd thought crossed Harriet's mind, had Spencer designed his costume to match hers?

"Harriet..."

"Nope. *No.* You stole my inheritance from me. You insulted my father by pretending to be him. You destroyed Turbish's priceless masterpiece, burned a massive pile of *my* money. I'm not going to willingly sit down and eat a meal with you. Just *no*," Harriet blurted out, crossing her arms in defiance. The fact that Spencer believed that getting slapped on his rump a few times absolved him of all of his transgressions, irritated her greatly. Yet, she could see that one way or another Spencer intended to get his way. He was watching her patiently, and, though he was frowning slightly, showed no signs of backing down.

Harriet turned and strode toward the door of the bathroom. Spencer walked over to her and dropped to his knees at her feet. Hearing the clunk of Spencer's bony calves hit the marble floor, Harriet spun around to glare at him.

"Please?" Spencer implored. "I'm sorry I took your house, ok? I don't even really want it, there's like, a crap load of servants living here and it's super weird. Kind of like living in a huge apartment building where strangers constantly break into your room to clean up after you...and it should be yours anyway. I'll give it back. You can have it all back."

"Yea, well, I'm taking it back, anyway. I'm still want nothing to do with you."

"I said I'm sorry."

"Did you?"

"Well, I'm saying it now. I'm sorry. That's why I let you give me a punishment," said Spencer, rubbing his sore behind with both hands. "Ow...*ow*...it still really hurts."

"Oh, shut up, you know you loved it."

"You can punish me again if it'll make you feel better," Spencer said, bowing his head in supplication. He grabbed one of her hands with both of his and said: "Dominate me. Humiliate me. I'll do whatever you want me to do. I'm yours to command. Your willing slave."

"My willing slave, huh?" Harriet repeated, arching an eyebrow. This proposition peaked her interest. "But what about your self respect?"

"Haven't got any," Spencer boasted frankly.

"*Promise?*" Harriet inquired skeptically.

"Cross my heart."

"So then...the henchmen?" Harriet asked.

"My henchmen are your henchmen."

"And The Ross Manor?"

"It's all yours."

"What about Headless Records?"

"You're the boss now. Everything that I used to control, is now controlled by you. Because you control me, get it?"

"Huh..." Harriet murmured in a lighter tone, as she considered the implications of this. With Death Laser's henchmen at her command, she effectively controlled an army. What she would do with an army, she had not the slightest clue. Yet, still she liked the idea of having one. "That's...*huh*...Well, I've got to say, Mr. Tuckerson, you sure can be persuasive," she said with a flicker of a smile. Then, she took his hand, which still clasped hers tightly and shook it as though they were agreeing upon a business deal. He grinned at her and rose to his feet.

"But if this is a trick, you're going to be s–" Harriet started but she stopped in the middle of the word "sorry" as she was interrupted by Spencer's nervous chuckle.

"Heheheh..heh..."

"...Oh what's the point of even threatening you?" she finished with a defeated groan. It seemed her attempts at intimidation were only turning her nemesis on.

"Well, then let's get something to eat," Spencer said, his voice goofy with lust-drunk admiration.

"Ugh...fine," Harriet replied with a sigh. She followed him as he exited the bathroom and walked back into the bedroom, stretching his arms wide as he yawned. Harriet trudged behind him, keeping him in her sight. His aura felt strange, sort of flickering and racing in a way that was difficult to accurately describe with English words. She could not identify what it meant. This frustrated her because it seemed increasingly obvious that her aura sensing ability was a useless side effect of her contact with the radiation, more brain damage than superpower.

The manor was large and for awhile, they walked in silence. Harriet continued to watch Spencer closely. Ever suspicious that he may be plotting something sinister, she never dared to take her eyes off of him. Ignoring the confusing flashing signal that his aura gave off when she stood too close to him, Harriet observed her nemesis with a sense that she knew she could trust: her vision. The man seemed simultaneously relaxed and wound up. His dark hair was a little bit too long. It spilled over his ears and stopped at the curve of his jaw, sliding over his face as he slouched and put his hands in his pockets. He was wearing what he probably would have considered pajamas, not her father's pajamas (thank god), but a pair of black boxers and a loose t-shirt with a local band logo printed on it that were probably his own.

"When I met you, you were trying to make it as a musician..." Harriet said as they entered a long hallway, lined with onyx pillars. "But then...you left the band right before they were discovered."

"I didn't leave the band, I was kicked out," Spencer corrected with some bitterness."

"Oh," Harriet said conversationally, "Why's that?"

Spencer stopped walking and sucked in air as though the explanation required some effort on his part: "Well....that's um...an interesting question. Devin said that it was because my playing sucked but the truth is he's always been trying to get rid of me. I just didn't think that the rest of them would start listening to him. I mean....I was wrong...but...there wasn't really anything I could do about it anyway. At some point it was just inevitable. They all turned against me in the end. It's kind of like, when they all started hanging around Devin, then all they'd do is talk shit behind my back and then sometimes talk shit to my face, to the point that, on a certain level, I just didn't want to be around them anymore."

"Jesus, what shitty friends," Harriet offered as a condolence. In truth Spencer's scenario reminded her much of her own. With Benjamin constantly sowing uncertainty about her around The Sexy Rad Super Pals, it was probably just a matter of time until she was phased out of her social circle as well.

"I don't know...maybe he was right maybe my base playing is bad," Spencer said as he started to walk again. Harriet increased her pace to walk next to him.

"That's not true at all. I've heard you play," said Harriet. She recalled Spencer's performances as well as Devin's, and it was clear to her that Spencer had been classically trained where as Devin had not. To her, the difference in quality was apparent. "And you're objectively much better than Devin. Take it from someone who hates your guts, he probably got rid of you because you make him look bad by comparison."

"You really think so?"

"Yea, dude, he's like Carlotta from the Phantom of the Opera and you're like Christine," Harriet confirmed.

"Heheh...heh...if Devin's Carlotta and I'm Christine,

then who are you?"

"I'm the fucking Phantom of the Opera," Harriet muttered dryly.

"Well, as long as everyone here can agree that Devin sucks..." said Spencer.

"Yup, ok. Whatever," said Harriet.

They entered the dining area. Once a long white table lined with boxy minimalist chairs, it was now a cafeteria of smaller square, dark wood tables.

"You eat with the help?" Harriet deduced, as she observed the multiple tables that were now dispersed throughout her father's grand dining room.

"Sometimes. Usually, I just have food delivered to my room. Huh...but there doesn't seem to be anyone in here today. That's really weird, I mean, this place is usually swarming with henchmen in the morning," said Spencer, sounding a bit worried.

He walked over to the adjoining kitchen and peered inside. The rows of stainless steel stoves and ovens stood deserted. The countertops were devoid of meat, poultry, produce, and cookware. The kitchen was devoid of people.

"...Hello?" Spencer called. His voice echoed back. No manor staff member replied to his call.

Spencer walked back toward Harriet who was now sitting at one of the small, square, tables, looking thoroughly unamused. He shrugged. She scowled in response, and shouted so that her voice would carry across the large room: "So, what's the problem? Where's my food?"

"Uh..." Spencer fumbled, "There's actually...nobody there..."

"What?" Harriet shouted and her voice echoed off of the steep, arched ceiling. The room was large and his voice was not carrying well.

"There's nobody there!" Spencer shouted back.

"*What?*"

"There's nobody—"

"I heard you!"

Spencer walked back to the place where Harriet was sitting.

"Why is there nobody there?" she grumbled with annoyance.

"...I swear I have no idea."

"There's no servants here at all?"

"Just me."

"Fabulous," grumbled Harriet sarcastically.

"But consider me the best servant you've got," Spencer said with some determination, he was not about to let his sudden and mysterious lack of staff, ruin his chance to impress The Justice Bitch.

"Whatever, just get me something to eat already," Harriet said with a sigh.

"Yes, ma'am," Spencer replied, with a short bow that made Harriet roll her eyes. Then, he turned and scurried back to the kitchen.

Harriet waited for ten minutes or so in the empty, quiet, room tapping her fingers against the dark polished finish of the table, and thinking about the snowstorm. Clearly this freakish blizzard was the result of some radiation altered villain but what radiation altered villain was doing this and why? Did Spencer have anything to do with this? His aura seemed to indicate that he was telling the truth when he said that the snow storm and the lack of henchmen at the manor confused him as well. However, he had managed to lie to her before without a problem. She quickly pushed the idea out of her mind. It seemed that the aura sense was just a bit of trippy chemical malfunction.

Harriet stared up at the ornate wood paneling in the ceiling for a moment. How much snow was piled up on top of it? How long would it take for the ceiling to simply collapse and kill her? Spencer returned from the kitchen, dressed as Death Laser, with a black mask and long black cape. He held a silver tray covered in a large cloche, in the flat palms of both hands. Harriet watched with suspicion as he lowered the tray down in front of her and removed the cloche. Underneath, there was a bowl of brightly colored sugar cereal, a glass of orange juice, two pieces of buttered toast, and a couple of overcooked, broken and ugly looking eggs.

"Sorry, it's not too fancy. I don't really know how to cook," said Spencer.

"It's fine. Thank you," Harriet said.

He sat down across from her, cringing slightly as his sore ass hit the seat of the chair. Seeing that he had neglected to get himself something to eat, he reached over the table and grabbed one of the pieces of toast off of Harriet's plate, which he then crammed into his mouth, crunching loudly.

Harriet watched him as she ate. The crimson glow of building eye lasers were not present, and in their absence, his eyes were dark brown. They reflected the glossy light of the chandeliers overhead. At this moment, Harriet could not help but feel that he was attractive. Not in the bulky, conservative way that Gary was attractive or even in the counter culture, too-cool-to-give-a-shit way that Devin Forress was appealing, but in a sweet, naive way. Despite his accomplishments as a villain, Spencer had the look of an inexperienced youth about him, and a certain carefully concealed nervousness, that Harriet was occasionally tempted to perceive as cute. Harriet finished her toast and moved to the cereal, watching as Spencer finished his meager breakfast.

"Hey, would you check outside and see if the snow is melted yet?" Harriet caught herself asking. Then, she shook her head and corrected herself: "You know what, never mind. I can't trust anything *you* say. I'll check it."

Harriet rose to her feet. The legs of her chair squeaked against polished marble.

"Hey, don't go yet," Spencer said a little pleadingly, "I wanted to play something for you."

Harriet ignored him and exited the dining room, walking out into the grand foyer, past a pair of steep marble staircases, and toward the front door. She could sense Spencer following her, and imagined, with accuracy, the worried look on his face as he slouched, instinctively sticking his hands into his front pockets.

Harriet opened the front door and was confronted by the same wall of solid snow which had prevented her escape the day before. Except it seemed to have melted slightly overnight, before refreezing into a solid sheet of ice. Harriet groaned and then tried punching it a few times but it refused to crack. Harriet stepped back from the door.

"Hey, Laser Doofus," she said, motioning toward Spencer. "Do you think that you could melt this with your lasers?"

"Um..." Spencer mused, straightening up a bit and rubbing his sore ass with the palm of one hand. "I'll try it. Stand back."

Harriet walked away from the front door and stood behind Spencer. His eyes began to glow and then he shot a pair of lasers at the ice. It cracked and melted slightly, but then, there was only more ice behind it.

"Again, again," Harriet goaded, now hopeful that they might be freed.

Spencer obeyed, closing his left eye and then unleashing a powerful beam of red light from his right eye. The beam hit the ice and a large chunk of it melted, but then an avalanche of jagged ice shards collapsed downward to replace it, before racing into the foyer, and gathering into an intimidating pile.

Spencer exhaled nervously and murmured: "Ok, so probably shouldn't try that again...incase it all pours in here and crushes us to death."

"Ok, what the hell are we doing? You can just phase through it," Harriet said.

"Yea, but I can't take other people with me."

"How does that make any sense? You took the money you stole back with you?"

"Yea, anything that's touching me will phase through too, but it doesn't always work with living stuff for whatever reason. I've lost a couple of pets that way."

"Ok, fine," said Harriet, "I'm going to *assume* that you're saying that because it's true and not because you want to keep me trapped here, but you can still get out, right?"

"...Maybe," Spencer replied unsurely, still looking at the precarious wall of ice which blocked their escape.

"What do you mean 'maybe'. Are you my slave or aren't you?"

"I am," Spencer replied.

"So, phase through that wall and get me a Danish from The Corner Mart," Harriet ordered. "Lemon not cheese. Though I will take cheese if there's nothing left but cherry. Also, tell me what's going on out there, when you get back."

"Um..." Spencer replied falteringly. Then, he straightened up and took a deep breath. He seemed afraid of the wall of ice in a way that Harriet did not understand. "...I'll try."

Spencer stood there for a moment as though gathering his strength and then inhaled deeply before closing his mouth and covering it with his hand to hold his breath. Then, he darted toward the wall of ice, phasing through it. A few long moments passed and then he ran back out, stumbling and blue-faced, hunched and gasping for breath.

"Oh god....oh shit...." he wheezed between labored breaths, leaning his hands against the wall as he hyperventilated.

"What's wrong?"

"The...the wall's too thick....I'll suffocate if I try to go any further."

"Well try anyway..."

"Harriet, I can't..." Spencer wheezed, some of the color returning to his face. "Ugh...so cold....It's...no...I'm sorry but I can't." He pointed to a small imperfection in the edge of one of his ears that she had not noticed before. "I lost a piece of my ear trying to breathe while I was halfway between a wall, as a kid....then, I did it again by accident a couple of years later and lost part of my pinky toe...What happens is that when I breathe I go solid again and then the metal and drywall sticks through my flesh and tears chucks off...sorry...but if I tried to breath in this, I'd probably die."

Harriet deflated a bit, disappointed to discover that this chink in Spencer's armor was going to prevent her from getting the Danish she wanted.

"Oh, well," she said with a shrug. "I guess the ice will melt by itself eventually."

The flat screen TV, on the wall, in the foyer was on and muted. Its colorful screen showed the Barbie-blond news anchor standing in front of a bunch of men in red tights, flying around and firing streams of lava at snow-covered roads and bridges, trying, with slow and limited success, to clear paths.

Spencer walked up to the flat screen and pushed a button on the side of it to un-mute it.

"It seems, that this god class storm has gotten a little more intense than meteorologist expected!" the news anchor informed them perkily, as icy winds tussled her blond locks, pulling her powder blue umbrella inside out. She shouted to be heard above its violent whirl. "But don't worry, those roads should be clear again by tomorrow morning!"

"Yea, that's what you said yesterday," Harriet muttered. She turned toward Spencer.

"So what do we do now?" she asked.

"Wait, I guess," Spencer replied with a shrug.

"Damn it. I hate waiting," Harriet fumed, crossing her arms.

"Aw, come on. It's not so bad," Spencer said and to her chagrin, he reached out as though to take her by the hand. "Come on, I'll play you a song."

Harriet, imitated Spencer's at-rest pose and stuck her hands in her pockets. Spencer lowered his hand and then scratched the back of his shaggy head with it awkwardly.

"Alright, so let's hear the song," Harriet said.

Spencer led her back to the dining room, and then, went back to the kitchen to retrieve his instrument. After a few moments, he returned with a black acoustic guitar slung over his shoulder. She watched him as he tuned it. He blushed slightly as he became aware of her cautious gaze. Uncharacteristically patient, she seemed strangely entranced by the rough notes that he strummed out as he turned the strings, drawing them tight. Finally satisfied, that the guitar had been tuned perfectly, Spencer strummed his pick across the strings and played an experimental chord. Harriet leaned back in her chair, still watching him carefully. He cleared his throat and then played a few chords before he began to sing:

"I wanted her but she was too beautiful to care that I was alive; too beautiful to care about anything. She was a goddess of sex and of war, a titan, a black-winged angel looking down upon us mere mortals with boredom and indifference. And I was *a hobo with a guitar*..."

He increased the tempo of his strumming and broke into a refrain, which expressed that this woman was beautiful, powerful, cruel, and unattainable by comparing her to wild, majestic beasts and forces of nature, before ending with the following lines:

"I saw her walking under the street lights, late last night. A black leather babe, always raring to fight. Are you the Venus who can truss me up tight and be the Wanda to my Severin tonight?"

The song went on for awhile in much the same way, and Harriet, whose secret weakness was her vanity, could not help but smile at it. Though the "black leather babe" from the song was never given a name, she understood that this personage was supposed to be her. When the song was finished, she nodded with subdued appreciation. Spencer lowered his guitar.

"So what did you think?" he asked.

Harriet shrugged.

"Well, it's pretty good, I guess."

"You really think so?"

"Yea. But there is one thing that I might change about it."

"Yea, what's that?"

"This hobo with a guitar character," she leaned close to him, breathing in the smell of his aftershave and feeling aroused. Hearing how great she was over and over again in song form had the effect of an aphrodisiac upon her. "You should change him to a...." she caught herself about to say something nice, and then, instead finished the sentence: "....a really dumb and annoying guy who loves to get his ass beat."

"Noted," Spencer responded with a grin, strumming all of the strings on his guitar at once.

There was an awkward silence between them, during which, Harriet, for the first time since meeting Spencer, found herself caring enough about what Spencer thought to not know what she should say to him.

"So...uh..." Harriet murmured. The words came out less detached and off-handed than she had intended. "...what now?"

Spencer put his guitar down on the table, walked over to her and dropped to his knees again, taking one of her hands in his and kissing it on the knuckle.

"My dark princess," he said. "I am repentant and yours to command, cleanse me of my transgressions against you, for I live only to worship your cruel beauty."

"Hmm...well, ok. If you insist," Harriet replied, still skeptical of Spencer's intentions. "But you'll have to prove your loyalty, I'm afraid, before I can realistically trust you at all."

"Like I said, babe, I'm your slave."

"Yeah, and about the whole 'slave' thing," Harriet said, failing to stifle a faint grin. "You can be my slave, but when we're out in public let's call you my 'butler'."

Spencer rose to his feet and ran a nervous hand

through his shaggy black hair, blushing slightly. He looked so happy about it that it was simply undignified: "Your 'butler' huh? I like that."

Harriet thought of her father and Reynolds, and how they were always together, constantly talking, constantly laughing, constantly bickering over little stupid, unimportant things, the way that married couples do. Reynolds had always been like a second father to Harriet and, in retrospect, it should have been obvious that he and her father were having an affair.

"My family has a long and proud tradition of fucking their butlers," Harriet informed Spencer with a bit of sentimental nostalgia.

Spencer chuckled and wrung his hands together nervously, still blushing.

It was then that the lights of the chandeliers overhead flickered out. With the light of the sun, (usually visible through the blinds) blocked out completely by snow, the Dining room was plunged into a sudden and complete blackness. Harriet stood in the dark, muscles tense, poised to strike. The only thing she could see were two pricks of crimson light in the darkness, the glow of Spencer's lit retinas.

Then, as suddenly as they had gone out, the lights flipped back on, leaving Harriet to wonder whether the power outage had been the result of snowfall crushing down the power lines, or a villain with malicious intent. It did not take long for this ambiguity to be resolved, as Harriet's eyes adjusted to the sudden reintroduction of light, she saw a line of people in costume, most of which she recognized (either because she had fought them before or because she had seen them on TV). From left to right, Trauma was present, followed by Miz Mayhem, The Jaywalker (who had shed his Richard Nixon mask in favor of a pruney, orange, Donald Trump), Crunchy Toast Muncher, and a villain that Harriet had never seen before. Crunchy Toast Muncher, she had yet to encounter in person. Though, she had seen him on TV before, his costume looked more foolish and less disturbingly out of place through the filter of a camera lens. Crunchy Toast Muncher wore a tan jumpsuit, painted to look like the surface of bread, and an eye-less mascot head, shaped like a bread slice, with a creepy, neutral line for a mouth. Through the large, empty eye holes of the mascot head, she saw that his eyes were green, like Benjamin's. The villain who stood next to Crunchy Toast Muncher, wore white trimmed in ice blue bands. His clear mask obscured only a small portion of his face. Even so, it still took Harriet more than a few moments to recognize him as Devin Forress. He seemed slightly different somehow. His tussled blond hair was slightly whiter, and his blue eyes had acquired an unearthly luminous quality. The cigarette in his mouth was unlit and he sucked on it, tried to light it, and then threw it down in frustration. It shattered into a thousand ice shards.

"Devin Forress?" Harriet murmured, perplexed by his sudden, bizarre reappearance.

"That's Freeze Out, to you, Bitch," Devin replied in his burnt-out, California draw. He pulled another cigarette out of his pocket and stuck it in his mouth, but it froze solid the second it touched his pale lips, and he did not bother attempting to light it.

"We are the League of evildoers!" The Jaywalker announced dramatically, stretching his arms wide. "And this is your *death*!"

The room was quiet for a moment and no one moved.

"The Justice Bitch and Laser Shithead will be slaughtered by ME, The Jaywalker!" The Jaywalker elaborated. He turned toward Bernice and whispered: "Bernice, do you have the camera ready?"

"You mean the thing what has all of the buttons and the metal bar thingies, lad?" Miz Mayhem replied with old-timey stupidity.

"Yes, that thing! Where is the thing? Who put *her* in charge of it!" The Jaywalker fumed.

"Oh, I think it's in the corner," said Trauma. He pointed to a camera, which was set up on a tripod. "I tried to help her turn it on back at the secret lair and then on the way over here but I can't seem to get it to work and Toast Muncher ate the manual *so*....here we are."

"Well, I'm not going to kill them if no one's filming it!" The Jaywalker fumed.

Spencer leaned against the nearest dining table, his lit eyes narrowed into slits, and he said:

"Well if you try to touch her, I'm going to kill you all," he pointed to Freeze Out. "Especially him. So please, take all the time you need. I'd like to murder you all on camera as a warning to the next goon who tries to touch her."

"Oh, eat a dick Fuckerson, I'm going to fuck your girlfriend after your dead, so fuck you," Freeze Out muttered.

"Yea, well, if that's the case, I can wait until that camera goes on to smash your face to shit, I want to remember that moment forever," Spencer said.

"Same here, Fuckerson."

Now, The Jaywalker, Trauma, Miz Mayhem, and Crunchy Toast Muncher were all gathered around the camera and tripod; pushing the buttons; plugging and unplugging the chord into different outlets.

"Uh, so..." Trauma called to them from across the room. "It might take us a few minutes to get the battery re-charged...so, Freeze Out, maybe keep them busy with your tragic backstory or something!"

Freeze Out grinned evilly and licked the edge of his frozen cigarette with a blue tongue.

"With pleasure," he said.

Chapter 53: Freeze Out:
An Origin Story Flashback

Devin Forress was born and raised in one of the more
pretentious beach communities off the coat of Southern
California. His mother, Evette Forress was a model; skinny,
ice blond and statuesque in a way that few women are by
nature. His father, Andy Forress was a professional surfer;
tall, tan, and muscular, he wore his curly, dark blond hair long
and tied into a ponytail. Yet, despite this, somehow, he
managed to appear very masculine. He had a strong, square
jaw, usually dotted with stubble, and a lot of tattoos covering
his muscular arms. Andy might not have possessed the
otherworldly beauty of his wife, Evette, but he was very
handsome in his own right.

Devin, who resembled both of his attractive parents to
some degree, had always been a good looking kid, and had
enjoyed the advantages that came with good looks from an
early age. People had always liked Devin and they had
always wanted Devin to like them. He never had to try very
hard to impress anyone; he could just show up somewhere, be
hot, say *anything* and everyone would gather in a circle and
laugh like it was the most funny and charming statement that
had ever passed through the lips of a human being. He was
confident, knew everyone, and had the ability to bend any
social group to his will with ease and predictability. As a
result, he sloughed off the innocence of youth fast, went to a
lot of parties, started smoking pot and cigarettes at 9, and lost
his virginity at 13.

From an early age, Devin found that he could be mean
and that people would still like him because he was
exceptionally good looking and could play the guitar. To
entertain himself, Devin, often made fun of people that he
perceived as ugly or stupid and influenced others to do the
same. He had the power to decide who would be accepted

and who would not be. Fat girls with pimples and one-piece bathing suits fled beach parties in tears due to his influence. Kids who were too weird, too timid, or too eager to please were quickly shredded by the lazy barbs of his razor tongue. Friendships and couples were broken up due to unflattering rumors he spread out of passive aggressive maliciousness. To Devin, the power to inflict emotional pain was a potent thrill, and became one of his most prized vices, second only to fucking, smoking, and drugs.

By high school, Devin's perfect body had blossomed into full manhood. Muscular and tall, he was tan from sitting out on the beach with a cigarette in his mouth all day, strumming his guitar, and well dressed due to the fact that both of his parents made a generous amount of money. Likewise, it did not take him long to make a lot of friends and control them completely.

In class one day, an annoying, perky teacher asked the students: "What do you want to be when you grow up?" When it came time for Devin to answer he replied: "Fuck, I dunno, maybe I'll be the lead singer in a band or something."

He leaned back in his chair and stared at the ceiling, rolling his eyes at the stupid question.

"Mr. Forress, that is hardly a realistic goal," the teacher chided, "Don't you have a backup plan?"

"Nah. 'Cause I'm amazing and it'll definitely happen for me," said Devin with laid back confidence. "Plus, my dad knows a guy."

Still, the question got Devin thinking about his future. College was no place for him. College parties, sure. But wasting his time in classes, not a chance. Instead, he decided, he was going to start a rock band and then use his father's fancy rich friends to turn that rock band into millions of dollars. He searched the school and quickly recruited two band members, Kalvin Pierce and Danny Plaxman. They were both decent musicians, and they both had the skinny, handsome look that helps rock musicians get famous. But there was a small problem, because Danny Plaxman had an annoying friend that he always took with him to practice and Devin decided quickly that this friend of his was not cool enough to hang out with them.

Spencer Tuckerson, was the name of Plaxman's annoying tagalong, and he had all of the traits that Devin loathed in another human being. At 16, Spencer was gangly, awkward, skittish, and unsure. This was before he had started wearing black clothing and leather, and he had more of a bookish, nonthreatening appearance, also he sometimes talked about how he liked to *read books*. This pretentious factoid drove Devin nearly to insanity. But what was more irritating than this: Spencer was in the marching band, he treated fat chicks like human beings, he was every teacher's pet, he was in the marching band, he played every instrument in existence including ones that Devin had never heard of, he was in the *marching band*, and most infuriatingly of all, he kept a notebook full of songs he was writing with him at all times and was always, *always* scribbling in it.

Before practice one day, before the other band members arrived, Devin said to Plaxman: "Why do you hang out with that fucking dildo, Tuckerson anyway?"

"Leave Spencer alone, ok," said Plaxman with a sigh. "I told you he was cool."

"Really? Because he seems *really weird*," Devin grumbled with distaste.

"Yea, he *is* really weird. But he's cool, I promise. And whether you like him or not he's probably the best musician here. Without him, we don't have much of a band," Plaxman said.

On some level this was true. Even though Spencer was the weirdest and least popular member of their party, he sang better than Devin and seemed to play every instrument on planet earth better than Devin could play the guitar. Even Devin had to admit that this was true, at least inwardly. Still hearing this previously unspoken truth acknowledged by

Plaxman, secretly enraged Devin and it was then and there that he decided not just to freeze Spencer Tuckerson out of the group, but to do so by destroying him completely.

Devin bided his time, for the most part tolerating Spencer's eccentricities and surplus enthusiasm. Devin's passive aggressive jabs were mostly shrugged off and ignored by the dweeb, who was too busy being socially retarded to understand the Devin hated his guts, his face, his voice, and basically everything about him. Aside, from the occasional "Why are we even friends with him? I mean, he doesn't even *smoke*." Devin eventually all but gave up on trying to dislodge him from the group. Still, he kept his eyes open, looking for an opportunity, something, anything, that could make the other two guys hate Spencer as well, effectively shoving him out of the picture. Devin was confident that, one way or another, he would eventually accomplish his goal. Yet this was never as easy as Devin had hoped or planned. By senior year, Spencer was dressing better. He was also taller and more muscular, and had shed his splattering of pimples in favor of pale, perfect skin. What was more, a lot of the other guys' coolness had rubbed off on him in his mannerisms and the way he spoke, so that he seemed to have absorbed some of their charisma. For the first time since he had joined the band, he looked like he belonged to it. He looked like one of them. But Devin knew the truth, Devin knew that underneath of his outward appearance, Spencer would *never* be one of them.

Devin pushed the idea out of his mind for awhile, tolerating Spencer with as much cool indifference stippled with passive aggressive venom as the group would tolerate. He chose to focus his attention on other things, like girls, in particular freshman girls, and in particular one Freshman girl above all of the others, Janet Laxley. With her long auburn hair, large breasts, and perfect, pointy nose and pert lips, she was the hottest one, and she was the hottest one without even *trying*. Devin approached her with confidence, talking to her everyday, waiting for her to become obsessed with him and beg to be his girlfriend as all girls eventually did.

Eventually, Janet Laxley did approach Devin, smiling and giggling to herself slightly, her cheeks flushed pink with excitement and embarrassment. She was flanked by two of her less attractive friends who kept saying things like: "Go ahead, ask him, ask him!"

"Uh, Devin..." Janet asked nervously. She had seen Devin every morning since the first day of high school, and he had always greeted her with an indifferent "*hey*" and a cool shrug of his muscular shoulders. So, to her, at least, he *seemed* friendly enough. "So, uh...so, Devin.... I know that the senior prom is coming up and I know that I'm just a freshman so this is really lame *but....* "

This was it. He was about to have her.

"But....your friends with Spencer Tuckerson, right?"

Devin, visibly twitched at the sound of her uttering the name of his hated rival.

"Oh god this is so lame....but if he doesn't have a date yet, maybe ask him if he likes me and then maybe we could go together. I know this is stupid, but...but I really want to get to know him."

"Why the hell would you like *him*?" Devin growled with annoyance and the girl flinched away from him, startled by his sudden harsh tone.

"Um....I don't know he's really cute and so nice and he's read Apocalypse Unending," the girl paused to giggle at some flashback that was happening inside of her head. "He makes me laugh..." she finished with a smile. "But I'm way too nervous to ask him myself. Maybe, since your his friend, you can just hint at it, see how he reacts and get back to me?"

"Uh, sure, no problem, babe," Devin responded indifferently, regaining his composure. This might have been the opportunity he was looking for.

The next day, Devin found Janet Laxley in front of her locker. Leaning against the locker adjacent to hers, he waited for her to notice him, and address him first. She slammed the locker shut and saw him standing there, recoiling slightly from the shock of having him appear so suddenly before her, she clutched her textbooks to her ample chest and smiled nervously.

"Devin!" she said a little too shrilly.

"Oh," Devin replied indifferently, as though he had not caught her eye on purpose and she were in no way more significant than the wall that she was standing in front of. *"Hey."*

"Did you talk to Spencer?"

"Uh, yeah about that...." Devin replied in the same indifferent tone.

"What did he say?"

"Well I could tell you," said Devin, "But you won't like it."

"Did he turn me down? If he did, I can take it. Spencer's really cool. I'm sure that he's got a really pretty girlfriend that he's taking to the senior prom already."

"Uh, so you're sure you can take it? Devin asked again.

"Yea, it's fine. I wasn't expecting him to say yes anyway," the girl replied.

"And you're sure, you're sure?"

"Yes."

"Yea, so he said that you were really ugly and annoying," Devin began. He, of course, had not said anything to Spencer about Janet Laxley having a crush on him and was making these insults up as he went along. "And that that mole on your neck grosses him out."

Janet Laxley brushed a strand of her auburn hair over the small mole at the nape of her neck, her eyes brimming with tears.

"Said it just makes him want to barf every time he looks at it," Devin said, "He was just a super dick about it. And also he told me to tell you that he thinks you're really stupid and never to talk to him again about that stupid book because he hates that book and he hates you and he says he'll look like a loser if people see you two hanging out together at all. But you know, what did you expect, that guy's just an asshole."

By the end of all of that Janet Laxley was sobbing.

"What a piece of shit..." she sniffled.

"Yea, but fuck him, right? And fuck the senior prom. It's for babies. I mean...I say you and me, we just ditch the prom and get shit-faced at a cool college party this weekend."

Janet Laxley smiled: "I would like that."

After a hazy weekend of making out with a drunk Janet Laxley and feeling up her boobs, Devin, returned to school, emboldened by his victory, and ready to make good on his inward promise to destroy Spencer Tuckerson completely.

In homeroom, he heard Janet Laxley yelling at Spencer when he tried to talk to her about the book they both liked: "*Never* talk to me again! You can shove that book up your ass!" Spencer shrunk away from her, blushing, hurt, and confused by the sudden change in her behavior toward him. "Jeese, sorry. I won't talk about the book anymore," he murmured timidly, slouching in his chair.

While Spencer was distracted by his misery, Devin, snuck close to his desk and snatched the small spiral notebook that Spencer kept his song lyrics in, quickly pocketing it. He spent the day reading it, looking for something, anything, that he could use to poison Spencer Tuckerson's name, thus making him so uncool that Plaxman and Kalvin would agree to throw him out of the band. It did not take Devin long to find the bits of gossip he was looking for.

At lunch, he grinned to himself evilly, thinking about how he would employ this new knowledge. He turned to Plaxman and inquired casually about something he had read in the notebook: "Hey Plaxman, didn't you and Spencer meet in juvie or something?"

"Oh, yeah," Plaxman replied, "Did he tell you that?"

"Uh yeah, but he didn't say what he was in juvie for. I mean, it makes a guy kind of curious...What was some lame-wad boy scout like Tuckerson doing in juvie anyway?"

"He doesn't like to talk about it," said Plaxman, "And I'm pretty sure he wouldn't like me spreading it around."

"Come on, bro, it's just me. And whom I gonna tell? We're all friends here, right?" Devin prodded.

"Yea."

"Oh, come on man. It's killin' me. I just gotta know."

Plaxman sighed and then conceded: "Ok, ok, *fine*. But just don't tell him I told you, ok? So, you know the laser eyes thing?"

"Yeah," Devin replied. He had seen Spencer Tuckerson lose control of those eye lasers before, usually when he was worked up about something. Freshman year, two of the sinks in the boys bathroom had been reduced to powder by his radiation induced ability, and the year after that, he had taken out a whole wall of lockers, leaving only a smoldering crater. Devin imagined that Spencer's juvie offense must have been related to some sort of laser-related property damage incident.

"Well," said Plaxman with a nonchalant shrug, like it was nothing. "He used it to murder his father."

Devin's mouth fell open.

"You've gotta be fuckin' me," he replied, nonplused. This was not the story he had been expecting to hear. "You've gotta tell me more."

"That's all I know," said Plaxman with a shrug, "I'm not even sure if it's true or not."

"Oh, come on, tell me more."

"I'm sorry. That's all I know," said Plaxman, "He doesn't like to talk about it."

Devin smirked to himself. Combined with the knowledge provided to him by Spencer's song notebook, this information would give him all of the ammo that he would need to knock Spencer right out of his social circle and subsequently, right out of the band.

After school, Devin caught Spencer in the hallway, headed to his locker. Devin waited until the bell rang and the crowd dispersed, its deafening roar, fading to near silence, before he approached. There were just a few students left in the hallway, milling about, packing their bags with textbooks and notepads. At this moment, it was just quiet enough for the conversation that Devin was planning to be overheard. And, what was more, there were just enough credible witnesses present to effectively spread it across the school like wildfire. Devin grinned to himself evilly. The time was right for him to strike.

"Yo, Tuckerson!" Devin shouted from across the hallway, waving Spencer's song notebook at him. "You dropped this."

Spencer walked over to Devin and Devin handed the book back to him.

"Thanks, man," Spencer said, "I was lookin' for that."

"Yeah, I kind of couldn't help but read it a little bit. Hope you don't mind."

"Nah, dude. It's just song lyrics," Spencer said with a noncommittal shrug as he returned the notebook to his backpack, and then slouched, putting his hands in his pockets.

"Yeah, *about that*...so there's this one song in there about you wanting to get your ass whooped. So, like, what's that about? Are you a faggot, Tuckerson?"

"No, I like girls. It's just that..." Spencer replied, now visibly uncomfortable with the conversation.

"Is that why you were hanging around Janet Laxley? Because you wanted her to dominate you? Are you a *spanko*, Tuckerson?" Devin said with a grin that was more of a sneer. He was talking so loudly that his voice echoed off of the walls. Everyone in the hallway was now silent and turned in Devin and Spencer's direction, as though spectators watching a play. "From now on I'm gonna call you *Spanky Fuckerson*."

"Um...maybe...*don't* do that?" Spencer replied falteringly, his eyes lighting crimson. "I don't really—" Devin interrupted him before he could finish the sentence: "—want people to know."

"What's a matter, Spanky? Can't take a joke? Or are

you just going to murder me with those eye lasers like you did your father....*psycho freak.* Why'd you do it, huh?"

"....I...I don't like to talk about it..." Spencer murmured, the color rising in his face, the crimson glow of his eyes growing brighter and radiating heat. It seemed Devin had struck a nerve.

"Why'd you do it, huh?"

"Please, I don't want to talk about it...just leave me alone, ok..." Spencer said, squeezing his glowing eyelids shut, in an effort to control his lasers.

Devin did not relent: "Huh? Are you a fucking nutcase or what? Why would you kill him? Did he fuck you up the ass or something?"

"D...don't talk about him like that, you fucking asshole!....He didn't deserve to die, ok?" Spencer said covering his glowing eyelids with his hand, a pair of tears trickled down his cringing face.

"Hahaha..." Devin chuckled, "You're such a pussy. So, why'd you kill him, *huh?* Are you just a fucking psycho, spanko murderer? Do you like killing? Huh, Fuckerson? Does it get your dick hard? Are you going to murder me? Are you going to run around murdering everyone at this school? Because I'm not going to put up with that kind of shit at *my school.* I'm going to make sure everyone knows to be afraid of you."

"*Fuck you,*" Spencer spat tearfully, his hand still pressed tightly over his glowing eyelids. He fumbled blindly through the hallway, feeling his way with his free hand. Devin followed him nonchalantly, continuing to bring up the murder of Spencer's father in a laid-back, conversational tone.

"What was the last thing he said to you before you killed him, huh? Was it: 'suck my big *dick*?' No wait, you said he didn't deserve to die, was it: 'Hey, son? Let's go get some icecream.' Devin mocked in his approximation of a dopey dad voice."

It was then that Spencer began sobbing outright,

stumbling blindly, in a desperate attempt to retreat to a place where his loud, undignified crying would not be overheard. He opened his eyes for a second to try and get a bearing on what direction he was facing, and a pair of lasers shot out of them, blowing up a row of lockers, and reducing them to ash. Five or six students, who had been standing in what would have been the line of fire, screamed and scrambled to flee his path of destruction.

At practice, the next day, Devin observed that Spencer was not present. Content that he had finally managed to ostracize his annoying rival from the group, he stretched and yawned, grinning with contentment. As he bent to plug his guitar into the amp, Plaxman and Kalvin arrived.

"What the fuck, man?" Plaxman shouted as he walked into the room. Devin straightened up and glowered in Plaxman's direction. This was not the reaction he had been hoping for. "I told you not to say anything about it to anyone."

"Anything about what?"

"You *know* what," Plaxman growled.

"Oh you mean how Fuckerson murdered his father," Devin said coolly, like it was nothing. "That was more of a public service announcement, you know, so *more* people don't get murdered. It would be being a dick *not* to tell people. I mean, he just blew up a whole wall out of nowhere that day. If you think about it, I mean really think about it, seriously, and without your head up your ass, somebody like that...he shouldn't be around normal people. He should be in an institution or something, in a straight jacket, with his eyes scooped out, and hopped up on Ritalin."

Kalvin, who was usually quiet and reserved during the band's confrontations, interjected calmly: "Devin, do you *hear* yourself?"

"Hey, dude, don't treat *me* like *I'm* insane. He could have killed like ten people yesterday. Are their lives really worth less than *his*?" Devin argued.

"Oh, *fuck you*, Devin, he only did it because you *egged him on*," muttered Plaxman with exasperation.

"Yeah, what the hell's wrong with you, man? You *know* how sensitive he is," interjected Kalvin.

"Whatever, asshole, I was just kidding around. Is it my fault that he can't take a joke?" Devin said, pulling a pack of cigarettes out of the pocket of his plaid, button-down shirt. He took a cigarette out of the pack, stuck it in his mouth, and lit it with a silver lighter shaped like a skull, then, returned the lighter to the pocket of his loose jeans. "He's a fuckin' dickhead. I say we kick him out of the band."

"How about we kick *you* out of the band," Plaxman said, angrily.

This statement made Devin drop his laid-back, cool demeanor. He got in Plaxman's face and started yelling: "You can't kick me out of the band! I *made* this band! I *am* this band! And what are you supposed to do without a lead singer anyway, huh? *Huh?*"

"Spencer could be the lead singer," Plaxman said through gritted teeth, staring Devin down.

"Spencer? The lead singer? You've gotta be fuckin' kiddin' me," Devin muttered indignantly, retreating slightly. Plaxman was still staring him down.

"What do you think, Kal?" Plaxman inquired of his band mate.

"Well," said Kalvin calmly and with a pleasant shrug. "When you think about it... how does it make any sense that our lead singer is the guy who smokes two packs a day?"

"Oh, *fuck you*, lots of singers smoke," Devin huffed, exhaling a puff of smoke. "You know what, though? If you're so dumb that you'd rather have Spanky as your lead singer than me, then you get what you deserve. You want to kick me out of the band? Fine. Fuck you. Fuck all of you. I'll just make another band."

Plaxman exhaled slowly and then put a hand to his forehead, in exasperation.

"No," Plaxman said a little apologetically, shaking his head. "You don't have to do that. I don't want to break up the band over some bullshit like this... *Just*...apologize to him, and we can pretend like this never happened."

Devin, who had not apologized to anyone for anything since the appearance of his first pubic hair, found the prospect of losing the band to Spencer, if he did not apologize to him, maddeningly infuriating. However, he hid the feeling well.

"Ugh..." Devin groaned with distaste, putting a hand to his forehead. "I don't know what I was thinking. Just tell him, I'm sorry, ok?"

This was a lie. In truth the only thing that he was sorry about was that his plan to get rid of Spencer had not worked.

Spencer never knew weather to trust Devin or not after that. Still, Spencer accepted Devin's indirect apology and the band was reunited. Though, for Spencer, high school never exactly went back to normal. There is a special place in hell reserved for teenagers (particularly teenaged boys) who cry in public, where the sinner is laughed at by strangers as they walk from class to class, or avoided and ignored out of fear that their social stigma may be contagious.

After graduation, Devin took the band to Propopolous city to play gigs at the numerous clubs there and try and get discovered. He had an unfair advantage over most other people trying to make it as professional musicians, because his dad had friends in the music industry. Rather than pull the strings he needed to get his career rolling right away, however, Devin bided his time and plotted a way to first dislodge Spencer Tuckerson from the band.

For a year, Devin was funded by his rich parents, who paid for his apartment and all of his expenses. Plaxman and Kalvin picked up menial jobs easily enough and got along fine. Spencer, however, had a hard time finding a job because of something called The Superhuman Labor Information Act, which was a law requiring that he list his superhuman abilities, and any damage which had been caused by them on any job application. It was common knowledge that anyone with the ability to pass through solid objects never got hired because it was too easy for them to sneak money out of a safe or cash register, so Spencer never listed this ability. However, the damage caused by his laser eyes ability was too well documented to really be denied, and he was rarely bold enough to risk prison by not mentioning it. The fear that someone might bother to build a cell with walls thick enough to contain him, prevented him from being comforted by the notion that he could escape prison easily just by walking out again. As a result, he ended up being homeless for a year, while he played with the band, receiving only small amounts of money for gigs, showering at the gym, and living out of his old, rusty car. Devin waited patiently for this harsh lifestyle to break Spencer, for him to give up and go back home, or simply go somewhere else. However, Spencer never seemed to give up on the idea that the band might make it big someday, and he never left EAR MUTILATOR of his own accord.

One day, as Spencer was wandering the city, he discovered a sign in a shop window which read: "We Hire High Risk Superhumans." The sign was telling the truth too, because for the first time in Spencer's young life, he was actually called in for an interview after having applied for something. Unfortunately, however, Devin overheard the news that Spencer had an interview to go to and scheduled the meeting with his dad's friend (who worked at Headless Records) for the same day and time.

This time, Devin's scheme paid off. He pulled the guy from headless records aside and told him that Spencer's guitar playing was no good, and that he was only a part of the band because they all felt sorry for him. With Spencer not there, this ploy was foolproof. There was no way that he could be proven wrong. Headless Records provided their own base player and the deal was signed.

However, it did not take Spencer long to figure out

that Devin had something to do with him being kicked out of the band prior to its success. He was not exactly sure how Devin had accomplished this but he knew that somehow, in some way, the devious bastard was behind it. As far as he was concerned Plaxman and Kalvin were guilty by association. Thus, after he assumed the identity of Death Laser (in hopes of incurring the wrath of Justice Bitch), one of his favorite groups of people to terrorize became his old band.

Headless Records became the sight of many of Spencer's first crimes, the ones which Justice Bitch ignored because her policy at the time had been to ignore him. He started by showing up a the beginning of EAR MUTILATOR concerts in order to blow holes in their equipment with his lasers until everything was so damaged that they had to cancel the performance and refund the fans their tickets.

One time, Spencer snuck onto the set five minutes before the start of an EAR MUTILATOR concert and replaced all of the band's instruments with different kinds of fish. He then got on the stadium's loud speaker and announced:

"Hey, what's up you bunch of douchebag hacks. It's me, *Death Laser*!"

At the time, Devin and the other members of the band hand been behind the set, scrambling to find their instruments.

"Looking for your instruments? Heheheheh....Well, look no further than the table, five inches to the left of the largest speaker."

Devin walked to the stage, behind the curtain, and found the table that Death Laser had been talking about. The other band members followed him.

"I'm not sure what I'm supposed to be looking at," Devin muttered, as he laid eyes upon a folding table, one that had not been present on the stage before this moment, as far as he was aware. It was lined with an assortment of different whole, raw fish with the heads and scales still on them: a sword fish, a tuna, a salmon, and a spiky puffer fish, to be exact.

"I used my fish ray to turn your instruments into different kinds of fish!" Death Laser explained dramatically over the loudspeaker. In truth he had no "fish ray." He had merely stolen the instruments, hid them in the walls, and then replaced them with fish. However, the people at the concert had no way of knowing that.

"Why was fish variety important to him?" Kalvin muttered incredulously.

"Uh, so, like, with The Fish Ray, different things become different fish. It's, like, *science* and stuff," Death Laser answered him over the loudspeaker.

The curtain on the stage was drawn back suddenly, as the band members picked the fish off the table and tried to figure out, while in a state of wide-eyed, incredulous shock, which fish used to be which instrument.

The audience gasped, having observed that Death Laser's wild statements about the instruments and the fish seemed to be true.

"People of the audience!" Death Laser announced dramatically, "I have my invisible fish laser ray directed at all of your heads at this very moment, as I am speaking to you. *And*, if you do not leave this concert within the next ten minutes, I will push the big, red, button that I am currently holding *and* turn you all into fish!"

A few screams rang out from the audience and many people stood up to scramble for the exits.

"And then you'll all be *dead*...or just *fish*! It might be, like, Princess and The Frog rules or something...I'm not really sure how it works. Anyway, either way, you'll definitely die pretty fast with out water...Heheheheheh....heh*heh*...*heh*!"

More screams broke out in the audience and the band watched with incredulity as people panicked, violently shoving each other out of the way to escape the stadium through the narrow exits. They behaved as though there were a shooter in their midst, firing off rounds.

"Oh and, uh, be sure to never come to another EAR MUTILATOR concert ever again, because I'll definitely be there...turning people into fish. So, if you don't want to be dead, don't give these crappy hacks anymore money," Death Laser informed the raving audience over the loudspeaker as pandemonium broke out in the crowd. Punches were flying. People were vying for supremacy, struggling to escape through the exits. Police and superheroes raced to the seen of the crime. However, seeing that Justice Bitch was not present among them, Death Laser simply sank through a wall and quietly escaped the scene of the crime before he would be expected to fight.

The fear that Death Laser would make an appearance at another EAR MUTILATOR concert and somehow murder the entire audience, for the most part, scared people from attending them. Many tours were canceled due to lack of tickets sales. Fortunately for Devin, however, the villain's dramatic stunts had the opposite effect upon EAR MUTILATOR's record sales, and soon a handful of their songs hit the top of the charts. Emboldened by the fact that no one had yet died at an EAR MUTILATOR concert, people stopped taking the villain's antics as a serious threat and simply attended EAR MUTILATOR concerts anyway. If anything, his occasional presence only bolstered sales. This unintended result, of course, irritated Spencer greatly. So much so that he became frustrated, shed his disguise, and simply used his stolen money to buy Headless Records outright.

By this time, Devin had achieved the celebrity status which he had always craved, and with it came more women, fast cars, private jets, and high price drug parties than he needed to fill a day. He bought a five million dollar apartment in Propopolous City's fanciest district, which he filled with expensive things, more so because they were expensive than because he actually wanted them. He married a model and aspiring actress named Lacey Ramirez, after having known her for only a week. Lacey had everything that

Devin desired in a woman: long, auburn hair, a mocha tan, double D cup breasts, a perfect, plastic, Barbie face, and most importantly, the Auschwitz emaciation of Devin's beloved mother.

While Devin sat on a two million dollar, white, leather couch and smoked weed out of a bong made entirely of crystal, Lacey walked to the bathroom, stuck her hand in her mouth and vomited six hundred thousand dollars worth of rare truffle into a diamond encrusted toilet. This was her post meal ritual, as the digestion of food was potentially disastrous to her modeling career.

After a month or so of making bad decisions for the band on purpose, hoping to tarnish their legacy, Spencer became frustrated by their continued success and simply dropped them from the record label, citing a clause in their original contract that would prevent them from receiving revenue from continued sales of their existing records. Around the same time, Death Laser put out a public statement threatening to murder the owner of any record company who agreed to pick them up. Devin, now unemployed but coasting comfortably on the money that he had already made, thought about this strange coincidence as he inhaled cannabis deep into his raspy throat and tortured lungs. It was almost as though Spencer and Death Laser were working together.

"Ugh....*fuck*...." Devin grunted in Lacey's direction as she emerged from the bathroom. He exhaled a puff of smoke and shifted to face her. "....I think they might be...maybe they're...the same person...No that can't be it...Spanky's such a fuckin' dildo...it must be his uncle or something..."

"Jesus...you talk about the dumbest shit when you're high, Devin," Lacey said, her voice was shrill, and cracked as though eroded from long exposure to the acidity of her own vomit.

"He fucking sucks and *I'm great*...so why's he the only one who get's to have magic powers, *huh*? Why don't *I* get to have magic powers?" Devin slurred through the haze of a gathering pot cloud.

"If you want magic powers so bad, there's, like, a Ross Foundation chemical plant around the slums or something."

"Yeah....fuck that place....the fumes are like...it smells like horse shit and orange juice...Fuck it...I'm going....Fire me will you, you fuckin'....you fuckin' dickhead....After I'm super....I'm going to kick your teeth in...hahaha..."

Devin walked past Lacey and through the door. He exited the apartment building got in his white Lamborghini, and drove it at 20 miles an hour down to the bad part of town, where he stopped clumsily, crashing it into a telephone poll in slow motion. As soon as he stumbled out of the Lamborghini, a man emerged from the shadows, pried the driver's side door open with a crowbar, jumped into the front seat, and started trying to hotwire it. Devin was too high and too rich to notice or care that this was happening. He stumbled toward The Ross Foundation chemical plant, broke one of the windows with a rock, and then, climbed inside. The effects of the marijuana and some pills he had taken earlier, had eased him into a state of relaxed, detached elation, so that he did not fear the radiation as he should have. He could not feel the shards of glass lodged in his hands from having climbed through the broken window. The smell of horse shit and orange juice omitted from the bubbling green liquid, which surrounded him in steep vats, came as a distant, surreal sensation.

A fat security guard holding a half-eaten donut in one hand and a steaming mug of coffee in the other shouted: "Hey! You can't be in here!"

Startled by this sudden, unexpected, and loud stimulus, Devin reacted with a paranoid spasm and he slipped on a bubbling green puddle on the slick floor, falling backwards into a vat of radioactive chemicals and quickly sinking to the bottom of it.

The security guard stared down at the place in the sunken vat of acid, where Devin had disappeared, still holding the coffee and donut in each hand. His mouth fell open as he watched air bubbles rise to the top and slowly pop until there were none. Content to believe that the intruder must had drowned, the security guard walked back to his chair, sat down, and finished his donut and coffee.

...

The next morning, Devin emerged from the tank with a gasp, coughing up a mixture of vomit and foul-smelling green ooze, before he staggered to his feet. The effects of the marijuana and pills had worn off by that point but they had been replaced by a powerful hangover; the mental effects of long exposure to the green ooze, which were their own kind of high, a painful, disorienting high which stabbed at the frontal lobe with sadistic, relentless malice. Overnight, the radiation had eaten his clothing and erased his tan, turning his blond hair white, and his blue eyes bizarrely luminous. He stood there for a moment, dripping and naked. His skin and eyes burned with cold. The pain was so great that he wept, but his tears were frozen and tore at the corners of his retinas, so that instead of water, he cried thick, freezing blood, which, far from providing comfort, sent a fresh spasm of agony coursing through his shivering body. His vision blurred and he willed himself to staunch the flow of painful, blinding tears. He then knelt down and retrieved his bong, which had slipped from his hand last night. It froze and cracked, shattering as he touched it.

He climbed back through the window he had broken and stumbled naked through the bad part of town, growing a large, thick icicle from one hand and then snapping it off with the other. Taking the large icicle in both hands, he swung it like a baseball bat as he stumbled drunkenly along, smashing the windows and the hoods of people's cars.

It started to snow. Only moments ago the atmosphere had been thick with muggy 80 degree heat. But then, in an instant, the air around Devin had plummeted to 15 degrees below zero. Soon, a thin blanket of snow covered the ground. As he moved, he left a trail of frosted pavement behind him, like a snail leaves a trail of slime.

A cop car pulled over and two police officers got out of the car, their hands on their weapons.

"You!" One of the police officers addressed Devin, as he clutched the hilt of his gun with trembling fingers. "Put the weapon down and put your hands were I can see them!"

"Oh...oh *fuck you*....goddamn pig..." Devin slurred drunkenly, swinging his frozen bat at the base of a street light and missing badly.

"Put the weapon down and put your hands were I can see them!" the cop shouted again, his body trembling both from fear and as a response to the freezing weather. The air around him was so cold that he exhaled white clouds of fog as he breathed.

Devin ignored the cop and swung the icicle again, this time hitting the windshield of the cop car. In his euphoric, post-radiation state, this action made as much sense as any. He laid waste the cop car; crushing club sized dents in the metal roof; shattering every window. His once healthy body burned and throbbed as though being assaulted by a thousand wasps with icicles for stingers, and he was angry, angry because he had not expected this unpleasant side effect; angry because he did not know whether the sensation would fade with time or only become more unbearable. He did not notice as both cops raised their guns and opened fire on him. Their bullets merely froze and shattered as they made contact with his skin.

Devin heard one of the cops on his walkie-talkie: "We have a high risk superhuman, possibly category four or higher. Yeah, he's a cold weather environmental threat. Send us some heroes with heat and fire related abilities."

Devin stumbled into the front seat of the cop car, which was unlocked. The keys were still in the ignition, so he put his foot on the gas and sped away with it, back to his apartment, where the heroes with heat and fire related abilities caught up with him. Soon Devin found himself bent over a squad car, as his face was smashed against its metal surface by a ginger superhuman with a fire engine red sunburn. The superhuman's peeling, red hands radiated heat against the back of Devin's white-blond head.

"Let go of me, asshole, do you have any idea who I am?" Devin yelled impotently as he struggled to free himself from the heat man's grip. Though still naked and still frothing with violent rage, he was beginning to come down from his post radiation exposure high and feel the indignity of the situation.

Money, however, has a way of protecting those who possess it from answering to the law. It was not difficult, therefore, for Devin to stave off property damage and resisting arrest charges by writing a few fat checks. He tolerated the six month long community service penalty that was administered to him, for the first two days, with much indignant distain and muttering to himself. Then, he hired a shape-shifting superhuman to carryout the rest of the sentence for him.

When Devin was in his apartment, Lacey avoided him due to the circle of cold air which enshrouded him, frosting the furniture with ice crystals, making the living space so unpleasant to inhabit, that she soon started having an affair, just so that she could avoid the place. Devin was too enveloped in his bitter, frozen hell to notice her long absences. He withdrew a pack of cigarettes from the pocket of his furry white jacket, opened the box, withdrew a cigarette, and stuck it in his mouth. It froze solid. He tried to light it but it would not light, so instead he sucked on the frozen cigarette in a spastic fit of desperation, like an infant attempting to draw milk from a dry teat. Later, he tried satisfying his craving with chewing tobacco, but this froze solid as well, cracking his teeth so that blood seeped over his gums and dribbled down his pointed white chin.

He tried taking intravenous drugs but the needles froze and cracked, no longer capable of penetrating his skin. He tried drinking and taking pills but found that pills and alcohol no longer had an effect on him. His altered body shielded itself against their effects by encasing the walls of the stomach and intestines in a protective layer of ice when a threat was detected, making intoxication near impossible.

Suffering intense withdraws from a sudden and forced sobriety, Devin sat at the center of the white leather couch in the living room of his apartment, shivering and hugging himself with muscular arms covered in frozen nicotine patches. For the first time in a long time, Lacey walked close to him, a look of distain twisting her beautiful face. She was silent, staring, apprehensive, and behaved as though she were observing a terrifying monster that had been put on display for her amusement.

"You're cold, Devin," she observed grimly, "I mean, *like*, you were always cold in the figurative sense but now you're literally *cold.*"

"...I want to touch you..." Devin murmured painfully, reaching out a shaking hand. She backed away from him. He had not touched her since his contact with the radiation. She had not wanted him to touch her. He was too cold. "Please..."

Devin stood up.

"No!" she shouted, backing away from him.

"*Please*..." he gasped again, sounding weak and strained as though the word hurt him to say it.

She hesitated out of pity and he took that as an invitation to cradle her face in both of his hands. But as he did this, she screamed in pain. He withdrew his hands but it was too late; ugly flakes of frozen flesh slid off of her jaw in bloody chunks. She screamed and screamed and clutched a melted, asymmetrical face, trailing strings of loose skin over bare jaw muscles, cauterized by frost. In an instant she had been mutilated to the point of having become monstrous.

In the future, a series of reconstructive surgeries would fail to restore Lacey's former beauty and her modeling career would come to an end, instead she would find work having her ruined face filmed and photographed in domestic violence PSAs.

Lacey received everything in the divorce. The judge, moved by Lacey's disfigurement and her claims that Devin had inflicted it upon her in a fit of jealous rage, ruled that Devin be shipped to a prison camp on the South Pole, where dangerous ice villains who pose major environmental threats are contained.

It was in the aftermath of this ruling, that The Jaywalker intercepted the armored car headed for the prison camp at the South Pole. He recruited Devon to The League of Evil Doers with a quick scribble on his yellow notepad, while the other two ice villains in the car, five-year-old twin girls who had gone blind from weeping ice crystals, were turned into bread statues, and then, eaten by Crunchy Toast Muncher. The girls were too weak by The Jaywalker's estimation; their youth and disability would only be an impediment to his cause. Devin, on the other hand, Devin was strong, angry, devious, remorseless, able-bodied, and cold. He had the power to create the kind of storm that The Jaywalker's plan to kill his enemies required. And, what was more, he possessed a hatred for The Jaywalker's soon to be former boss, Death Laser, that could only be described as ideal for the job.

Chapter 54:
A Battle for Possession of the Ross Manor Ensues

Devin monologue for a long time, disclosing his tragic backstory in a tone of cool indifference as The League of Evildoers sat in a circle around the camera and tripod, waiting for the battery to recharge. The thing was refusing to turn back on until the battery recharged to a certain percentage.

After some time, Devin completed his longwinded backstory, with a shrug of his muscular shoulders, and a casual flick of his frozen cigarette. The gesture was an old habit that no longer served any purpose as the cigarette, in its current state, was now no more than a nostalgic oral fixation.

"So, yeah," Devin concluded for an audience of Harriet and Spencer. "*My* life is over, so I thought, you know, fuck it, why does everybody else get to keep living? Why not join The League of Evildoers and find a way to freeze the whole fucking world dead before I off myself? So, yeah, and here we are. Motivation explained. Fuckerson ruined my life, so I'm going to finally kill that little shit and settle the score."

"But....*did he* ruined your life? Because it sounds like *you* ruined your life," Harriet observed boredly. While Devin had been talking she had leaned back in her chair and put her black leather boot clad feet up on the table. Spencer was standing near her, leaning against the table with his arms folded and his glowing eye glaring at Devin suspiciously.

"Oh and before I kill him, I've decided I'm going to *kill you*, Justice Bitch. It's nothing personally really, I just want to see the look on Spanky's stupid face when he has to watch you die. Jaywalker wants to be the one to kill you," Devin said and then he dropped his voice to a whisper so that The Jaywalker (who did not know that Devin had plans to usurp his position as the murderer of Justice Bitch) would not overhear. "But that little psycho doesn't stand a chance. You'll be a dead-ass frozen bitch-cicle before he can even reach you."

Before Harriet could retort, Spencer growled indignantly: "Whatever, frosty the fuck-face, let's see you *try* to touch her. I doubt you'll get very far."

"Ok, the camera's rolling," Gordeau announced cheerfully, as though he were some hapless substitute teacher, who had just managed to figure out how the classroom VCR worked, and he was about to pop in a G-rated movie.

"Finally!" The Jaywalker exhaled in an exasperated voice. He stood in front of the camera, assuming a villainous pose and proclaimed: "Justice Bitch! Death Laser! We are the League of Evildoers! And *this*...this is YOUR DEATH!"

Chapter 55:
Justice Bitch and Death Laser vs. The League of Evildoers

The Jaywalker ran at Harriet with his hand outstretched, a yellow notepad hanging off of the palm of his hand. Harriet did not read it. Instead, she leapt out of her chair, pushed Devin roughly to the side, and ran towards the group's ringleader with her fists raised. Touching Devin had been a bit of an accident, as she was not sure how her super resiliency attribute would respond to the extreme temperatures that his body emitted. But he had been standing in her way, with his fists clenched and freezing into massive balls of ice, which he apparently intended to bludgeon her with. The sight had enraged her, pushing out all other emotions, leaving no room for caution. But the gamble, it seemed, was worth it, because the palm of her hand, where she had touched Devin's muscular, white-spandex-clad chest, was now very cold, but otherwise, undamaged.

Harriet approached with her eyes unfocused, failing to read the message on The Jaywalker's notepad. The Jaywalker lost his nerve, and emitted a shrill scream of terror as he turned and ran from her.

Scowling slightly, Devin coolly snuck up behind Harriet and shoved her back. Caught by surprise, Harriet stumbled on a floor slick with ice, and fell flat on her face. She climbed back to her feet, seething with rage, but before she could run at Devin, and crack his frozen jaw into a thousand irreparable, frozen splinters, Spencer got between them and shouted: "Don't fucking touch her, asshole!"

Far from being intimidated, Devin nonchalantly walked up to Spencer, drew back his fist and punched him square in the eye, blackening it shut. A pair of lasers reflexively shot out of Spencer's eyes as his head was being driven back by the force of the powerful blow. The lasers hit

Devin in the face, but they had no effect on his frozen skin, other than to warm it slightly, relieving its stinging, freezer burned, sensation, as did the flame of his lighter at times when out of desperation, he attempted to light a frozen cigarette. Devin laughed derisively. His exposure to the radiation had achieved its intended effect. He was finally laser proof.

Harriet spotted The Jaywalker writing some kind of a message on a large piece of poster paper with a huge, black, dry erase marker. This message would be too large for her not to read when she blurred her eyes.

"Shit," Harriet swore under her breath and she ran to incapacitate The Jaywalker before he could complete his message. He ran from her.

But that's fine, Harriet thought. *As long as he's running he can't be writing.* She continued to chase The Jaywalker in circles as Spencer put a hand over his swollen eye and swore, then, drew back his fist and socked Devin square in the nose. There was a sick crunching noise, as Devin's nose collapsed, squirting blood.

"Now, you're going to die, Fuckerson," Devin growled confidently, swinging his fist to punch Spencer in the stomach. Spencer dodged the blow and struck back, hitting Devin in the face again. Soon, the two men were shuffling around on a floor slick with ice, throwing punches at each other. Despite the slipperiness of the floor, however, Spencer was a lot faster and more evasive than his opponent, dodging most of his blows. That was until he tripped, falling painfully backwards on the ice. He flinched and put his hands over his face as Devin's foot was about to slam into his mouth, reflexively phasing through what would have been a very painful and damaging blow.

"What the fuck," Devin muttered in disbelief as his foot simply phased through Spencer's head without damaging it. He tried kicking his opponent again and again, but all of his blows phased through and Spencer simply rose to his feet, smirking.

"I should have figured that the stuff would make you a wall phaser," Devin muttered, "You were always such a slippery, weasel-ly son-of-a-bitch.

Now that Spencer's secret ability had been revealed to his opponent, it only made sense to continue using it. He advanced on Devin, with far more confidence, raising his fists and ready to strike without fear of recompense.

Meanwhile, Harriet slowed to a crawl as she continued to run toward The Jaywalker, weaving between tables, panting and clutching her side. Trauma and Miz Mayhem had sat down at one of the many tables in the room and simply watched. The Jaywalker had ordered them to stand back and guard the camera as he murdered Justice Bitch, thereby proving his supremacy as a villain. Trauma and Miz Mayhem, who did not, in truth, care very much about whether The Justice Bitch lived or died, were happy to cooperate with The Jaywalker's plan. So far, it required minimal effort on their part. They watched the camera, from time to time, redirecting its lens to where The Jaywalker was standing; occasionally, warding back a stray superhuman who threatened to topple the tripod. The mere threat of their terrifying abilities, it seemed, was enough to keep that camera untouched by deliberate meddlers.

Devin swung a punch at Spencer but he held his breath and it phased through. Frustrated, Devin swung wildly at Spencer's face and chest but Spencer merely chuckled derisively as each blow phased through, and then, punched Devin in the mouth. Devin was noticing a pattern here. It seemed, his opponent had to hold his breath in order to shed his corporeal qualities. As Spencer opened his mouth to breathe, Devin grew a large icicle from one of his palms, snapped it off with his other hand, and then swung it at Spencer's face. This time the blow struck and Spencer was sent sprawling onto the ice. Devin stepped over his bleeding, unconscious body and moved toward Harriet, who was now very tired from running, and had collapsed onto the floor, clutching her side and panting hard to catch her breath. He raised the icicle high, ready to strike her over the head with it. The cold surrounding him enveloped her like an oncoming storm. She could sense his desire to kill and with it a corresponding drop in temperature, which seemed to freeze her very blood solid. The effect was paralyzing.

"You know," Devin said conversationally as he advanced on her, the shadow of his ice club enveloping her huddled frame. "It kinda sucks. I wanted to kill you before him. But, you know, *whatever.* I guess I'll just have to settle for killing you second."

It was then that The Jaywalker snuck up behind Devin and slapped a yellow note over his forehead.

"What part of 'Only I get to kill her' do you not understand? I'm the boss here, got that, you washed-up, one hit wonder? If you're alive it's only because I fucking tolerate you. Piss me off again, and Crunchy Toast Muncher will be picking you out of his teeth."

"Yes...yes....Jaywalker..." Devin replied as though struggling to break free of a trance, and then he bonked himself over the head with his ice club and collapsed face-first onto the slippery floor. The temperature rose considerably. Her mobility restored, Harriet rose to her feet and scrambled away. Crunchy Toast Muncher, who throughout all of this, stood silent and creepily still, at the center of the room, as he imagined the flavors of each person present with lustful anticipation, did not speak. Instead he turned his head in Devin's direction with a predatory gaze, and undid the zipper mouth of his mascot head, revealing a pair of slender, expressionless lips.

Devin stayed down, playing dead, listening to Crunchy Toast Muncher's amorous breathing as he crept slowly closer, perhaps hoping that he would not be noticed. The Jaywalker, however, did notice.

"Don't eat him yet," he huffed with irritation in

Crunchy Toast Muncher's direction, straightening the orange parking cone that was strapped to his head, with one gloved hand. "We can still use him."

Crunchy Toast Muncher inched forward a bit, his expressionless lips falling open with a moist *clack*.

"If you're hungry go eat Laser Fucker. I'm done with *him*," The Jaywalker said, his voice muffled slightly by the rubber mask.

Crunchy Toast Muncher obliged, turning slowly and shuffling gradually toward Spencer, who still lay face down, unconscious on the floor. Beneath the open zipper of the mascot head, which covered Crunchy Toast Muncher's face, a gaping mouth produced an obscene amount of saliva, dripping over white teeth, in thick, grotesque rivulets. A yellow beam shot from the depths of Crunchy Toast Muncher's throat, hitting the marble floor as he inched along slowly, perhaps savoring the promise of his delectable victim. As he moved, the beam of yellow-gold light moved with him, trailing a path of lightly toasted bread where there used to be floor.

Seeing this, Harriet roughly elbowed The Jaywalker out of her way, while at the same time, ripping the large piece of poster board, which he had been carrying, out of his hands, and then, tearing it in half. She watched as Crunchy Toast Muncher moved toward Spencer, hesitating for a moment, considering whether or not she should let him die. Could his promise to serve her faithfully have been a lie; a mere ploy to make her let her guard down? Or was he sincerely as enamored with her as he claimed? Did it matter? He was a human being and one who had been badly injured attempting to protect her.

"Eat his legs off, Toast Muncher. Then, I'll finish him off!" The Jaywalker shouted from across the room.

Harriet flung her body at Crunchy Toast Muncher, hitting him in the chest. She felt all of his ribs collapse like dry twigs and he was knocked backward into the tripod of the camera.

"Watch it!" Trauma shouted, as the camera wobbled precariously, having been momentarily destabilized by Crunchy Toast Muncher's head as he slid across the floor.

Harriet had a sudden idea. *If I destroy the camera,* she thought. *Then they'll have no choice but to leave and go get another one.* As soon as she thought this, however, she felt Trauma's invisible tendrils violate the confidentiality of her mind. *I can't let you do that, I'm afraid,* he thought back at her. *You see, it took me forever to steal this camera and then set it up and charge it—and there's no way I'm wasting another Saturday doing that again.*

Crunchy Toast Muncher rose, clutching his broken ribs and cursing her in German. He opened his mouth wide and shot a yellow beam in her direction, which she dodged easily. She ran toward Trauma, who was now standing behind the camera, filming her as she approached. There was no time for tact or caution, no room for subtly or restraint, and no opportunity for the element of surprise. He knew what she was doing and he had the power to stop her in an instant. To succeed, she would have to incapacitate him in a fraction of an instant.

Crunchy Toast Muncher turned toward her. Reassuming his creepy, doll-like performance, he crept slowly, quietly, as though hoping that he would not be noticed. In the background, The Jaywalker attempted to write another message, but then, found that both his blue ballpoint pen and his black dry erase marker were running out of ink. His attempts to write with them were very slow and frustrating.

Harriet stared at Trauma for a moment, remembering how he had overtaken her mind before, hardly daring to contemplate attacking him. Trauma stared back, unintimidated and waiting patiently for his boss to get around to killing her. He guided the camera with both hands, toward her face, and zoomed in on her worried scowl.

She clutched her forehead and screamed as her vision flickered, and an image of the wreckage left from the limousine after the crash flashed in her mind. She struggled to remain conscious; to avoid slipping into another dreamlike vivid flashback, which would leave her immobile on the floor; vulnerable to having her limbs consumed by the slowly approaching Crunchy Toast Muncher.

It's Will. He's Dead. He's fucking dead! she heard Reynolds shout frantically in the back of her mind. She could all but feel the martini glass that she had been holding on the day of the crash pressed into the palm of her hand. Its glass shards seemed to penetrate her skin. Her vision flickered again—and then, she jumped forward, knocking Trauma to the floor and ripping the camera from his hands. She heard something snap, one or more of Gordeau's bones, no doubt. He screamed and clutched at a broken arm. And, in that instant, she felt his mental tendrils withdraw as though having been beaten back with a club.

"What have you done to him?" Miz Mayhem demanded angrily as she observed Trauma's mangled arm, which now possessed all of the pronounced and misshapen angles of a crushed accordion. She stood and sashayed over to Harriet, long skirts billowing around her as she moved. Then, grabbed Harriet by the throat and tried to strangle her. Before Harriet could pull away from the week grip, she felt some of her life force leave her. For a moment, she felt paralyzed, unable to resist, as her skin shriveled, her tits sank, and streaks of grey snaked up and down her dark hair. Harriet's hand opened slowly and she dropped the camera. Miz Mayhem was growing younger before her eyes, younger and younger, until she had shrunken down to a flat-chested preteen, a size or two too small for her now sack-like gown. Feeling the terror of her mortality, Harriet reached a hand out and started strangling the preteen, who gasped for breath, unable to free herself from Harriet's powerful grip. Miz Mayhem's fingers loosened on Harriet's throat and her arms fell down to her sides. Harriet felt Crunchy Toast Muncher's breath on the back of her neck and swung around quickly, clocking him in the face with Miz Mayhem's limp body. The force of the blow flung him across the room.

"Give my life force back or I'm going to crush your windpipe and kill you," Harriet rasped through cracking lips, her voice distorted by age.

Miz Mayhem, gasped for air, kicking her legs as Harriet held her above the floor. She was growing taller and older, expanding to fill her gown. Harriet felt her life force return. Her skin became smooth again and regained the glow of youth. The grey streaks in her hair faded to black. She released Miz Mayhem and her opponent collapsed onto the floor, wheezing and clutching her lacerated neck.

Harriet quickly knelt down and grabbed the camera, crushing it into a ball between her hands.

"Jaywalker!" Harriet shouted, throwing the ruined camera at Crunchy Toast Muncher as he moved in range to kill her again. The ball of metal hit him in the face, sending him sprawling backward. The Jaywalker lowered his useless writing utensils and turned in her direction. "Your camera is *done!* Now, if you kill me, you'll have no proof that it was you. And if I kill you, *far more likely,* by the way—*You'll be dead!* There isn't a way this fight could end that you're going to like! So take your freaks," she walked over to Devin, whom she could sense was still conscious, and spat on him in disgust. Her saliva froze in his platinum hair. "And *go home!*"

"Shit, she's right," The Jaywalker muttered in frustration, throwing down his dry erase marker in disgust. The words tasted like poison on his tongue but he had to admit that they were true. Without video footage to prove that it was him and no other super villain who had murdered The Justice Bitch, anyone else might claim credit and be believed. Perhaps Freeze Out. Perhaps Super Annoyo. Perhaps some villain he had never seen or heard of before, trying to make a name for himself. No one would know what a heinous motherfucker The Jaywalker truly was. The normals would not comprehend the depths of his unfathomable power. They would not fear him as he desired to be feared. They would not worship him as he craved to be worshipped.

"Alright, pack it up guys! Let's go!" The Jaywalker seethed, defeated.

The League of Evildoers assembled before him. Devin rose to his feet and trudged toward him obediently, though a look of indignant reluctance twisted his pale face. In an instant, the temperature in the room grew warmer. Harriet could hear bits of ice melting outside, sliding down the sides of the darkened sunroof like rain.

Chapter 56:
To Be Continued...

After the League of Evildoers left the Ross Manor, Harriet walked over to the place were Spencer lay, and stared down at his unconscious body. She could sense his trembling aura, his heartbeat, the warmth of his still flowing blood. He was alive. She knelt down and picked him up in her arms, lifting him easily. He was taller and larger than her, so this looked a bit awkward. His legs and torso folded into the fetal position as she held him tightly in her short, slender, freakishly powerful arms.

She carried him to the nearest room with a bed, a servant's quarters, near the kitchen, usually reserved for the head chef. There were pictures on the wall here of people that Harriet did not recognize, as well as personal effects such as a man's watch and a glass of water on the bedside table. This was a room that somebody still lived in, a staff member who was mysteriously absent. Harriet wondered what had happened to this absent person. Was the person dead? Or had The Jaywalker merely hypnotized him to stay away during the planned fight between herself and The League of Evildoers?

Harriet laid Spencer's unconscious body down on the nearby bed. He shifted slightly and moaned, his eyelids flickering. There was a dark purple bruise on his forehead, indicating the kind of damage that might have killed a normal human. Superhumans, Harriet observed, did not seem to die as easily.

Agh! what am I doing here? Why am I doing this?, Harriet thought with exasperation as she walked to the adjoining kitchen, opened the freezer, and found a tray of ice. *He's my enemy. Why should I believe him when he says he's changed? He's probably lying.*

She tapped the ice out of its tray, accidentally cracking

the plastic as she did so. Then, wrapped the ice in a towel, walked back over to the bed, and held the ice-filled towel over Spencer's bruised head.

The sound of water melting and pouring down the shingles on the roof of the manor filled Harriet's ears. She sat there for awhile and listened to it, pressing the ice against Spencer's damaged head. She watched him breathe.

Time passed. Spencer's eyes flickered open and he moaned, shifting slightly.

"H...*Harriet*?" he slurred unsurely. He spoke as though he believed she were a dream.

"Sh...hey, it's ok...How are you doing?" Harriet replied quietly.

"Ugh...good I guess....I'm alright..." he replied weakly.

"Are you sure you're not brain damaged or anything, because Freeze Out smashed your head pretty good. I think he thought you were dead or he would have finished you off."

"No...I think I'm ok....kinda sleepy, though..."

"Don't fall asleep. You might have a concussion."

Spencer shut his eyes and murmured groggily: "...Yes, ma'am."

Harriet shook him awake.

"Keep your eyes open," she ordered.

"...Ok," Spencer replied groggily.

Water was pouring off of the roof like rain now. Its constant sloshing against the sides of the building filled the room. A clock on the wall, above the bed, clicked slowly.

"...Thank you for helping me out here...." Spencer murmured as he struggled to keep his eyelids from sliding closed against her wishes.

"Well," Harriet sighed, touching one of his muscular, leather-clad shoulders with cautious tenderness. "You *are* my butler."

Spencer chuckled weakly.

"....I suppose I am, aren't I?" he said, smiling slightly.

He shut his eyes again. Harriet shook him awake.

"Do you need a hospital?" Harriet asked him.

"Nah...I'm ok. *Really*," Spencer said, sitting up slowly. "I'm super fine."

"I'll take your word for it."

Spencer stood up, shakily steadying himself against the side of the bed. He forced a few groggy, experimental steps and then said: "I think it'll be easier to stay awake if I walk around a little bit. Anyway, if he smashed me in the head real good, it's what I deserve for not being able to protect you..."

"Uh..." Harriet replied, taken aback by the sudden expression of such a bizarre and probably unhealthy mentality. "Well, I'll give you points for trying," she finished in an awkward, joking tone.

Spencer walked across the room, observing the framed photographs, which decorated an island between the kitchen and living room. There were people in the photographs that he did not recognize: a man with a thick mustache; a plump woman holding a baby; an elderly couple sitting in plush chairs.

"Are these friends of yours?" Spencer inquired of Harriet conversationally.

"No, this is just a servant's quarters. Somebody lives here. But I'm not sure where he went," Harriet replied.

Spencer turned toward Harriet. He frowned and slouched, leaning against the side of the kitchen island as his bangs slid down, obscuring the bruise on his forehead: "Do you think The Jaywalker killed him?"

"I'm not sure," Harriet said, "There's no way to really know until the snow melts. I don't feel a presence here, though, other than ours. The place seems to be deserted."

"A presence?" Spencer repeated curiously, his interest peaked. "What do you mean by that?"

"It's hard to explain," Harriet replied. Spencer's eyes were on her, attentively awaiting the explanation. "And I'm not going to waste my time explaining it to *you*."

"Fair enough," Spencer said, as he wandered around

the room, taking in all of the personal details of this private home with curious passivity. Harriet watched him suspiciously, waiting for him to try and snatch something from the home, before shoving it into one of his pockets. But this never happened. Instead, Spencer circled the room once and then wandered back over to her, asking: "Will you show me how to be a butler?"

"What?"

"You said that I was your butler," said Spencer, putting his hands in his pockets. "But I'm not exactly sure what uh...what butlers do. Do they stand by the door and just wait for someone to ring the doorbell all day and then answer it? I mean...the butlers on TV shows do that."

"Come with me," Harriet instructed with a groan. She walked across the room and through the door connecting this apartment to the rest of The Ross Manor. Spencer shuffled behind her nervously.

Harriet walked for awhile through the large manor, keeping her eyes on Spencer as he shuffled along. As they were moving, past onyx pillars and seventeenth century Christian paintings of the damned burning in hell, Harriet said for Spencer's benefit: "A butler is a domestic servant in charge of a large estate, like this one."

She entered a large room with a high ceiling and Spencer followed her. This was a bedroom, with a dresser, an old fashioned lamp, and a large mahogany cabinet in it.

"The butler, is the highest ranking servant and sometimes behaves as an intermediary between the master of the house and the rest of the staff," Harriet explained, "His duties can vary depending upon what is needed and depending upon how big the staff is."

"...My cruel angel, you know I'm not worthy of such a rank," Spencer sighed overdramatically, gazing upon her with nervous lust.

Harriet groaned.

"That's true," she said, "But your henchmen are used to

taking orders from you, so it only makes sense that I used you as the intermediary between myself and them."

Harriet opened the mahogany cabinet, and sifted through the clothing that was hung there until she found what she had been looking for, a black tuxedo. Harriet picked the tuxedo up and held it out in front of her.

"Put this on," she said.

"Heheh...heh...what like right now?" Spencer giggled dumbly, the color rising in his face slightly.

"Did I stutter?"

Spencer took the hanger with the tuxedo out of Harriet's hands and then laid it out on the bed, before stripping off his cape and shirt and then tossing them onto the floor. His chest and arms were muscular and pale. Harriet was not surprised to observe that there was a tattoo of a grinning skull on his right bicep and that both of his nipples were pierced through with vertical metal bars. She watched as though she did not care as he stripped off his pants, revealing long, skinny, legs and a pair of black, skull-print boxer shorts.

Spencer looked up at her and grinned, silently inviting her to be impressed by his well maintained body. Then, he began dressing himself in the black tuxedo. She watched as he buttoned the black slacks, slid the white shirt over his muscular arms, and then, buttoned it up to his neck. He slipped on the black tuxedo jacket—then, tried and failed to tie the black bowtie around the collar of the white shirt. It hung loosely and awkwardly around his neck, like a twist tie on a bag of groceries, as he pulled on a pair of white socks, followed by a pair of black loafers.

"What kind of a butler doesn't know how to tie a bowtie?" Harriet groaned, narrowing her eyes with annoyance. "And didn't you wear a bowtie once, to the art exhibition? How did you tie it then?"

"It was a clip-on," Spencer explained lamely.

Harriet walked up to him. His heart rate increased as

she approached and his eyes got big. His aura flashed wildly. It was obvious by the look on his face that he was all at once terrified, delighted, and aroused by her close proximity to him. She extended her hands upward, toward his neck, untied the incompetent attempt at a bow and then retied it, so that it was perfect.

"There," she said, "Now you look less like an idiot."

Spencer stared at her, grinning foolishly, his eyes alight with the thrill of the terror which she inspired in him. She stared back, frowning slightly; still standing very close. Her hands lingered on the bowtie. Before she knew what she was doing, she leaned into him, and kissed him briefly on the lips, feeling his stubble against her skin, and the heat of his blush as she breathed in his musky, masculine odor. She felt his lips press cautiously; experimentally back against hers, and then, she withdrew as though nothing had happened. He grinned and chuckled, scratching the back of his shaggy head so that he would have something to do with his hand.

"But what about whatisface, you know, the lawyer?" Spencer inquired cautiously, hardly daring to believe that Harriet's affection at that moment, was his and his alone.

"What about him? We broke up," Harriet replied with a noncommittal shrug.

"Heheheh...heh...sucks for him," Spencer said with a grin. "So uh...now what?"

Harriet flopped down on to the red comforter of the nearby queen-sized bed, and rolled onto her side, so that she was facing him, posing seductively, staring at him through narrowed, dangerous eyes:

"Now, you go to the corner store and get me a Danish," she ordered.

About the Author

Coyote Paria is the alias of an agoraphobic hikikomori who writes and illustrates science fiction and fantasy novels. You can get information about Coyote Paria's upcoming novels, audio books, and creative projects (Including *Justice Bitch Issue 2*) by following this author on Facebook or on Twitter (@CoyoteParia).

www.ingramcontent.com/pod-product-compliance
Lightning Source LLC
Chambersburg PA
CBHW060348260626
47160CB00006B/2244